A POWDERKEG IN THE DESERT

From all over they had come, flocking to Diablo in droves. Prospectors, miners, promoters, gamblers, confidence artists, fallen doves, gunmen, thieves, vagrants, and even a few homesteaders could be found milling in pursuit of their private passions at any hour of the day or night.

They hailed from the ranges of Wyoming and Nebraska, from the rugged vastness of Montana, from Texas and New Mexico and Kansas, from the fertile farmlands of Illinois and Iowa and points east as well. From wherever men and women were down on their luck and heard about the bonanza to be reaped in the silver-laden mountains or the sin-strewn streets.

In that respect Diablo was no different from all the previous boomtowns, but those in the know, those who had been to other boomtowns, were unanimous in their belief that Diablo was the very worst.

DAVID ROBBINS

DIABLO

LEISURE BOOKS **NEW YORK CITY**

To Judy, Joshua, and Shane.

A LEISURE BOOK®
May 1997
Published by

Dorchester Publishing Co., Inc.
276 Fifth Avenue
New York, NY 10001

DIABLO

Chapter One

The rider appeared on a ridge five hundred yards northeast of the relay station. His lean frame sat slumped in the saddle; his horse hung its head in exhaustion. Clearly, both had been stretched to the limit of their endurance by the ordeal of crossing the parched, blistering landscape.

Salazar spotted the stranger first. Busy getting the team ready for the arrival of the stage, he idly glanced at the ridge, and froze. His first thought was that it must be an Indian, since only an Indian would dare cross the desert alone. Fear gushed up inside of him like water spouting from a geyser.

Many years ago, when he was a boy, Salazar had seen what was left of his favorite uncle after the Apaches got through with him. Ever since, he had been deathly afraid of all Indians. Even being around peaceful ones, like the Pimas and Maricopas, gave him a queasy feeling.

Squinting in the bright morning sunlight, Salazar used his left hand to screen his eyes and studied the horseman's silhouette. He was relieved to see that the rider must be white or Mexican.

The door to the station opened and out tramped Clarence Wynn, the owner, a rooster of a man notorious for his short fuse and his ability to use nine cusswords in a ten-word sentence.

Not one to live by the rules and laws set down by others, Wynn had established the relay station twelve years ago as a means of eking out a living with little intrusion on his cherished privacy. Except for when the stage arrived, his time was his own. As he damn well liked it.

"Salazar!" Wynn barked. "You got them horses ready yet?"

Ordinarily prompt to reply to avoid a tongue-lashing, Salazar was climbing to the top corral rail for a better view of the distant rider, who had not moved.

"Did you hear me, you lazy no-account?" Wynn demanded, advancing. His stringy form was clad in brown pants and a green shirt, both spattered with greasy food stains.

Salazar glanced at his employer, resisting an urge to question the identity of Wynn's mother. Wynn was a *bastardo*, he reflected, but the man paid well, and Salazar needed the money. His wife and five children were counting on him to save enough to cover the expense of moving in the spring to Pueblo, Colorado, where they had close relatives—and there were no hostile Indians.

Pointing at the ridge, Salazar said, "We have a visitor. Should I get the rifle, *senor?*"

Wynn halted several yards from the corral and turned to scan the horizon. His brown eyes widened when he spied the horseman. "Damn."

8

"Trouble, you think?" Salazar asked.

Wynn scratched the stubble on his chin, his devious mind pondering the possibilities. "Ain't no red devil," he deduced aloud. "Can't be no greenhorn, either. No blamed tenderfoot could make it across the Painted Desert." He paused. "Might be a longrider. Yep, I reckon you'd best fetch Old Bess for me."

It never ceased to amuse Salazar that white men gave their rifles names. Guns were guns, nothing more. Why, they might as well bestow names on chamber pots! Jumping to the ground, he noted, "The stage will be here soon. Do you think he plans to rob it?"

"How the hell should I know?" Wynn grumbled. "Go get Bess, pronto."

Salazar hurried toward the station. He could tell that his employer was in one of *those* moods.

Clarence Wynn pulled his hat brim low against the sun. What *was* that hombre doing up yonder? he wondered. Checking the lay of the land? A smart man, or an outlaw, always rode on the high side until satisfied the coast was clear.

Wynn was inclined to the opinion that the horseman was the former. Outlaws, like wolves and coyotes, tended to run in packs.

If the rider had, indeed, crossed the brain-baking stretch of godforsaken hell the Spaniards had named El Desierto Pintado, then either he was amazingly lucky, or the man knew how to live off the land the way an Apache or Navajo would.

Wynn's gaze strayed to the ribbon of road winding from his station in the direction of the ridge. Two hundred yards from the base of the rise, the road angled abruptly to the southeast. In thirty-one miles it would angle again, to the east, eventually meandering all the way to Gallup in the neighboring Territory of New Mexico.

Founded just one year ago, in 1879, Gallup served as the jumping-off place for those souls brave or foolhardy enough to confront the dangers of the Arizona Territory: the scorching desert, hostile Indians, and more cutthroats and hardcases than a person could shake a stick at, all greedy for their share of the wealth to be found in Arizona's booming mining towns.

Despite the risks, Wynn preferred Arizona over New Mexico for the simple fact that there were fewer people, and fewer people always meant greater freedom. If a man wanted to get falling-down drunk and raise a ruckus, he could do so without the neighbors raising a stink or complaining to the law.

Salazar emerged from the station holding Wynn's Winchester. "He's coming, *senor*. What should we do?"

"You finish gettin' the team ready," Wynn directed, looking at the ridge. Sure enough, the rider was descending. "I'll keep an eye on our visitor."

"As you wish," Salazar responded, his tone showing that he doubted the wisdom of staying in the open.

Wynn took the .44-40 and ambled to the northeast corner of the station where he commanded an unobstructed view of the horseman's approach. Leaning against the wall, he cradled Bess and pursed his thin lips.

Maybe he was getting all worked up over nothing. A fair number of solitary riders had stopped at the relay station over the years. But every one, as near as he could recollect, had followed the road, had stuck to that rutted, serpentine track as if their lives depended on it—which they did. Anyone who strayed into the desert risked becoming lost, and once adrift in that arid wasteland, death was almost inevitable, whether from thirst, snakebite, or Indians.

Small swirls of dust rose from under the hooves of the rider's mount. The man had spotted Wynn and slowed.

Wynn glanced around. Salazar was leading one of the team to a water trough located five yards from the station door, near the hitch post. That made no sense, since there was another trough by the corral. Then Wynn realized that Salazar wanted to keep an eye on the stranger, too, just in case, and Wynn grinned. The station hand was smarter than he had given him credit for being.

Nobody, Wynn mused wryly, had ever died from too much caution, although too little had planted more men in graves than smallpox.

The stranger had angled onto the road to cover the last fifty yards.

"You let me do the talkin'," Wynn said.

"If he tries anything, I will get your *pistola* from behind the counter."

"Just don't shoot yourself in the foot. It's got a hair trigger."

Both horse and rider were now close enough for Wynn to note details. The man was tall and well-built and had black hair worn long, down to his broad shoulders. A mustache framed his upper lip. On his square chin was a week's worth of growth. Atop his head perched a wide-brimmed black hat, its dusty condition matching that of the man's sweat-soaked white shirt and gray trousers. In a holster on his left hip, butt forward, nestled an ivory-handled revolver.

The trademark of a gun hand.

But not everyone who preferred a fancy six-shooter was a gunman, Wynn reminded himself. A lot of cowboys and miners went in for elaborate hoglegs with nickel plating, artistic engraving, and expensive grips. Why, the man responsible for founding Tombstone, a prospector by the name of Ed Schiefflin, liked to strap on a pair of Smith & Wessons with ivory grips. Yet he was a peaceable sort and had never shot anyone.

It was the times, Wynn reflected. In that day and age, many a man added a touch of vanity to his belt hardware.

Wynn straightened to move away from the corner, adopting a reasonably pleasant expression since he didn't care to rile the stranger. Some longriders were downright touchy over trifles. Being too quick with the tongue or too surly without cause was enough to bring out the worst in them.

Stopping, Wynn waited until the horseman was ten yards off before calling out, "Howdy, stranger! Welcome to my station."

The man reined up. Piercing blue eyes raked Wynn from head to toe, shifted to Salazar, and finally went to the faded sign suspended above the open front door. "Wynn's Stage Stop," he read aloud in a low, deep voice. "I'd be obliged for a drink for me and my horse. We're thirsty enough to drain a river."

"Help yourself," Wynn offered. He trailed the long-hair to the trough, admiring the man's sturdy roan, and catalogued his impressions. The man's accent was likely southern, his manner polite enough to show he wasn't a run-of-the-mill hardcase.

Salazar displayed remarkable agility in moving the team horse aside so the rider could get to the water. "Hello, *senor*," he said.

Wynn heard the stranger address the station hand in a string of perfect Spanish. He had never learned the language, himself, even though half the folks in Arizona spoke it. Too much bother.

Surprise flitting across his features, Salazar grinned and nodded. "Yes, *senor*. To a man who has crossed the desert, water is more precious than all the gold in the world."

The rider dismounted slowly, then arched his spine to relieve the stiffness.

"You must have been in the saddle a long time," Wynn commented.

"A long time," the stranger agreed, letting the roan drink first, his left hand holding the reins, his right close to his fancy pistol.

Wynn carefully skirted the hind end of the roan, noticing a black frock coat draped over the man's saddlebags and tied down with strips of leather. Gamblers were partial to frock coats; the garment served as the emblem of their fraternity. But a typical gambler would no more tackle the Painted Desert than he would a cornered rattler.

"Any chance of having you rustle up some grub?" the man asked in that distinct southern drawl.

"There's a stage due in soon," Wynn said. "If you don't mind waitin' a short spell, you're more than welcome to eat with the passengers."

"Sounds good."

As surreptitiously as he could, Wynn studied the stranger's belt gun, recognizing the model as a short-barreled Colt Peacemaker. They were tremendously popular on the frontier. Nickel plating made the gun gleam when struck by the sun. The caliber was most likely .44-40 or .45. Anyone who knew the business of killing wanted a certain man-stopper.

"I'll tend to your horse, *senor*," Salazar said.

"Thanks just the same, but I'll do it," replied the stranger, finally bending to cup water to his lips.

Wynn strolled to the doorway, pausing to watch the horseman go about the business of unsaddling. Long ago he had learned to judge the character of a man by how the man treated his horse. Greenhorns always betrayed their ignorance by treating their an-

David Robbins

imals as if they were made of fine china. This stranger impressed him. The man removed his Texas-style rig in no time flat, everything done just right with an economy of movement that spoke of long experience.

Salazar was also watching. Like Wynn, he was impressed. Nodding at the roan, he remarked, "You have a fine animal, *senor.*"

"Never owned better."

"I have worked around horses all my life," Salazar revealed. "I have a knack, as some might say. The secret is to be gentle with them. A horse will do—"

Wynn suddenly straightened, thinking of the time. "Quit your jawin', dammit. That stage is due, remember? Finish with the team before it gets here."

"*Sí, senor,*" Salazar answered. With a nod at the rider, he sheepishly led the team horse toward the corral. It was not like him to open up to a stranger, especially a gringo, but there had been genuine friendliness in the man's eyes.

Clarence Wynn lowered his voice so only the southerner could hear. "You have to ride them Mexicans all the time or they'll slack off every chance they get."

The corners of the man's mouth tugged downward. Wynn, staring after his station hand, did not see it.

"If you don't think highly of those with Spanish blood, why bother hiring them?" the rider asked.

Wynn sighed. "There ain't many white men willing to shovel horse crap for a livin'. Besides, the Mexicans work just as hard, and I can pay them less."

"You're a shrewd businessman, Wynn."

"Bet your britches I am."

"You hire cheap labor, then stand around and do practically nothing most of the day, I'll bet."

The station owner snickered. "There you have it!

14

That's the secret of good business. Keep expenses low and the profit high."

"You've missed your calling. You should be working for the railroad."

"How come?" Wynn asked, puzzled by the reference.

"Never mind," the longhair replied. Having already draped his saddlebags and the black coat over his right shoulder, he now effortlessly slung his saddle over his left and looked at Wynn. "Shouldn't you be getting that food ready?" he asked in the very same tone Wynn had used a minute before on Salazar.

Wynn abruptly saw that his remarks had offended the rider, and that the man had been mocking him moments earlier. A flinty narrowing of the stranger's eyes prompted him to check the indignant retort he was about to make. Instead, he mustered a feeble grin and nodded. "Some grub, comin' right up."

To try to make amends, Wynn pointed at the stable. "You can put your horse in one of the stalls if you want. There's plenty of hay and some oats, but the oats will cost. They're hard to come by."

"Thanks," the stranger said coldly.

Wheeling, Wynn entered the station, his mind awhirl, appalled by his lapse. He should have realized that the stranger might not look down his nose at Mexicans, as most did. The man spoke Spanish fluently, after all. For all Wynn knew, the longhair might even have some Spanish blood in him. If he wasn't real careful, he could find himself looking down the barrel of that Peacemaker.

Resolving to be more cautious, Wynn crossed to the cooking area along the west wall, passing four large tables set up for the benefit of the customers. After propping the Winchester in a corner, he checked a huge pot on the stove.

In it, stew was simmering nicely. Stew was Wynn's

specialty, the only meal he ever served the passengers. For one thing, it was easy to make. All he had to do was take his rifle and go for a stroll. Any critter unlucky enough to come under his sights wound up in the pot.

For another, Wynn always got a chuckle out of watching the pilgrims wolf down chunks of rattlesnake and lizard meat without their being the wiser. Every now and then he was tempted to tell what was in his concoctions. But he knew if he did, the tenderfeet would have a fit, or else puke their guts out. They'd also probably complain to the head office, and he could do without *that* aggravation.

Wynn went to the sink, where the skin of a six-foot sidewinder lay. Since it wouldn't do to have any of the stage line's squeamish customers catch sight of it, he tossed the skin out the rear door, onto the scrap heap, then set about placing plates and silverware on the tables.

He had to have everything ready to go. The stage never stayed more than half an hour, if that, barely enough time for the passengers to heed nature's call and down a quick meal.

Turning, Wynn was startled to see the stranger a few feet inside the doorway. "I didn't hear you come in," he blurted.

Despite the heat, the man now wore his frock coat. His saddlebags were draped over his shoulder, a Henry repeater in his left hand. He stepped to the table farthest from the entrance and sat facing it, his back to the wall, propping the Henry against his chair.

The precautions were not lost on Wynn. "Care for a drink, mister?" he asked to cover his nervousness.

"Water will do."

"Comin' right up." Wynn quickly poured a glass from a pitcher he kept on the sink. On his way over, he noted that the man held his right hand under the table, no doubt near the Colt.

If the stranger wasn't a gunman, then Wynn had missed his guess.

"Here you are, friend."

"Obliged," the tall man said, taking the glass with his left hand.

"The stew will be ready soon," Wynn said absently.

"When is the stage due?"

"Anytime now."

Sipping slowly, the man smiled as he quenched his thirst. "More precious than gold," he repeated softly, as if to himself.

"Mind if I sit and chew the fat?" Wynn proposed, reaching for another chair.

The rider locked his steely eyes on Wynn's. "I'm a mite particular about the company I keep," he said in that deceptively lazy drawl of his.

Offended, Wynn started to return to the sink, then mustered his courage and pivoted. "Listen, sonny," he said amiably enough, "I didn't mean to get your goat a while ago. It's not as if I think poorly of Mexicans or anything like that."

"You could have fooled me," the man said, and gave a little shrug. "But what you do is your affair, not mine."

"True, true," Wynn said. "I'd just like for you to know the truth so there's no hard feelin's. I don't get many visitors worth wastin' a breath on, but you're different." He leaned on the table. "Hell, it's as plain as the nose on your face that you're your own man, and so am I."

"Oh?"

"I live my life my way and I don't give a tinker's damn what other folks think," Wynn declared. He glanced at the door to make sure Salazar wasn't anywhere near. "Sure, I pay Mexicans less than I'd pay whites. But everybody does it, not just me. Truth is, I pay better than most. You can ask Salazar if you don't believe me."

"Like I said, what you do is your affair."

Wynn was more mystified than ever. Why was the stranger so put out by a practice so common that everyone else, including the Mexicans, took it for granted? "I'm not a Mex hater, if that's what you're thinkin'," he said. "It's just my nature. Believe it or not, I'm not a joy to be around."

"So I gathered," the man said, and grinned.

Pleased the ice had been broken, Wynn extended his hand. "Can we start over on the right foot?" He introduced himself.

The tall man considered Wynn's hand a moment before shaking. When he did so, he used his left hand, shaking crossways rather than raise his right arm. "Lee Scurlock."

"Scurlock?" Wynn said, the name jarring recollections of a notorious man-killer whose reputation had spread throughout the Southwest due to the gunman's involvement in a bloody fracas over in Lincoln County, New Mexico. Choosing his words with care, he mentioned, "A short while back I heard tell that a man by that name was riding with the runt they call Billy the Kid. Are you Doc Scurlock?"

"Doc is my older brother."

"You don't say!" Wynn declared, delighted to make the acquaintance of someone related to a real celebrity. He took a seat. "Your brother is a famous man in these parts."

Lee gazed out the window. "I reckon."

"That Billy Bonney has been the talk of the territory for months now," Wynn went on. "Hell, I hear he's made a big name for himself back in the East, too, thanks to the papers."

"As big as Hickok ever was," Lee said wearily.

Wynn leaned forward. "So tell me, what's the latest news? Have they caught the Kid yet?"

"Not yet."

"Is it true he's vowed never to be taken alive?"

"Yes."

"What about your brother?"

"What about him?"

"They say Doc has killed seven men in gunfights," Wynn said. "And the newspapers claimed he was involved in that big scrape in Lincoln."

"He was."

Something in the younger man's manner stopped Wynn from asking another question. Cocking his head, he said, "Ain't the talkative type, are you, sonny?"

"So I've been told." Lee Scurlock tilted his glass and downed the rest of the water in a single gulp, then smacked the glass on the tabletop.

"I didn't mean to pry," Wynn said. "I just—" He stopped when hooves drummed outside, and listened for the telltale creak and rattle of the stage. Not hearing it, he rose and headed for the door. "Now, who could that be? Tarnation, this place is gettin' worse than a train depot in a big city!"

Just then, into the stage station strutted trouble with a capital *T*.

Chapter Two

"Long time no see, old-timer."

The speaker was a wolfish, muscular man in his early twenties. Curly blond hair ringed rounded ears, a golden halo to contrast with his devilishly handsome features. Blessed with flawless good looks, he had turned the head of many an unwed filly and quite a few married females, besides. In addition to his vanity, Nate Collins was notorious for his speed with a six-shooter, as well as his readiness to resort to one at the most innocent of slights.

"To what do I owe this honor?" Clarence Wynn asked. He disliked Collins only slightly less than the two men the young tough was with.

Hooking his thumbs in his gunbelt, Nate chuckled. "If I didn't know better, Morco," he said, "I'd swear old Clarence ain't glad to see us." He figured that secretly the old station owner was afraid of them, and it tickled him. Inspiring fear always gave him a thrill.

"Sounds that way to me, amigo," said Morco, a husky, hairy Mexican who wore a brown sombrero and adorned his left hip with a Remington. A recent arrival in Arizona, he had drifted north of the border after murdering three people in Sonora.

"Me, too," added their companion, a weasel of a character dressed in grungy range clothes. Although as thin as a rail, he wore a Smith & Wesson on either hip. Gristy, he called himself. Few believed it was his real name. Rumor had it that he was wanted for killings in Texas and elsewhere.

Wynn refused to be cowed. "The last time you three were here, you shot holes in my ceiling," he snapped. "I want your word that you'll behave yourselves this time around."

"Or what?" Nate Collins taunted, casually resting his hand on the smooth butt of his Colt.

The three hardcases reminded Wynn of rabid wolves about to pounce. He wanted no part of them. Not when he was standing there unarmed. "All I'm askin' is that you keep your irons in their leather," he said, and made for the kitchen area to be closer to his rifle.

Nate let the old geezer walk off. He had to. The stage wouldn't linger if he shot the owner dead, which meant he wouldn't be able to do as his boss wanted, which in turn would make his boss mad. And the last thing Nate wanted was to anger his employer. "So what if we put a few holes in your roof?" he said. "At least we didn't put them in *you*."

Wynn decided to change the subject. "On your way back to the Bar K?"

"What if we are? Are you pryin' into our business, old man?" Nate responded.

There had been a time when no one would have

talked to Clarence Wynn in so insolent a manner. Wrinkles, he had learned, bred disrespect in the young. It should be the other way around, but life was seldom fair. Swallowing his pride, he said, "Not me. I'm not loco."

Nate Collins chortled. "You're a smart man, Clarence. No wonder you've lived so long." Nodding at a shelf behind the counter, he said, "Rustle us up a bottle of your best coffin varnish. We rode hard to get here before the stage arrives, and we're thirsty as hell."

"The stage?" Wynn said, concerned.

"The whiskey," Nate reminded him. As the station owner hustled to comply, Nate's gaze alighted on Lee Scurlock. "Well, what have we here?" he inquired of no one in particular.

Morco had already seen the man, and he did not like what he saw. A shrewd judge of character, he rated men on how dangerous he felt they were. This one, he sensed, was more dangerous than most.

Wynn halted and glanced from Scurlock to Collins. "He's a customer, and I'll thank you to leave him be."

"I do as I damn well please," Nate said, echoing the sentiments Wynn had expressed a short while ago. "Now, produce that rotgut, fast." Motioning to Morco and Gristy, Nate sauntered to the stranger's table. "Howdy, mister. I guess no one told you that this table is reserved for us."

Lee Scurlock sat impassively, the empty glass in his left hand.

Gristy fidgeted. He disliked it when anyone treated them as if they were dirt, and that was exactly what the man in the frock coat was doing. "Didn't you hear me, pard?" he demanded.

"He must be deaf," Nate said.

Morco was a few feet behind his friends. He nearly

recoiled when the stranger looked up at them; an icy chill rippled down his spine. His every instinct screamed at him to do as Wynn had advised. He wanted to suggest that they pick another table, but he held his tongue. His friends would think he was yellow. They would laugh at his expense. That, he could not allow.

Gristy sidled to the left. "Maybe this jasper needs new holes in his ears," he said, sneering wickedly.

"Maybe he does," Nate agreed. He'd never met anyone so all-fired eager to inflict pain as the weasel. Once, just to show how the Apaches had tortured an acquaintance, Gristy did the same to a puppy he stole. It had taken that dog six hours to die.

"I'll do the honors," Gristy said, rather nonchalantly lowering his hands to the Smith & Wessons.

The sharp, unmistakable click of a gun hammer being cocked caused the trio to stiffen. Clarence Wynn also heard, and tensed, hoping Scurlock would put windows in the skulls of all three.

Nate Collins stared at the top of the table. It dawned on him that the stranger's right hand was out of sight, and he mentally cursed himself for being a jackass. Licking his lips, he said with forced levity, "What are you hidin' under there, friend?"

"I'm not your friend," came the harsh reply. "And if that son of a bitch next to you doesn't take his hands off his hoglegs, I'm liable to start shooting."

Clarence Wynn suppressed an urge to guffaw at the expressions the three gunmen wore. He hoped one of them would be dumb enough to pull on Scurlock, but they disappointed him.

Nate elevated his hands, palms out. "There's no call to get so tetchy, mister. We were just funnin' you, is all."

Gristy eased his spread fingers from the Smith & Wessons. "That's right. Just pokin' fun," he parroted.

"Do you see me laughing?" Lee Scurlock said.

None of them answered.

The man in the frock coat slowly stood, the Henry in his left hand, the cocked Colt held rock steady in his right. "If you ever hooraw me again," he warned, "you'll be worm food." With measured steps he skirted the table and backed to the doorway. Nodding at Wynn, he departed.

"Wheee-oh!" Nate Collins exclaimed, letting out the breath he had not been aware of holding.

Gristy clenched and unclenched his hands. "The gall of that hombre! Who does he think he is, anyhow?" He swung toward the station owner. "What's his handle, you old buzzard?"

"How should I know?" Wynn fibbed. "I never laid eyes on the gent until a short while before you got here. He wasn't much for conversation."

Morco said nothing. He thought it unwise to constantly push others, as his newfound friends were forever doing. Sooner or later they were bound to meet someone who would not bend, and he did not care to be with them when that happened. It was stupid to die for nothing.

When Morco killed, he did so for a reason, as had been the case with the three men he murdered in Mexico. One had made the mistake of flashing around a thick wad of bills at a cantina, another had owned a fine sorrel that was now Morco's, and the third had suspected him of slaying the second.

Morco had dropped all three from ambush, then buried the bodies where no one would ever find them. Or so he thought, until a boy out playing with a dog stumbled on the last grave and the dog, drawn by the scent of blood, dug down, exposing part of the body. The *federales* had been called in, of course, leaving Morco only one option.

So here he was, north of the border, working for

a man who had as few scruples as he did.

Nate Collins walked around the table Lee Scurlock had vacated and sat down in Scurlock's chair. It hit him that although the man in the frock coat had thrown down on them and lived to tell of it, they had buffaloed the bastard into leaving. That counted for something.

Ever since he was knee high to a calf, Nate had taken considerable pleasure in making others do as he wanted. He could remember beating up his brothers and sisters as a kid when they had something he wanted and they would not hand it over. At the age of eleven he'd nearly kicked a neighbor boy to death because the boy refused to give him a folding knife he had taken a shine to.

The way Nate saw things, there were two kinds of people in the world: the sheep and the wolves. The sheep were there to be sheared, and he was one of those who truly loved shearing.

"I don't like anyone runnin' roughshod over me," Gristy declared, sinking into a chair on his friend's left. He was so mad he could hardly think straight. No one was allowed to get the better of him, ever.

Gristy's pa was to blame. Until he turned fifteen, his old man had beaten the tar out of him every time he turned around, walloping him for things like not chopping enough wood for the fireplace or forgetting to feed the chickens. It had gotten so bad that Gristy ran away from home.

The first thing Gristy did when he was on his own was to scrimp and save up enough money to buy a pistol. He'd practiced and practiced until he was as slick as a greased gopher snake when he drew. No one had laid a finger on him since.

Angrily pounding the table, Gristy hollered, "Where's that red-eye, old man? You'd best put some spring in your step!"

"It's on the way," Wynn responded, retrieving a bottle he had watered down the week before. He grabbed three dirty glasses from the sink, wiped them with an even dirtier apron, and hurried over. "Here. Help yourself."

Moving to the stove, Wynn made a show of inspecting the stew, even going so far as to dip in the ladle and sip as if tasting it. In reality, he had his ears pricked to catch snatches of their conversation.

"I don't like backin' down to any man," Gristy was saying. "I've half a mind to follow that coyote and settle accounts."

"Simmer down," Nate said. "We have us a job to do, remember? That comes first. As for the dandy in the frock coat, he'll get his eventually. As my dear sainted ma used to say, all things come to those who wait."

"Maybe so," Gristy groused, "but I've never been long on patience." After pouring himself a glass, he gulped thirstily, savoring the burning sensation that seared his parched throat.

"Only a jackass bucks a rigged deck," Nate said. "If we'd touched our hardware, that son of a bitch would have blown out our lamps. So I let him walk away until I can repay the courtesy when the odds are in our favor. Savvy?"

"I savvy," Gristy said, "but I still don't like it."

Nate took a swig straight from the bottle, smacked his lips, then wiped his mouth with the left sleeve of his red shirt. "That temper of yours will be the death of you one day," he predicted.

Morco motioned at the whiskey. "Let me have a taste, amigo."

Wynn lingered at the stew, stirring it. For the life of him, he couldn't imagine why those three had shown up when they did. Whatever they were up to, it was bound to be no good. Which was why their mention of the stage had him so worried.

"I hope we don't have too long to wait," Gristy remarked.

"We'll stick as long as it takes," Nate said. "Mr. Kemp gave us orders, and we'll follow them to the letter."

At that moment Salazar appeared, calling out, "*Senor* Wynn, the stage is coming."

"Thanks," Wynn said, his stomach churning. "Take care of the team, will you? I have things to do in here."

"*Si, senor,*" Salazar said, mildly surprised. His employer always greeted the stages to swap good-natured insults with the drivers. Something must be wrong, but it was not his place to question. So he left.

Gristy bent toward Nate. "What if he ain't on it?" he asked. "Do we wait for the next one?"

"He'll be on it," Nate said. "The boss was sure."

"I hope so," Morco said. There was a certain *senorita* counting on him to show up in town that night, and he did not care to let her down.

Intense curiosity burned in Wynn, mingled with rising dread. He hoped they would say more, but they fell silent as the racket made by the approaching stage grew louder and louder, until with a clatter of hooves and a rhythmic creaking the coach rumbled to a halt outside the relay station. A billowing cloud of fine dust eddied at the open door.

Voices punctuated its arrival. Horses whinnied at the tempting scent of water. Footfalls neared the building. Wynn walked to the counter and tied the apron around his middle.

First to enter was a portly man attired in an ill-fitting suit, his balding pate crowned by a muley.

A citified slicker, Wynn decided. A drummer, by

the looks of him. Or maybe a dentist. It was hard to tell the two types apart.

Next came a stately gray-haired matron in a prim blue dress. She was using a fan to lessen the effect of the awful July heat on her pale neck.

Wynn's interest perked up substantially.

The slicker and the matron took seats at separate tables without saying a word, the latter bestowing a charming smile on the station owner.

Flustered, Wynn returned the favor. There should be others, he mused. The front office rarely sent a run down the line without at least four paying passengers on board. Were they availing themselves of the facilities out back? He made for the stove with an armful of bowls.

Wynn saw the three hardcases glance sharply at the entrance. Just entering were a man and a young woman. They were obviously related. Both had full heads of flaming red hair, the man's partly covered by a Stetson, the woman's falling to shapely slim shoulders. Both had frank blue eyes and pointed chins. The man wore a costly brown suit, the woman a stylish beige dress.

Gristy whispered excitedly to Nate.

"Make yourselves comfortable, folks," Wynn announced. "Vittles are just about to be served."

With a wave of a hand, the handsome man indicated the table at which the matron sat. "Shall we, my dear?" he said. He held a chair for the young woman, then, with a sigh, slid into another. "It's nice to be sitting on something that isn't bouncing up and down," he quipped.

Wynn hurried over, aware of the evil looks the three toughs cast at the pair. "Howdy," he said, and informed them who he was. He wished there were something he could say to warn them, but he dared not with the gunmen eavesdropping. "I hope none of you object to stew and biscuits. If you're so inclined, I've got liquid refreshment, too." Winking, he bobbed his chin at the shelf containing the hard stuff.

"A simple glass of water for the two of us will suffice," said the man in the Stetson, indicating the lovely young redhead. "This is my daughter, Allison. I'm Jim Hays."

"Pleased to meet you," Wynn said, with a hopeful look at the matron. "How about you, ma'am?"

"Water, if you please," she said softly.

The drummer at the other table piped up and said, "I'll take some whiskey, sir. Nothing less will wash down all the dust I've swallowed today."

"Hold your britches," Wynn said, giving the matron his best smile. As much as he liked living alone, he was not above being friendly to an occasional female. Some things a man just couldn't do without.

It took no time at all to fetch the water. As Wynn turned to the shelf for the bug juice, he glimpsed Nate Collins rising, wearing a malevolent smirk. His stomach did flip-flops.

Nate raised his voice so everyone could hear. "Water, mister? Did I hear you say that you're only drinkin' water?"

Jim Hays, taken aback, scrutinized the gunman closely. "Are you addressing me, young man?"

Like a cougar stalking prey, Nate Collins moved toward their table, his smirk widening, his spurs jangling with each step. "I sure ain't talkin' to that potbelly over yonder," he said, jerking his thumb at the drummer.

"Who are you calling a potbelly, sir?" the slicker asked, taking offense.

Nate swiveled, his right hand hovering near his Colt. His tone became thick with menace. "You're the only one here with more fat on him than my grandpappy's hog. 'Course, if you don't like me pointin' it out, you're perfectly welcome to show how much grit you've got."

Totally flustered, the portly passenger averted his red face and folded his hands in front of him.

"What's the matter?" Nate would not let it be. "No gumption? Make smoke anytime you're ready."

"I'm not armed," the drummer said.

"Whose fault is that?" Nate retorted, eliciting laughter from Gristy and Morco. "If you're too stupid to go around heeled, you'd better be ready to curl your tail when you meddle in matters that don't concern you."

Jim Hays cleared his throat and drew a grateful look from the drummer by saying, "He's done nothing to you, young man. You should let him alone."

Nate wheeled, a vicious gleam animating his eyes. "Should I, now? And who are you to be telling me what I should be doing?"

Hays was a big man, and he was not intimidated. "You act as if you're on the prod. If so, maybe you should go elsewhere. None of us want any trouble."

"Is that a fact? And who's going to put me in my place if I don't? You, mister?"

Wynn saw Hays's eyes narrow. The man in the Stetson realized that Collins was up to something, that he was prodding them on purpose. Hays or the drummer had to be the one the three gunmen were waiting for. Whoever it was, their potential victim was as good as dead. When Nate Collins worked himself into a killing mood, lead was bound to fly.

Jim Hays controlled himself with a visible effort. "I'm warning you, young man," he said severely. "Either desist with this juvenile behavior or I'll report you to the first law office I see."

Raucous laughter burst from the Bar K riders. "Oh, my!" Gristy squealed in mock terror. "He's going to tell the law on us! I'm tremblin' in my boots!"

Diablo

Allison Hays had been sitting quietly, her features inscrutable. Abruptly, she straightened, demanding with fiery passion, "Why don't you stick your head in the horse trough and cool off? We haven't done a thing to deserve this barbaric treatment." She was about to say more, but her father gripped her wrist and shook his head.

Nate blinked, feigning shock. He had hoped the girl would speak up. She was as fine a looker as he had ever seen, and he was strongly tempted to run his fingers through her luxurious red mane. Lecherously ogling her figure, he said, "A regular firebrand, ain't you, lady?"

Allison would have risen if not for her father's restraining hand. "If I were a man, I'd teach you manners."

"I believe you," Nate said soberly. "It's plain who wears the britches in your family."

Morco and Gristy cackled.

"See here!" Jim Hays said hotly. "This has gone far enough. I won't have you insulting my daughter."

Nate resorted to his customary smirk. "Well, I apologize, then. All I wanted was to offer you a taste of a man's drink. Water is for pussy-kittens. Have a glass of whiskey with me."

"No," Jim Hays said.

"Come on. *Por favor,*" Nate coaxed. "I'm being real sociable, mister. The least you can do is accept to show there are no hard feelings."

Jim Hays hesitated. He exchanged a peculiar look with his daughter, then said, "I can't."

"Can't? Or won't?"

It was Allison who answered. "All we want is water."

"What's wrong? Ain't I good enough to drink with?"

Clarence Wynn knew he should do something. As

31

station master, he was responsible for the welfare of the passengers. But he had no hankering to get himself shot full of holes, which was bound to happen if he butted in. He saw now that it was Hays the trio were after, that Collins was determined to provoke the man into doing something rash.

"I don't care for any whiskey," Jim Hays stressed emphatically.

Nate backed up a stride and bent his elbow so his hand was almost touching his six-shooter. He had followed his boss's instructions to the letter, and now was the moment of truth. "Seems to me I'm the one who has just been insulted. Stand up and take your medicine."

Before the father could respond, Allison Hays leaped to her feet and shook a finger at their tormentor. "How dare you threaten us, you vermin!" Her face blazed, matching the hue of her hair. "You're an animal! Go away, or else!"

"Or else what?" Nate said. "Are you aimin' to slap me for misbehavin'? I'd like that. I admire a female who plays rough."

Jim Hays stood, his fists balled. "That's enough!" he thundered. "I will not sit still and let you abuse my daughter."

Gristy, then Morco, also rose.

A palpable tension seized the room, crackling with the energy of a lightning bolt, threatening to erupt into violence at any second. Nate Collins was poised to draw on Jim Hays, and his two partners were set to back his play. A careless word or hasty movement by Hays would result in his instant death.

At that moment, when the ominous atmosphere was on the verge of unleashing a leaden hailstorm, a calm voice spoke from the front doorway. "Are these polecats badgering you, ma'am?"

All eyes swung toward the square-shouldered form

of Lee Scurlock. His striking blue eyes were on Allison Hays. The left side of his frock coat had been swept back, revealing his ivory-handled Peacemaker.

Jim Hays replied, "Yes, they are."

Scurlock said nothing. He stared at Allison, waiting for her to acknowledge his question. It was as if they were the only people in the station. Or the only ones who mattered to him.

Allison Hays met his stare. With a toss of her head, she said, "These ruffians are trying to goad my father into a fight. I would like for them to desist."

"Then they will," the man in the frock coat said, and he shifted toward the gunmen.

Chapter Three

It was not the first time Lee Scurlock had confronted killers on the prod.

As clearly as if it had just happened, Lee recalled the day his brother, Josiah—whose nickname was "Doc"—taught him how to use a pistol, and the words of wisdom Josiah had imparted: "Never let yourself get flustered. The man who loses his head loses his life. Keep your nerves as steady as steel, and don't let your mind drift."

Lee had learned his lessons well. Willing himself to relax, he scanned the three gunmen, taking their measure. The blond leader seemed flabbergasted that anyone had opposed them. The Mexican had cold but wary eyes; he would not draw unless drawn on. The greatest danger came from the weasel, whose fury was barely contained.

Gristy sidled to the right to be clear of the table. "If you know what's good for you, mister, you'll get the hell out of here while you still can."

Clarence Wynn edged toward his Winchester, intending to side with the southerner if gunplay broke out. No one could handle all three gunmen alone. They were too fast.

Gristy had not gotten a reply, and his fury was mounting. "Didn't you hear me?" he rasped. "Vamoose."

Lee Scurlock took a step to the left and planted his feet firmly. Out of the corner of his eye he noticed the redhead gazing at him in wide-eyed wonder, and he shut her from his thoughts, just as his brother had taught him. "I want the three of you to shed your irons," he directed.

"Do *what?*" Gristy snarled.

"We're not backin' down this time," Nate Collins said. Not that he expected it to make a difference. As incredible as it seemed, the stranger actually had enough sand to take on the three of them. No one had ever done that before.

Morco found his voice. "Hit the breeze, hombre," he said, the short hairs at the nape of his neck prickling. Something about the gringo bothered him, something he could not quite put his finger on, something that told him not to go for his revolver. But he had to if the others did. They were his *compadres.*

Again a terrible tension charged the room. More than a minute went by and no one uttered a sound.

The strain began to take a toll on Gristy. Nervously switching his weight from the ball of one foot to the other, he licked his thin lips and scowled. It rankled him, being put upon—and twice by the same upstart. *"Damn your hide!"* he roared, more to bolster his bloodlust than anything else. "I'll show you!" With that, he clawed at his Smith & Wessons.

Gristy's enraged act served as the signal for his two

companions to unlimber their pistols. Their arms were blurs. Gristy wore a smile of triumph, born of supreme confidence in his speed and accuracy. In the blink of an eye he had the Smith & Wessons out and leveled. To his amazement, though, the air rocked to the boom of the tall man's Colt even as his fingers were tightening on the triggers.

Lee Scurlock fired at the two-gun hothead, pivoted, and sent another slug into their blond leader. He pivoted again to fire at Morco, but the hairy Mexican had frozen with the Remington partway out.

It all happened so swiftly that the onlookers were not quite sure of the sequence of events. They saw Gristy smashed backward, blood spurting from his chest. They saw him crash into the wall with his arms outspread, then crumple like a toppled house of cards.

They also saw Nate Collins whipped around, his six-shooter sent flying. He was jolted to the floor, where he clutched at his bloody right shoulder in agony.

Transfixed by the astounding turn of events, Morco stood with the tip of his revolver's barrel hooked in the top of his holster. His skin itched as if from a rash. A tingle rippled down his backbone, and he thrust his left hand at the man in the frock coat, crying, "Don't shoot!"

"Get to fighting or drop the gun," Lee instructed.

The Remington hit the dirt floor with a thud. Morco elevated his arms, not caring one whit if his *compadres* branded him a coward. He would rather live than die any day.

Gristy was propped against the wall, a scarlet stain working down the front of his shirt. "Help me!" he whined, dizziness assailing him. "Dear God! Someone help me!"

No one moved to his aid. A cloud of gun smoke

slowly spread outward, causing the drummer to hack and sputter.

"You bored me!" Gristy fumed at Lee. "I'm dyin'!"

"Good riddance," Lee drawled. He had known men like the weasel before, and the world was a better place without them and their evil.

The scrawny gunman looked at Morco. "Get word to my brother," he pleaded. Blood was trickling from the corner of his mouth and dribbling down his chin. "You owe me that much."

Morco nodded.

Everyone was dumbfounded when the kindly matron unexpectedly rose and hastened over to the stricken gun-shark. "There, there," she said to soothe him, clasping his shoulders.

Wynn had the Winchester in his hands, but he did not remember picking it up. Going to the matron's side, he said gently, "Don't bother with that no-account, ma'am. He's not worth the bother."

She focused on him in reproach. "He's a human being, isn't he?"

"Barely," Wynn said.

"The Good Book says we must do unto others as we would have them do unto us," the matron said. "Even sinners need comfort when it's their time to cast off this earthly coil."

Wynn didn't know what to say. Bible-thumpers always left him tongue-tied. Arguing with them was like arguing with living Bibles, and he wasn't about to slur Scripture. Although never much of a church-goer, he favored not doing anything to get on the Almighty's bad side.

Gristy was having a hard time breathing. He had lost all sensation in his body and the world around him was blurring. "I don't want to die!" he groaned.

"Do you have any last requests?" the matron politely inquired.

A stupid question, Gristy thought. Sure he had a last request! He'd like to live! He yearned to spit in her face but could not gather the spittle he needed.

Lee Scurlock had no more interest in the weasel. Advancing, he towered over the blond gunman. "On your feet."

"I can't," Nate said through clenched teeth. He had lost a lot of blood and was feeling woozy. Torment racked him with every breath. When he tried to move, his shoulder shrieked with anguish.

"Your legs aren't busted," Lee said, and roughly yanked the hard case to his feet, heedless of Nate's stifled outcry. Anyone who tried to kill him deserved no sympathy. "Take your *compañero* and make yourself scarce."

"I need a doctor," Nate complained.

"If I hadn't rushed my shot, you'd need an undertaker," Lee informed him. "Count your blessings and skedaddle before I change my mind."

Morco was not about to tempt fate twice. Darting to his friend's side, he braced Nate under one arm and angled toward the door. "Let's go, amigo," he said. "There will be other days."

"But Gristy—!" Nate said.

The weasel's head flopped to the right and left. Eyes wide, blood oozing thickly over his lower lip, he whimpered like a puppy. "I hurt!" he wailed. "Lordy, I hurt!"

"Downright pathetic," Wynn commented. He didn't know why it was, but the scum who made a habit of bucking other folks out in a haze of gun smoke were usually the ones who fell all to pieces when their own time came.

"Go to hell!" Gristy said. Marshaling his fading strength, he stared at the man who had mortally wounded him. A spasm racked him as he huffed, "I'll have the last laugh, you bastard! When my brother hears about this, he'll come gunnin' for you. You'll be dead before the year is out. Mark my words."

"If your brother comes after me, your parents will lose two sons," Lee promised.

"May you rot in—" Gristy began to say, but couldn't. Stiffening, he raggedly sucked air, quivered spastically, then pitched onto his right side and was still.

Wynn snorted. "One less bad apple."

Over by the entrance, Morco firmed his grip on Nate, who plucked at the Mexican's elbow. "Wait! My hogleg. I dropped it."

Lee Scurlock wagged his Colt. "Leave it."

"You can't take a man's gun," Nate said venomously.

"When you want it back, I won't be hard to find."

Feral hatred animated Nate's countenance as Morco carted him from the premises. He was in a funk, craving to curse a blue streak, but he lacked the energy. "This ain't over," he vowed weakly.

For a few moments no one said anything. Clarence Wynn felt sorry for the southerner. Scurlock should have killed all three when he had the chance. "You've made a mortal enemy today, son," he said. "That curly wolf won't rest until you're six feet under."

Lee had gone to the door to be sure the pair departed. Morco boosted the blond into the saddle of a dun, forked leather himself, and gripped the dun's reins. Without a backward glance, the Mexican headed westward.

Wynn's boot nudged something, and he looked down to find Collins's pistol. "I reckon this is yours now," he said, carrying it over to Lee.

Still watching the gunmen, Lee accepted the Colt and hefted it. Like his, it was a Peacemaker, but plain in comparison, with walnut grips and no nickel plating. Still, the balance was superb, the single action smooth.

"Excuse me," the matron said anxiously.

Lee checked to verify that the killers were gone, then turned to learn why she was upset. Two men stood close to the rear door, the shorter of the pair holding a scattergun aimed in his direction. The other fellow, a scarecrow in buckskins and a floppy hat, was armed with a Sharps rifle. Automatically, he covered them both with the two Colts, assuming they were friends of the gunmen.

Wynn took one look and sprang in front of Scurlock to avert more bloodshed. "Buckskin, you danged idiot!" he yelled at the man with the Sharps. "What do you think you're doing? This hombre just saved one of your passengers from being made into wolf meat."

Buckskin promptly lowered the big buffalo gun. "What the Sam Hill went on here, Wynn? We heard the shooting and snuck around back to get the drop on whoever was being rambunctious."

"Rambunctious, my foot!" Wynn said. "Those Bar K hands were fixin' to murder Mr. Hays." He thrust his own rifle at the man bearing the scattergun. "Shorty, didn't you hear me? Put that cannon away before you cut someone in half."

Shorty sheepishly complied.

Stepping aside, Wynn introduced the two men to Lee Scurlock, adding, "There's no cause for alarm. Buckskin, here, drives the stage, and Shorty rides shotgun when they're carryin' valuables."

Lee had been in the stable when the stage pulled in and had not paid much attention to anyone once he spied Allison Hays. Her beauty had caught his breath in his throat, and he had not taken his eyes off her until she disappeared inside. It was strange, how he reacted. He couldn't recall ever being so frazzled by a pretty face before.

Buckskin was talking. "We were tending to the stock and giving Salazar a hand switching the team when we heard the shots. Any idea why they'd be after Mr. Hays?"

Everyone faced the father and daughter. Lee twirled his Colt into his holster with a flourish and began to wedge the spare revolver under his belt. That was when he noticed the blatant admiration that the redheaded beauty was lavishing on him. He met her sweet, wonderful, awed gaze, drinking in the loveliness she unconsciously radiated. The proper thing to do was introduce himself, but his tongue refused to work. To cover his embarrassment, he swiped at the acrid gun smoke.

Her father came around the table, offered his hand, and explained who he was. "I don't know what got into those men. I'd never seen them before. But I do know I'd be dead right now if you hadn't stepped in."

Lee swore he could feel his cheeks burn. Shrugging, he made light of the incident. "I heard them giving your daughter a hard time," he said lamely. "What man worthy of the name wouldn't help out?"

Jim Hays glanced at the ivory-handled Colt. "I don't believe I've ever seen anyone as quick as you, and I've witnessed more than my share of gunplay over the years."

Lee shrugged again. "I was lucky."

"You were magnificent!" Allison Hays declared, then pressed a hand over her mouth, shocked by her own declaration. "I mean," she corrected herself, grinning in an effort to be lighthearted, "only a magnificent gentleman would come to the rescue of a damsel in distress."

Lee's legs moved toward her of their own accord.

"Thanks, ma'am. I don't often get compliments from a lady like yourself."

"Will you join us?" Allison asked hopefully, pushing out a chair to her right. She would never admit as much, but she found her rescuer irresistibly handsome.

"Please do," her father said.

The southerner looked at Gristy. Since he was responsible for gunning the man down, by rights he should dispose of the body. As if the station owner could read his thoughts, Wynn clapped him on the back and said, "We'll take care of the trash."

Nodding, Lee lowered himself, instantly pushing up again when he realized that the redhead was still standing. It had been so long since he was around a well-mannered woman that he forgot his own manners. "Allow me," he said, holding her chair for her.

Jim Hays took his seat.

The matron knowingly appraised the young woman and her knight-errant, then moved to the drummer's table. Wynn, Buckskin, and Shorty briskly attended to the corpse, whispering all the while, now and again secretly studying the man who had brought Gristy low.

The redhead looked into her benefactor's lake-blue eyes and felt her pulse quicken. "I didn't catch your name," she said softly.

"Lee Scurlock, ma'am."

"Please, call me Allison."

"All right, Allison," Lee said, rolling her name off his tongue as if it were golden honey. He could not take his eyes off her smooth complexion or her full, rosy lips.

"Scurlock?" Jim Hays repeated quizzically. "Are you any relation to the one they call Doc Scurlock?"

"He's my older brother," Lee admitted.

Allison found the news interesting. "Your brother

is a physician?" Her childhood ambition had been to become a doctor, but she had been sidetracked by a later desire to follow in her father's footsteps.

"No, ma'—Allison," Lee corrected himself.

"Doc Scurlock is a gunman," Jim Hays said. "A man-killer who operates in New Mexico Territory, if I'm not mistaken. There was a story about him in the newspaper last year, about his escapades with Billy the Kid."

Lee mightily regretted ever getting to know the happy-go-lucky youngster who was now touted as the "Terror of the Southwest" by a hack journalist slavering after sensational headlines. But then, who could have foreseen how events would unfold? How famous Billy would become?

Allison's forehead furrowed, and she glanced at the scarlet stain on the wall. "Is *everyone* in your family a gunman, Mr. Scurlock?"

"Call me Lee," he coaxed, and felt it prudent to stare at the table instead of at her face for fear of the stirrings deep within him. "To answer your question, no. My brother and I are the only ones who have acquired a bit of a reputation for slinging six-shooters, and not by choice, I can assure you." He paused, feeling a strange compulsion to explain so she would not think ill of him. "My sister lives in Tennessee with her husband and five younguns. Two other brothers have their own farms there. As for my ma and pa, they were killed in a flood five years ago."

"My own mother passed on to her reward last year," Allison disclosed sadly. She could not say why, but she felt a peculiar kinship to the handsome stranger, an instinctive liking that was stimulating and discomfiting at the same time.

"I'm right sorry to hear that," Lee said sincerely. Losing a parent was one of the worst calamities he could think of.

David Robbins

"How do you make your living, then?" Allison inquired. "Do you kill people for money?"

Jim Hays stiffened, saying sternly, "Allison Hays! You know better than to pry into this fellow's personal life." His daughter had always displayed a knack for being brutally blunt. Most of the time he admired her honesty, but there were instances, such as now, when she overstepped the bounds of propriety.

"It's all right," Lee said. Had a man asked him that, he would have pistol-whipped the cur. But he could not find it in him to be offended by the redhead. "As a matter of fact," he went on, "of late, I've been making ends meet in a rather footloose fashion."

"How?" Allison brazenly prompted. She could not say why, but she wanted to learn all there was to know about him.

"At poker."

"You're a gambler?" Allison said, unable to keep a hint of distaste out of her tone. It had long been her opinion that men who made their living at cards were too lazy to secure decent work. And here her knight in shining armor did just that! She felt let down, as if he had failed her somehow.

"Afraid so," Lee confirmed. It was common knowledge that many folks frowned on the gambling fraternity, but until that moment it had never bothered him before.

Allison arched an eyebrow. "Correct me if I'm wrong. I admit that I don't know a lot about your profession, but there doesn't seem to be much of a future in your line of *work*." She emphasized the last word to show that it was anything but.

"So they say," Lee hedged. It was beginning to peeve him that she was being so critical when she had no notion of the circumstances that had led him to his current state.

"Don't you agree?" Allison asked earnestly.

"I'll confess I haven't cogitated the matter much," Lee said, his drawl more pronounced than ever. It always was when he became defensive. "I like to take each day as it comes along, without much thought for what lies ahead."

"You live hand to mouth, you mean," Allison said, her displeasure mounting. That in itself disturbed her. She had no earthly excuse for being so annoyed. If Lee Scurlock wanted to fritter his life away at a senseless occupation, that was his right. What should it matter to her?

Jim Hays was sipping his water when he saw something mirrored by his daughter's features that only someone who knew her as intimately as he did would have noticed. It was there, then it was gone. He glanced at the gunman again, not knowing whether to be happy or distressed. In the strained silence that had fallen between the two, he said, "Are you taking the stage, Lee?"

"I've got a horse," Lee said without really thinking about the question. He was preoccupied by Allison's beauty. She had tilted her head to stare out the window, and her face, caught in profile, was positively breathtaking.

"There's room for one more inside," Jim Hays suggested. It would be an ideal way of getting more acquainted with their benefactor, and give Hays an opportunity to confirm his suspicion about his daughter.

"If he doesn't want to come, we shouldn't prod him," Allison commented. "He probably has an important gambling engagement somewhere."

Her words, spoken quietly yet tinged with sarcasm, ate into Lee's conscience. He thought of all the women he had known in the past seven years, all those he'd met since he lit out from Tennessee with his brother, all the saloon fillies and dance-hall girls and the doves of the night who made their money on their backs, and a feeling he had not experienced in ages washed over him: guilt. Allison Hays qualified as the first genuine lady he had spoken to in a coon's age, and her acidic rebuke was like having a red-hot branding iron scorch his soul. With a start, he realized that her father was speaking to him again.

". . . our way to Diablo. Have you ever been there?"

"Can't say I ever heard of it," Lee said.

"The town is twenty-one miles west of here, the next stop down the line," Jim detailed. "An old friend of mine, Bob Delony, lives there. He's why we came. About two weeks ago we received word from him to come as fast as we could, so I suspect he's in a fix of some sort. A legal fix, that is. You see, I'm a lawyer."

"Oh?" Lee said, to be polite. He would rather talk to Allison, but she was acting distant.

"We live in Denver, Colorado," Jim said. He did not add that they had been there more than ten years, that they lived in a well-to-do section of the Mile High City, and that he enjoyed a thriving, lucrative practice. "I wanted to come to Diablo alone, but my daughter insisted on accompanying me. It might not be safe, though, with the situation as tense as it is."

"How do you mean?" Lee asked, aroused by the implied threat to Allison.

The lawyer's answer was forestalled by Clarence Wynn, who came over to their table bearing a grimy bandanna in his left hand. "Will you look at this?" he said. "We just found it in one of Gristy's pockets."

It was a human finger.

Chapter Four

Lee Scurlock could not say, exactly, why he did what he did next. Maybe it was the look of horror that came over Allison Hays's face. Maybe it was the notion, bred into him by his folks, that showing such a gruesome trophy to a lady was not proper. Whichever, he suddenly swatted the station owner's arm to one side and snapped, "There are women present."

Wynn was so stunned that he nearly lost his grip on the bandanna. Anger brought an oath to his lips, an oath he stifled when he realized that the pretty young redhead had recoiled and the matron was looking at him in disapproval. "Sorry," he blurted.

Allison recovered quickly, curiosity overriding her loathing. "Whatever would prompt a man to carry a grisly thing like that?"

Wynn covered it, saying, "Some men are peculiar, missy. I knew a trapper once who toted a coin pouch made from the breast of an Apache woman. And

47

there's a bartender in Texas said to keep a pickled Comanche kidney in a jar on his bar." He hefted the bandanna. "This here finger is an Indian's, too, unless I miss my guess. Gristy probably liked to take it out and fondle it when he was sittin' around a campfire at night and had nothin' better to do."

"How sick," Allison declared.

"Life in Arizona ain't for the squeamish, ma'am," Wynn said. "There are bad men like the three who braced your pa everywhere, and the Apaches and the Navajos are forever taking scalps and such." He paused. "I couldn't help but overhear that you're headed for Diablo. If'n you'll take my advice, you'll get on the first stage back out once you get there. It's no place for decent women, though a few call it home." He rejoined the stage driver and the shotgun.

Lee was reminded of Jim Hays's statement. "What was that about a tense situation?" he asked.

Hays finished his water. "My friend wasn't specific, but I gather that various factions are at odds and he's caught in the middle."

"What does your friend do?"

"He's a lawyer also. We went through school together back east, years ago."

A shuffling and scraping noise heralded the removal of Gristy's body. Wynn, Buckskin, and Shorty carted it out the back door, having to tug when one of Gristy's spurs snagged on the frame.

Allison worried that soon the stage would leave and she might never see the Tennessean again. "Where are you headed, if I may ask?"

Given how she had looked down her nose at his cardplaying, Lee was almost ashamed to say, "Nowhere special. I'm just sort of drifting at the moment."

"Drifting," Allison repeated, with all the enthusiasm she would have uttered the word "plague." She could not help herself. Her parents had instilled a strong work ethic in her. It was simply unthinkable that anyone would wander aimlessly through life like a piece of wood adrift on the sea.

Jim Hays coughed. "Why don't you tag along with us to Diablo? We wouldn't mind the company."

"Papa," Allison said, "I'm sure Mr. Scurlock doesn't have time to spare, what with his gambling and drifting and all."

Her father frowned. "You must forgive my daughter, Lee. She tends to be too critical sometimes, a failing she picked up from her mother, God bless her soul."

"Papa!" Allison exclaimed.

"Only twenty, and she thinks she can judge people like cowboys judge cattle," Jim continued, grinning impishly. As much as he loved his offspring, she had to be put in her place every now and then for her own benefit.

"I never!" Allison huffed. Her father had the disconcerting knack of making her feel as if she were ten instead of twenty, and he invariably did it in public.

Lee forgot himself and laughed. Immediately, he regretted it when Allison's eyes flashed with indignation.

"And how old might you be?" she asked.

"Twenty-seven next month," Lee divulged.

"Mercy. Yet you don't have a wife?"

"No, ma'am."

"Never married?"

"Allison, that's enough," Jim Hays said. "The poor man won't have any secrets left by the time you get done with him."

"I don't mind," Lee said, meeting her inquisitive look. "No, I've never been halterbroke."

Allison smiled smugly. "You make it sound as if

marriage is the same as breaking a new horse."

"They're acquainted, I reckon."

"How so?"

"Whether it's a horse or a woman, a man should always pick quality."

Jim Hays burst into mirth. "Doggone it, son! I like you! There aren't many men who can hold their own with my daughter."

Lee saw Allison blush and rushed to her defense without hesitation. "Most men, I've found, are intimidated by beautiful women."

The compliment flattered Allison immensely, but she was not about to let on that it did. "Intimidated?" she said. "Such a big word for a man who makes his living reading cards."

"My ma was real keen on book learning," Lee said. "All of us younguns had to read out loud every night."

"What would she say if she knew you were a gambler?" Allison pressed. She knew it was wrong. She knew that she had overstepped herself. But she wanted him to see it as she did.

"That's enough out of you," Jim Hays said strictly, and nodded at the southerner. "What about my proposition? You can ride along with the stage if you don't care to ride in it."

"I was thinking of heading to Tucson," Lee said. In truth he had been thinking no such thing, but it was apparent that the redhead was not as attracted to him as he was to her.

"You can always go on to Tucson later," Jim said, then had an inspiration. "If it's gambling you're after, Diablo might be to your liking. There are several reputable gaming establishments."

"Several?" Allison broke in. "It's more like two dozen."

"I said reputable," Jim pointed out, not taking his eyes off Scurlock. "What do you say?"

"I don't know . . ." Lee wavered.

"I'm not asking for myself so much as I am for Allison and the other passengers," Jim said. "Those rowdies headed west, didn't they? For all I know, we might encounter them again."

The man had a point, Lee reflected. The Mexican was bound to light a shuck for town and the nearest sawbones. If Hays bumped into them again, Lee wouldn't give two bits for the law wrangler's life. Allison might be harmed, too. "You've convinced me," he drawled. "I reckon I'll tag along.

"Excellent," Jim Hays said, beaming.

Allison did not think so. Or, rather, she did not quite know what to think. On the one hand, she was pleased that they were not parting company. On the other, her feelings toward the handsome southerner troubled her. She had never felt like this toward any man before. Yet she hardly knew him. What was the matter with her?

Forty minutes later, and half an hour behind schedule, the stage pulled out from the relay station. Wynn and Salazar stood waving as the coach rattled into the distance and was swallowed by the haze.

Lee Scurlock, astride his roan, rode beside the stage. He would rather have been in it so he could talk to Allison, but that would require him to tie his horse to the back. The poor animal would breathe dust all the way to Diablo. He could not put it through that, not after the ordeal of crossing the Painted Desert.

Although tired and sore and barely refreshed, the roan gamely stayed abreast of the stage. Lee rode on the right side, nearest the window at which Allison sat. He would gaze at her when he thought she was not looking.

The heat gave birth to rivulets of sweat that trickled down his back and front. His frock coat was once again tied behind the cantle. Thanks to his hat, his eyes were shielded from the harsh glare.

Lee's mind strayed to the meal at the relay station, to his enjoyable conversation with Jim Hays. Allison, oddly, had not said much after his comment about her beauty. He'd figured she would be flattered, but she didn't treat him as if she were.

Lee wasn't dumb. He knew that he had somehow offended her, and he reasoned that it had something to do with what he did for a living. While being a gambler did have a certain stigma attached to it, she had no call to treat him with contempt.

It would not have bothered him so much, except that every time he glanced at her, a tingle shot through his body. The irony of his infatuation was not lost on him, provoking a self-conscious grin.

Leave it to a chucklehead like him!

A man on the run had no time to dally, no time for luxuries like a woman, not if he wanted to keep one step ahead of those on his trail.

Lee had no doubt that his pursuers were still after him. In a rush, the memories played themselves across his mind. He recalled the talk Doc had given him the night before he left, how his brother felt that the Lincoln County War, as the newspapers dubbed it, would end in disaster for everyone who had sided with Alexander McSween and John Tunstall, both long since dead.

That included Billy the Kid, Bowdre, O'Folliard, and the Scurlock brothers. Billy and the others were still fighting, but the law now regarded them as outlaws. "It's only a question of time before we're hunted down," Doc had said. "But it doesn't have to happen to you."

It still galled Lee that his brother insisted he leave. It galled him more that he had done it, but then, ever since they forsook the rolling green hills of Tennessee to strike out on their own, he had been in the habit of doing whatever Doc wanted. How could he not? Doc was older. Doc was bigger. And he'd always rated Doc as smarter.

Sighing, Lee scanned the horizon for sign of the town. It was as much his own fault as Doc's that he was now on his own. If he had left well enough alone, if he had minded his own business and kept his mouth shut, if he had not indulged in a rash act of gunplay, he would not be a marked man.

He tossed his head, clearing the mental cobwebs. Ahead, the landscape was subtly changing. The desert had gradually given way to sage, which was now blending into scrub brush and stunted trees. Scattered buttes broke the monotony of the flatland. Soon hills replaced them, and when the stagecoach clattered through a gap between two of them, Lee found himself on a switchback above an incredibly lush valley, an oasis sheltered by mountains to the north and more hills far off to the west and the south.

It was startling, the change in the terrain. A meandering river was the cause, a sparkling blue ribbon that literally meant the difference between life and death for the plant and animal life that depended on it for survival. To say nothing of the two-legged inhabitants of the town, several of whom Lee spotted some two miles off.

Buckskin brought the coach to a stop on a shelf that afforded a panoramic vista of the verdant paradise. "Climb on out and stretch your legs, folks," he hollered. "I need to rest the team a bit before we take to the steep grade ahead."

Lee reined up and eased to the ground. Sunlight played off the buildings in the distance, pinpoints of light marking windows and metal. The river, he observed, flowed out of the mountains to the north, crossed the valley, and looped to the southwest along the base of the far hills. The town of Diablo was located on its east bank.

Lee strolled to the coach as Jim Hays was helping Allison down. "I never have been fond of stage travel," he remarked. "All that jostling jars a man's innards something terrible."

"Isn't that the truth," Jim said, stretching. "I feel as if every bone in my body is out of joint."

Allison was as perfectly composed as if she were in a sitting room. "I don't mind," she said. Truth was, she loved to travel, to see new sights, to meet new people.

Jim stepped to the edge of the shelf. "Isn't this extraordinary?" he said, encompassing the valley with a gesture. "We've been here several times, and I still can't get over how splendid it is. No wonder my friend Bob Delony likes it so much." He regarded Lee a moment. "Where will you stay once we hit town?"

"A hotel, I reckon."

"We'll be staying with Delony," Jim said. "I'll give you his address so you can pay us a visit sometime. I'm sure he'd like to meet you."

Allison was befuddled by her father's behavior. For someone who had always been critical of every suitor who ever courted her, he was being uncommonly friendly to Lee Scurlock. It made no sense. They hardly knew the southerner.

"We'll see," Lee said, unwilling to commit himself unless Allison showed a spark of interest in him. She still would not look him in the eyes. "I might only stay long enough to check on the whereabouts of those two I tangled with." He did not mention that he was doing it for them.

The driver, Buckskin, had been adjusting the traces, and overheard. "If you don't mind my sayin' so, sonny," he chimed in, "you'd best tread lightly if you go on the prod after Collins and Morco, or you'll find the whole Bar K outfit gunnin' for you. Wynn says you jerk a pistol like greased lightning, but there's just one of you and Allister Kemp has twenty top hands ridin' for him, every one loyal to the brand."

"Where does this Kemp fit in?" Lee asked.

Jim Hays answered. "Allister Kemp is an Englishman. He was the first white man to settle in this valley, years before silver was discovered and the town sprang up." He pointed at a vast stretch of grassland visible beyond the town. "That's part of Kemp's ranch, the Bar K, one of the biggest in Arizona. It stretches from west of the river clear to those hilly specks to the west. Most of the valley is his."

"He came to our country to make his fortune, and he succeeded," Allison interjected with a touch of excitement.

"You sound as if you know him personally," Lee said.

"We do," Jim Hays confirmed. "Two years ago, on one of my visits to Bob Delony, we were introduced. Since then, whenever we come to see Bob, Kemp makes it a point to look us up. The last time, he even invited us to his ranch for supper."

"Right friendly of him," Lee commented.

"I think he's stuck on Allison," Jim said, and he did not sound particularly pleased.

"Oh?" Lee looked at her, but she turned, foiling his attempt to learn if Kemp's attention pleased her.

"Allister Kemp is a gentleman," Allison said. "He's worked hard to get where he is. You wouldn't catch him making his living as a cardsharp." She checked to see if her barb had scored and was rewarded by a tightening of the Tennessean's jaw muscles.

Buckskin made a clucking noise. "Kemp ain't to be trusted, lady. Who do you think those three gun-sharks who tried to make wolf meat of your pa work for?"

With an airy laugh, Allison dismissed the idea. "Don't be ridiculous. Allister Kemp would never harm a soul."

"He wiped out the Indians who were here before him, didn't he? And he's made no secret of the fact that he'd like to drive off every last prospector and settler in these parts."

"If those three were his men, and that hasn't been proven yet, then they were drunk and acting on their own," Allison said. "You can't blame Allister for their actions."

"I'm afraid I have to agree with my daughter," Jim said. "Kemp has always been cordial to us. There is no reason in the world for him to harm us."

Buckskin clucked again. "Be that as it may, those three were his hands. I know, 'cause I've laid eyes on his outfit when they've come into town to raise hell and those three are always along." He patted one of the horses and walked off with a parting shot: "Ask anyone if you don't believe me."

Lee had taken a dislike to the Englishman the moment he saw that Allison appeared to be fond of him. It gratified him that his dislike was justified, since it was highly unlikely that the three hardcases would risk their boss's wrath by picking on a known friend of his. There had to be a lot more to the affair than was apparent.

Jim thoughtfully gazed westward. "Kemp owns over five thousand acres, or thereabouts," he said. "Until four years ago, he had this whole valley to himself. Then the prospectors came. A small town sprang up, mainly businesses supplying their needs. But it wasn't long before squatters moved in."

Allison took up the account. "Allister didn't mind at first, because he owned all the prime land. He expected the settlers to drift elsewhere after a while, but the town kept growing and they stayed on."

"You mentioned prospectors," Lee said to her father. "Did they find gold?"

"Silver. An old geezer struck a rich vein in those mountains to the north and prospectors poured in from all over. A strike always draws like honey does bears. Diablo grew from a population of sixty or so to over two thousand in the span of a month. It caught Kemp by surprise. He didn't like it much, but there was nothing he could do."

Lee studied the buildings once more. "Where did the town get its name?"

"Where else? That's the Diablo River next to it," Jim said. "Or, to be more precise, Rio de Diablo, as the Spaniards named it way back when. If memory serves, they called it that after a flood wiped out a third of their expedition. So now everything is named Diablo." He indicated the mountains. "Those are the Diablo Mountains, and the valley is Diablo Valley, and those hills to the south are—"

"The Diablo Hills," Lee guessed.

Jim chuckled. "You learn quick. Why, even the main creek that feeds into the river is called Diablo Creek. That's where silver was initially discovered."

Lee took in the sprawling expanse of the Englishman's ranch in silent contemplation. His cherished dream, confided to no one but Doc, was to one day own a cattle spread of his own, a place where he could hang up his pistols and raise a family. But the likelihood of attaining his dream was as remote as the moon in light of his current difficulty.

"The Diablo Creek Mine is one of the best producers in the Southwest," Jim said. "The old buzzard who made the claim, Abe Howard, is a real character."

"Half the town thinks he's loco," Allison mentioned. "All because he donated the money needed to build a school and a church, then set up his own general store."

In the past two minutes Lee had learned more about Diablo than he ever knew about his hometown of Possum Hollow. And there was more to come.

"You see, there already was a general store," Jim Hays explained. "It's run by a man named Frank Lowe, who had a monopoly until Old Abe opened his and undercut Lowe's prices. Lowe has had it in for Old Abe ever since." He surveyed the valley. "Hate and spite are the real problems here. The homesteaders look down their noses at the prospectors and miners, and boths sides despise the cowboys and their employer, Kemp."

"With the town caught in the middle," Lee said.

"Diablo is a tinderbox just waiting for the fuse to be lit," Hays said.

Buckskin whooped for everyone to climb on board. Lee walked to the roan and stepped into the stirrups. As he rode beside the stage down the incline, he mulled over everything he had been told. He could ill afford to get caught up in the brewing conflict, not when the three gents on his trail would hound him to the gates of hell and back again in their quest to bring him to justice.

"Is there a lawman in town?" Lee asked through the window.

"Not yet," Jim replied. "When Allison and I were there last, there was talk about the council appointing a marshal. I don't know if anything ever came of it. Why?"

"Just curious," Lee lied.

"They need one badly," Jim said. "Seldom a day goes by that there isn't a fight or a shooting."

"It doesn't sound like a fitting place for your daughter to be," Lee commented, and knew he had made a mistake when Allison's color deepened.

"Why? Because I'm a *woman?*" Few things riled Allison more than being treated as if she were helpless or incompetent. Some men did that, though, carrying on as if women were incapable of doing whatever men did. As if men were in some respect superior! "I suppose it's fitting for you, being a man and all?"

"That's not what I meant."

Allison looked, and saw that he was telling the truth. "I beg your pardon. I suppose it's more fitting for you because you're a gambler and the place is crawling with dens of iniquity?"

"It's a living," Lee said, piqued.

"So is cattle rustling, but neither will take you very far in life."

Lee spurred the roan on past the stage. He had been a fool to think she favored him. Every time he opened his mouth, she jumped down his throat. He couldn't wait to reach Diablo so they could part company.

In the stagecoach, Allison told her father, "I don't see why you've been so nice to him. I can't wait to bid him good-bye."

To her astonishment, the kindly matron, who had hardly uttered three words since leaving the relay station, laughed lightly and said, "You can't fool us, my dear. Please keep me in mind when you send out the invitations. I do so love weddings."

Chapter Five

Wild and woolly didn't begin to describe Diablo.

Like an enormous beehive, the town swarmed with activity twenty-four hours of the day. It was already a turbulent boomtown, and if it kept growing as many foresaw, it would soon outpace every other town in Arizona to claim the crown as the largest.

Divided in half from east to west by a wide, dusty thoroughfare, Diablo displayed two faces to the world at large.

North of the central street, called Cottonwood, existed scores of tents, shacks, and even a few frame houses. This was the residential section, at its heart a towering white church sporting a needle-thin steeple that reared skyward as if striving to reach heaven itself.

South of Cottonwood Street flourished dens of iniquity devoted to every sensual pleasure imaginable. Saloons, dance halls, places of prostitution, and sundry other dives lined both sides of every artery, beckoning the foolish and the carefree with the tinkle of glasses, raucous laughter, and the come-hither looks of painted females wearing dresses no woman north of Cottonwood would be caught dead in.

If Diablo south of Cottonwood qualified as an inferno, then Hell Street served as the focal point for the burning vices on parade. It was the next wide east-west thoroughfare, six blocks south of the central avenue.

Hell Street attracted the hardest element with its higher class of saloons and working girls. Half a dozen gaming establishments, in particular, received the dubious distinction of being viperous dens the equal of any the West had ever spawned.

From all over they had come, flocking to Diablo in droves. Prospectors, miners, promoters, gamblers, confidence artists, fallen doves, gunmen, thieves, vagrants, and even a few homesteaders could be found milling in pursuit of their private passions at any hour of the day or night.

They hailed from the ranges of Wyoming and Nebraska, from the rugged vastness of Montana, from Texas and New Mexico and Kansas, from the fertile farmlands of Illinois and Iowa and points east as well. From wherever men and women were down on their luck and heard about the bonanza to be reaped in the silver-laden mountains or the sin-strewn streets.

In that respect Diablo was no different from all the previous boomtowns, but those in the know, those who had been to other boomtowns, were unanimous in their belief that Diablo was the very worst.

Hardly a day went by without a new marker being placed on the aptly named Boot Hill, a solitary windswept knoll on the northeast outskirts.

Diablo, as the saying went, was a wide-open town

where anything went, and usually did.

As Lee Scurlock trailed the stagecoach down Cottonwood Street and gazed at the sea of humanity flowing back and forth in a torrent, he felt a tingle of excitement. He'd seen his share of rowdy places in his travels with Doc, but nothing like this.

Doc. Thinking of his brother saddened Lee. It had been a fluke of chance that Josiah's skill with a six-shooter had earned him that nickname. Josiah was no healer. No, the nickname came from the fact that Josiah had sent so many men *to* doctors. Naturally, when journalists latched on to the Billy the Kid story and learned that one of Billy's partisans was a rangy Tennessean called "Doc," they just had to write him up as they had done Bonney. Small wonder Doc was now halfway to famous, and Lee could not go anywhere his brother's handle was not known.

The crack of Buckskin's whip shattered Lee's reverie. The stage angled toward a building on the right, pedestrians scattering like chickens to get out of its way.

Lee reined up shy of the stage office and patted the roan. He surveyed Cottonwood Street, debating his next move.

Jim Hays stepped down and held up his hand for his daughter and then the matron. "Say, Lee!" he called. "I want you to promise to pay Allison and me a visit tomorrow."

Allison did not know whether to be upset or glad. Her father's strange attachment to the southerner continued to baffle her. By the same token, she would secretly have liked to see Lee again, but she was not going to admit it to him.

Lee took his time answering. He'd rather get on with his own life, yet he did want to spend more time around Allison. He'd never admit it, for fear she would fling his feelings back in his face. "If you want," he said.

Jim Hays came over. "We'll look forward to it. Bob Delony's house is on Allen Street, three blocks north. Seventeen Allen Street. You can't miss it. Say about noon?"

"I'll be there," Lee promised.

Allison joined them. It was on the tip of her tongue to say that she would also be glad to have him for company. Instead, her traitor tongue declared, "Off to the gaming tables, I presume?"

Lee gripped the reins tighter. "I reckon I'll take in the sights" was all he would say. By sheer happenstance, a pair of doves in tight dresses sashayed past, one playfully winking at him while the other tittered. Unconsciously, he grinned back.

"Enjoy yourself," Allison said, her temper flaring. She never had understood women who would sell their bodies for money; she had never been one to throw herself at men for any reason.

Lee's grin aggravated her further. Men could be such animals! "Come, Papa," she said, flouncing toward the office. "We don't want to keep Mr. Scurlock from his carnal pleasures."

Jim clapped Lee on the leg. "Don't pay her no mind, son," he said quietly. "She thinks highly of you. I can tell."

"She has a mighty peculiar way of showing it," Lee said, watching her enter the building. "An Apache would treat me with more respect than she does."

"Some women, and men too, have a hard time coping with emotions that are new to them," Jim said. "Allison's problem is that most of those interested in her in the past were mere boys. You're the first real man to come along, if you don't count Kemp."

Lee had no idea what to say to that, so he changed

63

the subject. "Do you happen to know where the nearest stable is?"

"At the corner of Cottonwood and Cedar," Jim said, pointing westward. "The Kayser Livery. The rates are high, but you'll find that everything in Diablo is spendy. Greed is the order of the day here." Smiling, Jim walked off.

Kneeing the roan, Lee rode on down the street. As he passed the stage office, he glimpsed Allison peering out at him. She neither waved nor smiled.

Women! Lee reflected. When the good Lord made them, He must have been drunk!

The stable was situated less than half a block from an imposing hotel that called itself the Arizona Imperial. Although it was only a mediocre lodging house, its plump owner acted as if it were the Ritz in New York City.

Lee checked into the Imperial, stored his meager personal effects, shaved, and washed using a basin. After dusting his clothes with his hairbrush, he locked the door and ventured out into the whirlwind that was Diablo.

In addition to the ivory-handled Peacemaker, Lee had wedged the Colt he took from Nate Collins under his belt, butt forward, on his right hip under his coat. It never hurt to have a hideout.

The last lingering rays of sunlight streaked the western horizon with brilliant shades of red, pink, and orange. From the northwest wafted a cool breeze, stirring the sluggish air.

Lee took a walk down Cottonwood until he came to an intersection. Turning southward, he ambled along for blocks until he came to the next broad avenue, designated by a crudely lettered sign: HELL STREET. Under the name someone had scrawled in barely legible handwriting, "Beware."

The noise rose to a steady din. It was as if someone

had opened a floodgate to permit the dregs of the earth to roam loose. Hard faces were everywhere. Drunks were commonplace. Enticing women beckoned from windows and doorways. Shifty no-accounts stood in shadows, their money-hungry eyes measuring passersby for likely prospects. All kinds of humanity mingled freely, reveling in life, in lust, in greed.

Curious onlookers appraised Lee as he went by, and he knew that everyone who saw him branded him as trouble. Which was just fine by him.

A saloon dead ahead arrested Lee's attention. It was a grand edifice with elegant glass doors and ornate windows.

Lee recognized a quality establishment when he saw one. He pushed through the glass doors to take in a lively scene the likes of which stirred his blood to pump faster.

Off to the left ran a polished mahogany bar crammed with rowdy patrons guzzling their favorite drinks. Gaming tables devoted to faro, poker, and keno filled the center of the spacious room. On a recessed platform at the rear sat a piano player, accommodating requests. And a huge sign emblazoned in gold letters proudly proclaimed that this was the Applejack Saloon.

Lee had taken only three strides when a blond woman in a black skintight dress materialized at his elbow.

"Howdy, stranger."

The fragrant scent of lilacs tingled Lee's nose. "Howdy, yourself," he said as she gently placed her slender hand on his arm.

"Care to treat a girl to a drink?" the blonde asked. When he did not answer right away, she joked, "Don't worry. I don't bite."

"That's what they all say," Lee said, drinking in her

finely chiseled features. Here was a beauty to rival
Allison Hays, but with none of the pretentious airs
Allison adopted. Throughout the afternoon he had
pondered the enigma of the redhead, how at first she
had been warm, then cold, then ice. All because she
disliked his being a gambler. Yet who was she to
judge him?

"My name's Nelly," the blonde said.

"Sure it is," Lee responded. Often doves took false
names, either from shame or to protect the reputa-
tions of their more respectable kin.

"Do you have one?"

"One what?" Lee toyed.

"A name, silly."

"Lee."

"Lee? That's all? Very well." Nelly did not pry. She
had been in the business long enough to know that
men with shady pasts were not to be grilled. The
wrong question could earn a working girl a cuffed
ear, or much worse. Although, if she was any judge,
the man she had latched on to was not the type to
strike a woman. "It fits a handsome hombre like
you," she said, going through the motions.

"One of us is handsome, and that's for certain
sure," Lee said.

Beaming, Nelly steered him toward the bar. "Want
an escort this evening, my fine sir?"

"I'd have to be plumb loco to say no," Lee said. But
even as the words left his mouth, a vivid image of
Allison Hays filled his mind and a twinge of guilt
pricked him. Why that should be, he couldn't say. He
was under no obligation to her.

Nelly laughed again, her green eyes scrutinizing
him with heightened interest. "Well, what have we
here, anyway? You don't smell of cows like most
cowpunchers do, and you don't smell of worse like
most miners do." She let her gaze rest meaningfully

on his Colt. "And you're sure not no tinhorn."

"What I am is thirsty," Lee said. Thumping the bar to get the attention of the barkeep, he said, "Care for a drink?"

"My second-worst weakness," Nelly admitted with a wan grin.

"What's your first?"

"Handsome desperadoes like you."

The drinks were served. As Lee tipped his whiskey to his lips, he leaned against the bar and observed the goings-on at nearby tables. A poker game was in progress at one. Four men were beginning a new round of five-card stud. Three had to be prospectors or miners, judging by their filthy clothes. The fourth, a stocky man attired in a Prince Albert coat and a brown bowler, was unmistakably a professional gambler.

The gambler started the bidding at fifty dollars and the pot climbed in short order to two hundred. Two of the miners were forced to drop out, but the biggest, a bear of a man with a yellow beard stained by tobacco smears, stayed in. Three hundred and ten dollars constituted the stakes when the big miner declared roughly, "Call!"

"Read 'em and weep, friend," said the gambler with a faint brogue as he flipped over his cards. "Three tens and a pair of eights. Where I come from, they call that a full house."

Snarling in disgust, the miner tossed his hand on the table. "You sure have a nasty habit of winning, Shannon."

The gambler became as taut as wire, his thin lips compressing. "Are you saying what I think you're saying, Wilson?"

Their eyes widening in alarm, the other two miners suddenly looked as if they keenly desired to be somewhere else.

David Robbins

Wilson did not seem to notice the gambler's tone. "All I'm saying is that you win a lot, damn your bones," he groused.

Shannon had acquired an icy calm. "In some circles that remark could be construed as an insult."

"What?" Wilson said, looking up from the pile of money he had just lost. Comprehension dawned, and he blanched. "Now, hold on, Shannon. I wasn't callin' you a cheat."

"I hope not."

The big miner squirmed, motioning at his companions. "Ask them. I know better than to insult you. Everyone knows that you play an honest game. Hell, you're one of the few who do."

Deliberately, Shannon rested his right forearm on the edge of the table. An audible sound, like the rasp of metal on wood, let all those present know that there was a derringer up his sleeve. "I'm glad to hear you think that way, because I wouldn't want to hear that you've been spreading stories about me. You lose all the time, Wilson, because you're a lousy card-player. You never know when to fold."

"I do so," Wilson said, but he lacked conviction. Shoving his chair back, he rose. "Anyhow, you have no cause to complain. If I was a better player, you wouldn't be gettin' rich off of me."

Shannon relaxed. Chuckling, he said, "True enough. Tell you what. For being so sensible, take this and treat your friends to drinks and whatever else you're hankering for." Counting out fifty dollars, he pushed the coins across the table.

The miners were stupefied. "Thanks," Wilson exclaimed, scooping up the money quickly as if afraid the gambler would change his mind. Laughing and clapping one another, the three men made off.

Shannon began to stack his winnings, then sensed he was being watched. He saw Lee staring at him curiously and said, "It's good business, laddie. They'll tell all their friends what a great guy I am, and the next time they have a full poke and are in the mood for cards, it's me they'll come to see."

It was a new ruse on Lee. Most cardsharps were so greedy, they'd sooner part with their lives than with any of their hard-won earnings. "I bet you're right popular with the mining crowd."

"And with anyone else who admires a fair game. Care to try your skill?"

Lee noticed that the Irishman said "skill," not "luck." "Maybe another time."

Turning his chair, the professional offered his hand. "Ike Shannon, my blessed mother named me. Been playing the circuit long?"

"Lee Scurlock. No. A year or so, is all."

As Shannon released Lee's hand, his brown eyes flicked at the Peacemaker, then at Lee's right side where the spare Colt was neatly hidden. "It's not an unheard-of handle in these parts, lad. I'll look forward to taking your money someday soon."

Two men arrived to take seats, and the Irishman turned to do battle. Lee swallowed the rest of his drink and was going to order another round when he saw that Nelly had hardly touched hers. "Not thirsty?" he said, leaning close to be heard.

The dove tapped her glass and scowled. "After a while you get sick of the stuff. If I wasn't required to order some, I never would."

Sensing that she would rather discuss something else, Lee asked, "How long have you been here?"

"In Diablo? Oh, only four months or so. Before that I lived in Denver, and before that—" Melancholy etched her face. "Well, let's just say that I'm widely traveled, kind sir, and leave it at that."

It was not Lee's habit to delve into the personal lives of doves. Most resented it. But he said anyway,

David Robbins

"If you don't like the work, get out."

Nelly sighed. "If only it were that simple. Besides, what would I do? Where would I go?"

Touched by her sadness, Lee said, "You're young. You're attractive. You could go anywhere you want, do whatever you like." He meant to bolster her spirits, but it had the opposite effect.

"If only things were that simple," Nelly said forlornly.

Lee was going to inquire why they shouldn't be when a complete hush fell over the Applejack. All voices fell silent. Dealers stopped shuffling, players stopped clattering coins, even the bartenders paused to do as everyone else was doing and gaze at the glass doors.

A lanky figure stood to the right of the entrance, thumbs hooked in twin gunbelts that slanted over his slender hips. In the holsters rested a matched pair of Colts with mother-of-pearl grips. A black sombrero crowned curly black hair. His clothes were those any cowboy would wear: a brown shirt, jeans, black boots, and a blue bandanna.

"Vint Evers!" Nelly whispered, her voice fluttering with emotion.

"The Texas gunfighter?"

"One and the same."

Lee straightened for a better look. Vint Evers justifiably rated a reputation as one of the deadliest shootists in the entire Southwest. From the mighty Mississippi to California, from Montana to the Lone Star State, his name was a household word, rivaling Wild Bill Hickok's and John Wesley Hardin's. Thanks to dime novels that had embellished his career in sensational tales, Evers was unique in being a genuine legend in his own time.

Lee had heard all the stories. How the Texan had single-handedly cleaned up Bozeman, Newton, and

70

Diablo

Enid, three of the roughest towns that ever were, how his swift guns were credited with planting more than thirty-six enemies, how he had once held off a war party of forty Comanches with the help of a handful of men. Even allowing for exaggeration, there was no denying that Evers was a man to be reckoned with.

To the Texan's credit, most of those he was reputed to have shot were slain in his various capacities as a lawman. Constable, sheriff, marshal—he had been all of them at one time or another.

"Vint was in a gunfight several nights ago," Nelly said. "Right at that table." She pointed at the one where Ike Shannon sat. "Two lowlifes tried to back-shoot him while he was playing with Ike, but he got wise and slapped leather as they cut loose. One died on the spot; the other will be laid up for months with a punctured lung." Vehemently, she added, "Serves the bastards right!"

The way she talked gave Lee the impression that she was on more familiar terms with the Texan than he might otherwise suspect. Her tone alone implied that she cared for him—cared a lot, in fact.

As if to confirm the Tennessean's hunch, Vint Evers spied the blonde and sauntered toward her, his gray eyes shifting back and forth, always razor keen.

Gradually the patrons of the Applejack resumed whatever they had been doing when the living legend entered. Men whispered excitedly behind his back, some pointing, some openly awed. Others, a very few, looked as if they were inclined to test whether the Texan merited his fame.

Evers nodded at the Irishman. Shannon returned the greeting by touching the brim of his bowler. Four paces from the bar, Evers halted and regarded Lee closely. "And what might your name be, stranger?" he asked in a thick-as-molasses Texas twang.

David Robbins

A hint of suspicion laced the query, suspicion and something else Lee could not quite put his finger on. It galled him, being treated so curtly. "My name is my business," he drawled.

The Texan's mouth crinkled. "I reckon you know who I am. So you can understand that a person like me can't be too careful, not if he's partial to breathin'. I'm bait for any polecat out to make a name for himself. Which makes me naturally curious about anyone who impresses me as being a gun hand." He paused. "You impress me."

"Are you saying I'm a polecat?" Lee demanded, louder than he really had to. He couldn't say what made him do it, unless it was a case of raw nerves.

Suddenly everyone within ten paces was putting more distance between them.

Ike Shannon abruptly rose and moved to the right.

Nelly placed a hand on Lee's wrist, and he shrugged it off. He hadn't meant to antagonize the Texan, but that was just what he had done.

For Vint Evers had dropped his oddly slender hands to his sides—those deadly hands that could find his guns in less time than it took a man to blink—and they were ready to draw.

Chapter Six

Ike Shannon picked that moment to step forward. His head gave a barely perceptible nod, a nod only Vint Evers—and Lee Scurlock—caught.

The Texan slowly relaxed, his thumbs returning to his crossed belts. "Well, now," he said, "I'd be the last person to insult another without cause. No, I reckon you're not a polecat." He tilted his head. "Sure you know who I am?"

"Who doesn't?" Lee countered.

The flattery rolled off the Texan like water off a duck's back. "I admire any man who has fightin' tallow. Something tells me you'd do to ride the river with." His smile was the real article.

Shannon put his hand on Evers's elbow. "Vint, allow me to have you make the acquaintance of Lee Scurlock."

The saloon had come to a standstill, with all eyes fixed on the Tennessean and the Texan. Cards were held in midair, glasses halfway to waiting mouths.

"Are you Doc's kin?" Evers asked.

"We're brothers."

"You don't say?" The Texan smacked his thigh. "Ain't it a small world? I met him once down to Tascosa. He's a straight shooter if ever there was one."

The praise, from a man of Evers's stature, sparked a feeling of intuitive friendship in Lee. "How about if I buy you a drink to make up for acting like I'm ten years old?"

"Only if you let me buy you one after," the Texan said, sidling to the counter. As if on cue, the customers took up where they had left off, the piano player launching into a lively rendition of "The Texas Cowboy."

Evers glanced at the bartender. "The usual, Hank."

"Coming right up, Mr. Evers, sir."

The Texan braced his back against the mahogany and surveyed the room with hawkish eyes that did not miss so much as the curl of a finger. Many customers were openly gawking at him, and at Lee. "What a pack of vultures," he remarked dryly. "They'd like it better if blood were spilt."

The drinks arrived. Lee was about to down his when Evers tapped their glasses together in a salute.

"To Tennessee and Texas, the two finest states ever."

As the tarantula juice seared his throat, Lee commented with a nod at Ike Shannon, "I take it that the two of you know each other?"

"We go back seven years," the Texan disclosed. "Ike saved my hide in Kansas once and we've been pards ever since. Wherever I go, he drifts there too. You'd think the idiot would learn his lesson, lasso a filly, and settle down. But he's too fond of Lady Luck to court any others."

"You're a fine one to talk," the gambler bantered.

Diablo

"I don't see you with a wife and sprouts."

Evers grew wistful. "Never had the inclination." His gaze strayed to the blonde and he said softly, "But people have been known to change. Good evenin', Miss Rosell. It's a pleasure to see you again."

"The honor is mine, Mr. Evers, sir," Nelly said. In that short statement she managed to convey more affection than many people express in a lifetime.

Lee pretended not to notice and saw Shannon do the same. Vint Evers did, and he had to clear his throat before he replied.

"Call me Vint, ma'am, or you'll have me feelin' old before my time. I'll put up with that nonsense from barkeeps and bootlickers, but not from the loveliest woman this side of Creation."

An awkward moment followed, with Lee unwilling to intrude on the special sentiments the two so plainly shared. He need not have bothered. They were intruded on anyway, and all thanks to him.

Through the glass doors shoved the Mexican gunman called Morco. Beside him were two gun-hung cowboys, both as hard as tacks, their skin leathery and bronzed from long exposure to the elements, their countenances more reptilian than human. Or that was the illusion Lee had as Morco swept the saloon, caught sight of him, and bent to say something to the pair.

Vint Evers set down his shot glass. "Somethin' up, Lee?" he inquired.

With exaggerated swaggers the pair of hard cases, dogged by Morco, shouldered through the throng. In the lead was a bull of a man packing a pair of Starr double-action .44 revolvers, worn butts forward, as Lee wore his. A high-crowned, dusty brown hat topped a thatch of brown hair slightly lighter than his bushy mustache. His boots were scuffed, his pants dotted with grime. He was a living man-mountain, and the patrons parted before him like blades of grass before an avalanche.

"*You!*" the bull thundered, once again bringing the bustling establishment to a dead stop.

"What's this, then?" Ike Shannon asked.

"Stay out of it," Lee said, taking strides to the right so Nelly, Evers, and the gambler would not be caught by a stray slug if the worst came to pass. The threesome halted ten feet away, spreading apart so they would be harder to hit. "Do I know you, mister?" he challenged.

"I'm told that you're the one who put lead into Nate Collins and sent Bran Gristy to the hereafter," the bull rumbled.

"What's it to you?" Lee said, pricked by the wicked grin on Morco's face.

"I'm foreman at the Bar K," stated the bull. "Nate Collins is one of my punchers. So was Gristy. I hear tell that you threw down on them without cause."

"That's a damned lie," Lee said, bristling. Recollecting Doc's teaching, he capped his temper and stared straight at Morco. "Show me the four-flusher who made the claim."

The Mexican was offended. "Why are we wasting time, amigo?" he asked the bull. "Let's do what we came to do, eh? This cub must have his claws trimmed."

The other cowboy, a skinny bundle of whipcord and arrogance, grinned. He shouldn't have. Four front teeth were gone.

Light, carefree laughter smothered the grin and added a trace of confusion to the bull's rough-hewn features. Vint Evers, of all people, was doing the laughing. "Who do you figure will pay for your funerals, boys?" he addressed the Bar K riders. "Your boss?"

"This ain't your concern, Evers," the bull said.

Diablo

"Sure it is, Bodine," the Texan said. "When anyone accuses a pard of mine with no just cause, I take it real personal. It's one of my many flaws."

Bodine could not hide his surprise. "A pard of yours?" he said, and gave Morco a look that would have withered a plant. "You damned Mex. You didn't tell me that he knew Evers."

"How was I to know?" Morco complained.

Vint Evers, as innocent as could be, swirled the liquor in his glass. "You weren't aware that Lee Scurlock and I are acquainted? For shame."

"Scurlock?" Bodine said, and Lee could practically see the gear turn inside the man's skull. "That's something else I didn't know."

"Dog my cats!" Evers declared. "I'm surprised at an old hand like you not checkin' his facts before he goes on the prod." Evers winked at Lee. "By the way, this here is Jesse Bodine. Maybe you've heard of him?"

The name rang a bell. Lee realized that Evers had cleverly let him know who the ramrod was to ensure he wasn't too quick on the trigger.

Jesse Bodine was a Texan, like Evers. He had played a leading role in the Simms-Harkey feud, reportedly rubbing out five of the Simms family in one fell swoop. Later Bodine took a herd north to Kansas, three thousand head, all hardy longhorns. In Indian Territory six hungry Osage requested ten head over and above the tribe's usual cut. Bodine refused, a warrior lifted his rifle, and Bodine shot all six dead.

Near Kansas, another herd crowded Bodine's from the rear. When Bodine objected, the other trail boss made an insulting reference to Bodine's mother. It was costly. The trail boss and three punchers who were with him were added to Bodine's string.

And this was the same Jesse Bodine, the White Oaks Man-Killer.

Evers turned to Lee. "What did Collins and Gristy do, anyhow?"

"Tried to provoke an unarmed man into a fight by insulting his daughter. When I pointed out their lack of manners, they went for their hardware." Lee added, to show that he was not going to back down to any man, "It's not my fault, Bodine, if your men suffer from a bad case of slow."

Evers wanted to learn more. "Who was this hombre they picked on?"

"A law wrangler by the name of Jim Hays."

"Now, ain't that interestin'?" Evers twanged thoughtfully.

Jesse Bodine glanced from his fellow Texan to the Tennessean, his bushy brows knit. When Ike Shannon took a step from the bar, he seemed to come to a decision, and pivoted. "If I had proof, Scurlock, I'd settle accounts. As it stands, it's your word against Morco's and Nate's."

Morco clutched Bodine's sleeve. "But I told you the truth, *compadre. Es verdad!*"

Lee could feel a welcome warmth spreading through his abdomen courtesy of the whiskey. He also felt a rising outrage that the Mexican killer had goaded Bodine into throwing down on him. Added to that was a chilling insight. Morco had tried to kill Jim Hays once. What was to stop him from trying again? Morco and his friends had not been drunk, as Allison halfheartedly suggested. There had to be another reason they had braced her father, a reason that might prompt Morco and Nate Collins to try again.

"We're leavin'," Bodine announced, leading the other two off.

"Not so fast!" Lee challenged, his voice cracking like a bullwhip. Customers hastened to clear out from behind the trio. He took a few paces so he had a clear view of the Mexican, then said, "Where I come from, anyone who would shoot an unarmed man is scum."

Morco scowled. He had not counted on this. Just as he had not counted on Bodine backing down. The fire in the Tennessean's stare warned him of what was to come and he wanted no part of it, but he saw no way out other than to turn tail in front of everyone there.

"I'm accusing you of being a lying, low-down coward," Lee went on. He had never deliberately goaded anyone into drawing before, but he had no qualms about doing so. It was for Jim Hays's sake. And for Allison's.

"You push your luck, gringo," Morco blustered. He looked at Bodine and the other man, hoping they would back him if push came to shove, but it was apparent that neither was going to help. He suspected that the presence of Vint Evers was to blame.

"Didn't you hear me, Morco?" Lee said. "I say that you're yellow. That you prefer to fight women, and men who can't defend themselves."

The indignity of the public humiliation grated on Morco. Many were staring at him with contempt, some in ridicule. He could abide many things, but not that. No man who was a man would stand for having his manhood questioned. "I warn you!" he cried.

Lee saw the Mexican tremble with indignation. All it would take was a few choice words and he would get his wish. He never hesitated. Spurred by the image of the redhead, he lashed out, "Save your breath, you miserable son of a bitch. If I'm wrong, prove it. If not, leave this valley and don't ever show your face again."

"*Bastardo!*" Morco fumed. At the back of his mind a tiny voice screamed for him to stay calm, for him not to let the gringo bait him. But he silenced the voice with a choking sob of fury and jerked at his Remington. He was, after all, not without skill with a pistol. He had a chance.

Lee's hand flew in a cross-draw, the Colt leaping from its holster. He fired once as Morco's Remington cleared leather, fired again as Morco tottered backward, fired a third time as Morco twisted and crashed onto a faro table, spilling the table and everything on top of it into an untidy heap.

Smoke curled from the Peacemaker as Lee warily walked over. The table had landed on its side, partially covering Morco from the waist up. Lee kicked the Remington away from the Mexican's hand.

Never again would the *pistolero* dance the fandango or savor a tequila. Never again would he ride the range or thrill to a woman's embrace. His sombrero lay a yard from his head, upended, spattered with blood. A jagged entry hole low on his forehead explained why. Framing his tousled hair was a growing scarlet pool. Over his sternum were two neat holes, pumping more blood.

The patter of onrushing boots brought Lee around in a flash to cover three men who were running toward him. The foremost was a short, dapper individual in an expensive suit, whose clipped sideburns and trimmed handlebar mustache testified to a streak of vanity. The other two were burly underlings. "That's far enough!" Lee barked.

They stopped, not one going for a weapon. The dapper leader stared at Morco, then at Bodine and Evers.

"What's your mix in this?" Lee demanded.

"I'm Frank Lowe," the dapper man said in a voice reminiscent of sandpaper grating on metal. "I own this establishment."

Frank Lowe. Lee remembered Jim Hays telling

him that a man by that name owned one of the general stores in Diablo. Apparently, Lowe had his hand in more than one business enterprise.

"I don't tolerate gunplay in the Applejack," Lowe said. "Unless a shooting is justified, I post the hombre responsible from the premises."

"Are you aiming to post me?" Lee asked, irked by the man's smug air.

"That depends on what happened."

Vint Evers came to Lee's defense. "Morco had it comin', Lowe. He was spreadin' a pack of lies about Mr. Scurlock, here. When Lee called him on it, Morco slapped leather."

Lowe faced Jesse Bodine. "Is that the way it went?"

The bullish Texan was gazing at the body, his features rippling with resentment. "Morco went for his gun first," he reluctantly admitted.

"Then you're off the hook," Lowe told Lee. "My men will tend to the body. In the future, though, I'd be grateful if you settled your scores outside." At a gesture from him, the two burly underlings each grabbed one of Morco's arms and dragged the body toward the rear of the saloon.

Lee had yet to lower his smoking Colt. Turning toward Morco's companions, he waited to see if they were going to call him on what he had done. That was the way of things west of the Mississippi. Kill a man, and the man's friends invariably came after you.

Jesse Bodine hitched at his gunbelt. "This ain't over, Scurlock," he said gruffly. "There'll be hell to pay." So saying, he stalked from the Applejack with the skinny cowboy dogging his spurs.

The saloon slowly galvanized into life again, most of its occupants speaking in muted tones. Lee was given a wide berth as he walked to the bar, where he began replacing the spent cartridges.

Ike Shannon clapped him on the shoulder. "Pure quicksilver, laddie," he said. "There aren't many who can match you. Vint, for sure. Maybe Bodine, too, and five or six others I can think of. But that's all."

"My brother is one of them," Lee idly mentioned. "We used to practice all the time, and I never could beat him." He slid the reloaded Colt into his holster.

Nelly handed him his glass. "Here. You could probably use this." She watched him gulp the contents, then said, "Between you and me, I'm glad you shot that bastard. A week ago he got drunk and beat up one of the girls for no excuse at all."

As Lee lowered his arm, he spotted several men in the middle of the room. One, a pocket hunter by the looks of him, had a red stain on his shoulder and was being tended by two friends.

Vint Evers noticed. "Your second shot went clean through Morco and hit that prospector. Happens a lot, I'm sorry to say. Once, in Newton, three men tried to bushwhack me as I came out of a store. They sprayed so much lead that they hit everything except me. One of their shots went through a wall and killed a little girl."

Lee strode toward the wounded man, who glanced up and took a step back. The pair bandaging him froze, unsure of what would occur. "You were clipped," Lee said, stating the obvious.

"My own fault," the prospector grumbled. "I ought to know to make myself scarce when a shooting scrape breaks out. A smart man hits the floor first thing."

Unimpeded, Lee inspected the wound. "It's only a crease," he said, relieved. Gunning down a cold-blooded killer like Morco was one thing; to slay an innocent man would be a burden he did not care to bear.

"Don't fret yourself on my account," the prospector

said. "I've been hurt a lot worse. Hell, you should have seen me the time a tunnel caved in on top of a bunch of us. Busted my shoulder and both legs besides. I was in agony for weeks."

Be that as it may, Lee had to make it up to him. "Are you a drinking man?"

"Does a bear crap in the woods?"

"How about if I treat you to one? Consider it my way of apologizing."

The man grinned slyly. "How about if you treat me to a bottle?"

"Tell the barkeep to set you up, on me."

Chortling, the prospector elbowed one of his friends. "Don't this beat all? Maybe I should get shot more often. I'd spend a heap less on liquor."

Their laughter was the catalyst that restored the Applejack to normal. In the short time it took Lee to reach the bar, the saloon was its noisy, turbulent self again.

"That was a mighty fine thing to do," Vint Evers said.

Lee glanced at Shannon. "I learned it from a friend of yours."

The Texan rested his forearms on the mahogany. "I reckon it's only fair that I warn you. By killin' Morco, you've made yourself some powerful enemies."

"Don't forget what I did to Gristy and Collins," Lee said dryly.

"I'm not forgettin', and neither will those who pulled their strings." Evers paused. "You say that they were proddin' Jim Hays?"

"Yep. Do you know him?"

"I've seen him around. He's a decent enough gent, for a lawyer. Mind you, they could take the whole kit and caboodle and toss 'em off a cliff and we'd all be better off."

"Who are these powerful enemies you mentioned?" Lee asked.

"Allister Kemp and Frank Lowe, for starters," Evers answered. "You just met Lowe. I don't know if you know it, but he also owns a general store and runs the bank. Kemp owns most of Diablo Valley. The two of them are the leaders of what the newspaper is callin' the Cowboy Faction." He paused, and Ike Shannon took up the account.

"Then there's the Mining Faction, which is led by old Abe Howard, the prospector who first struck silver, and his business partner, a man by the name of Parsons who runs Howard's general store."

"As if that ain't complicated enough," Evers resumed, "there's the Homesteader Faction, headed by a farmer, Will Dyer. All three factions despise one another, and there's been no end of trouble. All that hatred is bound to come to a head."

Lee waved a hand. "I don't intend to get involved with one side or the other."

"You're already involved whether you want to be or not," Vint Evers said. "By killin' two of Kemp's men and woundin' his favorite, Nate Collins, you've set yourself up against Kemp and Lowe."

"Lowe seemed cordial enough," Lee noted.

Ike Shannon snorted. "Frank Lowe is a snake in the grass. He's the kind who would smile while he stuck a knife into your back. You can't trust him any further than you could chuck his horse."

"Ain't that the truth," Nelly said so bitterly that all three of them looked at her.

"I still don't intend to get involved," Lee insisted. His only interest was in safeguarding Jim and Allison Hays.

"Staying neutral is impossible, laddie," Shannon said.

The Texan pushed back his hat. "Maybe not. I can

think of a way, Lee. Become a lawman. The town council is fixin' to pick a marshal next Tuesday. I've applied, and word is I'll get the badge. If so, I'll need two or three deputies I can rely on. I'd like you to be one of them."

The offer tantalized Lee. Never in his wildest dreams had he ever considered being a lawdog. Perhaps, once, he would have leaped at the opportunity, but now he was a wanted man, a fugitive from justice. "I can't," he said. To justify his refusal, he added, "I don't expect to be here more than a few days."

Evers shrugged. "Suit yourself. But if you change your mind, look me up." He smacked Shannon's shoulder. "What say we play some cards? I need some spendin' money."

"Then you'd better go rob some poor old lady, 'cause you sure won't be taking any of mine," the gambler said as they walked to his table.

Nelly could not take her eyes off Vint Evers. "He's something, isn't he?" she said, her longing thick enough to be cut with a knife.

"Why don't you go join them?" Lee proposed.

"Do you mean it?" Nelly said hopefully, brightening. "I mean, I shouldn't. I latched on to you first, and my boss might not take kindly to my being with Vint."

Lee gave her a playful push. "Go ahead before you bust your corset. It's not as if we're engaged or anything."

The blonde dove squeezed him. "Thanks, Lee Scurlock. I owe you." Her dress swirling around her ankles, she fluttered to the Texan's side, a gaily colored butterfly drawn to the nectar she desired.

Sighing, Lee ordered another drink. Now that he had a moment to think clearly, he realized that killing Morco had been unwise. Word was bound to spread, as words of gunfights always did. It would pass from town to town, saloon to saloon, until it reached New Mexico, and Lincoln. The men who were after him would know right where to come.

Lee made a decision. Tomorrow he would pay his respects to the Hayses, then he would leave. Maybe, one day, if he was very lucky, he'd find a nice woman to fawn over him the way Nelly did over Vint Evers.

One thing was for sure.

It certainly wouldn't be Allison Hays.

Chapter Seven

Lee Scurlock slept late the next morning. He had gotten in after two, his poke forty dollars richer thanks to a winning streak at poker. After shaving, washing up, and donning clean clothes, he strapped on his ivory-handled Colt, shrugged into his frock coat, and ambled out into the harsh glare of the Arizona sunlight.

Almost immediately Lee noticed a change toward him. Where the day before he had walked down the street without attracting much notice, now some of those he passed gave him second looks. Some pointed, some whispered. It was not difficult to guess why.

Lee didn't help matters any by keeping his frock coat swept back behind the Colt and his right thumb forked under his belt close to his holster. He acted as if he was ready to unlimber at a moment's notice, and he was. Jesse Bodine's parting words and Vint

Evers's warning were fresh on his mind.

Lee reached the Delony residence without mishap.

The lawyer lived in a white frame home a block from the church. A picket fence, a rarity in Diablo, protected the dwelling and its garden from passersby. Flowerpots on the porch and drapes in the windows denoted a woman's touch, while alphabet blocks on a green bench on the porch were a clue that Delony had children.

Lee knocked loudly. Seconds later a petite brunette in a yellow dress answered.

"Yes?"

"Howdy, ma'am," Lee said, doffing his hat and stating his name. "I believe I'm expected." He hid the slight nervousness he felt at imposing on a family he didn't know.

"Why, yes, you are, Mr. Scurlock," the woman said with a pointed glance at his Peacemaker. "Come on in. We'll be eating in a few minutes."

"No one said anything about a meal," Lee commented as he stepped into a narrow hallway. "Jim Hays invited me. I don't want to inconvenience you."

"Nonsense," the brunette said in kindly fashion. "I'm Ethel Delony, Bob's wife. Any friend of Jim's is a friend of ours. Make yourself to home."

A boy of ten or so dashed from a parlor on the left and hugged Ethel about the legs, his fascinated gaze rising to Lee. "Is he the one, Mommy?"

"Hush, Kenneth," Ethel scolded. "Run along and play."

The boy spun and ran up a flight of stairs at the end of the hall.

"This way, if you please," Ethel said, guiding Lee to the parlor. "Our guest has arrived," she announced for the benefit of those within.

Lee was taken aback to discover more people in the room than he had expected. Allison and her father were there, of course, Allison standing near a front window, her father in a nearby chair. Seated on a sofa was a man with brown hair and eyes, wearing a blue suit. In a rocking chair sat an old-timer in grungy jeans, scuffed boots, and a faded white shirt.

"Lee!" Allison exclaimed happily. She had been up half the night thinking about him, reviewing every word he said, recalling his every gesture, his every mannerism. Try as she might, and she had made a few feeble attempts, she could not put the handsome southerner from her mind.

That morning Allison had pondered heavily and vowed not to be carried away by her feelings. After all, her knight-errant was a footloose gambler and gunman, hardly an ideal prospect for someone who one day wanted a home and a family.

Now, catching herself, Allison fell into the same detached reserve she had used the day before to shield herself from her own feelings. "I'm glad to see you could tear yourself away from your card games long enough to join us."

Lee almost turned and left then and there. He had not seen her since the day before, and the first words out of her mouth were more criticism. Some women, he mused, just naturally liked to nag men to death.

Jim Hays stood to shake his hand. "I'm happy you came, too," he said, and sobered. "We heard about last night. It's all over town. I'm afraid you've made some powerful enemies."

"So everyone keeps telling me."

The man in the blue suit was next to greet their guest. "I'm Bob Delony. Jim has been telling us all about you."

"What little I know," Jim amended.

Lee acknowledged Delony's warm handshake with a nod and a self-conscious smile, then faced the old-timer, who hadn't budged. "And who might this be? Your pa or an uncle?"

The oldster belly-laughed. "Not hardly, sonny! Any kin I have long since disowned me." He rose with spry agility for one of his years. "I'm Abe Howard, and I'll let you know up front that I don't cotton to shootists."

"Abe!" Jim Hays said in reproach.

"Well, I don't," Old Abe snapped. "Would you have me lie? I'd sooner cut out my tongue."

Lee was more amused than offended. So this was the man who had started the stampede of silver-hungry prospectors? The man Diablo owed its existence to? Howard had a flowing white beard and long white hair, more wrinkles than a hound dog had fleas, and, in contrast, lively green eyes. "I don't see myself as a shootist," he replied.

"Then you shouldn't go around shootin' people," Abe retorted. "First those whippersnappers at Wynn's place, then that *pistolero*. At the rate you're goin', our undertaker will make a mint." He wagged a finger. "The word is out on you, mister. You're considered real bad medicine."

"The word is out on you, too, Howard," Lee replied, holding his ground. "You're considered a crazy old fool. But then, all you do is go around building churches and such."

For a few seconds their wills locked and clashed in mutual defiance. Finally the prospector's mouth creased in a lopsided smirk. "I reckon I had that comin', Reb. Maybe you ain't a bad man, after all."

"Oh, no," Allison said, unaccountably annoyed at how well Abe and Lee were hitting it off. "He's just a gambler and a gunslinger."

Jim Hays addressed his daughter sternly, saying, "Lee is our friend, and I won't have you treating him with disrespect. Or have you forgotten that he saved my life yesterday?"

Chastened, Allison retreated into the shell she always did when she had overstepped herself.

Her father cleared his throat. "Before we drop the subject, Lee, there's something I need to know. It's about Morco. Did you kill him on our account, because you thought he might come after us again, or was his death unrelated to the incident at Wynn's?"

Lee hesitated, mulling whether to admit the truth. It was bad enough that shooting Morco had confirmed Allison's low opinion of him. If she learned that he had done it to protect them, she might be offended and claim it was just his excuse for throwing lead. The intense look she was giving him increased his unease.

"Well?" Jim goaded.

"He was spreading lies about me," Lee said. "When I called him on it, he slapped leather."

"That was all there was to it?"

Lee fiddled with his hat. "What more do you want?" he rejoined.

Old Abe clucked. "A definite man-killer," he said without rancor.

Bob Delony stepped to the doorway. "Why don't we head for the dining room?" he suggested eagerly. "I don't know about the rest of you, but I'm starved enough to eat a steer." He winked at Lee. "In case no one told you, you're in for a treat. My wife is the best cook this side of the Mississippi."

"Oh, Bob," Ethel protested, though not too strongly.

The lawyer's praise proved well-founded. Lee had never tasted more delicious fried chicken. Baked potatoes, peas, buttery biscuits, and stewed apples completed the meal.

For so modest a home, the dining room was elegantly decorated, down to the fine white china on which the meal was served. Lee wound up between Allison and Jim Hays, while across from him were

Old Abe, Ethel, and the boy. Bob sat at the head of the table.

"You're a superb cook, ma'am," Lee said as he started on his second helping.

"Why, thank you," Ethel said sweetly. "But I'm not the only one. Did you know that the lovely young lady beside you bakes the tastiest cherry pie in the Territory?"

Jim Hays grunted. "I'll vouch for that. Allison makes it hard for a man my age to keep a tight rein on his middle."

Bob Delony smacked his lips. "Trust us, Mr. Scurlock. There's nothing quite like coming home to a freshly prepared meal steeped in love."

"Steeped in love?" Lee said.

Ethel tittered. "He gets that from me. My grandmother used to say that a woman should always have love in her heart when she cooks. That way, everything she makes is manna from heaven."

Lee dipped his fork into the potatoes. "A home-cooked meal is a luxury I haven't enjoyed in ages." It stirred memories of Tennessee, of his ma bent over their big black kettle, of his pa smoking a pipe and his brothers and sisters scampering around like wild chipmunks.

Old Abe was about to chomp down on a chicken leg. "What you need is a wife, Reb. I've had me three in my time, and as much aggravation as they were, I've learned that it's better for a man to live with a woman than without one."

Allison became conscious of her father staring at her, and she was glad her long hair hid her burning ears. "Speaking for myself, the man I marry must be dependable and considerate. He has to be my partner in life, not just looking for someone to fill his belly."

Jim Hays pursed his lips. His daughter did not fool

him for one minute. That comment had been her way of tactfully stressing the point she had hammered into their guest over and over. "Allison, don't start in on Lee again. He's here at my invitation."

All during the meal, Lee had been conscious of questioning glances thrown in his direction. Not only by Jim, but by the Delonys and even Abe Howard. The logical conclusion was that they had something on their mind, that their invite had a hidden motivation. "Why am I here?" he asked to get to the bottom of it.

"How do you mean?" Jim Hays said.

"I wasn't born yesterday," Lee said.

Abe Howard chortled. "You're not pullin' the wool over this feller's eyes, Jim. Might as well come out with it."

"Tell Lee what you have in mind, Father," Allison added.

Jim Hays appeared uncomfortable. Setting down his spoon, he said, "I'd rather wait until after our meal is over, but if you insist—"

"I do," Lee said.

Scanning those at the table, Jim leaned back. "What do you think of Diablo?"

"What's to think? It's a boomtown like a hundred others."

"To you, perhaps. To the people who live here, it's much more. Bob and Ethel and Abe foresee a great future if certain elements don't ruin it. As you've heard, Old Abe went so far as to donate the money needed to construct a church and a school. All of us want Diablo to flourish."

"What's your stake in this?" Lee asked. "You live in Denver."

"Now we do, true, but I've given some thought to relocating my practice here a few years down the road. My main stake is my friendship with Bob and

Ethel. He's in a tight spot, Lee, and I'd like to help him out. If certain elements aren't stopped, Diablo might wither and die from a blight of violence and bloodshed."

"That's twice you've mentioned 'certain elements.'"

Jim's face clouded. "You know who I mean. Allister Kemp, Frank Lowe, and the rest of their cohorts."

Lee deliberately turned to Allison. "That's funny. I recollect someone telling me that Kemp is more of a gentleman than anyone else around these parts," he said, quoting her.

"My daughter still thinks highly of him, but I don't," Jim stated. "Even her faith has been shaken in light of recent developments."

Lee could not resist. "What did he do? Play a game of cards?"

"No," Allison said, stung but not offended. "He's going to court."

"That's right," her father confirmed. "The reason Bob sent for me is that Kemp is in the process of trying to take control of Diablo."

"Hell, he's been trying that ever since the town sprang up," Old Abe said. "That varmint has used every nasty trick you can think of to force the homesteaders and us ore hounds to leave. Since that hasn't worked, now he's tryin' to run roughshod over us. He has the misguided notion that the valley and all the land around it are rightfully his."

Lee did not see where any of this had anything to do with him. "What has Kemp done so far?"

"What hasn't he done?" Abe shot back. "Take the homesteaders. His punchers have threatened them time and again. Their livestock has been slaughtered in the dead of night. Their gardens have been trod under, their irrigation ditches filled in. They get up in the morning and find their plows busted, their tools smashed. All thanks to Kemp."

"There's no proof he's involved," Allison said.

Old Abe sputtered. "Who the hell needs proof, missy? Everyone knows he's to blame."

Ethel, reaching for a pitcher of water, shook her head. "Watch your language, Abe, with ladies present. I won't have swearing under my roof."

"Sorry, Ethel," Abe said, not sounding sorry at all. To Lee, he said, "As for us prospectors and miners, Kemp's cowboys gave us a hard time from the very beginnin'. They'd cuss us, hopin' we'd go for our guns. A few fools did, and Jesse Bodine and his crowd made short work of them. But the town grew anyway, and before long prospectors and miners were being found dead. Others were robbed by masked bandits."

"Yet most of you stayed on," Lee guessed.

"Those with gumption," Old Abe said. "So when all that didn't scare us off, Kemp brought in Frank Lowe. They opened a store, started the bank, and took over a few of the dives."

"I thought Kemp wanted to shut the town down, not build it up."

"Not anymore. Not since he saw that it was hopeless. Now he wants to run it, lock, stock, and barrel. So Kemp has Lowe fleece everyone except the cowboys who work for him."

Jim Hays took up the account. "I think the church and the school were the last straw for Kemp. They made him realize the homesteaders and the miners are here for the long haul. So now he's taking legal action. He's hired three top lawyers, who have filed a motion claiming that Kemp has exclusive water rights in Diablo Valley."

Old Abe bristled like a he-bear. "Do you have any idea what would happen if the court agrees? Everybody would end up paying through the nose for every drop of water they use. Kemp would have us all under his thumb."

"No judge would ever go along with such a hare-brained notion," Lee said.

Jim Hays let loose a brittle laugh. "You don't know much about the legal system, do you? It's not always whether a legal argument is based on solid law or even common justice that matters. It's how much money one side or the other can spend to influence the verdict."

"You're saying the court can be bought?"

"Any court can. We suspect that Kemp has influence where it counts. The preliminary hearing on his motion has been moved up, even though Bob asked for more time to prepare his case."

Bob Delony nodded. "Old Abe, on behalf of the Miners Association, asked me to represent him, and I sent for Jim because I'm in over my head on this one."

Lee got to the heart of the issue. "What does all of this have to do with me?"

The law wranglers and the gristle-heel exchanged glances. "I'll do the honors," Old Abe said. "You see, Lee, Diablo is slowly but surely gettin' civilized. Seven of us have been elected to a town council, and next Tuesday we're votin' in a town marshal."

"So I've heard."

"Who we pick is crucial. If the Cowboy Faction appoint their man, they'll have the local law in their pocket. So far we have two candidates. One is Jesse Bodine, foreman at the Bar K. The other is a Texian called Vint Evers."

"Know them both," Lee said.

"Bodine is a Kemp man, bought and paid. Three idiots on the council will vote for whoever Kemp wants. Two others will vote with me to pick who I want. That leaves Will Dyer. He'll vote with us to spite the Englishman."

"So what's your problem? Pick Evers and be done with it."

"I don't want Evers."

"Why not?"

Abe plucked at his beard. "Evers is a lone wolf. He blew into town and applied on his own. Kemp didn't ask him, and neither did I."

"What's wrong with that? Vint's a straight shooter," Lee declared, pleased to be able to do the Texan a good turn.

"I ain't so sure, Reb. I've been askin' around, studyin' his history, and I can't guarantee he won't throw in with the Kemp crowd. He was a cowboy before he pinned on a star, so he's apt to be a mite too partial to the Cowboy Faction for my tastes."

"Evers will do the job better than anyone else you could find."

A hawkish smile lit Old Abe's craggy visage. "Better than you, you reckon?"

"Me?"

Jim Hays spoke. "That's why I invited you here today. I knew Abe would agree once I proposed the idea. We need someone reliable. We want you to put in for the position."

The full implications bunched Lee's gut into a knot. Like most Tennessee hill folk, he tended to take others at face value. It shocked and angered him whenever he found that he was being used—especially by people he had taken to be friends. "So you had it in the back of your mind to ask me to apply even before we got to town yesterday, didn't you?"

"Yes, but—"

"So that's the real reason you invited me here," Lee said, and he could not keep an edge of disappointment and rising resentment out of his voice.

"Now, hold on," Jim said defensively. "I think I see where this is leading, and nothing could be further from the truth. I happen to think highly of you or I wouldn't have even considered asking you over."

Lee's appetite had evaporated like dew under a blistering sun. Pushing the plate back, he said to Ethel, "I want to thank you, ma'am, for your hospitality. I reckon it's time I was on my way."

Old Abe sat up. "Hold on, young hoss. Don't go off half-cocked. Stay and hear us out."

"My answer is no."

"Just like that?" Abe said, his cheeks hardening. "Stop and think a moment, won't you? Unless we appoint an impartial lawdog, there will be hell to pay. Diablo will run red with the blood of innocent men and women. Do you want that to happen?"

"Vint Evers is your man," Lee said. Nodding at the Delonys, he wheeled and stalked toward the front hall, not caring one whit that they were shocked by his rudeness.

Allison Hays watched the Tennessean's retreating broad shoulders a moment, her heart torn by the thought that she might never see him again. Flinging her napkin onto the table, she dashed after him, calling out, "Lee! Wait! Please!"

If it had been anyone else, the Tennessean would have kept going. Halting, he turned, jamming his hat onto his head so that the brim hid his eyes. He could not quite decipher Allison's visage. Was she upset over what had happened, or was she upset with him?

"I want you to know that I had no idea what my father was up to," Allison explained. "When he told me, I tried to talk him out of it, but he refused to listen." She laid a hand on his arm. "Please don't think badly of him, or of Old Abe. They honestly feel that appointing you marshal is best for the town and everyone in it."

Diablo

"A man has the right to do what he believes is best for *him*," Lee said. He did not mention what was really upsetting him.

"Are you mad at us?"

"Why should you care?"

The verbal lashing caused Allison's skin to prick. "What?" she said, aghast at the vehemence that suddenly twisted his handsome face.

Her question opened the floodgates of Lee's pent-up frustration. It was as if a finger had been yanked from a hole in a dike and all the water came crashing through at once. "Why should you care?" he repeated himself. "You've been riding roughshod over me since you found out how I make my living. I didn't try to hide it from you, but that didn't count for much. You decided I was no more than a jug-headed no-account." In his anger he reared over her in dark and ominous profile.

Allison was chilled to the depths of her marrow. Not by fear for her safety, for her intuition assured her that he would never, ever, do her physical harm. No, she was scared because she saw that in some unfathomable manner she and her father had hurt him more than a bullet ever could, that her childish carping and her father's subtle manipulation had wounded the southerner severely.

"Who are you to judge me?" Lee voiced the question that had seared him from the beginning. "Did you ever think to ask about all the steady work I've done in the past? No. You thought the worst of me and branded me as less than decent." He paused, righteous with wrath. "Well, I have news for you, Miss Hays. Whatever I've done, whatever mistakes I've made, I've never done anything I'm ashamed of. I may not be a Bible-thumper, but I'm not as worthless as you seem to think. And I won't abide being treated as such."

The words trickled to a stop and Lee paused, waiting for a reply, but there was none.

Allison's mouth had slackened at the tirade, and she gazed at him in frank astonishment, at a loss for words.

"I've said my piece," Lee said, rotating on a boot heel. "Tell your pa that neither of you will be bothered by my presence again." With that, he stormed to the door, thrust it wide, and was gone.

In shock, Allison ran to the doorway. "Lee, I didn't—!" she yelled, stopping when she realized that nothing she could say would stop him from going. Inexplicably, her knees went weak, and she clutched at the jamb for support.

Chapter Eight

Ike Shannon loved to gamble. He loved it with a passion that defied description. He loved it more than he did fine liquor, or willing women, or any of the other pleasures men were addicted to.

A combination of factors contributed to his zeal. There was the rush of excitement, the lure of a challenge, that came from pitting his intellect and skill against others'. There was added spice in the fickle element of pure luck that more often than not decided the outcome.

The very first time Shannon had sat in on a poker game, he'd been hooked. It had not been all that long ago, actually. Seven years had passed since he saw the handwriting on the wall and gave up his previous profession to ply the craft of cardsmanship. Not once had he regretted his decision.

But there were days like this one when the hours dragged. It was early afternoon, and only a handful

David Robbins

of patrons were in the Applejack. None showed an interest in parting with their money, so Shannon sat alone at his table, glumly playing solitaire, depressed as much by boredom as by the weight of worry for his best friend in all the world: Vint Evers.

Two less similar people would be hard to find. Where Shannon was coldly logical, even methodical, in all he did, the Texan was a man of fire and action, further marred by a wild streak that had nearly been the death of him on several occasions. For a man who made his living by enforcing the law, it was a potentially fatal flaw. The hellholes that Evers tamed festered with the flotsam of humanity, with callous brutes and razor-honed gunnies who would give anything to be the one who brought the Texan down.

Shannon had seen Evers's flaw right off. Yet he had been oddly drawn to the formidable *pistolero*, and had risked his own life to save the Texan's time and again.

Why did he keep doing it? He was under no obligation to follow Vint from town to town, to always be there when Evers needed a helping hand. Vint had certainly never asked him to do it. He had taken it on himself, as if it were the most natural thing in the world for him to do.

Friendship. That was the answer. For most people, friendship meant sharing a drink or a meal or going out on the town now and then, or lending tools or helping out when a roof needed to be repaired or a field needed tilling.

In the name of friendship Shannon was willing to do much more; he was willing to die for Vint Evers, something he would do for no other human being, not even some of his own relatives. The bond between them was as profound a mystery as life itself, one he could no more deny than he could willingly stop breathing.

Shannon accepted it. He lived by it. And on this particular day, he worried that his friend was making the biggest mistake yet, a mistake that might cost both of them their lives.

The rush of air and the tramp of heavy boots brought Shannon out of his reverie. Into the saloon had stalked the Tennessean, another man Shannon had taken an instinctive liking to. Immediately, he saw that something was wrong, that a thunderstorm roiled on the southerner's forehead.

A trio of miners were near the entrance, in Scurlock's path. Shannon saw them hastily step aside, one saying, "Afternoon, Mr. Scurlock, sir."

Lee tromped past them without comment. His gaze was fixed inward, not outward, and he stepped to the bar oblivious to his surroundings. All he could think of was how the Hayses had let him down, and how he had let himself down by being stupid enough to get interested in a woman who saw him as so much dirt.

"Howdy, Mr. Scurlock," the bartender greeted him. "The same as last night?"

Lee absently nodded. He wanted to jolt his anger out of his system with a few shots of rotgut. Intent on the barkeep, he started when a hand fell lightly on his shoulder.

"Whoa there, fella! It's me," Nelly Rosell said, sliding up beside him. She had been at the back of the room when he entered, and recalling how kind he had been the night before, she had hurried over before any of the other doves snagged him for their own.

"Nelly," Lee said sourly. He wanted to be alone, but he could not bring himself to ask her to leave.

"What's eating you?" Nelly asked.

"Nothing."

Nelly almost laughed. Men liked to pride themselves on being as hard as nails and keeping their feelings a secret, but the truth was that most wore their emotions on their sleeves and were no harder to read than an open book. They were boys, the whole lot of them, only bigger. And brasher. "If you say so," she responded. "But you sure are a terrible liar."

Lee bit his lower lip, mad at himself. It wasn't bad enough that he had let the Hayses make a fool of him. Now he was doing it to himself. "It's that obvious?" he said.

"Afraid so. Woman trouble would be my guess."

"It would be a good one," Lee confessed. But he did not elaborate. His problems were his own. He would not burden others with them.

Nelly did not pry. A lifetime ago she had learned that men were touchy when it came to personal matters. She'd learned it long before she ever set foot in a saloon. Her husband had taught her.

No finer man had ever drawn breath than John Rosell. Nelly's heart had fluttered the first time she laid eyes on him. Wonder of wonders, his had done the same on being introduced to her. After a whirlwind courtship they had wed, and John persuaded her to leave Ohio for the frontier.

Nelly had not really wanted to. She would have been content to stay in Ohio the rest of her life. But her man had a dream. John was a farmer, and he had heard that all the farmland he could ever want was in western Kansas, just sitting there, ripe for the taking. All he had to do was file a claim. A few years of hard toil and sweat, and he would have a farm the size of a county and be able to provide all his family's wants.

That was the dream. The reality was that they filed on a windswept stretch of arid prairie that seemed to resent their presence as much as Nelly resented being there.

No one had told them about the awful summer heat, about the bleak winter cold when their sod house was buried in snow clear up to the roof and there wasn't a lick of wood to be had anywhere.

No one had told them about the wind, the constant, buffeting wind, that scattered precious seed as if it were chaff, the wind that was forever tangling her hair even when she wore bonnets, the wind that fanned her face day in and day out until her cheeks felt like leather.

Nor had anyone told them about the dust. It was everywhere. It got into their eyes, into their ears, into their nostrils. It covered every article in the house. She would clean until the place was spotless, then go to bed, only to wake up the next morning to find a fine layer of dust again covering everything.

Then there were the thunderstorms. They had to be seen to be believed, awesome tantrums of nature, violent, raging upheavals that tore portions of their roof off or damaged their stable or blew down fences.

Hail as big as hen's eggs. Deluges that turned dry gullies into seething torrents, grassland into soggy ruin. Tornadoes that destroyed everything in their path. Nelly had seen them all.

Little by little, the steady wear and tear took its toll on her husband. Crop after crop failed, and with each failure the gleam of hope dwindled a bit more in John's eyes, eventually to be replaced by a horrible despondency. He went about his daily toil mechanically, seldom laughing, never joking.

Nelly had done what she could to bolster his spirits. When he would not respond, she had tactfully suggested that they go back to Ohio and start over. But John would not listen. His pride would not let him give up. He toiled on and on, losing more and more of his self-esteem as the days went by, until that nightmarish morning when he went out to plow and she never saw him again.

Indians, the Army said. A marauding band of Cheyennes, some claimed. No, it was Kiowas, others said. A patrol followed their trail until the tracks were wiped out by a storm.

For days Nelly had wept, until she had cried herself into a state of total emotional and physical exhaustion. Left all alone, virtually penniless, she'd had no one to turn to.

Returning to Ohio had been her only option. But her few friends did not have any money to spare. So, in desperation, she had done what everyone claimed no decent woman would ever do.

It had seemed like a harmless idea at the time. Nelly had gone to Dodge and applied at a saloon that happened to be run by Frank Lowe. How many years had it been now? she mused sadly, and suddenly grew aware that Lee Scurlock was studying her.

"Are you all right, ma'am?"

"Never better," Nelly said. For once she meant it, but she hesitated to tell him why. Leaning closer, she warned, "I saw you blow in. You should know enough not to waltz around with your guard down. Take a gander to your left."

Lee did, and saw Jesse Bodine and three cowboys at a faro table. The human bull of a ramrod was staring at him.

"Bodine was asking about you earlier," Nelly said. "He seemed real interested in knowing if you'd be in tonight."

"I wonder why," Lee said.

"I don't think he's on the peck."

"If he is, it's his mistake," Lee vowed. He was in no mood to be pushed by anyone.

Diablo

Nelly made a *tsk-tsk-tsk* sound. "Vint's right about you, Tennessee. You'd better watch yourself."

"You two have been talking about me?"

The sparkle in Nelly's eyes grew brighter. "We hit it off last night, Lee. That Texan sure is special." Catching herself, she said, "Anyway, we got to gabbing about you and he told me that you remind him of an hombre who's never forked an ornery horse. You don't know when to rein up, because you've never been thrown."

Lee could have told her differently, but Jesse Bodine had risen and was walking toward him. "Maybe you should skedaddle," Lee suggested in case there was gunplay.

"Not on your life," Nelly said. Just as she had stood by her husband's side until the very end, so she would stick by her newfound friend.

Taking a casual step, Lee aligned his back to the counter, his elbow propped so his right hand was near the ivory butt of his Colt. Bodine did not have a threatening air about him, but a man could never be too careful. Intent on the Texan, he did not realize someone was at his other elbow until the person spoke.

"Care for some company, lad?" Ike Shannon asked. He, too, had heard Bodine asking about the Tennessean, and he wanted to be on hand to learn why. Not that he would interfere if Bodine called Lee out. He liked the southerner, but his true loyalty lay with Vint Evers.

"Ike," Lee said, noting a Remington on the gambler's right hip. "I see you're packing more hardware than before."

"Not by choice. A belt gun is damned uncomfortable to wear for hours at a stretch at a gaming table," Shannon remarked, "but I need something to swat the flies with." He grinned at Bodine. "Here comes one now."

Jesse Bodine had halved the distance to the bar when he said, "Hello, Scurlock. I've been looking for you."

"So I've heard."

"I need to talk to you," Bodine said, glancing at Shannon and Nelly as if they were intruding.

"So talk."

Bodine did not like it, but he said, "My boss sent me in to find you. He wants to extend an invite to you to come visit his ranch."

One thing Lee could safely say about his short stay in Diablo: One surprise was piled on another. "Why does Allister Kemp want to see me?"

The huge man shrugged. "He's not in the habit of explaining why he does things, and I'm not about to ask. All I know is that you're invited to supper tonight at six. Head due west out of town. You can't hardly miss his spread, since it's all there is between here and the hills to the west." Chortling at his own warped humor, Bodine walked off.

Nelly waited until the giant was out of earshot, then slapped the Tennessean's arm. "Are you insane?"

"I'm beginning to think that most everyone in Arizona is a mite touched in the head," Lee said wryly.

"I'm serious," Nelly said. "How can you be loco enough to accept Kemp's invitation? After what you've done, he's just waiting for a chance to kill you."

"You know this for a fact?"

Ike Shannon answered. "Anyone with half a brain knows that Kemp is your enemy. You've killed two of his men, wounded another, and he's not the forgiving kind, laddie. You're playing into his hands by going out there. Don't do it."

Lee turned to his drink to gain time to focus his thoughts. They had a point, he granted, but if he didn't go, there would be talk. Some people might brand him a coward. He mentioned as much, adding, "There's no harm in riding out to see what the man wants. Kemp is not about to have me killed in his own house." He jerked a thumb at each of them. "I have witnesses that he invited me."

"You're forgetting that there ain't no law in these parts yet," Nelly said.

"Besides which, witnesses don't count for much when lead is flying thick and fast," Shannon reminded him.

Half in jest, Lee said, "Well, then, if the Englishman does make wolf meat of me, I'll expect the two of you to see that he gets his due."

"You're on," Shannon said sincerely.

Lee was surprised. "You'd call him out on my account?"

"No, I'd use a Sharps fifty-caliber and drop him from a quarter of a mile away," Shannon said, straight-faced.

When it came to killing, Shannon was not like Vint. His friend was so inherently fair-minded that he would never shoot anyone from ambush. Vint would rather brace an enemy to the enemy's face. Not so with Shannon. To him, killing was killing, plain and simple. How the deed was done was of no consequence. *Doing it* was what counted, and Shannon would do it in whatever way was best guaranteed to get the job done.

Lee's interest in the Irishman perked. "Not many gamblers can use a Sharps worth a hoot," he said. The big rifles were immensely powerful, able to drop a bull buffalo at five hundred yards.

"I haven't always made my living at cards," Shannon said. Though he rarely talked about his past, he confided, "I was born and raised in Illinois, and when I was sixteen I got a hankering to travel. I did some buffalo hunting for a spell, until the big hairy brutes pretty near died off and there was no money to be made."

Lee tried to picture the nattily dressed gambler in grimy buckskins and reeking of the stench of blood and death. He couldn't do it.

"Then one evening in Cheyenne, for the hell of it, I sat in on a poker game. That was all it took. I've been playing the cards ever since. Likely I'll go on gambling until the day they plant my carcass on a Boot Hill somewhere."

"I'm flattered that you would kill Kemp over me," Lee remarked.

Shannon smirked. "Over you? No, laddie, if I kill that arrogant Englishman, it will be because of Vint."

"You've lost me."

"Vint and I are pards. To you that might not mean much. To me it means that I won't abide any man being a threat to him." Shannon removed his bowler to run a hand through his hair. "If Kemp has you cut to ribbons, then he has more brass than I give him credit for, and I'd kill him in a heartbeat to ensure he doesn't endanger Vint once the council picks Vint to be the marshal."

"You're awful confident they will."

"Who else is there to choose from? Bodine is the only other man in the running, and not enough will vote for him."

Lee did not relate his noontime meeting with Old Abe and Jim Hays. "You'd do to ride the river with, Ike," he said. "Not many men would be as loyal to a friend as you are." He turned to the blonde, whose full figure was sheathed in a sheer red dress. "I owe you thanks for warning me about Jesse."

"Think nothing of it," Nelly said. "Consider it my

way of paying you back for last night. If you hadn't let me latch on to Vint, I would have missed out on the most fun I've had in years." A haunted longing crept into her tone. "I'd forgotten what it was like to live for myself. Once a woman is lured into the saloon trade, her life is no longer her own. She's branded forever."

Lee intended to ask what she meant, but Ike Shannon muttered, "Here comes another bastard I'd like to fill with lead."

Frank Lowe and Lowe's ever-present bodyguards were approaching. Attired in an expensive suit, a diamond stickpin scintillating in the light, Lowe notched a thumb in a vest pocket. "Gentlemen," he declared grandly. To the Tennessean, he said, "I'm flattered that you've made the Applejack your regular waterin' hole."

"What difference does it make?" Lee responded.

"You're good for business, Scurlock," Lowe said. "Gunmen always are, provided they don't let the liquor and their temper get the best of them." Puffing up like a peacock, he motioned at the spot where Morco had fallen. "Shootin' that damned greaser was the best thing that's happened in months. Word has spread all over town. Tonight everyone will be stoppin' by in the hope of catchin' a glimpse of you. I'll do three times my normal business."

"Maybe you should pay Lee a percentage of the take," Shannon said to spite the man.

Frank Lowe forced a laugh. "Now, why didn't I think of that?" He sobered. "Tell you what I will do, though. All your drinks tonight, Scurlock, are on the house."

"Your generosity is overwhelming," Shannon said.

Resentment flickered across Lowe's swarthy features. Suddenly spinning on Nelly, he snapped, "Workin' hard, woman, or hardly workin'?"

"I'm doing my job," she said softly.

"Are you?" Lowe said viciously. "Your job, in case you've forgotten, is to mingle with the customers, to smile and be friendly and persuade them to partake of the hard stuff." He sniffed. "I don't see you minglin' or smilin', even."

"I was talking to Lee."

"And I was just about to buy her a drink," Lee fibbed, agitated by Lowe's domineering attitude. The man treated the woman as if she were his personal property to do with as he saw fit. It wasn't right.

"Maybe later," Lowe said, stepping close and seizing her roughly by the wrist. "Last night I let you get away with doing as you saw fit. Not tonight. You're paid to use your charm on anyone and everyone who comes through that door, not just on those you're fond of."

"Let go," Nelly said, twisting her arm to no avail.

Lowe shook her. "I'll do what I damn well please! Or have you forgotten our little arrangement?"

"How could I ever forget?"

The dandy sneered and puffed his chest out even farther. "You're all alike, you trollops. You think that you can take advantage of me, that you can slack off whenever you like. Well, you're wrong."

"Take your hands off her!"

The command was roared like the primal growl of a panther. There, mere yards away, stood Vint Evers, his sinewy frame coiled, menace and fury transforming him into a brooding inhuman engine of destruction. As everyone turned, his hands swooped to his pistols.

Chapter Nine

Allison Hays sat in a rocking chair on the front porch of the Delony home and thought about her life. Not that a lot of memorable events had befallen her. Except for the death of her mother after a long and wearying illness, she had suffered no great tragedies.

If anything, Allison had led a fairly sheltered existence, living in the best of neighborhoods, attending the best of schools. Hunger and want had not left their stamp on her character.

It was to her credit that she had not turned out as spoiled as some of her friends. Those born with proverbial silver spoons in their mouths often grew up thinking that life owed them a living, when in truth the only thing that life owed anyone was the priceless gift of being alive.

Still, Allison would be the first to admit that she was not as mature as she should be. Her temper was too volatile, her patience too short. And, as she had shown with Lee Scurlock, she was prone to look down her nose at anyone who did not measure up to her standards of upright conduct.

Was that wrong? Allison had never doubted herself before, but now, her heart torn by the abrupt departure of the handsome southerner, she doubted, and doubted deeply.

Allison could not bear the thought of never seeing Lee again. At no other time in her life had she ever felt similarly about any man, even those who had wooed her with lavish gifts and elegant dinners and nights at the theater.

She could not shake Lee's image from her mind's eye if she tried—though she did not try very hard. She saw again those flashing eyes, his carefree smile. She reviewed his lithe economy of motion, and how warm his hand had been when she touched it.

Was this what it was like to fall in love?

The mental query jarred her. Allison had always been of the opinion that true love was a fiction, the handiwork of writers of sensational novels, who must all be hopeless romantics. Marriage and raising a family of her own had always been alien concepts, perhaps fit for other women but definitely not for her. She was different, she'd told herself time and again. She was destined for a more exotic destiny.

But now Allison wondered if maybe she was more normal than she had ever been willing to admit. The blood of her mother and her grandmother and her great-grandmother flowed in her veins, and maybe the blood of untold others for as far back as the family line extended. In an unbroken chain they had done what women had been doing since the dawn of time: They had passed on the spark of life from one generation to the next by marrying and rearing families as best they were able. Thus had it always been; thus would it always be.

Diablo

For the very first time in her life Allison seriously considered that she, too, would follow in the footsteps of those before her, and wed. Once, the notion would have sparked mirth. Now she rested her chin in her hand and envisioned what it would be like being the wife of Lee Scurlock.

Allison had to admit that she knew very little about him. Other than where he came from and a few meager facts about his family, he was an enigma, a man of mystery. Strangely, that added to his appeal. She felt that unplumbed depths lurked in the wellspring of his being, depths that only someone who cared for him with a supreme and total devotion would be permitted to delve into. And she liked the idea of that someone being herself.

There was only one hitch. Lee had made it clear that he never intended to see either her father or her ever again. She still did not quite comprehend why he had become so upset, but there was no denying that they had hurt him to the quick.

How could she make it up to him?

That burning issue occupied her for the better part of an hour, until the hinges on the front door creaked and out walked the one person in whom she could confide. "How did you know that Bob was the right man for you, Ethel?" she bluntly asked.

Ethel Delony's wise eyes kindled with understanding. She did not ask why Allison wanted to know. She did not badger Allison with probing curiosity. Smiling in the knowing way that feminine intuition lent her gender, she said, "I just did. I can't give you the how and why of it, because I doubt I know them myself. Suffice it to say that in my innermost soul I was drawn to him like metal to a magnet, or a moth to a flame. Some might call it instinct. Some might say it was nothing more than primitive longing. I say it was true love."

"True love," Allison softly echoed the words.

Ethel leaned against a post and folded her arms. "My grandmother used to say that for every woman, somewhere in the world is the right man. A woman might need to wander long and far to find him, but if she perseveres, then the powers that be will ensure that she does."

A silly idea, Allison thought. Or was it? How else could she explain her unshakable attachment to a man she hardly knew? A gambler, no less, and a gunman to boot?

Ethel stared skyward. "I like to think that our guardian angels are responsible, that they watch out over us and lead us in paths that will benefit us best."

"Angels as Cupid?" Allison said, grinning. "Well, Cupid *is* supposed to have wings."

The older woman laughed. "Poke fun all you want. The fact remains that women and men are drawn to one another, and there's no explaining why. It's more than animal lust, more than human passion. It goes deeper, to the core of what we are."

Allison had always admired her friend's insights, never more than now. "You'd think, though, that two people meant to be together would hit it off from the moment they met."

"That's not always the case," Ethel said. "It's like that old saying, 'You can lead a horse to water, but you can't make it drink.' Well, the angels or Cupid or whatever can lead two people together, but they can't force the couple to fall in love. Sometimes the people balk. Sometimes either the man or the woman or both are too selfish or too childish or just too plain stupid to realize the gift they have been given, and they go their separate ways."

The thought of losing Lee forever sent a chill through Allison, and she shivered.

"Are you cold, my dear?"

"No," Allison said, bending so the sun was full on her face. "But I am at a loss." She tried not to betray how distraught she was when she asked, "What can a person do when the man she thinks is right for her doesn't want to see her ever again?"

The corners of Ethel's eyes crinkled. "A woman in that situation has two choices, it seems to me. Either she can let the pigheaded man have his way and deprive both of them of lifelong happiness, or she can seek him out and, as the saying goes, put all her cards on the table. What will be, will be."

"Funny that you should mention cards," Allison said.

"Yes. Isn't it."

"Evers!" Frank Lowe exclaimed, a sickly pallor creeping over his features. He snatched his hand from Nelly Rosell as if he had brushed against burning coals and stepped to the right, his palms held outward. "Now, you hold on, mister! You have no call to throw down on me!"

Only the fear that laced Lowe's voice and was betrayed by his widened eyes prevented the enraged Texan from drawing. Gradually, his whipcord muscles relaxed. Slowly, he released the pearl butts of his sheathed pistols and squared his broad shoulders. The red haze that had fallen before his eyes faded, but not the gnawing fury boiling at the core of his being.

Vint Evers had known men like Frank Lowe before. They were as common as rattlesnakes, but much more vile. They lived off the misery of others, lining their pockets through commerce in lust and greed. They were the embodiment of all that was wicked and despicable in human nature. And as such, they were symbols of all that Vint Evers opposed.

David Robbins

Frank Lowe's fright faded when he realized that the Texan was not going to shoot him. Regaining his customary bluster, he rasped, "You had no call to butt in like that. This doesn't concern you."

Vint glanced at Nelly, who glowed with gratitude, and he thought of the previous night, of the glorious, magical hours they had shared, the likes of which he had not experienced in his whole short but eventful life.

Lowe did not know when to leave well enough alone. "I have a perfect right to address my girls as I see fit," he crowed.

Vint Evers stalked closer. Ever a man of action, he came to a swift decision, stating ominously, "Nelly is no longer yours to boss around."

Lee saw the blonde clutch at her throat, saw undiluted affection wash over her countenance like a stream of crystal-clear water over a waterfall, and in that moment knew that something had transpired between the Texas gunfighter and the soiled dove, the same thing that he had once hoped would blossom between Allison and him, and he felt a twinge of envy overridden by happiness. It could not have happened to two more deserving people.

Frank Lowe sputtered in incoherent anger. "What the devil are you talking about, no longer mine?" he fumed.

"You heard me," Vint said. "Nelly is done workin' for you as of this very minute."

"She's one of my best workers!" Lowe protested. This from the man who a few moments ago had accused her of slacking off.

"I'm takin' her out of here," the Texan announced.

Only Frank Lowe reacted with shock at the news. Ike Shannon frowned, for he had known it was coming and dreaded it. He didn't begrudge Vint the companionship; he dreaded that it would distract his

118

friend to the point where Vint would no longer keep his mind on what had to be done. For someone in Vint's line of work, the consequences could be fatal.

Lowe looked around in amazement, as if to confirm he was awake and not dreaming, then sneered at the Texan. "Think so, do you? Well, think again! You can't just waltz out of here with her, and she knows it."

Vint Evers had never been one to take it kindly whenever someone told him that he could not do something he was of a mind to do. Hitching at his gunbelts, he said, "Who's to stop me?"

"Not who. What," Frank Lowe said, sinister triumph crowning him as he gestured at the blonde. "She has a contract with me. All my girls do. It keeps them honest."

Vint looked at Nelly again, his gut bunching into a tight ball at the despair that marred her beauty. Fresh in his memory were the hours they had spent in the saloon the night before, Nelly glued to his elbow, the two of them whispering and laughing like kids.

It had been Vint's brainstorm to take her for a stroll, and they had wound through Diablo's darkened streets until the wee hours of the morning, shoulder to shoulder, sharing their good experiences and their bad. Now and again shadowy figures had made toward them as if inclined to rob them or do them harm. But when the footpads recognized the famous Texan, they melted away as soundlessly as specters.

Vint and Nelly had bent their steps to the river. Under a spreading cottonwood, on a carpet of lush grass, bathed by the glow of the full moon, they had sat and cuddled, Vint awkward and timid, Nelly warm and tender. As a man-killer Vint had few equals, but as a lady-killer, he was as green as the grass on which they had sat.

Later, Vint had walked Nelly to the shack he shared with Ike Shannon, where they had sat at the small table and talked, talked, talked until a rosy glow painted the eastern sky, heralding the advent of a new day.

It had been the grandest night of Vint's entire life, a night such as he had occasionally dreamed but never dared to actually think would take place. He had been floating on air when he escorted her to her hotel, and then had the audacity to give her a kiss in public. He could still taste her incredibly sweet tongue and feel the delicious pressure of her pillowy lips.

Now here was a mangy polecat of a pimp telling him that he couldn't free her from the shackles of saloon life? Vint Evers edged nearer to Frank Lowe, his eyes ablaze with raw hatred. "What are you on about?"

Lowe lost some of his swagger, coughed, and said, "When she first came to work for me in Dodge, I had her sign a standard contract. She didn't have a penny to her name, so I advanced her five hundred dollars to pay off her debts and use however else she pleased."

"She hasn't paid it off?" Vint asked.

Nelly responded, in a voice so frail that Lee Scurlock would not have recognized it as hers if he had not seen her lips move. "I've tried, but he'll only take a dollar a week from my pay, no matter how much I earn."

"A dollar a week?" Vint snarled at Lowe. "At that rate, it will take her ten years to pay it all off!"

The saloon owner chuckled evilly. "Can I help it if most of the women who apply for work are too dumb to read the fine print? I have the right to set the amount they'll repay each week. And they're obligated to abide by it, whether they want to or not."

Like a flower shriveled by drought, Nelly wilted, bowing her head. The previous night with the lanky Texan had been too glorious for words, a night like none she had enjoyed since her husband's death, and which she had never expected to enjoy again. Now her stupidity had trapped her, depriving her of the chance to start over. It wasn't fair.

Ike Shannon pulled out his poke and wagged it at Lowe. "How much does she still owe on her contract? I'll pay it off right here and now, plus throw in an extra hundred besides for your trouble."

A serpentine sneer was Lowe's response. "Keep your money. I aim to hold her to her contract." He was no fool. Nelly was a favorite with his customers. In a single week she earned him more than a hundred on drinks alone. "What will it be, Evers?" he demanded. "Does she honor her word, or will you take her out of here by force? I'm not jackass enough to try and stop you. But if you do, then you'll be in the wrong, and we both know it. I can go to the judge, and she'll be back at work before the sun sets."

A shadow fell across Vint Evers. Inwardly, he wrestled with himself, torn between his desire to free Nelly from Lowe's clutches and his personal code that required he must always abide by the letter of the law. It was ingrained into him, like a knot into wood. Most of his adult life, after all, had been spent wearing a badge.

Legally, Frank Lowe had the right to require that Nelly live up to the terms of the contract. So long as she had signed it willingly, she was bound by its dictates. Legally, there was not a thing in the world Vint could do. The realization hit him harder than any fist ever could, and those observing him saw his shoulders sag and his mouth compress into a slit.

"What's your decision?" Lowe said.

Lee Scurlock yearned to intervene on the Texan's behalf, but what could he do short of whipping out his Colt and shooting Frank Lowe dead?

Ike Shannon could not bear to see his one and only friend in the grip of inner torment. "Be decent for once in your life, Lowe," he said. "Let me pay off her contract. I'll make it well worth your while."

"Nope. Nelly is one of the most attractive girls I've got, and I won't let her go until I'm damned good and ready."

For a few tense moments Lee had the impression that the gambler was going to resort to his steel, but Shannon looked at Vint, frowned, and swung toward the bar in blatant disgust.

Nelly stepped forward. For one brief night she had felt what it was like to live as a human being again, and for the first time since John died she had dared to hope, to aspire to a way of life other than that of alcohol and lust. She wanted more than anything to be free of Frank Lowe's clutches, but she would not do it at the cost of all that Vint Evers held dear.

The Texan had told her about his life. How his folks had been massacred by Comanches when he was twelve and he had struck off on his own, drifting south of the Rio Grande where he had fallen in with a Mexican *pistolero* who had taught him how to use a pistol.

At sixteen, Vint had gone to San Antonio with the *pistolero* and they had been involved in a gunfight in a cantina. The *pistolero* died. Vint was arrested, but a Texas Ranger took the youth under his wing. It was a turning point in Vint's life. At nineteen he pinned on a tin star, and had been doing so ever since.

If Vint were to buck Frank Lowe on her behalf, it would put him on the wrong side of the law for the first time since he hooked up with the *pistolero*. Nelly would not let that happen. "I appreciate the offer,"

Diablo

she told him, fighting back a flood of tears. "But there's nothing you can do." She spun, her eyes moistening, and hastened toward the rear of the Applejack so the Texan would not see.

"Glad that *that's* settled," Lowe said expansively, checking his gloat when the lean Texan abruptly reared over him.

"I reckon you've got me over a barrel, mister," Vint Evers hissed, "but I'm lettin' you know, straight out, that if you try and use that gal for anything other than peddlin' drinks, I'll come gunnin' for you, badge or no badge. Savvy?"

"It's my—" Lowe began, his vocal cords freezing at the icy chill the Texan radiated. He was as close to death at that instant as he had ever been. Shrugging, he said, "Whatever you want, Evers. Consider it a personal favor."

Vint glanced at the door through which Nelly had disappeared, his heartstrings tugging at his conscience. Wheeling before he did something he would regret, he stormed from the saloon, shoving past two prospectors who were entering.

Frank Lowe chuckled and turned to leave.

"You must have been born under a lucky star," Lee noted. "If it were me, I'd have emptied my Colt into you."

Snorting, Lowe departed. His victory lent spring to his step and he barked orders at his employees like an imperious military commander.

"Damn! Damn! Damn!" Ike Shannon barked, venting his spleen.

"Things will work out," Lee said, the assurance sounding childish even to him. There were no guarantees in life.

"Now Lowe and Kemp will have a hold over Vint," Shannon said, voicing his innermost fear. "If Vint becomes town marshal, I wouldn't put it past those two to use the woman against him." Once again the gambler eloquently summed up the situation with a heartfelt, resounding *"Damn!"*

Vint Evers stormed from the saloon in a blind fury. He neither saw nor heard those around him. In the iron grip of a seething vortex of emotion, he aimlessly roamed the streets of Diablo, walking off the fiery steam pent up inside of him. It might have been an hour later, it might have been two, when the clomp of hooves and brittle laughter from a second-floor window snapped him out of it.

Swiveling, Vint discovered that he had drifted toward the river. Toward, in fact, the very grove Nelly and he had visited the night before. He went to the exact spot and stood staring at the grass. The outline of where they had lain was still vaguely impressed on the bent stems, and he imagined them as they had been, locked so close together it was as if they were trying to crawl into each other's skin.

Vint could not bear to think of his clash with Lowe. It was all he could do to keep himself from marching back to the Applejack and exterminating the vermin. But if he did, he could forget about being appointed marshal. His prospects of being a lawman ever again would be slim.

In despair, the lean Texan wandered toward the shack he shared with Shannon. He balked at going in, since it would provoke more bittersweet memories of the hours Nelly and he spent there, but at last he pushed back his sombrero and shoved the rickety door inward.

Right away the Texan was struck by something odd. It was the middle of the afternoon, yet the shack was as gloomy as a tomb. Over the single window had been draped a blanket that normally covered Shannon's bed. For the life of him, he could not explain why the gambler had done it.

"Ike?" Vint said, entering. He left the door open to have light enough to see by, and it was well he did, for as he crossed toward the window to take down the blanket, boots scuffed on the floor behind him while at the same split second the small table in the center of the room heaved upward and out from under it sprang a dusky man armed with a Bowie knife.

The flying table saved Vint's life. For as he leaped back to avoid it, behind him a six-shooter blasted three times in swift succession, the slugs thudding into the wall below the covered window.

In a twinkling Vint had spun and brought both of his Colts into play. He thumbed their hammers as the assassin who had tried to backshoot him was leveling a smoking Smith & Wesson. The twin shots boomed like thunder. An invisible hammer slammed into the cutthroat's chest, flinging him into the corner, where he crumpled in a miserable disjointed heap.

That left the man with the Bowie. Vint spun again, but the dusky attacker was on him with pantherish speed. The big knife flashed. Pain seared Vint's left forearm. Despite himself, he dropped the pistol in his left hand.

There was still the other short-barreled Colt. Vint pivoted, the barrel arcing around. As it did, the other man speared the Bowie straight at his chest.

Chapter Ten

Texans were a peculiar breed.

No one would deny that they loved to fight. When insulted, or at the *hint* of an insult, they were prone to unlimber their hardware and blast away. Hairtrigger tempers were their stock-in-trade. But the violent code by which they lived had a strange quirk. As prone as they were to violence, they disdained using their fists. It wasn't that they couldn't hold their own man-to-man. Many a Texan had proved that, in countless barroom brawls. But when set upon, their natural instinct was to resort to a revolver.

The Texan disdain for using fists explained why, when Vint Evers found himself locked in grim combat with the man who sought his life, he never once thought to punch the man in the face or stomach.

It happened that as the Bowie streaked at Vint's chest, by pure chance his Colt clanged against it, steel ringing on steel, deflecting the blow. The knife

126

seared his ribs, not digging very deep. In a heartbeat he tried to take a bead, but the dusky man seized the wrist of his gun hand.

To save himself from the Bowie, Vint, in turn, lunged and seized the man's knife arm.

Locked in a grim life-or-death struggle, they rocked back and forth and around and around, each exerting himself to the utmost. Vint's sinewy muscles bulged. The veins on his temples resembled carved marble.

All this while the man with the Bowie was striving fiercely to wrench his arm loose from Vint's grasp. In their flailing around they happened to crash into the upturned table. The man's arm hit against a leg, numbing his fingers, jarring the Bowie from his grasp. The blow also jolted Vint's grasping fingers off the man's wrist.

That was the moment when the lawman should have slugged the assassin. One punch, and he could have driven the man back, enabling him to employ his Colt. But instead of swinging, he clamped his left hand on the other's arm in an attempt to free his gun hand.

It was then that the killer braced his legs and shoved. Caught off guard, Vint was flung backward, tripping over the table. In a flurry of limbs he toppled, rolling as he landed so that he came up into a crouch with his hand poised to fan the Colt.

Fanning was held in low regard by gun sharks, except when an enemy was so close that the shooter could not miss, and at that range Vint Evers could have split the edge of a coin.

Only, there was no one to shoot. For the man had vaulted through the doorway in a powerful leap and was off like a rabbit being chased by hounds, bounding down an alley that bordered the shack.

Vint ran after him, pausing at the alley mouth. He

had a clear shot—at the man's back. Slight pressure on the trigger was all it would take. He pointed the Colt, but his finger never tightened. He could not bring himself to backshoot someone, not even a man who moments ago had tried to take his life.

Giving chase would be futile. The assassin was as fleet as an antelope. At the far corner of the alley he glanced back, saw Vint, and bestowed a mocking smile on the Texan. Another second and he was gone.

Automatically, Vint reloaded his pistol. It was the cardinal rule, one he never, ever violated. Not with as many enemies as he had.

Voices were raised in outcry nearby. Feet pounded as the curious converged. Ignoring them, Vint returned to the shack, reclaiming the pistol he had dropped.

The dead man was not anyone Vint recollected. It might be someone with a grudge, someone whose kin Vint had slain at one time or another in the performance of his duties. He'd had to kill so many, it was hard to keep track. Somehow, though, he doubted it.

A shadow filled the doorway. Vint flung himself backward, his right hand stabbing downward.

"What the hell!" Ike Shannon growled. The gunshots had carried far on the sluggish afternoon air. He had pinpointed the direction, and fearing the worst, had raced from the saloon.

Lee Scurlock looked in. He saw a crimson stain on the Texan's shirt and fresh scarlet drops forming at the ends of Evers's fingers. "You're hurt," he said.

"Just a couple of scratches," Vint responded.

"Let me see it," Shannon said, angrily tearing the blanket from the window. It scared him to think how close his friend must have come to being murdered, and he partly blamed himself. He was supposed to stick close to Vint at all times, to always be there to cover Vint's back. But he had not figured on someone making an attempt on the lawman's life before the council rendered its decision.

Rolling Vint's sleeve up, Shannon found a three-inch-long gash. Already the blood was congealing, but that did not stop him from cleaning the wound and bandaging it with a strip torn from one of his white shirts. Next he tended Vint's cut side.

"You know who's responsible, don't you?" Shannon said as he carefully tied a knot.

"We can't say for certain," Vint said.

Shannon jerked on the knot so hard that the Texan grimaced. "The hell we can't! Kemp is behind this. He doesn't want you wearing the tin, so he took steps to remove you from consideration."

The likelihood made sense to Lee. But he had to agree with the Texan when Evers replied, "Unless we can dig up proof, there's nothin' we can do about it."

"There's something *I* can do," Shannon declared.

Vint shook his head. "No. That's not our way. We do everything accordin' to the law or we're no better than those we're up against. If you did what you're implyin', I'd have to haul you in myself."

Shannon pushed to his feet. "That damn honor of yours is going to be the death of you one day. When fighting rats, you kill them before they have a chance to bite you. You don't sit around waiting for them to pounce."

"You heard me, Ike," Vint said sternly.

It would not be the first time his friend had gone against his wishes.

Once, in Newton, a tough by the name of Clem Starling had bushwhacked Vint. The bullet had gone clean through his shoulder, sparing his vitals. Shannon had been so incensed that he'd taken his big buffalo gun and gone after Starling. Ike would have blown the man's brains out, if Vint had not risen from his sickbed and stopped him.

Shannon flung past Lee, saying gruffly, "You try and talk some sense into that hard Texan head of his. He never listens to me."

Outside a crowd had gathered. Many were pressing forward for a glimpse of the body. Pausing, Ike glared like a grizzly at bay and roared, "What's the matter with you coyotes? One of you fetch the undertaker, and the rest of you skedaddle!" His hand fell to his Remington, but it was his wrath more than the threat that sparked a general exodus.

Lee watched the Irishman tromp off. "If he's right, Kemp will try again."

Vint slowly rose. "I hope he does. I've tangled with a lot like him in my time, and they all have one thing in common." He pulled his sleeve down over the bandage. "They always trip themselves up sooner or later."

"But what do you do in the meantime?"

"What I always do, friend," Vint Evers said. "I try my best to stay alive."

Why would a man who owned thousands and thousands of acres resent a handful of homesteaders for squatting on a trifling few hundred? That was the question Lee Scurlock asked himself as he rode westward from Diablo, toward the bloodred setting sun.

The ranch, he had been told, was seven miles west of town, on a high rise. He saw it from a long way off, and noticed how it afforded a sweeping view of the valley in all directions.

What a valley! Lee mused. A cowman's paradise, lush with sweet grass. Streams fed by the Diablo River quenched the thirst of huge herds. Cattle lolled or grazed or drank in total ignorance of their eventual fate in the beef-hungry East.

Kemp's hands were everywhere. The looks they gave him were not friendly. At one point, a pair rode to within forty yards but did not do anything, so word must have gone out not to molest him.

As the roan climbed a grassy slope toward a palatial white structure on the rise, Lee heard the whoop of cowboys and the whinny of a horse. Clearing the rim, he counted nine punchers ringing a corral attached to a stable. Half a dozen outbuildings flanked it. A tall man perched on the top rail waved to him, so Lee angled over, unconsciously loosening his Colt in its holster.

The whooping and hollering rose to a crescendo. The punchers were urging on Jesse Bodine, who was astride a bronc saddle on a piebald mustang wrinkling its spine in a frenzy to pitch Bodine off. The horse bucked and kicked in savage abandon, even jumping skyward and coming down stiff-legged, the nastiest of tricks, but Bodine refused to be thrown.

The man on the top rail hopped down. In contrast to the dusty hats, shirts, jeans, and boots of the punchers, he affected an elegant style of dress. His tall frame was clad in an immaculate blue suit and polished black shoes, a type rarely seen on anyone except rich Wall Street tycoons or railroad barons. A full head of thick, slicked black hair crowned an angular aristocratic face. Green eyes regarded the Tennessean with no warmth whatsoever.

Lee reined up. "You must be Allister Kemp," he deduced.

"How do you do, Mr. Scurlock," Kemp said in a clipped accent. "I'm grateful you could make it." The Englishman's handshake was surprisingly strong. Steel flowed in Kemp's veins, the same steel that glittered in his eyes.

"I was a mite surprised to get the invite," Lee admitted.

"Really?" Kemp said. "I should think that you would have anticipated it, given the situation."

Before Lee could ask him to clarify his statement, a chorus of laughter erupted from the ranch hands as the rebellious mustang sent Jesse Bodine sailing. The foreman landed on his side, then instantly rolled to the left toward the fence and kept on rolling. It was an unusual tactic for a broncobuster. The good ones always climbed right back on. Letting a horse think it had won invited more trouble later on.

The reason for Bodine's action became apparent when the mustang went after him like a bat out of hell, front legs pounding like hammers. It was trying to stomp him to death, and it nearly succeeded. Bodine slid under the bottom rail a fraction of a second before those driving hooves thudded into the patch of earth he had just vacated.

One of the cowhands cackled. "You're losin' your grip, Jesse!"

"Hurricane is still too much for you!" declared another.

Bodine rose slowly and slapped dirt and dust from his shirt and chaps. The piebald pranced to the rails and tried to bite him, but he was just out of reach. Grinning, Bodine said, "You never give up, do you, fella?"

The bullish Texan turned, spied Lee, and the grin became a wary look. Walking to the skinny cowboy who had been with him at the Applejack when Morco was killed, and who now held his gunbelt and revolvers, Bodine took his irons and strapped them on. Spurs jangling, he came over, nodding at the Tennessean. "We meet again, Scurlock."

"You seemed to enjoy that," Lee commented.

"I did," Bodine said proudly, casting an admiring look at the mustang. "Six times I've forked that-

cayuse, and each time I've eaten dirt. No horse has ever done that to me before."

Allister Kemp dipped a hand at the corral. "Perhaps you would care to try, Mr. Scurlock?"

"Much obliged, but I'll pass," Lee said, patting his roan. "Mine is already broke, and I didn't come here to have my bones busted."

Jesse Bodine chuckled. "Busted bones would be the least of your worries, mister. Hurricane has already killed two bronc peelers."

Lee straightened, eyeing the mustang. "The hell you say!" he exclaimed. Few outfits would allow such an animal to live, let alone permit anyone to ride it. Once a horse killed someone, it was useless. No wrangler would want it in a cavvy.

"True enough, sir," Allister Kemp said. "Hurricane is a bona fide man-killer, the worst I've ever come across. He's as devious as he is vicious."

The mustang stood glaring at the men outside the corral with what could only be described as bestial bloodlust. Lee had never seen the like.

"He'll let us get a rig on him with no problem," the Englishman continued. "But once someone forks leather, he turns into a raging whirlwind. I know. I try to ride him at least once a month."

Lee was perplexed and did not try to hide it. "You can take your pick of the finest horseflesh anywhere, and you risk your hide on a man-killer? That doesn't make any sense at all."

Kemp gazed fondly at the piebald, much as a parent might at a naughty child. "I do it for the challenge, Mr. Scurlock. Hurricane refuses to break, refuses to knuckle under to any man. His spirit is indomitable. We can't intimidate him as we do most horses, because he confronts life on his own terms. Either we respect him for what he is or we shoot him dead, and I, for one, would consider that a tragic waste."

The lord of Diablo Valley clasped his manicured hands behind his back. "Some men are the same way, Mr. Scurlock. They take life on their terms. They have certain rules that they live by, which may or may not be the same rules set by society. If someone violates those rules, they die."

Lee had a hunch that his host was now talking about the powder keg in Diablo, and Kemp's next statements confirmed it.

"Of course, once a man refuses to be broken, once he draws a line over which others dare not tread and enforces his will by killing whoever crosses that line, then society brands him a man-killer. Whether it's a horse or a man or even a cougar or a bear, it makes no difference. Once that line is crossed, there is no turning back."

A dread suspicion crept over Lee that maybe he was wrong, that maybe Kemp was making a sly reference to his own difficulty in New Mexico. Was it possible Kemp knew?

"I keep Hurricane because he is a magnificent living allegory," the Englishman went on. "In him lies the secret to all success." He glanced up. "If you want to succeed in life, Mr. Scurlock, if you want to be your own man, you must set the terms. You must wrest whatever you want from those who have it, and you must crush anyone who opposes your will. Only a bloody fool allows himself to be stepped on, and I'm not a bloody fool."

It was not a boast or an angry outburst. It was stated matter-of-factly, which made it all the more chilling. Lee eased to the ground, saying amiably, "I still say you're loco to keep a man-killer around."

Kemp's brow furrowed. "Can it be that you've missed my point? Man-killers, Mr. Scurlock, have their purpose, as do we all."

"I suppose," Lee said.

Kemp would not let the issue drop. "Take, for instance, your mate—sorry, your friend—Vint Evers."

"What about him?"

"Evers has a reputation as a man-killer. True, so far all his killings have been on the side of the law, but he is a man-killer nonetheless."

"Some might see it that way," Lee said. In his eyes there was a crucial difference between men like, say, John Wesley Hardin, whose violent natures compelled them to kill again and again over trifles, and men like Vint Evers, who killed only when necessary to stop those like Hardin.

More was on the tip of the Englishman's tongue, but for some reason he fell silent a few moments, then shrugged and indicated his stately residence. "Shall we adjourn to my drawing room, sir, for a brandy before our meal?"

"Suits me."

"Excellent," Kemp said politely. To his foreman, he said, "Take care of our guest's horse, Mr. Bodine. See that it is groomed and fed and watered."

"Yes, sir," Bodine replied dutifully, taking the reins when offered them by Lee.

As the tall Briton led the southerner across a trimmed yard, he commented, "An acquaintance of yours wanted to be on hand today to greet you, but I discouraged him."

"Who might that be?" Lee idly asked, walking on his host's right so that his gun hand was on Kemp's off side.

"Nate Collins." The Englishman negligently waved at a long, low building near the stable, evidently the bunkhouse. "He wanted to apologize for his atrocious behavior at Wynn's relay station, but he's still not up to being on his feet, so I forbade him."

The blond gunman did not strike Lee as the sort to say he was sorry for anything, and he mentioned as much.

"Quite. But the blighter has confessed to me that he and his friends were drunk when they insulted Jim Hays and drew on you. The physician has instructed him to stay in bed for a minimum of two weeks, and then Nate will have another two weeks of convalescence. So I'm apologizing for him."

Lee said nothing. But he noted that Kemp avoided saying whether the apology was Kemp's idea or Nate's.

"And I also want you to know that I hold no hard feelings about what happened to Ed Gristy and Morco. If Gristy was going to shoot innocent people, he deserved his fate. As for the Mexican, I've heard that he tried to justify their actions at the stage station by spreading lies about you. Anyone who has lived in this country any length of time knows that small lies lead to big bullets."

First a veiled warning, then a pardon for past offenses. Lee did not know what to make of it, but he had the impression that he was being treated like some kind of menial serf from back in the Old Country.

"I try to hire dependable men," Kemp rattled on, "but you can't really judge character by outward appearances, now can you?"

"Everyone makes mistakes," Lee said to hold up his end of the conversation. His gaze swept the sprawling Bar K. "But it doesn't appear that you made one in coming to the United States."

Allister Kemp inhaled deeply, smiling as he surveyed his vast domain. Pride and passion shone on his face. "Venturing to your country was the best idea I ever had. Who would have thought that this would be my destiny?" They were almost to a wide portico bordered by massive marble columns that must have cost a fortune in themselves. "Forty-five years ago I was a bloody brat in a London slum, eking a living by pinching bread and grog for my old man. Today, I own the biggest ranch in all of Arizona."

"You've come a long way," Lee agreed, hoping to prompt the Englishman into revealing more of his past. It worked.

"You don't know the half of it, Mr. Scurlock. I stole aboard a freighter when I was fourteen and wound up in New York City. The first mate put me up with his brother's family, where I lived until I was eighteen. Then I came west to make my fortune." Kemp chortled. "I was no different from the thousands of common people who fed their dreams on the fantasies of pulp fiction and saw the frontier as Utopia. I need not tell you the rude awakening I received."

A servant, an elderly Navajo, had appeared at a wide door, opening it and standing back so they could enter.

Kemp paused. "I took a job as a cowpuncher and worked on several spreads until I was twenty-five. That's when the lure of this new territory brought me to Diablo Valley. The rest, as they say, is history."

"Now you're a cattle baron," Lee said.

"Yes. Now I'm a cattle baron," the Englishman said. "The position weighs heavily on my shoulders at times. So many important decisions must be made, matters of life and death to some."

Was that for his benefit? Lee wondered. He stared at the enormous mansion and felt a twinge of homesickness. "Your place reminds me of the estates in the South."

"I shall take that as a compliment," Kemp said loftily. "I took the idea from a plantation I visited shortly before the Civil War broke out. Next to the West, I've

David Robbins

always been most fond of the South. You hail from Tennessee, I understand?"

"Yes."

"Do you ever miss your home and your people?"

"Home is where I hang my hat."

"Quite," Kemp said, using his pet expression. "Myself, I miss England occasionally, but I always come to my senses when I recall those terrible years spent in the slum. I'll never go back again."

"A man can never return to his roots. He's likely to have outgrown them."

The cattle baron smiled. "An astute observation. I never cease to be amazed by the practical wisdom westerners exhibit. Living life in the raw matures people before their time."

"Experience is the best teacher," Lee allowed.

"I know I've learned from mine," Kemp said, and gave his head a shake. "But enough! I'm talking you to death, and you must be famished after your long ride. Come."

Lee figured that his host would introduce the Navajo, but Kemp treated the servant as if he were not there. A spacious hall adorned with paintings and a suit of armor on a pedestal led to the drawing room, which was more plushly furnished than the finest hotel Lee had ever been in.

"I promised you a brandy," Kemp said, striding to an oak cabinet on the west wall. Inside were dozens of bottles, many imported brands. "You're undoubtedly curious about why I invited you here," he said as he set out two sparkling glasses and opened the brandy. "It has to do with the situation in Diablo Valley."

"I know that you're not too fond of the homesteaders and the miners," Lee remarked, which he knew was putting it mildly.

"Fond! I detest the buggers!" For a fleeting few seconds stark, feral hatred animated Allister Kemp's patrician profile, hatred so deep, so intense, that it rolled off him in elemental waves.

Lee was shocked, and just had to ask the question uppermost on his mind. "With all the land you have, Mr. Kemp, why get so upset over a few nesters and silver-hunters? They're not doing you any harm, are they?"

The Englishman composed himself, but his skin was chalky white with suppressed fury as he strolled to a window on the south wall and contemplated the rolling sea of grass and cattle. "You've missed my whole point, then. This valley is *mine*, Mr. Scurlock. Twenty years of hard work, of sweat and sacrifice, have culminated in the Bar K. I clawed my way up out of the London slums to rule a ranch the size of London itself. I have carved a virtual empire from the open range, and I will not stand still while my land is threatened by outsiders." His voice dropped to a savage snarl. "I'll see them dead first. Every last one!"

Chapter Eleven

A brilliant full moon bathed Diablo Valley in a
ghostly glow. The high grass swayed in a brisk north-
westerly breeze, casting shadows that rippled and
seethed as if they were alive. Occasional trees
loomed like immense creatures from a bygone age,
their leaves rustling in secretive whispers.

Lee Scurlock stuck to the rutted track that served
as the road between the ranch house proper and the
town. He was deep in thought, reviewing the evening
and the many ominous comments the Englishman
had made.

All during the meal Kemp had gone on and on
about the threat to his ranch. An aged Navajo
woman, possibly the wife of the servant who had
opened the front door, waited on them hand and
foot, always in stony silence, never allowing her eyes
to meet Lee's. As with the other Navajo, Kemp did
not deign to introduce her. The few remarks Lee

made in praise of her cooking failed to elicit a reply.

Shortly after they sat down, Lee had mentioned that there must be a way for Kemp and the homesteaders to live in peace.

"Peace?" The cattle baron sneered. "How naive do you think I am? The same thing will happen here that has already taken place in parts of Wyoming, Montana, and elsewhere. I'm hemmed in by the settlers to the south, the prospectors and miners to the north, and the town to the east. Little by little they'll chip away at the Bar K. They'll trespass. They'll hunt game on my property. My water rights will be challenged. And I won't be able to graze my stock where I please."

"Aren't you making a mountain out of a molehill?" Lee could not resist saying.

"If you were in my boots, you wouldn't be so nonchalant," Kemp said. "I will not stand by and let those bloody vultures ruin everything I've worked so hard to build up. Did you know that some of the nesters are letting their stock cross onto my property and mingle with my herds? Did you know that my punchers have found pigs running loose on the Bar K? *Pigs*, for God's sake!"

"I didn't know."

"That's not the worst!" Kemp said irritably. "My hands have found six head slaughtered on the north range. Three guesses who is to blame. The bloody miners are helping themselves to my beef to feed themselves."

"So you aim to drive them off?"

Kemp did not appear to hear. "My big mistake," he said more to himself than to the Tennessean, "was in looking the other way when the homesteaders first moved in. Even before that, I shouldn't have laughed at the fool prospectors grubbing in the mountains for ore. I should have driven both out the minute they appeared. But I was too soft, too complacent."

Somehow, Lee found it hard to believe that Allister Kemp had *ever* been soft. Suddenly, those blazing green eyes fixed on him.

"Enough beating around the bush. I need to know whose side you are on, Mr. Scurlock."

"I'm not on one side or the other."

"Come, now. You can tell me the truth. I happen to know that Jim Hays and you are mates, and Hays has sided with Abe Howard and Will Dyer. Have you joined forces with them also?"

Lee was puzzled that Kemp knew. "No," he answered.

The rancher drummed his fingers on the table. "You seem to be an honest man, sir, so I'll be honest with you. When I first heard about the incident at Wynn's, I reasoned that the miners or the nesters had brought in a gunman of their own. After you disposed of Morco, I learned your identity. Your name, or rather, your brother's, is well-known in these parts. Although many of my men wanted to go after you, I restrained them. The last thing I need is to have your brother and a bunch of his friends show up to avenge you."

Only then had Lee understood the real reason for the invitation. The likelihood of Doc and some of Doc's pards riding to his aid had the Englishman spooked. "I'm not taking sides in this mess," Lee had stated. "I don't intend to be here that much longer. As for Doc, he has his hands full in New Mexico."

"I've been informed that Vint Evers would like you to be his deputy if he's selected as marshal. Is this true?"

Lee had hesitated. Was there anything the man did not know? "He asked, but I turned him down."

"And you have no other interests to keep you in Diablo?"

"None."

Allister Kemp had not spoken for more than a minute, his features a blank slate. At length he had smiled and slapped his thigh. "I'm glad we've cleared the air, sir. It's good you're leaving Diablo soon. I've taken all I am going to take off the scum who infest my valley. Very shortly they shall learn to their regret who rules this roost."

"You?"

"Is there any doubt? By the time I'm through, no one will dare trespass on the Bar K ever again."

All in all, it had been an educational evening. Lee knew beyond a doubt that blood would flow thick and heavy before too long, and that whoever accepted the tin star might live to regret it.

Faintly, to the west, a dull thud sounded. Lee twisted in the saddle, peering out over the sea of shadow and gloom. Twice now he had heard that sound, but it was impossible to say whether a horse or one of the countless head of cattle was to blame. Probably the latter, he reflected. He was just edgy because of his host's parting words.

"I've studied you all evening, Mr. Scurlock, and I like what I see," Kemp had said as they strolled to the corral to claim the roan. "Why don't you come work for me?"

"No, thanks. I make my living at cards nowadays, not eating the dust raised by cows."

"You wouldn't have to be a puncher," Kemp said. "I've other positions for a man of your particular talents."

"I didn't know I had any," Lee joked.

"Please. You're too modest. No ordinary gunman could beat Nate Collins to the draw. I'm thinking of creating a group of range enforcers. You would be perfect for the post."

Range enforcers. That was a fancy way of saying

"vigilantes." "I'm not interested," Lee declined.

Kemp sighed as Lee mounted. "Most unfortunate," he had said. "Oh, well. I tried." Offering his hand, Kemp's parting words were "Farewell, sir. We won't be seeing each other again."

That last comment bothered Lee. It had been so sincere, so final, as if Kemp knew something that he did not. Lee watched his back trail for over a mile, but there had been no hint of anyone skulking along behind him. Now he had covered two and a half miles, and nothing had happened—except for the hoofbeats.

Somewhere to the west a coyote yipped and was answered by another to the south. To the north an owl uttered the eternal question of its kind.

Stifling a yawn, Lee decided that his nerves were getting the better of him. He was looking forward to a night of cards and whiskey, to forgetting all about Allister Kemp and the storm clouds brewing on Diablo's horizon.

Ahead grew an isolated stand of trees. Lee had passed them on the way out. Seven separate trunks, crowned by thick foliage. He did not recollect seeing any bushes among them, but as he drew nearer he saw that there was one, a big one, uncommonly dense, growing close to the bole nearest the road. Then the "bush" moved.

Lee's first thought was that it must be a cow. Almost too late he registered the lean frame unfurling on top of it. Without delay he reined to the left.

An unseen force smashed into the southerner's left shoulder and he was hurled from the saddle. The thunder of the shot rumbled off across the grassland as he crashed onto the hard ground and lay dazed, vaguely aware that the roan had snorted and bolted.

Flat on his back, his hat askew, his left side seared by anguish that caused him to gnash his teeth to

144

keep from crying out, Lee struggled to overcome the shock of being shot. *Someone bushwhacked me!* pealed over and over in his brain. Although he had half figured on something like that happening, the reality numbed him. Gripping grass, he tensed his abdomen to roll over, freezing when he heard the *clop-clop-clop* of hooves and realized his ambusher was coming over to verify that he was dead.

"I knew I got him!" the man cried.

"We check to be sure," said another.

"Shut up, you jackasses!" barked a third. "He might not be finished."

So there were three, possibly more. Lee stifled an urge to leap up and bolt for cover. There was none to speak of, and they would cut him down before he took a dozen strides. Sliding his right hand across his hips, he groped for the Peacemaker, his relief unbounded when his fingers closed on the ivory grips.

Bile rose in Lee's gorge, not due to his wound but due to Allister Kemp's callous bid to eliminate him. Since he was still on the Bar K, the bushwhackers had to be some of the Englishman's men. But the next comment he overheard absolved the cattle baron of blame.

"This wasn't as hard as I thought it would be," said the first man. "Kemp's hands ain't so tough."

"Shut up, damn it!" ordered the one who appeared to be in charge.

Lee had no time to ponder the mystery. Their horses were so close that he could hear the animals breathing, and at any moment another slug might tear into his body. Flinging himself to the left, he winced against the pain as he heaved to his knees and extended his Colt. A pair of inky forms loomed out of the night, the foremost bearing a rifle.

"Look out!" that one cried.

Lee thumbed the hammer twice, the Colt spitting

flame and lead. The rifleman was punched backward and toppled, his mount fleeing in fright as the roan had done. The second man produced a pistol and snapped off a shot that went wide even as he cut his animal toward the high grass to get away. Lee banged a shot after him and was rewarded with a shriek and the thump of a heavy body.

Near the trees fireflies blossomed as more guns boomed. Three of them, two rifles and a pistol. Lead buzzed like hornets past Lee's head and shoulders. Replying in kind, he pitched toward the grass to the south, weaving unsteadily, his shoulder a dizzying quagmire of torture that would suck his consciousness into oblivion if he succumbed.

The trio charged, spreading out, the darkness molding rider and horse into a single blurred being. Their guns rocked the night, but they were hasty.

Bullets chewed the soil at Lee's feet as he plunged into the grass, dropped onto all fours, and scrambled to the southwest. His left shoulder was next to useless, his arm and chest already slick with blood. He sucked in air, realized he was making too much noise, and breathed shallowly.

The riders pounded past the spot where he had entered the grass. They fired wildly, at shadows, and one of them bawled, "Where the hell did he go?"

Lee hugged the earth, its dank scent mingled with the pungent scent of his blood. Like most who were gun wise, as a rule he kept only five pills in the wheel. For safety's sake, the chamber under the hammer was left empty. So he had only one shot.

Snorting and tramping, the three horses were moving in different directions. A bay trotted steadily closer to him. Lee stayed motionless, praying he would blend into the background. The man looked right at him, and Lee started to lift his Colt. Cursing, the rider reined to the left, zigzagging, moving farther off with each step.

Stifling a grunt, Lee rolled onto his side. He had to reload, but his left arm was useless. Wedging his thumbnail under the edge of the loading gate, he flipped it open. Replacing the spent cartridges one-handed when he couldn't see what he was doing taxed his skill, but he had loaded his pistol so many times that he could do it blindfolded if he had to.

As the last cartridge slid home, the same rider hove out of the plain, head cocked as if he had heard something but was not quite sure what it had been.

Seething resentment lent strength to Lee's limbs. Bushwhackers were the lowest of the low; they deserved swift and merciless retribution. Lurching upright, he sighted on the center of the black mass atop the saddle. His Colt cracked and kicked in his hand.

A gurgling death-screech wavered shrilly as the killer keeled off his mount. From out of the murk rushed his companions, rifles crackling. Lee sidestepped, squeezed off a shot, sidestepped, and fired at the other one.

Both veered wide. One hollered, "He got Winslow, too! I'm for gettin' the hell out of here!"

A parting shot sizzled the air over the southerner's head, then they were gone, their mounts' hoofbeats receding into the distance until the only sounds were those of the rustling grass and Lee's labored breathing. Plus one other: From the vicinity of the road rose blubbering moans.

Lee shuffled to the man he had shot last. A hole in the bushwhacker's jugular spouted a dwindling geyser and his eyes were locked on the stars in mute astonishment at his own end. Lee searched his pockets, finding some loose change, a broken comb, tobacco, odds and ends, and a wad of bills, one hundred dollars in all.

Stuffing the money into his frock coat, Lee walked toward the man who was moaning. His shoulder throbbed. He held his right arm pressed to his side to reduce the torment.

The bushwhacker saw him. "Help me, mister! Please, for the love of God!"

"Don't so much as twitch!" Lee warned.

"I couldn't if I tried! Honest!" The man cried out, flooded by agony. "Oh, Lord, it hurts!"

Wary of a ruse, Lee carefully knelt, shoving the muzzle against the bushwhacker's temple. The man was on his side. Evidently the slug had caught him high in the shoulder, shearing through flesh and bone into his back. A few feet away lay a small cap. "Who are you? Why did you try to kill me?"

The man whimpered, trembled, and said plaintively, "It wasn't supposed to be like this! We were told it would be easy!"

Lee grabbed him by the shoulder. "Who told you? Who are you?"

"Meers," the man husked. "My name is Carl Meers."

"Why did you jump me?"

"The money."

Someone had *paid* them to dry-gulch one of Kemp's men? "Who hired you?" Lee asked, shaking him without remorse. "What did they hope to gain?"

Meers gasped, his fingers clawing at empty air. "I can't stand the pain! Do something, won't you? Help me! Fetch a sawbones!"

"Not until you tell me who is responsible," Lee fumed, shaking him harder. "I'm not one of Kemp's hands, damn you. You ambushed the wrong man." He leaned lower so he could see the would-be killer's pale face better. "What are you, Meers? A hired gun?"

"Me?" Meers tried to laugh and spit blood instead.

"Hell, mister. I ain't no damned gunman. I'm a miner. Or I was, anyway."

"Who was it paid you? Abe Howard?"

Meers tried to respond, but only gurgling and groaning came from his froth-flecked lips. Rigid as a broomstick, he broke into convulsions that set his teeth to chattering. "I wish—" he bleated. "I wish—" Whatever he longed for was lost to posterity. Exhaling loudly, he gave up the ghost.

"Damn," Lee muttered. Rummaging through the man's pockets, he found another crisp wad that totaled one hundred dollars, exactly. Rising, he walked to the first man slain, a bearded, unkempt devil whose pockets contained a few paltry coins and that was it. On a hunch, Lee tugged off one boot, then the other. In the second was the blood money.

His head swimming, Lee shambled erect and trudged eastward. He had lost so much blood that he was growing weak. As he walked, he pondered.

Someone had hired the five miners to kill one of Kemp's men. Had they been after someone in particular, or had they picked their victim at random? The latter seemed likely, since they had no way of knowing who would be going into town at any given time. In the dark they could easily have mistaken him for a cowboy, what with his wide-brimmed hat and all.

Who had done the hiring? Lee could think of only one person who hated Kemp badly enough and had enough money, the richest prospector in the region: Abe Howard. But would Old Abe stoop so low?

A wave of dizziness brought an end to Lee's musing. His legs weighed a ton, his shoulder was aflame. He could still feel blood trickling down his side, despite the hand he pressed over the entry hole. If he lost too much more he might pass out, and he had miles to go yet before he reached town.

He fervently hoped that the roan had not run far.

David Robbins

It was as dependable as the day was long, and the few times it had given in to fright, it had soon recovered. Squinting to pierce a gray haze that blurred his vision, he sought some sign of the animal. Hundreds of yards he covered, and his legs were faltering under him when he spied an indistinct shape to one side of the rutted track.

In his condition Lee could not tell if it was his horse, a steer, or one of the men who had tried to kill him. He put his hand on his Colt, learning to his horror that he was barely strong enough to draw it. If that shape was an enemy, he would be cut down before he got off a shot.

A nicker preceded a flurry of hooves, and the roan rushed out of the veil to nuzzle him. Elated, Lee weakly patted its neck, gripped the bridle to keep from falling, and shambled to the saddle.

Mounting became a test of endurance. Lee hooked an arm over the saddle horn and tried to leverage himself up, but he could not bear his own weight. He slipped, and would have sprawled onto his face if not for his hold on the apple.

Marshaling his swiftly fading reserve of energy, Lee tried again. He had to boost his leg with his free arm to fork the stirrup with his toes. Then, every muscle taut, his shoulder hammering mercilessly, the world spinning madly, he struggled to gain the saddle.

His sole hope to survive was to reach Diablo. Should he collapse, he would lie there with his lifeblood seeping into the soil until someone came along, and who knew how long that might be?

Unbidden, a groan escaped his lips. Clamping them tight, Lee surged higher, his face a wolfish statue of grim resolve, his muscles carved in marble. Panting, his whole body quivering, he rose high enough to slump across the hurricane deck. It took the last iota of strength he had to slide one leg over the other side.

Doubled over, an arm clasping the horn for dear life, Lee nudged the roan eastward.

The trek was a blur. A misty sheen seemed to hover over the grassland, a sheen so thick that he could not see much more than a few feet with any clarity. The plodding of the roan's hooves was like the peal of his death knell, to which his shoulder throbbed in pulsing rhythm.

His sense of direction, the unerring instinct that had seen him safely across the Painted Desert and guided him in his many travels, deserted him. He worried that the horse would stray off the road and he would pass out in the middle of nowhere, to be found days or weeks later by roving Bar K cowhands.

An icy sensation crept over him. Beginning in his fingers and toes, it chilled him to the marrow, spreading slowly but inevitably up his limbs. His teeth chattered of their own accord, and he craved nothing so much as to be beside a roaring fire.

The cold settled in his chest, an icy fist that enclosed his heart and threatened to stop its beating forever. Lee shook himself like a stricken panther. He moved his arms as feebly as he was able. He even smacked his face a few times. The cold persisted, though, so that shortly, when delirium set in, he imagined that he was caught in a blizzard and that he was slowly but surely becoming a human icicle.

Dying time was near.

Somewhere—in the innermost recesses of his mind or the depths of his soul—he sensed that his time had come. In the extremity of the moment his thoughts congealed into the image of another's face. It wasn't his brother's, or his ma's or pa's or that of any of his kin in Tennessee. It wasn't that of a southern belle he had courted before he left home, nor that of a certain South American she-cat.

The image was that of a lovely young woman with flaming red hair and features as smooth and pure as snow. She was smiling and carefree, a beautiful vision, more angelic than earthly. He reached out to touch her but she dissolved before his fading gaze, breaking into tiny glistening shards that rained down around him like broken bits and pieces of a rainbow.

The grip of ice grew worse. Lee looked up just as the world went black around him. He blinked, and knew it was not the world but his eyesight that had gone. His hearing, too, for he no longer heard the roan. He felt himself falling, but there was nothing he could do. As he faded into a black chasm, he voiced the name of the angel.

"Allison!"

Chapter Twelve

From the depths of a bottomless well, Lee Scurlock looked up and saw a pinpoint of light. He flew toward it, literally, sailing upward as would a bird of prey soaring on air currents. How he was able to perform this miracle, he did not know. Arms wide, he soared higher and higher, the pinpoint expanding into a doorway that in turn widened into a blazing glare.

Suddenly Lee was awake, back among the world of the living. His eyes shifted. He was stunned to find that he was in his own room in his hotel, lying on his bed, covered with blankets. Someone had propped him on a pair of downy pillows. His right shoulder had been expertly bandaged. It flared with torment when he tried to straighten.

"I wouldn't move around much if I were you, young man. You're liable to open the wound."

Startled, Lee swiveled his neck to the left. Seated

in a chair in the corner was a heavyset man in a rumpled suit, spectacles perched on his bulbous nose. Pink cheeks lent him youthful vitality although he had to be in his sixties, judging by his silver hair.

"Who are you?" Lee croaked, his throat exceptionally dry and coarse.

"Dr. Franklyn, Mr. Scurlock. I'm the one and only sawbones in this marvelous town of ours." The physician's sarcasm was thick enough to cut with a butter knife. From an inside jacket pocket he produced a silver flask. Opening it, he tipped the contents to his mouth and swallowed greedily. "Ahhhh," he said, smacking his lips. "The elixir of the gods."

Lee saw sunlight streaming in the window behind the doctor. It was the middle of the afternoon, at least.

"How do you feel?" Dr. Franklyn asked, lowering and capping the flask.

"I've felt better," Lee responded. His clothes had been strewn at the foot of the bed. Lying on top of them were his gunbelt and Colt.

Franklyn chuckled. "I should think so. You're most fortunate. Another couple of inches lower and you would be lying on Boot Hill." He leaned toward the bed. "The angle of penetration was most propitious. The humerus sustained a slight nick—"

"Whoa, Doc," Lee interrupted. "Don't use those highfalutin words or you'll lose me."

"Very well. Your heart and lungs were spared, but one of your minor arteries was severed. That accounts for your large loss of blood. The lead grazed the bone that extends from your shoulder to the elbow as it exited your body, which will limit your mobility until it heals. All in all, I'd say you have a lot to be thankful for."

"I'm alive," Lee agreed.

Franklyn rose to inspect the dressing. "This should

suffice for a few days, then I shall have to return and change it. We can't let the wound fester or infection will set in." He probed Lee's arm, but gently. "You also sustained some damage to the deep fascia, the deltoid, and—"

It was Lee's turn to chuckle. "You're doing it again, sawbones."

"Sorry. Old habits are hard to break." Franklyn sat on the edge of the bed. "The bullet tore some muscle. If you want to regain full mobility, I'd advise you not to use your arm at all for the next two weeks." He adjusted his spectacles. "In fact, I recommend complete bed rest for that period."

"Two whole weeks?" Lee said bleakly. He had never taken to being cooped up for very long. Fourteen days flat on his back would be an ordeal in itself.

"It's not the end of the world," Dr. Franklyn said. "The choice is yours, but remember what is at stake." Sighing, he rose and crossed to the chest of drawers. On top of it was a black bag. "It would please me greatly if you would comply. Too many of my patients do as they damn well please, with dire results." He picked up the bag. "Just two weeks ago an older woman came down with a bad cold. Her lungs were horribly congested. I told her to drink a lot of warm fluids and to stay off her feet. But would she listen? No, she went on with her life as usual, and now her condition has deteriorated to the point of pneumonia. She might die."

Lee did not want the physician to go just yet. "How did I get here, Doc? The last thing I can recollect is falling off my horse."

"That you did, right outside of the hotel," Franklyn said. "The desk clerk had you brought up and sent for me."

"What about my horse?"

"At the stable down the street, I believe someone

mentioned." The doctor glanced at his bag, then set it on the bed. "Almost forgot. That shoulder is bound to bother you something awful. I can leave a bottle of painkiller, if you'd like."

"Will the stuff make me woozy?" Lee was thinking about the enemies he had made, and how happy they would be to hear that he had a clipped wing.

"Laudanum can have that effect, yes. You'll be drowsy at times and you'll sleep a lot, but sleep is good for you right now."

"No, thanks, Doc."

"The bottle isn't expensive," Franklyn said.

"It's not the cost."

The physician was not pleased, but he closed his black bag. "I won't press it, sir. I know who you are. It's all over how you shot Morco the other night, and those other two before that." Unbending, he was about to depart when he did something that endeared him to Lee. He brought the gunbelt to the head of the bed, depositing it within easy reach.

"I'm obliged."

Dr. Franklyn stepped to the door. "I fail to understand how anyone can live the life you do, young man. I'm surprised you don't have an ulcer."

"Ulcers are for those who worry too much and die young. Me, I aim to live to a ripe old age."

The physician worked the latch. "Don't take this in the wrong vein, Mr. Scurlock, but at the rate you're going, you'll be lucky if you last out the year."

Confinement made Lee irritable and uneasy. By the second day he could barely stand to stay in bed. The gnawing pangs that racked his shoulder were added aggravation, but he refused to change his mind about the laudanum. The only break in the monotony was when the desk clerk brought up his meals.

Then he had a visitor.

Diablo

It was late in the afternoon and shadows were spreading along Diablo's streets. Lee had positioned the gunbelt so he could draw the Colt with ease, and at a creak outside his door he did just that, his thumb resting lightly on the hammer. He listened, and thought he heard someone shift uneasily. Training the barrel on the center of the panel, he waited for the crash of a heavy boot on the wood. Instead, someone rapped lightly, almost as if they were scared to do so.

"Who is it?"

"Me, Lee. Allison Hays."

The last person Lee expected. Dumbfounded, he fumbled at sliding the Colt into its holster and nearly dropped the pistol on the floor. Shoving it in, he sat back and covered himself as high as his chest. He had not shaved and his hair was disheveled, and his hat was clear across the room.

"May I come in?"

"Oh. Sure. Please do."

Allison slowly opened the door. She was nervous, unsure of the reception she would receive. It had taken all her courage to swallow her pride and pay the southerner a visit, but she could not have stayed away if she had been chained and gagged.

Word had reached her the night before. She had been on the front porch, rocking in the cool air. Half an hour earlier her father and Bob Delony had gone to play billiards, so she had been surprised to see them hurrying up the street. The look in her father's eyes had alerted her that something dreadful had happened, and she had steeled herself. Even so, her heart had nearly burst on hearing what it was.

"Lee Scurlock has been shot."

Allison had leaped up, driven by an impulse to rush to Lee's side. She would have, too, if her father had not taken her by the arm and steered her to a corner of the porch where they could talk in private.

"I know what you're thinking, but you'd only be in the way. They've carried Lee up to his room and Dr. Franklyn is working on him. The word is that Lee's condition is serious, but he'll live."

"Who shot him?" Allison had asked, filled with a rare lust to see another human being suffer. Whoever had done the deed deserved to be severely punished—or hanged.

"No one knows yet. But I did learn that he was invited out to Allister Kemp's ranch tonight. It happened either there, or while he was on his way back."

"I can't believe Allister would do such a thing," Allison had said, and she meant it. From the moment she met him, she had been grandly impressed by the Englishman's suave manner and glib tongue. He was cultured. He was well-traveled. He had a flair for elegant manners. In short, he was the sterling prince she had always imagined would be perfect for her. The fact that he had shown an interest was immensely flattering, although, strangely enough, she could never bring herself to feel more than friendly toward him.

Now, staring at Lee's bandaged shoulder, seeing his pallor and how weak he was, she forgot all about the suave Englishman in her anxiety over the southerner. "I would have stopped by sooner, but they said that you needed rest."

Lee was awhirl with emotion. After their last meeting, he had not figured to ever talk to her again. Yet here she was, and he was reminded of the image of her branded in his brain before he passed out. "I never thought to see you again," he blurted.

Allison walked to the end of the bed. She considered telling him she was only staying for a few minutes. She considered saying that she had stopped by just to be polite, or to repay him for saving her father at the relay station. But an irresistible urge came over her, an urge to admit the truth, though in doing so she was exposing more of her inner self than she had ever exposed to anyone. "Wild horses couldn't have kept me away," she compromised.

Lee did not take her seriously. That she would actually care for him was beyond belief; that she would admit it, improbable. "I'm glad you found the time," he said lamely.

Their relationship was at a cusp, a moment when their future balanced precariously on the conflict of their past. Allison sensed that whether they would grow closer or farther apart depended on what she said next. "How could I not, the way I feel about you?"

Lee would have sworn he had been drugged without his knowledge. She couldn't be implying what he thought she was. "I know all too well how you feel. Gamblers aren't your cup of tea, remember?"

No malice tinged his tone, yet Allison blushed and stepped to the window to gaze into the bustling street. "I deserved that, I suppose. I know that I've treated you horribly, childishly. And I'd like to make amends." She could not look him in the eyes, but she could say, "I apologize for how I behaved."

Lee wanted to pinch himself to verify he was awake. Better yet, he should pound his head against the wall once or twice. "I'm the one who ought to say he's sorry," he said. "It was rude of me to talk to you the way I did."

Allison shook her head. Now that the moment had come, she wanted to get everything off her chest. "The fault was all mine. I was so disappointed, I couldn't see straight."

"Because I didn't live up to your expectations?

"Yes," Allison admitted, cringing inwardly. "I'm probably making a fool of myself, but if we don't clear the air now, we may never say what has to be said." She stopped, regret drooping her chin.

Lee knew that she was upset, but he could not gauge how much. To spare her from having to say more, he responded, "Hold your horses, beautiful. I have something to say, too." He took a breath. "I want to confess that I cottoned to you from the very start—"

Allison's back stiffened.

"—but I haven't enjoyed the company of a genuine lady in ages. I reckon that I plumb forgot how a woman like you looks at the world. Gambling and gunfighting don't go hand in hand with a sterling character."

Allison pivoted, her heart alight with joy and something else, something deeper. A gleam lit her eyes as she moved to the side of the bed. "Do you mean that, Lee? Do you honestly and truly mean it?"

"You're right, and I was wrong," Lee said as succinctly as he could.

Impulsively, Allison bent and clasped his hand. "Could you give up cards for my sake?"

"I don't aim to gamble the rest of my life away."

"You're evading the question," Allison said, fearful that his words were empty of meaning, that he was saying what he suspected she wanted to hear. "Can you stop gambling if you try? Some men can't once they start. With them, cards are an addiction. They stay out until all hours of the night, betting their last dollars if they have to." She squeezed his fingers. "I'm sorry, but if I'm to commit myself to a man, it has to be someone who places more value on me than on three of a kind or a royal flush."

Lee still could not accept the evidence of his own ears. "Are you proposing to make a decent man out of me?" he quipped.

Allison grew stern. "I've seen too many of my

friends led down the primrose path by handsome galoots who later put their own selfish interests above their love. You say you care for me, and I wouldn't be here now if I didn't care for you, but I won't allow you to use me like so many women are used." She paused, embarrassed by what she had to say next but compelled to say it anyway. "Call me silly if you want. Call me old-fashioned. But I've gone to a lot of trouble to save myself for the man I wed, and I want that man to be as true to me as I'll be to him."

Another bout of dizziness assailed Lee, only whether from his wound or her revelations, it was hard to determine. She had actually mentioned marriage and him in the same breath! Yet he had not even courted her!

Then it sank in. The deeper meaning. "I've gone to a lot of trouble to save myself," she had said. Having been around fallen doves so long, he'd forgotten that there *were* women who put their virtue before all else. He thought of poor Nelly Rosell, and then envisioned Allison in a saloon girl's tight, revealing dress. He'd die before he'd let her sink to Nelly's level of despair and misery.

"So what will it be?" Allison demanded. "Can we start over on the right foot?"

"I reckon I'd be honored if you would let me come calling," Lee said formally.

Allison beamed. "You'd better, or I'll shoot myself."

Lee forgot his wound, and laughed. His quaking shoulder lanced with agony. Grimacing, he clutched himself. Allison clutched him too. For a moment their faces were nose to nose, her warm breath on his cheek, his on hers. He desired to kiss her more than anything in creation, but he could not bring himself to do it. He, who had faced down cold killers, could not plant his lips on those of the woman he adored.

David Robbins

Allison wanted him to. She tensed, expecting him to move that extra half an inch. When he sat there like a bump on a log, she took the initiative. *She* kissed *him*.

The ice was broken. Allison sat on the bed, and for the next two hours they talked about everything under the sun. They shared their innermost longings, their plans and dreams, everything and anything that was important, and when Allison rose to go, a heaviness came over Lee's heart unlike any he had ever felt.

"You'll be back tomorrow?"

"And every day after that," Allison pledged. She left with a new bounce in her step and a smile that rivaled the sun.

Lee Scurlock sank back onto his pillows, his toes curling under the covers. If he had been whole and well, he would have leaped about the room like a madman and whooped for joy at the top of his lungs. Suddenly, all was right with the world. Suddenly, life was worth living again.

His euphoria did not last long. Twin clouds hovered over him. First, he remembered that he was a wanted man, and that before long lawmen from New Mexico were bound to arrive in Diablo seeking him.

Second, hardly had Allison's footsteps faded when someone else knocked on the door. It was a heavier, masculine knock, and Lee had the Colt in his hand before his visitor stopped. "Yeah?" he called out.

"Ike Shannon."

The door was slowly pushed open to reveal the gambler with his hands out from his sides. Entering, he closed it behind him, not saying a word until he had straddled the same chair the doctor had used. Cocking his bowler, he regarded the southerner's shoulder, then said, "Who did it?"

"I can't say," Lee lied. That morning he had made

162

up his mind not to tell until he knew beyond a shadow of a doubt who was to blame. Otherwise, the hatred that boiled under Diablo's surface might burst its bounds and result in a needless bloodshed.

"Can't, or won't?" Shannon said, since it was apparent the Tennessean was hiding something. "It's your life. But Vint and I are ready to stand beside you if you need us."

"I appreciate that," Lee said in all honesty. Reminded of the Texan, he asked, "How is Evers doing? Has he gotten Nelly away from Frank Lowe?"

"I wish," Shannon said. "No, he's in one of his funks. I saw him go to pieces over a girl once in Kansas, but it was nothing like this. She was just a friend who took a bullet meant for him. This is different." The gambler rubbed his forehead as if to erase worry lines. "Vint has been drinking pretty heavily. I'm watching him closely to make sure he doesn't do anything stupid before the new marshal is picked."

"Think he'll go after Lowe?"

"I sure as hell would, but Vint won't cross the line. He's too damned noble."

"How is Nelly holding up?"

Shannon scowled. "Are you kidding? She's doing worse than he is. I never saw a woman drink so much. And no, I haven't told Vint. Today is Friday. If I can keep him out of trouble for three more days, he'll be the law in this town. Then he can do as he pleases."

Lee leaned back. "You didn't stop by just to see how I was doing, did you?"

"No," Shannon said. "I've talked to Dr. Franklyn, so I know you'll pull through." He rubbed his hands together, stalling, leery of overstepping himself. "I'd be obliged if you would let me speak my piece before you give me the boot."

"I'd never throw you out."

Shannon's laugh was as brittle as china. "You haven't heard what I've got to say." He made a tepee of his hands. "I want you to reconsider Vint's offer. He'll have his hands full keeping a lid on this town, and you're one of the few reliable hombres around. I'd hate to see him dry-gulched for lack of a good deputy."

Lee glanced at his shoulder, recalling the shock of being shot. He wouldn't like to see it happen to the Texan, either.

"But that's only part of the reason," Shannon said. "You should pin on a star because it's in your own best interest. Someone obviously has you in their gun sights. Knowing you as I do, you're not going to take this lying down. So why not go after them legal-like? You can question whoever you want, go wherever you please. Hell, you can gun them down and claim it was in self-defense and no one will lift an eyebrow."

"You've got this all thought out, don't you?"

"I've tried," Shannon conceded, seeing no need to mention that he would do whatever it took to protect Vint.

Lee Scurlock plucked at the blanket. A day ago he would have flatly refused. Now . . . Shannon had not voiced any points that he had not already mulled over himself. Except one. As a deputy, he would be in a better position to protect Jim and Allison Hays. "All right," he said softly. "Go find Vint and tell him that he has himself a lawdog."

Ike Shannon was ecstatic. "Thanks, Lee. You won't regret this."

That remained to be seen.

Chapter Thirteen

The news that the Tennessean had agreed to wear a badge did little to cheer Vint Evers. Alone in the shack, he poured himself another glass of coffin varnish and gulped most of it. Added to the half a bottle he had polished off earlier, it was enough to cause the room to spin and his temples to pound.

It was stupid for him to be drinking so heavily, but Vint didn't care. So what if someone wanted him dead? So what if the liquor would dull his reflexes and negate the instincts he had relied on for so long to keep him alive? He didn't care. Maybe he deserved to be buzzard bait for his failure to help Nelly when she needed help the most.

Ike was upset with him, Vint knew. Ordinarily that would have been enough to get him to change his ways, but not this time. Vint Evers drank and moped and wished to high heaven he was not so almighty self-righteous that he couldn't bend the law for Nelly's sake.

Shannon wouldn't let Frank Lowe get away with it. Nor would Lee Scurlock. Only a fanatic like him, someone who believed that the law was all that separated humankind from the animals and that it had to be respected above all else, would sit there drinking himself under the table while scum like Lowe crushed the spirit from the woman Vint cared for.

It was enough to make a man sick.

The Texan suddenly flung the glass down. Flying shards scraped his boots, stung his shins. Pushing his chair back, he rose, chuckling when his traitor legs swayed like tree trunks in a tornado. He hadn't downed enough to be really drunk, but neither had he eaten a meal in a day and a half. His stomach was bone empty.

Twilight claimed Diablo. Vint drank deep of the air, but it had no effect. Carelessly leaving the door partway open, he ambled toward the alley. Ike had told him to stay put, but he had a hankering to stretch his legs.

At the cross street, the Texan tilted his black sombrero and strolled westward, the jangle of his spurs keeping time with the melancholy song he hummed. People looked at him as they might a jaguar on the prowl.

Haughty with booze, Vint stared them down. He wandered aimlessly, or so it might appear to the casual onlookers. In reality, he studied each face he passed, seeking a dusky individual whose cruel features were indelibly seared into his memory.

Vint doubted that he would find his quarry. Who in their right mind would stick around Diablo after the attempt on his life? But, then again, the would-be killer might think himself safe among thousands of others. Or the man might plan to try again later on.

On a whim, Vint shoved through the batwing doors to a small saloon, one of the dozens of unsavory dives that infested the south end of town. Where first-rate establishments like the Applejack were all glitter and brass, this hole was dank and dark, filled with shadows and whispers and furtive movement. He paused in the doorway so his eyes could adjust, then sauntered to the near corner of the bar.

Scruffy men who seemed more animal than human moved aside at his approach. Eyes that glittered balefully regarded him as if he were beef on the hoof. He thumped the counter and a portly, sweaty barman came over.

A wad of tobacco bulged the man's cheek. Chomping heavily, he slurred, "What's your poison, mister?"

"I'm huntin' a man," Vint said.

Nearby figures rustled and huddled. Some moved elsewhere. Others fingered weapons.

The bartender was indifferent. Swiping a smudge from the bar with a cloth rag that was itself filthy, he shrugged. "Is that so? Well, I have this policy, friend. I don't get involved with what others do. It's healthier that way."

"He's a black man," Vint detailed. "Favors a Bowie."

One of the man's pudgy hands delved under an armpit to scratch and pick. "Hell, mister," he sniffed. "Do you have any idea how many blacks there are in this town? I don't keep track of every damn one that comes into my place."

There were quite a few whom Vint knew. Many were miners. A few were homesteaders. Realizing that he would get nothing out of the barkeep, he rotated to leave and saw three black men playing cards at a table. They studiously ignored him as he walked over. "You heard what I told the barman," he said.

None of the three paid any attention to him. Two wore homespun clothes; the third was an ex-soldier who had on a battered Army hat and faded Army pants.

"Do you know the man I'm after?"

One of the players said without glancing up, "What if we do, white man? We don't tell on our own."

"Don't hold it against us, Texas," said the other man in homespun. He was older, more polite. "Black folks learn at an early age that we've got to stick together. We learn the hard way that it's our kind against yours." He touched a jagged scar on his cheek. "Being cussed at and beat just 'cause of the color of your skin will do that, you know."

Vint was wasting his time. He turned to go, saying, "You're scratchin' at the wrong tree. One of my best friends when I was young was a black boy who lived on the river. We used to spend hours swimmin' an fishin' and catchin' crawdads. I'm not one of those who runs around at night with a white sheet over my head."

"Hold on there, mister," said the ex-soldier. "Why are you after this fella? What did he ever do to you?"

"He tried to stick his Bowie between my ribs."

"You give him call?"

"If you know who I am, then you know that there are some people who don't want me to pin on a badge. I suspect that he was hired to make sure that I don't."

The soldier ran a finger over the top of his cards. "That ain't hardly right."

The one who did not like whites poked a finger at the soldier. "You keep quiet, Sam. You hear? This ain't none of our affair."

"It ain't hardly right," Sam repeated.

"Maybe so. But you don't want to do anything that

will get the likes of *him* mad at you. He'd as soon stick that Bowie into you as a whitey."

Sam looked up. "That black cracker don't scare me. In my day I've fought the Sioux, fought the Cheyenne, fought the Rebs under Sherman. If he comes around wavin' that pigsticker of his, I'll shove·it up his ass." Sam shifted toward Vint. "Teego is his name. Out of New Orleans."

"I'm obliged."

The soldier had already turned back to his cards. "Trash is trash, mister, no matter what color the skin."

It was a busy day for Lee. That evening he had his third visitor.

Allister Kemp, dressed in impeccable clothes as always, stood by the chest of drawers with his hat in hand. "Some of my hands found three bodies on my property. Miners, by the looks of them. We slung them into a buckboard and brought them into town. That's when I heard about you." His anger was almost a tangible force. "Are they the ones who did it?"

There was no denying the obvious. "Yes," Lee admitted.

"But you didn't let everybody know?"

"Not yet, no."

Kemp nearly crushed his hat, shaking it. "For God's sake, man, what were you waiting for? Don't you realize that *I'm* being blamed? That there's talk I had you ambushed on your way back from my ranch? The bloody homesteaders and the miners are having a field day with this!"

"I didn't want to say anything until I knew who put them up to it," Lee explained.

"They're miners, aren't they? Who else but Abe Howard could it be?" Kemp shook his head as if baffled. "You mystify me, Mr. Scurlock. You truly do. I would have thought that you would know who your friends are by now—and who are your enemies."

What was Lee to say? That he had reached the point where he didn't trust any of them? That he wasn't prepared to share all the details until he knew for certain who was to blame? He kept quiet.

"There's one aspect that puzzles me," the cattle baron said. "Why would the miners want to see you dead? Did any of those you shot say anything to you before they died? Were they in fact after you, or were the blighters after me?"

Lee gazed out the window. Revealing his suspicion that the bushwhackers had been after Bar K riders might spark Kemp into unleashing Bodine and company on the miners and prospectors. "No," he lied. "They never said a word."

"Too bad. I'm glad you survived. If I can be of any assistance, just let me know."

Lee sat for hours after the Englishman left, trying to put together the puzzle. It was hopeless. Too many important pieces were missing, pieces he was going to uncover once he was on his feet again.

The next morning, Allison showed up bright and early and stayed until late in the afternoon. They could not get enough of each other. For hours on end they talked and talked. Lee, who had never been one of those who liked to flap their gums nonstop, found himself chattering like a chipmunk, and enjoying it.

Day after day was the same until Wednesday, shortly after noon, when Allison showed up with her father in tow.

"It's official," Jim Hays said. "Last night the town council selected Vint Evers to be marshal."

"You don't sound none too happy," Lee observed.

"I still have reservations about him," Jim said. "And it doesn't help matters any that his first act after taking office was to swear in that gambler, Ike Shannon, as his deputy. It's a poor choice, if you ask me."

"Ike isn't his only deputy," Lee said casually.

Jim was leaning against the window jamb. He looked around. "Are you telling me that he's sworn in someone else since last night? I'll bet it was another gambler."

"You'd be half right," Lee said, and reached under his pillow to produce the tin star that the Texan and the Irishman had placed in his hands earlier. "Some might see me as one, but I've sworn off cards to please a filly I know."

Both father and daughter were stunned.

"You!" Jim exclaimed.

Allison moved closer, heartfelt gratitude and anxiety vying for dominance. While she was supremely glad that Lee was willing to change careers on her account, pinning on that badge would put him in daily danger.

"This is the best news I've heard since we got here!" Jim enthused, bustling to the door. "I've got to let Old Abe and some of the others know."

"Maybe he won't be as happy about it as you are," Lee remarked.

"Nonsense. Why wouldn't he be? He doesn't trust Evers." Donning his hat, Jim chortled. "Allister Kemp must be stewing right about now. Bodine lost out. Now this. I'll bet he's worried that you'll find out he was behind the attempt on your life."

"If he was," Lee corrected him.

"Who else could it have been?" In fine fettle, Jim Hays departed, whistling loudly.

Allison roosted on the bed. "You don't think Allister Kemp is to blame, do you? I could tell by your tone."

"I have my doubts." That was as far as Lee was willing to commit himself.

The next ten days were some of the most idyllic Lee had spent since childhood. Allison was at his side every minute. She brought his food, read to him, played cards and checkers, and went with him on regular strolls once Dr. Franklyn gave permission.

Lee healed rapidly. By the end of two weeks his left shoulder was still sore and flared if he tried to lift anything heavy, but he could get around just fine. He made plans to treat Allison and her father to a fancy meal at the very best restaurant in town. Then, half an hour before he was to head for the Delony house, as he stood before his mirror running a comb through his hair, heavy footsteps thumped in the hall and the next instant his door was flung wide to reveal Ike Shannon.

"Come with me!" the gambler declared. "Jim Hays has been shot!"

Fear spiked through Lee as he grabbed his hat and streaked from the room on the Irishman's heels. They dashed down the stairs and into the street, turning northward. In his haste he forgot his frock coat and the spare Colt, but he could not go back for them.

"How bad is he?" Lee asked anxiously.

"I have no idea. All I know is what a man told me at the Applejack," Shannon said. "He came running in and shouted that Hays had been shot in front of the Delony place. Since you have an interest in the Hays girl, I figured I should stop and get you on the way." He slowed as they came to an intersection. "Now, which way is it? I know where Delony lives, but I don't get up in this part of town that often—"

"Follow me," Lee said, racing past to take the lead. His heart beat wildly in his chest, as much out of dread for Jim Hays as alarm for Allison. Maybe she had been hit too. Maybe she was lying in the dirt, broken and dying. To take his mind off it, he asked, "Where's Evers?"

"Making his rounds. I left word at the Applejack," Shannon puffed. "Since the town fathers haven't gotten around to building us a jail yet, we've adopted the place as our headquarters." He was hard-pressed to keep up with the younger man and had to exert himself to the utmost. "By staying there," he said, "we kill two birds with one stone. Vint can keep an eye on Lowe and watch over Nelly at the same time."

Lee barely heard. He was straining to hear a commotion up ahead, and he was so worried about the future of his relationship with Allison that he felt fit to burst. A block from Delony's he saw a crowd gathered near the picket fence. People gestured and talked excitedly. Above the babble rose the wail of a woman whose soul had been torn asunder. "Allison! Oh, God!" he breathed, and ran faster, his left shoulder pounding. But he didn't care. "Move aside!" he roared. "Let me through!"

A beefy man at the edge of the throng started to turn. "Who the hell do you—?" he growled, and was flung aside as if he were not there. Others received the same treatment. All Lee could think of was reaching Allison. He pushed past the foremost ranks and drew up short, his breath catching in his throat.

Jim Hays lay on his back, arms outspread, his head tenderly cradled in his daughter's lap. Her dress, arms, and hands were covered with blood, her features a ghastly pasty white. Tears streaked her cheeks as she murmured to her father, whose eyes were closed and whose chest barely rose with each breath.

The crowd had pressed in so closely that some of them accidentally trod on Jim's fingers. Lee, seeing this, nearly went berserk. "Stand back, damn it!" he raged, pushing those who did not comply fast enough. "Give them room!"

Allison glanced up, her eyes pools of vibrant sorrow. "Lee! Oh, Lee!" she said woefully.

At a loss for words, Lee sank to one knee and took one of her bloody hands in his. He saw two bullet holes in her father, one in the chest and another high on the left temple. With a sinking sensation, he knew that Jim Hays would not live out the night, if that long.

"They've sent for Dr. Franklyn," Allison said, trembling. "Where is he? Why doesn't he get here?"

Bob and Ethel Delony materialized, and Ethel draped an arm over the younger woman's shoulders. "There, there, dear," she soothed. "I'm sure he'll come just as quickly as he can."

"I saw the whole thing," Bob said to Lee.

The southerner's whole body hardened, and he grated out, "How did it happen?"

"We were standing on the porch enjoying cigars when a man in a baggy black coat and a white straw hat came up the street. He stopped at the gate and asked if we knew where the Delony family lived. When I told him that I was Bob Delony, he looked at Jim and said, 'Then you must be that Hays fella. I've got a message for you.'" Bob stopped and motioned for Lee to step to one side.

Loath to do so, Lee balked until Ethel knelt beside Allison to comfort her. He rose, wiping his hand on his pants, and Bob guided him a few yards away.

"That poor, sweet girl. I don't want her to have to hear the details again." Delony ran a quaking hand across his brow and whispered, "Jim asked the man what the message was, and the man replied that it was for his ears alone. So Jim went down the walk and out the gate. That was when our visitor whipped out a revolver and shot him."

"Where's the bastard now?" Lee snarled.

"He ran off," Bob said. "A neighbor boy, Eddy Hall, was outside and saw what happened." He nodded at a house across the street. "Eddy is fourteen. He took off after the killer, but he hasn't returned yet. I'm getting worried."

"Allison!" Jim Hays suddenly cried, and everyone else fell silent. His eyelids fluttered, opened, and focused with immense difficulty on his daughter. "Is that you, precious?"

"I'm here, Papa," Allison confirmed, fighting back a tidal wave of tears. She had been inside at the kitchen table sharing coffee with Ethel when the two shots rang out, and she had trailed Ethel outdoors, never imagining that her father had been involved. Devastated, she clutched his hand to her bosom. "I'm here."

Jim had to work hard to speak. "I'm sorry. So, so sorry."

"For what?" Allison responded, her voice breaking.

"For leaving you all alone."

The cry that tore from Allison's throat brought Lee to her in a lithe bound. He held her close, her tears dampening his shirt. Placing a hand on Jim's shoulder, he vowed, "She's not alone, sir. She'll never be, so long as I'm alive."

"Lee, is that you?" Jim's eyes drifted back and forth. "Why is it so dark? I can't see a thing."

The southerner had to clear his throat to say, "Hush. You need to save your strength. The sawbones will be here any second."

Jim began to wheeze. His lungs were filling with blood, which seeped from his nose and trickled out the corners of his mouth. "I don't have much time, Lee, so I can't beat around the bush. My daughter is fond of you. Do you care for her?"

The question, posed publicly in front of dozens of onlookers, caught Lee unawares. He hesitated, reluctant to divulge his innermost feelings in front of so many strangers. A glance at Allison, though, was enough to make him respond, "Yes, you know I do."

Every vein in his neck standing out, Jim Hays twisted, blinking furiously. "Why can't I see?" he repeated, his free hand grasping at the air in front of the Tennessean.

Lee grasped it. The fingers were slick and sticky with blood, and as cold as snow.

"She could do a lot worse," Jim Hays said. "If things work out for the two of you, I want you both to know that you have my blessing. For what it's worth."

Allison was on the verge of hysterics. Her father had always been the most decent of men, had always respected her and treated her kindly. Losing her mother had been a test of her spirit; losing her father would be unbearable. She let go of Lee to hug him, saying, "Don't talk like that, Papa. You'll be all right once Dr. Franklyn gets here."

Either Jim Hays did not hear her, or he was solely intent on Lee, because he said, "She's a good woman, Lee. She'll stand by you through thick and thin. You could do a lot worse." A groan tore from his throat and he arched his back.

"Where's the doctor!" Allison cried, tears pouring in a deluge. "Please! Someone go find him!"

At that moment a figure hurried through the crowd, shouting for everyone to get out of his way. It was the elderly physician, who gave Jim Hays a cursory examination and promptly demanded that the stricken man be carried into the Delony house. Lee leaped to obey, along with Ike Shannon and half a dozen others. As considerately as they could, they lifted the groaning man and carried him up the walk to the porch.

Dr. Franklyn held the door. He directed them to

the kitchen, where he requested that blankets be brought and that water be put on the stove to boil. Ethel and another woman attended to the water while Bob went after the blankets.

Lee stood in a corner, out of the way, while the sawbones shooed the rest of the men out of the house. When their eyes met, the physician gave a slight shake of his head.

Lee concentrated on Allison. She was by her father, their hands locked together, her face glistening, her lips quaking. He longed to take her into his arms, to comfort her, to tell her that everything would be all right, that he would be by her side forever if she would have him.

Bob hastened in with an armful of blankets. Franklyn told him to stand back, and as he did, someone in the hallway called his name.

Lee looked around. A boy in his teens leaned against the wall, trying to catch his breath. It had to be Eddy Hall. Lee joined Delony, who asked the boy urgently, "Did you keep up with him? Where did he go?"

The youth sucked in air. "I was real careful, Mr. Delony. He looked back a lot, but I don't think he saw me." Eddy Hall paused. "I saw him go into the Silver Dollar. He should still be there."

That was all Lee had to hear. Whirling, he sprinted to the gate, nearly ripped it off its hinges barreling on through, then plowed through the crowd heedless of those he bumped into. Bursting into the clear, he sped through the night, vengeance a blazing flame at the core of his being.

Chapter Fourteen

The Silver Dollar was on Hell Street, a block east of the Applejack. Noted for a huge chandelier that had been brought in all the way from Philadelphia, it was the Applejack's chief rival for the honor of being the most elite establishment of its kind in all of Diablo.

Lee slowed at the sight of its ornate front doors. Perspiration caked his body, and his shirt clung to him like a second skin. The exertion had taken a toll on his left shoulder, which lanced with pangs every few steps. He was in no shape for a gunfight, but the thought of Jim Hays lying in a pool of spreading crimson fueled the anger that had brought him this far and now carried him through the doors like a battering ram, spilling him into the smoky den of rowdies and hardcases.

The two doors smashed into their adjoining walls, causing every head in the saloon to swing toward the entrance. Men and women gaped at the pale, grim apparition in their midst, and everyone there saw the right hand poised like a claw above the pearl-handled Colt.

A beak-nosed prospector at a card table squalled, "What in hell do you think you're doin', mister?"

"Shut up, you drunken jackass!" called out someone else. "That there is Lee Scurlock."

A deathly hush claimed the forty or fifty occupants of the room. To a man, they were riveted in place as the southerner stalked warily forward like a panther entering a den of jackals. A lean bartender, petrified in the act of lifting a glass, blanched when the Tennessean swung toward him.

"You!" Lee roared, his voice thick with menace. "An hombre in a black coat and a straw hat came in here a few minutes ago. Where is he?"

The bartender's mouth moved, but it was a full ten seconds before he could be coherent. "I don't know who you mean, mister. I've been busy tendin' bar."

Lee surveyed the room, probing the corners, the tables, the stairs to the second floor where the doves entertained in private. Men and women recoiled from his predatory glare as if it were a rapier. Halfway across, he spotted a patch of black among a group huddled near the east end of the bar. Wheeling, Lee pointed with his left hand, wincing at a spasm that seared his shoulder.

"You there! The one in the black coat!"

Patrons scrambled to the right and left, exposing a big bear of a man in a baggy black coat and a ratty straw hat. He slowly turned, a bristly beard and bushy brows adding to his bearish countenance. No weapon was apparent. "Are you talkin' to me, cub?" he challenged.

Lee's cry was a verbal blade cleaving the air like a thunderclap. "You're the one who just shot Jim Hays, you mangy son of a bitch!"

David Robbins

The man was not intimidated. Leaning back against the bar, glass in hand, he said mockingly, "Not me, cub. I've been here all night."

Incensed, Lee coiled to draw. "You're a filthy liar!" he fumed. "Now let's see how you do against someone who's armed!"

Grinning, the man took a swallow of whiskey, then said, "I don't know what you're talkin' about, cub. And as you can plainly see, I don't have a gun on me. So if you slap leather, you'll be shootin' an unarmed man yourself."

Uncertainty pierced Lee's fury like a pin pricking a bubble. He was nearly positive he had the killer, but what if he was wrong? He couldn't gun the man down without due cause, not now that he had been appointed a deputy. "I'm taking you to the new marshal," he announced. "Set down that glass, real slow, and let's go."

The brutish bear lost his cockiness. "Like hell you are. If the marshal wants to arrest me, he can do it his own self. I don't have to go with you."

"I'm one of his deputies," Lee disclosed.

"Is that so? Then where's your badge?"

Lee had left it back in his room. He had no proof that he was who he claimed, but he was not letting that stop him. "I'm taking you to Evers, and there's not a damn thing you can do about it."

"Not much, Mary Jane," the other responded, and with the quickness of an Apache he flung the glass at the Tennessean's head even as he dived to the right and produced a pistol as if by magic.

Lee threw himself to one side, his right hand doing magic of its own. His first shot was a fraction of a heartbeat after the killer's. Lead zipped past his ear so close that it nearly took off skin.

The man in the black coat grunted, buckled, and

rolled under a table. Prone, he fired twice without taking aim.

Lee hurtled under a table himself as bedlam erupted. Women were screaming. Men were yelling. Everyone in the Silver Dollar sought cover, some flying out the door, others cowering against the walls.

Rolling out from under the table, Lee pivoted, aiming at the spot where the murderer had been. But the man in the coat was gone, scrambling toward a side door like an oversized salamander. Lee fixed a hasty bead. As he was about to shoot, a panicked customer ran between them.

Growling like a wild beast, the bearded man upended a table, threw a chair. He was doing all he could to spur the bystanders into creating enough confusion for him to escape. A dove who blundered in front of him was seized and spun around. Using her as a living shield, the man backed toward the door.

Lee could not get a clear shot. He stepped to the right, danced to the left. The front sight settled on the man's head, but the killer quickly jerked back and pressed his own revolver against the dove's temple.

"Shoot, and this bitch dies!"

The people nearest the side door were doing everything in their power to get out of the bearish brute's path. Some were kicking chairs and tables over, others clawing across the upended furniture like four-legged crabs, while still others were clambering over the bar. A woman tripped, then screamed when several others trampled her. She was boosted to her feet by a man who literally threw her onto the counter.

Lee, meanwhile, angled to the left, his arm rock-steady, the hammer of his Colt cocked, his trigger finger caressing the trigger. All he craved was a clear shot. Just one! But the milling crowd and the terrified dove in the killer's grip thwarted him again and again.

The man was within a few strides of the door. He turned to get his bearings, and in doing so, his left shoulder poked out from behind his human shield.

In the blink of an eye, Lee fired. The slug jolted the murderer backward, spinning him half around, making him lose his grip on the woman. She skipped against the bar, tripped over her own feet, and shrieked loud enough to shatter the chandelier.

Lee methodically cocked the Colt again.

The killer tottered, recovered, faced him. Livid with rabid spite, he bellowed, "For Oscar!" and brought up his gun.

With a calculated precision that was breathtaking to behold, Lee emptied his pistol into the murderer's chest, the shots cracking in cadence, the bullets smacking into the man's sternum within a hair of one another. As the echoes of the last blast resounded throughout the saloon, the man in the black coat oozed to the floor, his glazing eyes wide, his face waxen.

Lee promptly reloaded. It hit him what he had done, and he wanted to shoot himself. Now he would never learn why the man had gunned down Allison's father.

Frowning, Lee crossed to the body and dropped to his left knee. The man's pockets held cigars, matches, a folding knife, a fob watch, and, of special interest, a thick roll of bills. Lee was amazed at the sum. Four hundred and ninety-four dollars, more than many people earned in a year. He rose, turning just as Vint Evers and Ike Shannon burst into the Silver Dollar.

The gambler took one look at the riddled corpse and glanced angrily at Lee. "Damn! I figured you had more sense than this."

"I tried to take him alive," Lee said.

"He sure did," chimed in one of the bystanders, which set half a dozen to wagging their tongues all at once, relating what they had witnessed.

Vint Evers listened for a bit, enough to get the gist, then held up his right hand for silence. They immediately quieted. "I reckon Ike owes you an apology, Lee," he drawled. "But I surely do wish you'd waited for us."

"I didn't want to chance him getting away," Lee said, which was only part of the reason he had taken out after the murderer as he did. And a small part, at that. Mainly, bloodlust was to blame. He'd been so consumed by fury that he had not been thinking straight.

The Texan hunkered and examined the killer. "Anyone know this hombre?" he asked loudly.

A grizzled prospector edged forward. "I knew 'im, Marshal. Not real well, but we did share drinks on occasion."

Vint waited for the prospector to say more, but the man fidgeted and gnawed on his lower lip. "Well? Cat got your tongue, old-timer?"

"Oh. His name was Joe Neff. He used to have a claim 'bout a quarter of a mile from mine, but it didn't pan out and he gave up a month or so ago. Been down on his luck ever since."

Lee extended the thick wad of bills and mentioned how much it was. "I found it on Neff. His luck couldn't have been all that bad."

Evers held the money in his left palm. "Mighty strange," he commented. Then again, he mused, maybe it wasn't. "Could be that someone paid Neff to kill Jim Hays. Question is, who?"

Lee remembered the night he had been shot. Was there a link? Had the same party who paid Neff also paid Meers and those other miners to ambush a Bar K rider?

Rising slowly, the Texan pocketed the money, then told Shannon, "I'd be obliged if you'd stay and take charge of cleanin' up this mess. Have four men cart Neff to the undertakers."

"Where will you be?" Ike asked, disguising his worry. He did not like to leave his friend's back unprotected for long spells.

Vint hitched at his gunbelt. "Walkin' our young friend back," he said, and led the southerner toward the doors.

The prospector who had been so helpful suddenly snapped his fingers. "Say, there's one more thing, Marshal."

Both the Texan and the Tennessean stopped.

"It's awful queer how Neff said Oscar's name before he pulled his persuader on Scurlock," the man said.

"Oscar?" Evers repeated.

"Yep. 'For Oscar!' Neff hollered. He must've been talkin' about poor Oscar Dieter."

Again Vint figured the man would go into detail. Again he had to prod him with a verbal spur.

"Sorry. I thought you would've heard. Oscar hit a rich vein three months ago. Somebody killed him one night and stuffed his body into a ravine, but a dog stumbled on it. We all put the blame on the Cowboys, but we never had no proof."

"And Dieter was murdered three months ago, you say?" Evers said, perplexed. What possible link could there be between the dead miner and Jim Hays that would make Neff want Hays dead?

"Yes, sir."

"Much obliged."

The night air was pleasantly cool on Lee's brow. The throngs in the street were going on about their business as if nothing out of the ordinary had happened. As far as they were concerned, it was just another in an endless string of shootings, hardly worth a second thought.

"I'm sorry about Jim Hays," Vint Evers said as they headed for the Delony place. "He's a decent gent. And Ike told me that you're keen on his daughter."

"I aim to marry her," Lee stated, surprising himself even more than the Texan. Until that very moment, he had not realized he truly intended to.

"I'm right pleased to hear it," Vint said sincerely. "I have high hopes of throwin' a loop over a certain fine filly one day soon, myself."

They walked in silence for a while.

"I haven't had a chance to properly thank you for agreein' to wear a badge," Evers continued. "I admit that I'll need all the help I can get. Tonight is just a taste of things to come, Lee. There'll be a right smart of trouble hereabouts before this is settled."

"Diablo Junction has seen bloodshed before," Lee noted absently, preoccupied by concern for Jim and Allison.

"Sure enough, but a few diggers and drunks here and there ain't nothin' compared to the blood spillin' to come. Whoever is behind all this is gettin' bolder and bolder as time goes by." Evers sighed. He had seen it all before, in other wild and woolly towns. "The fuse has been lit. It won't be long now before the powder keg goes up, with us caught smack in the middle."

Most of the crowd was gone from in front of the Delony residence.

The Texan halted at the gate. "This is as far as I go. Ike and me will nose around some, see if we can learn who's to blame for Jim. If you need us for anything, anything at all, give a yell."

Lee offered his hand and shook warmly. He had

found a genuine friend in the lanky lawman, and from that moment their bond was cemented. "That works both ways."

Bob Delony stood on the porch, head bowed, eyes glistening. "Doc Franklyn is still working on Jim," he said as Lee came up. "I tried to lend a hand, but I couldn't take all that blood and the sight of Jim being cut open."

"Where's Allison?" Lee asked.

"Upstairs with my wife. She wanted to stay in the kitchen and watch, but Doc wouldn't hear of it. He shooed her out. Ethel went along to comfort her."

Lee resisted an impulse to dash inside. It would only distract Franklyn. Besides, he reasoned, Mrs. Delony was probably better at this sort of thing. Still, it was hard for him to do.

"What about the man who shot Jim?"

"Dead," Lee said, and let it go at that.

Waiting was terrible. Every sound from within caused Lee to stiffen. At one point a fluttering moan made his heart grow heavy with foreboding. From where he stood at the edge of the porch, he could see a light in an upstairs window.

It must have been an hour later that the door creaked open and Doc Franklyn shuffled out, his hands and arms and the front of his white shirt soaked scarlet, his features haggard. Leaning on the rail, he said softly, "I tried. God, *how* I tried! But there is only so much a person can do."

Lee wanted to speak, but his tongue seemed twice as thick as it should be.

Delony put a hand on the sawbones's shoulder. "He's gone, then?"

Franklyn nodded. "I'm sorry, gentlemen. I know how much you cared for him."

Upstairs was someone who cared even more. A piercing wail rent the house, a cry torn from the very depths of a soul in abject torment. Without a word, drawn to Allison's cry as instinctively as a moth to a flame, Lee Scurlock whirled, hurrying to the side of the woman he loved.

Vint Evers decided to look in on Nelly before he joined Ike Shannon. Two days had gone by since he saw her last, two bitter days in which he had waged intense war with his own conscience.

He should have seen her every day. Several times a day, in fact. That was the right thing to do. But he could not bear to watch her in the company of other men, not knowing how she felt about him, not when he had to endure the haunted look in her eyes.

It wasn't so bad when she was sharing drinks. At the bar most men treated her politely enough. But when she was whisked over by the piano to dance, when the customers took to pawing her and treating her as if she were beef on the hoof, it was all he could do not to fill the bastards with lead.

Worst of all was the knowledge that he had let her down. He had failed her in the worst way a man could ever fail a woman.

Nelly loved him. She wanted him to save her from the sordid life she led. Instead, he allowed Frank Lowe to ride roughshod over her. All because the law was on Lowe's side.

Now, girding himself, Vint strode into the saloon and sidled to the left so his back was to the wall. It was a habit of his, a precaution to keep from being backshot. Far too many skulking cowards infested the world.

Right away Vint spotted a halo of golden hair. Nelly was by the bar, sharing drinks with a greasy drummer who frankly ogled her body between gulps.

Nelly Rosell saw the lawman at the same moment that he saw her. Hope soared within her, hope that at long last he had come to do what she had prayed he would do every day since that night they spent together.

"You must excuse me a moment," Nelly told the drummer, and hastened toward the Texan without waiting for approval. She did not care if Lowe noticed. Let him browbeat her later. He could rant all he wanted so long as he did not lay a finger on her.

Vint wanted to go to her, to take her into his arms and assure her that everything would turn out all right. But he was rooted in place by fiery spikes that tore at his innards like the claws of a cougar.

Nelly was almost to him when the lawman blanched. "Is something wrong?" she asked, dreading that he no longer shared their mutual affection. Why else had he taken to stopping by less and less?

"No," Vint lied, his tone betraying him. "I just came by to make sure you were all right." So much more needed to be said, but he could not bring himself to say it. The feeling that he had failed her was almost too agonizing to bear.

Hanging on his every word, his every gesture, Nelly glimpsed something in his eyes, something she could not quite place. For a moment she thought it might be fear, but the notion was silly. Vint Evers had never been afraid of anything, ever.

Yet if not fear, then what? Nelly clasped her hands, her anxiety mounting. Could it be that he *had* changed his mind? That he wanted to tell her but he feared hurting her feelings?

Vint mentally cursed himself for being a jackass. Nelly was upset. That was plain. He should say something to soothe her. But as he opened his mouth, someone else spoke.

"Marshal! Fancy seeing you here! You haven't been around much of late."

Frank Lowe swaggered over, his two beefy shadows at his heels. Smoothing his oiled mustache with a flip of a finger, he added, "I was beginning to think you weren't as fond of my establishment as you used to be."

Lowe's sneer made Vint's head swim red. His temples pounded. His fingers twitched. He came so close to shooting the man dead in cold blood that it took a supreme effort of will not to. He knew that if he lingered a few seconds longer, he might lose control. Accordingly, he wheeled and stalked out into the night.

Nelly Rosell was seared by dizziness. She had to dig her nails into her palms to keep from fainting. *Oh, Vint!* she yearned to cry. *Please don't leave me!*

Frank Lowe chuckled. "Now, what do you suppose got into him? If you ask me, the way that man is acting, he has no business wearing a badge."

"No one asked you!" Nelly responded. If she'd had a knife or a gun, she would have put an end to her misery on the spot, and hang the consequences. Turning, she took a step, but her elbow was snagged.

"Not so fast, dearie. You've been awful uppity of late. Keep it up and there will be hell to pay, Evers or no Evers. Savvy?"

Nelly jerked free. Incensed, she nearly spat in his face, but contented herself with shoving his arm. Her legs were cast in iron as she shuffled back to the bar.

"Everything okay, honey?" the drummer asked. "What was that all about?"

"None of your business," Nelly snapped. Her glass was empty and she ordered a refill, swallowing the whiskey in three swift gulps. Her throat felt as if it had been scorched by acid, but she didn't give a damn. The past few days she had been drinking much more than usual. At the moment she was inclined to get falling-down drunk.

The coffin varnish helped ease the pain. It numbed

her. It enabled her to forget, however briefly. It blunted the injustice and cruelty of her bleak existence, made all the more unbearable by the glimmer of sunshine that had entered her life and was now being slowly but surely snuffed out—if it had not been already.

Life stunk. Just when folks thought that things were going their way, life had a knack of jarring them with a brutal dose of reality.

Nelly had the bartender top off her glass again. Two or three more and she would be able to make it through the night without shedding tears or being sick to her stomach. Two or three more and she would be as dead inside as she was beginning to wish she really were.

My dear, sweet Vint! Nelly thought, then greedily gulped the tarantula juice. Her only regret was that it wasn't a real tarantula she held. That would put her out of her misery soon enough.

It was food for thought.

Chapter Fifteen

Vint Evers stormed from the Applejack saloon, shouldering aside a pair of clerks who were about to enter. Awash in seething emotion that buffeted him like storm-spawned waves crashing on a rocky shore, he plowed through the throng crowding Hell Street with no regard to where he was or what he was doing.

Faces were a blur. The night was a blur. Dazed by the intensity of his turmoil, he wandered aimlessly.

It occurred to him that he was being reckless, that any of his many enemies would give their weight in gold to get him in their gun sights when his guard was down. But he could not shake off the spell that gripped him in its seething coils.

Since first pinning on a tin star years ago, not once had Vint ever broken the law. He prided himself on that. Which made his lapse in the Applejack all the more abominable. For once he stepped over the line, once he crossed the invisible barrier that separated the law-abiding from the lawbreakers, he would be no better than the Frank Lowes of the world. He would never be able to look himself in the mirror again.

With a start, Vint became aware that the hubbub of voices around him had tapered to silence. Stopping short, he discovered that he had turned into an alley so dark that he could not see his hand six inches from his face.

Vint pivoted. It was well he did, for a shadow abruptly detached itself from the alley mouth and glided toward him. In the blink of an eye both pistols were in his hands and he cried out harshly, "Hold it right there, mister, or I'll drop you where you stand."

The figure halted. "I'm a friend, Mr. Evers, sir. There's no call for gunplay."

The voice was vaguely familiar. "Don't I know you?" Vint demanded.

"We met once," the shadow said. "I'm Sam Wilson. We talked about Teego, remember?"

Vint recalled the black ex-soldier who had ridden with Sherman, the one who told him about the killer from New Orleans. "Don't you know it's not smart to sneak up on someone like me?" he scolded. "I have too many enemies to give someone the benefit of the doubt."

"Sorry," Sam said, "but I didn't want to talk out in the open where we might be seen. What I have to say is for your ears alone."

"I'm listening."

Sam shifted to scan the street, then whispered. "My kind wouldn't take it kindly if they knew what I did, so this is just between you and me."

"You have my range word on it."

"Good." A clomp of hooves made Sam whip around. After a horseman passed, he said urgently,

"It's about Teego. Do you still want that worthless polecat?"

"More than ever," Vint said. *And in more ways than one.* "Why?"

"I found out where he's stayin'," Sam said. "Do you know those shacks on the south side of town, the ones over by the river? Well, Teego is livin' with a white gal in the one that has roses planted out front. He's been there ever since the two of you tangled."

Vint lowered his six-guns. "You did the right thing by tellin' me."

"My friends wouldn't think so," Sam replied. He waved aside a handful of coins Evers thrust at him. "Don't insult me by offerin' money. I didn't do this just so I can stake myself in a poker game. I came to you because what Teego did was wrong. Vermin like him have no business breathin'."

The man moved to the opening. "You be careful, friend. That Teego has all the moves of a copperhead, and he'll kill anyone, man or woman, if it suits his purpose. He's pure mean."

Sam blended into the flow of passersby, leaving Vint alone in the darkness to ponder the warning. The sensible thing to do was to fetch Shannon or Lee and try to take Teego into custody alive, so they could get some answers. But Lee would be tied up at the Delonys' for hours, and Ike was mopping up at the Silver Dollar.

Vint elected to go it alone. After the encounter with Lowe, he was feeling peckish. Bracing the killer by his lonesome would be just the thing to get his blood pumping and clear his head.

Consequently, the Texan soon found himself near the lush belt of vegetation that bordered the gurgling Diablo River. Here the air was cooler, danker.

Dozens of ramshackle shacks were home to the town's poorer element. Many were so dilapidated that it was a wonder they didn't topple in gusts of strong wind. Here and there windows covered by burlap or tattered sheets were illuminated by the glow of lanterns or candles.

A grunting brown hog rooted around a shattered stump. Mongrels sniffed at a reeking pile of garbage. One growled at the lawman as he walked by.

The shack Sam had mentioned was easy to find. It was one of the few that boasted neat, washed curtains, and the only one where someone had taken the time to plant a flower garden. Roses grew beside the small porch. Light glared within. Dancing shadows confirmed that someone was there.

Vint circled wide, hugging the shadows. The shack was on the riverbank, less than ten yards from the Diablo. At the water's edge grew a willow that overspread the roof. Tied to a rail at the back was a bay, unsaddled.

Vint was itching to barge right on in, relying on his reflexes to see him through as they had so many times before. But the black soldier had mentioned a woman, and Vint did not want her harmed if he could help it. She might be perfectly innocent, with no idea of what the man she had taken up with was really like.

At that exact moment the front and only door opened. Out sashayed a full-figured female in a pink blouse and long beige skirt. She toted a pitcher toward the river, humming softly.

It was an opportunity Vint could not let pass. Palming his right-hand Colt, he padded to the porch. A board shifted under his boot, squeaking like a mouse. Hardly enough noise to forewarn the killer. Or so Vint thought until he reached the jamb and peered past it.

Steel gleamed, flashing at his head. Barely in time, Vint threw himself backward and the Bowie swished past his cheek. As he backpedaled he leveled the Colt, but Teego was on him in a bound, the Bowie slamming against the pistol's barrel and knocking it from his hand.

Snarling, the curly-headed assassin pressed in close. Vint managed to grasp Teego's wrist and they grappled, Vint wincing when Teego's other hand closed on his throat. Locked toe to toe, they strained and heaved, Vint seeking to break Teego's grip, Teego striving to crush Vint's throat or embed the knife.

Someone yelled. Feet pattered, and suddenly the woman was there. The pitcher arced overhead as she swung it at the Texan's head with all her might.

"I'm the marshal!" Vint bellowed, rotating to the right and pulling Teego after him. The blow clipped the killer's shoulder; Teego roared lustily.

"Not me, bitch! Hit him, damn you!"

Obeying, the woman pranced to the left in search of an opening. "Leave my man be!" she howled. "I'll bust your skull wide open if you hurt him!"

Vint Evers tried to keep an eye on the enraged she-cat even while battling Teego for his life. The razor tip of the Bowie sliced into his shirt, nicking his flesh. Shoving, he pushed the naked steel back a few inches. All the while, the killer's steely fingers clamped tighter and tighter on his throat.

Only Vint's constant twisting and turning had saved him so far. It soon was apparent that Teego's strength was superior to his own, and that if he did not do something and do it quickly he would not live to greet the next dawn.

What slight disadvantage Vint had in sheer brawn, he more than made up for in speed and shrewdness. Since brute force would not prevail, he resorted to his wiles, throwing himself onto his back, wrenching Teego down on top of him.

As they toppled, Vint brought his boots up, slamming them against the dusky cutthroat's chest. His legs uncoiled like giant springs.

Teego was catapulted head over heels to crash against a porch post, then sprawled forward.

Vint started to rise. A rush of air behind him galvanized his limbs into a forward leap, but the heavy metal pitcher caught him across the back of his head. Bursts of light flared before his eyes, swirling around and around. His knees buckled. Dimly, he was aware that Teego had lifted his head.

"Kill him, Mavis! Now, before he recovers!"

The woman moved as if to brain Vint again but instead darted to the left, her outstretched fingers grasping at a metal object lying in the dust near the porch.

It was Vint's fallen pistol. "Leave it be!" Vint warned, dipping into the reservoir of stamina that had served him in good stead time and again. "This doesn't concern you!"

Mavis paid him no mind. She brought up the pistol, cocking the hammer as it rose, showing that she knew how to use a revolver. At that short distance she could not possibly miss. Simultaneously, Teego shoved onto his knees and clawed at the six-shooter on his hip.

Maybe, if Vint had been able to, if he had not been partially stunned and hurt and bleeding, he would have tried to wound the pair rather than slay them. More than anything he wanted Teego alive. But with his own life hanging in the balance, with two gaping muzzles rising toward him and two fingers curled to stroke hair triggers, he could not afford the luxury of being lenient.

Self-preservation flashed the Texan's left hand to his other pistol. Self-preservation streaked the Colt up and out. And it was that most basic of human instincts which tightened Vint's finger on the trigger.

Two shots rang out. Two forms pitched to the earth, the darker of the duo to rise again, foam flecking contorted lips as Teego elevated his pistol once more. Another report smashed him flat. His arms shook, his spine arched. An animal snarl was the last sound he uttered.

The she-cat lay where she had gone down, her face covered by her long raven tresses.

Vint Evers slowly stood. Sickness assailed him, a queasy, gut-wrenching sensation born of loathing and despair. He had never shot a woman before.

Teego did not rate another glance. The man had been a coldhearted fiend, a merciless assassin who killed for hire. No-account trash, through and through.

But the woman? To Vint's knowledge, her only crime had been that she was fond of the rabid wolf she lived with. That she had been all too willing to kill a lawman doing his duty in order to save her lover should have been enough to convince Vint that she deserved her fate, that maybe she was as callous and brutal as Teego himself.

But Vint had been reared to treat all women with respect. Boys living on the frontier were taught to always place females on pedestals; women were kinder, gentler, living visions of grace and charm. Even doves were held in high esteem, since more often than not how they earned their livelihood was more a result of circumstance than choice.

Now Vint had done something he would never have imagined doing. Filled with horror and self-reproach, he hunkered and gently placed a hand on the woman's dark mane. Blind to the shouts and rushing footfalls around him, he bowed his head and shuddered.

The Texan tried to tell himself that he had only

been doing his job, that he had tried to warn the woman off and she had not listened, that she would undoubtedly have shot him if he had not shot her.

It was small consolation. Coming, as it did, on the heels of his failure to save Nelly from the clutches of Frank Lowe, it made him doubly distraught at his own shortcomings, and for the first time in his career he questioned the wisdom of being a lawman.

What good was a badge if it could not right wrongs? What was the use of wearing one if it meant having to put up with all the insults and abuse and outright hatred of those he was sworn to protect? Why bother? Why inflict a burden on his soul that no man should have to endure?

Maybe, just maybe, it was high time he turned in the tin and hung up his pistols.

The afternoon sun blazed in a stark blue sky. To the north of Diablo Valley stark peaks reared in somber array.

Lush vegetation blanketed the valley floor, but on the arid slopes little grew besides shrub brush and occasional stunted trees. Ravines and gullies laced the rocky terrain like stitching on a quilt. Every few miles the rider in the wide-brimmed black hat came up on bubbling ribbons of water fed by an unknown source high up in the mountains, each winding down to drain into the Diablo River.

Lee Scurlock followed a dusty track westward from that river, steadily climbing. The badge pinned to his frock coat gleamed in the bright glare.

It was not the scenic splendor that drew Lee's interest. It was the swarm of humanity that covered the land like a plague of locusts.

Crude shacks, torn tents, and earthen dugouts were everywhere. Silver fever had lured prospectors in droves from all parts of the country. The fact that relatively few would make strikes worth their effort did not deter them from ranging over every square inch of the high country in dogged search of the precious metal.

To be fair, a number of major veins and immense pockets had been found, and that was where the miners came in. For when a prospector hit it big, he needed help to sink a tunnel, and if the mine proved ample enough, he soon had anywhere from a handful to dozens of miners working for him and had set himself up as a fledgling silver baron.

Old Abe had been one of the first, and he had the biggest operation of all. Thanks to Bob Delony's directions, Lee located the Diablo Creek Mine with no trouble. It was situated on the east bank of the only wide creek in the mountains. Several large log structures were proof of the mine's status in the hierarchy of wealth.

From a mine shaft rattled a laden ore cart pushed by a pair of brawny miners. Four men were working at a sluice, while a fifth stood guard on a ledge.

Lee shifted so the rifleman could see his badge plainly, then kneed the roan down to a hitch rail in front of the main building. A sign proudly proclaimed, "Diablo Creek Mine. Abe Howard, Proprietor."

Another man sat in a chair near the door, a greener on his lap. He stared at the tin star, then rose, cradling the shotgun. "Are you here about the shootin', lawdog?" he inquired.

"Yes," Lee admitted. The query sparked a vivid recollection of the hours he had spent in the Delony parlor, holding Allison, consoling her as she gave expression to her grief in a torrent of tears and heart-wrenching sobs. He had held her until the wee hours of the morning when she at last cried herself to sleep.

After placing her gently on the sofa, Lee had gone

outside and sat on the porch to ponder. He'd watched the sun rise, listened to the birds greet the new day. It was after eight when Allison woke up and came out to sit in his lap. She seemed to take it for granted that from then on they would be inseparable, and nothing could please him more.

During those lonely hours spent on the rocking chair, Lee had vowed that come what may, he was going to provide for her the best he could, and be the best damn husband any woman ever had.

First, though, he had to settle accounts. First he had to track down the party responsible for her father's death and see that the son of a bitch paid—and paid dearly.

Over a late breakfast cooked by Ethel, they had nibbled and poked and talked about the arrangements that had to be made for the funeral. Lee confided in her his belief that there was a link between her pa's murder and his being bushwhacked.

When they parted later, Allison had boldly kissed him on the mouth. He could still feel the pressure of her soft lips, still taste the salty tang of dried tears.

"How'd you hear about it so quick?" the man with the shotgun asked, ending Lee's reverie. "Old Abe didn't want any of us to spread the news that he'd taken a bullet."

Being a gambler came in handy at times. Such as now. Lee did not let his reaction to the startling news show as he lithely swung down and looped the reins around the rail.

"I reckon you can go right in," the man said.

To the right of the door stood a counter and a table, both littered with mining equipment that included a large scale and several pans, as well as sacks and assorted odds and ends. On the left, in a corner, was a green cot on which reclined the owner of the mine, his left thigh swaddled in crude bandages.

"Howdy, Scurlock," Abe Howard said. "Or should I call you Deputy Scurlock now?" His wise old eyes sparkled with satisfaction. "It's good to see that you came around to our way of thinkin' and accepted a badge."

"I didn't do it on your account," Lee said. He strode to a chair, straddled it, and nodded at the bandages. "What happened?"

"What's it look like, sonny?" Old Abe retorted, miffed by the southerner's curt manner.

"You've been shot."

Abe snorted. "Hell, now I understand why Jim wanted you to be a lawman. You're downright brilliant."

Lee's forehead furrowed, and a disturbing insight made him wish someone else could relay the bad tidings. "I take it that you haven't been into town today?"

"Two deductions in a row!" Abe said, chuckling. "How *do* you do it, sonny?" He paused. "No, I ain't been to Diablo today. I can't hardly ride with my leg the way it is, now can I? That must be why you're here, but for the life of me I can't figure out how you learned I'd been plugged."

"I had no idea."

The feisty prospector heaved himself onto his elbows and cocked his head. "What? Then why the blazes are you here? Is this a social call?"

"I wish it were."

Confused, Old Abe studied the younger man's features. "Uh-oh. Don't keep me in suspense, Deputy. What the hell has happened?"

"Jim Hays was murdered last night."

Old Abe turned chalky white. "No!"

"He was gunned down in front of the Delonys'. Allison is staying with them for the time being."

Grunting, Old Abe sat up, heedless of a stain that

appeared on his bandages. "This is terrible! Does anyone know who did it?"

"A miner named Joe Neff. I wanted to question him, but he threw down on me."

Abe slumped and closed his eyes. His whole body shook. Clenching his brawny hands, he pounded the cot, crying, "That bastard! That murderin', butcherin' bastard!"

"Who?"

"Who the hell else?" Abe responded, nearly rising in his indignation. "Allister Kemp has put us in a real tight spot. The nerve of that polecat! He tried to have Jim and me both killed on the same night, only I was lucky and Jim wasn't."

Lee rested his arms on the back of the chair. "Mind telling me what happened?"

"There's not much to it. I went outside last night about nine or so to smoke my pipe, and if I hadn't dropped the match and bent to pick it up, my brains would be plastered all over the wall outside. Whoever was up in the rocks took to sprayin' lead at me something fierce, and I got hit in the leg runnin' for cover. That was when my boys came chargin' out of the bunkhouse. The scalawag lit a shuck. That's all."

"Why didn't you send someone to let Marshal Evers know?"

Abe scowled. "I told you at the Delonys' that I don't trust two-gun Texians who strut around like they're the Almighty."

Lee sighed. "It's a shame you can't judge men as well as you do ore. Evers has grit, and he'll always treat you fair."

"Forget the Texian." Old Abe leaned forward, fires burning in his eyes. "What do you aim to do about that rotten Englishman? He has to be brought to account for what he's done."

"There's not much I can do until I can prove he's

behind the shootings," Lee said. "*If* he's even to blame."

The prospector swore a blue streak. "What in the hell does that mean? Are you addlepated? Who else would send gunmen to rub out Jim and me on the very same night?" Abe glowered, his knuckles white. "The bastard's timing is perfect."

"How so?"

"Don't you remember? The hearin' on Kemp's motion is set for a few days from now. Jim was gettin' set to leave for Phoenix tomorrow. He was a top-notch lawyer, and Kemp probably figured that Jim would give him a tussle in court. So Kemp had Jim killed."

"Where's your proof?"

Old Abe was so mad that he started to rise, but his leg gave way. Swearing another lusty string, he shook a fist at the Tennessean. "Proof! Proof! Is that all you ever go on about? We both know who's to blame. No one else stands to gain. So who needs proof?"

Lee tapped his badge. "I do. I can't arrest a man without cause. It's the law."

"Kemp doesn't need arrestin'. He needs killin'!" Old Abe declared. "If Henry Garfias was marshal in Diablo, this whole mess would have been cleaned up right quick," he added sarcastically.

The handle was familiar to Lee. Garfias was a tough lawman in Phoenix who had killed several bad men in bloody gunfights. Just the year before, a hard case named Juan Gallegos had gone amok at a horse race and cut up eight people with a saber. Garfias pursued Gallegos into Mexico and brought him back. One day, when Garfias was taking Gallegos to visit his lawyer, the desperado tried to cave in the lawman's head with a club. Garfias shot him dead on the spot.

"From what I hear," Lee mentioned, "Garfias goes by the book, too. He wouldn't gun Kemp down without cause."

Abe made no attempt to hide his disgust. "So that worthless Texian and you will sit on your backsides and wait for Kemp to oblige you by confessin'?"

"I intend to get to the bottom of this," Lee stated.

"Sure you do." Abe grumbled into his beard and lay back down. "Do me a favor and leave. You're stinkin' up the place."

Lee stayed where he was. "You're forgetting that I was shot, too. I'm not about to let that pass."

That gave Abe pause. It was no secret that Tennessee hill folk lived and died by the code of the blood feud. Kill one, and the whole clan came at you tooth and nail. So he didn't doubt that Scurlock was sincere. But that did not stop him from griping, "I'm sure Kemp is tremblin' in his boots, worried to death that you'll figure out he was to blame."

Lee had more to say, but just then feet pounded outside and voices rose in dispute. One of them was a woman's. The next moment a middle-aged woman in a brown homespun dress threw the door wide and glanced around.

"Deputy Scurlock! Please, you must come with me this minute! It's urgent!"

Chapter Sixteen

A red hawk wheeled high in the azure sky. On the stony trail the roan's hooves clinked loudly. Reins in hand, Lee Scurlock led his mount toward a knoll flanked by the creek. Ahead of him walked the woman.

Claire Russell was her name. She carried herself stiffly, as if she were not comfortable in his presence. Her chestnut hair had been pulled up into a tight bun, exposing a neck that had been bronzed like her face and hands. Tiny worry lines pinched her brown eyes.

Lee had no idea what was going on. All the woman would say was that her husband, Frank, needed to see him right away. Their camp was only a short distance from Old Abe's mine. He'd offered to let her ride double, but she had primly declined. And since she walked, he did.

"Why didn't your man just come on over to Abe's

if he needed to talk?" Lee asked.

"You'll understand once you meet him," Claire said quietly. Then, as if it were important, she remarked, "I was the one who saw you riding up the mountain and let him know."

A faded, patched tent sat in a clearing beyond the knoll. Mining utensils, many rusty, were scattered about. An old sorrel nibbled at a clump of weeds, while near the stream stood a mule that had seen better days.

"This is our claim," Claire said nervously. "Frank is inside. I'll wait out here, if you don't mind." She avoided his questioning gaze, her shoulders quaking, and started to sob softly.

Bewildered, Lee ground-hitched the roan and walked toward the tent. His suspicious nature asserted itself, his right hand drifting across his belt to his Colt. It might be a trap of some kind.

Then the stench hit his nostrils. Lee halted, nearly gagging, his gut doing flip-flops. He glanced at the woman, who had turned her back to him.

The rank odor was all too familiar. It reminded Lee of the time he found a rider and horse lying near a tainted water hole. Both had been dead for days, and both had reeked to high heaven with a stink that no man could describe and do justice. There is no smell in the world as revolting as that of rotting flesh.

Taking a shallow breath, Lee pushed the flap aside and entered.

Frank Russell lay on his back on a blanket on the ground, his pale, emaciated features ghastly to behold. It was like looking at a skeleton covered with skin. A second blanket covered him from his chin down.

Despite the scorching heat, Russell quivered, his teeth chattering. With a visible effort he focused on Lee. "Scurlock? Thanks for coming."

"Your missus said you wanted to see me," Lee said. The top blanket, he noticed, bore a yellowish-green stain. The stench came from under it.

Russell liked his thin lips. "That's right. Sorry I can't stand to greet you proper-like."

Squatting, Lee examined the prospector's features. "What's ailing you?"

About to answer, Russell winced in pain, then broke into a ragged coughing fit. "Damn these spells," he complained weakly when the bout passed.

"Do you want me to fetch the sawbones? I know Franklyn personally. He'll ride out here if I ask him."

"It's too late for the doc," Russell responded. "I should have sent for one two weeks ago, but I was scared."

Lee reached for the edge of the blanket.

"No! Don't!"

The reek thickened, so foul that Lee tasted bile in his mouth and had to fight it down. The left side of the prospector's chest was a decaying mass of putrid, discolored tissue festering with sores that oozed pus. Gulping, he quickly lowered the blanket.

"Gangrene," Russell said. "There's no hope for me."

"What caused this? How could you just lie here? Don't you want to live?"

Sorrow made bottomless pools of Russell's dark eyes. "Of course I do. But I couldn't hardly go to the doctor and have him blab. I was afraid you'd want to finish the job."

"Me?"

Frank Russell motioned at the stained blanket. "You're the reason I'm in the shape I am. You shot me about two weeks ago, on the Bar K spread."

The revelation shocked the Tennessean. "You were one of the men who ambushed me!" he exclaimed.

A feeble nod was the prospector's response. "That

I was, I'm ashamed to admit. I hightailed it all the way back here and collapsed out front just as the sun was rising. Claire dragged me inside before anybody saw me and did her best to nurse me back to health. But it was hopeless once infection set in."

Lee glanced at the man's ravaged body. "I never meant for you to suffer like this. I was only trying to save my hide that night."

"You're a hellion with a six-gun, that's for sure. I reckon I made a mistake when I agreed to go along, the latest in a long, long string."

Movement drew Lee's attention to the flap. Outside paced Claire Russell, wringing her hands. He was horrified by the thought of the anguish she must have endured.

"I didn't ask you here to poke blame," the prospector said. "I wanted to get some things off my chest while I still can." Russell paused to take a ragged breath. "I'm close to meeting our Maker, friend, and I'd like to have a clean slate when my rope is all played out." He paused once more. "I need to ask your forgiveness."

"What?" So much, so fast, made Lee's head whirl.

"My wife is a good Christian woman, Scurlock. She's been praying for my soul day and night, and reading from the Good Book to bolster my spirits. She says I need to ask your forgiveness or my soul will never know peace." Russell lifted a broomstick arm to wrap scarecrow fingers around the southerner's wrist. "Will you?"

The plea ran counter to Lee's nature. He had never been a forgiving person, not when wronged. In Tennessee he had spent weeks tracking down a man who insulted his sister just so he could beat the offender within an inch of his life. When a distant cousin had been shot by a rival suitor for the hand of a girl, he had joined dozens of other Scurlocks in a bloodbath that turned the green hills scarlet.

"Please?" Russell begged, his eyes watering. "I'd get on my knees if I could."

"I can say the words, but they won't mean much," Lee honestly confessed.

"They will to me."

"Then for what it's worth, I forgive you."

An expression of incredible happiness spread over the prospector's face. He beamed like a ten-year-old granted his heart's desire for a gift. "Thank you, Deputy. I wish I could return the favor."

Never one to let an opportunity pass, Lee replied, "You can. Who paid Meers and the rest of you to go gunning for cowboys on the Bar K? And what can you tell me about Joe Neff's role in the whole she-bang? I know there's a link."

Russell coughed some more, his frail form racked by a fleeting spasm. His lungs were reacting to the massive invasion of his system that was slowly wasting him away. Once the spasm passed, he cleared his throat. "You're right about the connection, but you've got the rest all wrong."

"Set me straight."

"Meers, me, and the others were paid to get revenge on the coyotes who had a hand in killing Oscar Dieter." Russell grunted and shifted. "Do you know who Oscar was?"

"A miner murdered three months ago."

"Yep. And he was well liked by every digger. So it wasn't hard to convince us to avenge him. Besides, we were all flat broke. We took the man up on his offer."

Tension gripped Lee from head to toe. "What man, Russell? Give me a name."

"I don't know who he was."

Disappointed to the point of anger, Lee straightened. "It won't wash, mister. A man pays hundreds of dollars to have some killing done, and you're not the least bit curious about who the gent might be?"

"Sure I was. We all were. But he wouldn't say, and none of us wanted to pry and risk losing our share of the money." Russell took a deep breath. "We were in the Silver Dollar one night when in walked this skinny runt of a miner. He bought us drinks, then asked if we'd like to pay back the bastards who killed Oscar and fill our pokes at the same time."

"Had you ever seen this skinny miner before?"

"Come to think of it, no. But he was wearing miner's duds and acted just like one of us." Russell's eyes glittered. "You should have seen the money he flashed around. He claimed he was speaking on behalf of a lot of the boys who wanted to see justice done. They'd learned who did in Oscar, and they needed a few brave men to even the score."

"Go on."

"The man told us there were two men who were to blame, that you were hired by a law wrangler named Jim Hays to blow out poor Oscar's lamp." Russell had to stop to take several breaths. "The skinny guy told us that we could get you the very next day, that you'd be riding alone out to the Bar K. He even told us where to wait for you on your way back, and described your hat and coat and your roan."

The Tennessean grew as rigid as a rod. So he had been the intended victim all along! They had not been gunning for Kemp's cowboys.

"We'd have done the job, sure enough, if you weren't so ungodly fast," the prospector said. "In all my born days I never saw anyone who can move and shoot like you."

"What about Joe Neff?" Lee prodded, his tone as hollow as a conch, as latent with suppressed violence as the rumble of a grizzly.

Diablo

"What about him? I know Neff, but he wasn't there that night. What's he done?"

Lee did not answer right away. It was possible, he mused, that the skinny hombre had hired Neff later, telling the miner the same pack of lies swallowed by the bunch who ambushed him.

"Russell, you are a damned fool," Lee growled. "First, I never had a hand in killing Oscar Dieter. Hell, I wasn't even in the Territory when that happened. Second, and worse, you threw your life away for a handful of money when right outside this tent is a treasure worth more than all the money in the world, someone who loves you with all her heart and will cry herself to sleep for years because of your stupidity."

Cut to the quick by the unexpected tongue-lashing, Frank Russell gaped, tears filling his eyes.

Lee wasn't finished. "Third, and worst of all, Joe Neff murdered an innocent man last night. Jim Hays was on your side. He traveled all the way here from Denver just to take on Kemp in court on your behalf."

The tears streamed down Russell's pasty cheeks.

"Whoever told you that Hays and I were to blame sold you a bill of goods. You were used. You should have stuck to prospecting, pay dirt or not." Lee shook his head, his features smoldering like a volcano about to erupt. "I take back what I said earlier. I can't forgive you for what you and your friends have done, you snake."

Wheeling, Lee stormed out. He bobbed his chin at Claire, swung onto the roan, and trotted up the gully. On a whim he turned toward the Diablo Creek Mine. To his surprise, Abe Howard was up, hobbling on a makeshift crutch on the porch. With the feisty old-timer was the guard toting a greener, who took one look at Lee and grew edgy.

"What are you doing back here, mister?"

Lee ignored the underling. "Howard, I just found out that a bunch of miners were paid to put windows in my skull that night I was shot. And Joe Neff, another ore hound down on his luck, was paid five hundred dollars to kill Jim Hays."

"There's the proof you needed," Old Abe said. "Only someone who is rich could afford to throw that much around, and we all know Allister Kemp has money to spare."

"The Englishman isn't the only one."

Abe blinked, then recoiled. "You can't mean me?"

"Can't I?" Lee countered. "The prospectors and miners all hate Kemp. They wouldn't hire out to him, ever. But they would to one of their own. And you have plenty of money to spare, yourself."

Old Abe chuckled.

"Something strike your funny bone?"

"You did, you idiot! Are you going to sit there and say that you honestly and truly suspect *me?* Do you really believe I would let harm come to Jim Hays?"

Lee was sick and tired of being played the fool. He was a living bullwhip about to lash out as he snapped, "Old age is no excuse for poor manners. I won't abide disrespect."

"Sorry, Scurlock," Abe said, still chuckling. "But you're barkin' up the wrong tree if you figure I was to blame."

Slowly Lee's anger faded. No, he did not think that Abe would ever hurt the lawyer. It sparked a train of thought. "Tell me, did all the pocket hunters in these mountains know that Jim was fixing to represent your side in court?"

"Hardly any of 'em did. I didn't call a meetin' and make a public announcement, if that's what you're gettin' at. I was waitin' to see how the hearin' turned out." Old Abe propped himself on his crutch and shook a gnarled finger at the southerner. "Believe it or not, I don't want a full-scale war. It wouldn't take much to spark one. Were all the boys to learn that Kemp is tryin' to drive us from our claims with legal shenanigans, they'd be liable to rise up and attack the Bar K in force."

Lee regarded Howard a moment. "I reckon you're telling the truth. But that leaves me with nothing to go on and no suspects other than the skinny miner who wanted Jim Hays and me dead."

"What's this?" Old Abe's interest perked. "What skinny miner?"

"He's been stirring up trouble, is all I know." Lee lifted the reins to depart. It had been a mistake to storm out on Russell. He should have stayed and gotten a description of the man who paid him.

The guard holding the shotgun coughed. "Say, you wouldn't mean that weasely character who makes the rounds of the saloons every now and then, would you?"

Both Lee and Old Abe turned. "You know who we're talkin' about, Bert?" asked the latter.

"I might," the miner said. "I've seen him a few times. He's always buying drinks for the boys, and he's forever talking about how we need to take the law into our own hands and drive Kemp from the valley."

"He have a name?" Lee pressed.

"Not that I recollect hearing. All I can tell you is that he has short hair and smells of lilac water." Bert scratched his chin. "Oh. And he has a heap of teeth missing."

"How's that?" Old Abe said.

"Four of his front teeth are gone. Two on the top, two on the bottom."

Every nerve in Lee's body jangled, and he stiffened as if shot. Hellfire flamed in the glare that he cast at the startled miner, whose mouth went as dry as dead grass. "Was his hair sandy? And did his chin have a cleft?"

Bert had to think. "Yep, now that you mention it. Do you know him?"

Lee knew everything. In a clear flood of crystal comprehension, he saw who was to blame for all the bloodshed. The intricate pattern unraveled, unthreading step by step to its source. He marveled at the culprit's diabolically crafty scheme, and wondered how anyone could be so utterly ruthless, so brazenly, viciously wicked.

"What's the matter?" Old Abe asked. "You look as if you just chugged a gallon of castor oil."

"I have to go," Lee declared, reining the roan around. "I'll be in touch." Abe called after him but he rode on, immersed in thought. Vint Evers had to be told, so they could plot how to bring the conniving demon to bay.

So preoccupied was the Tennessean that he covered more than a mile with no regard to his surroundings. He went by camp after camp, heedless of hostile glances thrown his way by many of the prospectors, not caring that more than a few patted revolvers or fondled rifles as if eager to use them. It had been the same on the way up.

Then Lee wound through a gulch that opened onto a ridge and drew rein on finding that his route was barred by three swarthy figures astride horses and a mule.

The trio were members of the pick-and-shovel fraternity. Dirty clothes, unkempt beards, and floppy hats were their trademark. In the center sat the largest, a hulk of a miner whose square jaw jutted like a spike and whose cheek swelled from a wad of chewing tobacco. Being cordial was not on their minds.

"What the hell are you doing up here, lawdog?" demanded the slab of beef. "Your jurisdiction is down yonder in town. The mountains are *ours*."

"I'm on official business," Lee said to placate them. He would avoid trouble if humanly possible.

"Maybe so," said the spokesman. "Or maybe you're up here scoutin' around for the skunks who have been robbin' us. Maybe you're workin' for them on the side."

"You're loco."

"No, we're just being mighty careful," said the human mountain.

Lee nudged the roan forward, saying, "I have no time for this nonsense. Out of my way." He angled between the man in the middle and the miner on the right, hoping against hope they would not do anything foolish. He should have known better. A hand the size of a hog haunch gripped the roan's bridle.

"Not so fast, lawdog. We ain't done jawin'."

"Oh, yes you are," Lee said, conscious that the other two were closing in. His Colt sprang from his holster, but instead of working the hammer, he struck the hulk across the temple with the barrel, a resounding blow that would have felled most any man.

Not the human mountain. The miner swayed but did not slacken his grip. And in that moment when Lee was off balance from his swing, the other two men pounced, urging their mounts in next to the roan and grabbing at his arms.

They did not intend to kill him, or they would have resorted to their revolvers. But that was small consolation. Once unhorsed, he would be beaten within an inch of his life and left lying senseless in the dust.

But not if Lee could help it. His Colt whistled right, hissed left, and the two miners toppled from their saddles, one with a pulped ear, the other with blood gushing from lips that would be swollen the size of bananas by the next morning.

Their mountainous leader roared and lunged, wrapping arms swollen like tree trunks around the Tennessean's chest and bearing them both to the ground.

It was like having a five-ton boulder fall on him. The breath spurted from Lee's lungs and his body went limp. Fingers made of stone seized him by the front of his shirt and hauled him erect. A fist bearing knuckles harder than walnuts was cocked to bash him in the face. Shaking himself, he raised the Colt, determined to fire if he had to.

Someone else did. The boom of a shotgun rooted the miners in place.

Fifteen feet away sat Bert on a skittish bay. Smoke curled from his greener. "That'll be enough, Hickman," he called to the human mountain. To Lee he said, "Old Abe figured something like this might happen and had me tag along."

Lee did not have time to waste. The incident was additional proof, as if any were needed, that he must act quickly. All it would take was a tiny spark of burning hatred to ignite the whole countryside in a raging inferno of blazing lead and violent death.

Forking leather, Lee said, "Tell Abe I owe him." With that he flew like the wind down the mountainside, the future of Diablo riding heavily on his broad shoulders.

Chapter Seventeen

Shortly past noon the next day two riders approached the Kemp ranch at a wary walk. Not a soul was in sight. The grand mansion, the brightly painted barn, the bunkhouse, all appeared to be deserted. The corral was empty save for the man-killer, Hurricane.

"What do you make of it?" Lee Scurlock asked, the heat of the sun on his back.

Vint Evers surveyed the rolling expanse of grassland. "Mighty peculiar," he drawled. "I don't even see any cattle."

Lee was watching the mansion. "Maybe he found out we were coming and lit a shuck."

"Takin' all his cows along?" The Texan grinned. "Not likely, hoss. Who could have leaked word? I know I didn't, and the only other person I told was Ike."

"The only one I confided in was Allison."

David Robbins

The lean lawman's smirk widened. "Maybe I should swear your filly in, too. That way she'd be obliged to keep our secrets to herself."

"I can't help myself," Lee said in his defense. "When I'm with her I babble like a kid."

"I know the feelin'. Folks call it love."

Lee suspected that his friend was thinking of Nelly Rosell, so he adroitly changed the topic. "If my hunch is right, Kemp isn't about to stand by and do nothing."

"There's no tellin' what that varmint will do," Vint said. "He's the slickest sidewinder I've ever gone up against."

It had been late the evening before when the Tennessean pounded up to the Texan's shack. Vint had been deep in his cups, trying in vain to blunt his torment with liquor. The news Lee brought had the same effect as a bucket of ice water dashed over his head. It had cleared the cobwebs from his brain and left him straining like a bloodhound at a leash, eager to bring the guilty parties to justice.

But they had to take it slow. If there was one lesson Vint had learned in his years upholding the law, it was that every lawman must play his cards close to his vest, and always, always, go by the book.

"What have we here?" Lee abruptly said.

A solitary figure stood on the great front porch, observing them. The slightly stooped physique was familiar. "That's an old Navajo who works for Kemp," Lee revealed. "There's also a Navajo woman who does the cooking and whatnot."

"Must be a warrior and his wife," Vint guessed. "But it beats me why Kemp would keep them on. From what I hear, he hates the red race with a passion."

The Navajo might as well have been carved from wood for all the life he showed.

"Howdy," Vint hailed as he halted near the steps and dismounted. "I'm Marshal Evers, and I'd be grateful if you'd fetch the gent you work for."

"Him not here," responded the Navajo.

"Where is he?" Vint asked.

The warrior raised a hand to the west. "Far."

"When do you expect him back?"

"Soon."

The Texan scanned the corral and the outbuildings. "Did all the hands go with him."

"Yes."

"Every cowpoke on the spread?"

"Yes."

Vint chuckled and winked at Lee. "This Injun has a bad case of medicine tongue." To the Navajo, he said, "Will you do me a favor and let Kemp know that we were here, and that we'd like to talk to him as soon as he can make it to town. It's important. Savvy?"

"You tell him," the man stated, pointing westward again. Head high, he pivoted and walked into the mansion, closing the door quietly.

A large group of horsemen were approaching the ranch from the west. Both the Texan and the Tennessean checked their equalizers, more out of habit than necessity, since both made it a point to keep their pistols loaded at all times.

In a swirl of dust, amid the drum of hooves, the riders bore toward the corral until a man at the forefront spotted the lawmen and raised an arm. At that, they swept on past the outbuildings in a compact body. By the dust that caked their clothes and mounts, it was apparent they had ridden long and hard.

The Englishman was in the lead. To his left rode Jesse Bodine. On his right trotted a certain skinny cowboy Lee had seen before, the first time being the night Lee tangled with Morco at the Applejack.

The outfit stopped when Kemp elevated an arm. "Hello, Marshal," he said amiably enough, though the glance he threw at Lee was coldly aloof. "Deputy Scurlock, too. To what do we owe the honor of this special visit?"

"We're tendin' to a legal matter," Vint said, his hands at his sides, brushing his twin holsters. Although he was facing the Englishman, his eyes darted from hand to hand, settling most often on Jesse Bodine and the beanpole of a galoot flanking Bodine.

"Nothing serious, I trust?" Allister Kemp said.

"Would you rate murder serious?" Vint asked.

Lee Scurlock was scrutinizing the Bar K hands. Bodine was leaning on his saddle horn and yawning, not the least bit concerned. The skinny puncher, however, was as tense as barbed wire and twice as prickly, judging by the spite he could barely hide. The rest did not seem particularly interested in the proceedings, but that could be a sham on their part to throw Vint and him off guard.

"Has someone been killed?" Kemp inquired innocently.

Vint had to admire the rancher's acting ability. "Didn't you hear?" he said, just as innocently. "Jim Hays was shot dead, and Old Abe Howard took a slug in the leg."

"Really? How bloody awful."

Maddened by the cattle baron's nonchalant attitude, Lee struggled with his chronic temper. "You're not exactly overflowing with sympathy, mister," he noted.

Kemp was unfazed. "Why should I be? It's no secret that Old Abe and I despise one another. The fool mistakenly believes he is a power to be reckoned with in this valley, when he is not." He sniffed. "As for Mr. Hays, I'm truly sorry to learn of his demise. But Diablo is a hotbed of bloodshed. A man has to have eyes in the back of his head every minute of every day."

"That's all you have to say?" Lee bristled, and would have pulled the smugly arrogant devil off his horse had Vint Evers not gripped his arm. "Here I thought Hays was your friend. Didn't you have him and his daughter over to supper?"

"I've had many people out to visit, including you," the Englishman said. "But speaking of lovely Allison, how is she, by the way? I've been meaning to pay her a visit, only I've been much too busy."

"She doesn't need you to comfort her," Lee said, relishing the blow he was about to strike. "She has me. You see . . ." Lee paused for effect, ". . . Allison and I are getting hitched."

"Do tell. Well, congratulations to you both. I think it's safe to say that you deserve each other."

Lee's hope of provoking Kemp fizzled. The man betrayed no hint of being the least bit upset. If anything, Kemp's stern countenance became more haughty. That last comment Lee took as a veiled insult, and he was going to reply in kind but Vint Evers spoke.

"I'm a mite surprised to find you at the Bar K, Mr. Kemp, what with that important trial you have comin' up soon in Phoenix."

"It's a hearing, not a trial," corrected the lordly baron. "And I don't need to attend in person. I've retained three of the best lawyers money can buy to represent my case. I'm positive I'll be legally vindicated."

"Maybe so," Vint said, and glanced at a hand brushing dust from his chaps. "Looks as if you've been in the saddle a spell."

"We've been busy moving all of my cattle out to

my west range," Kemp explained.

"*All* of 'em?"

"Yes, and we're all quite bushed. So if you have a reason for being here, kindly state what it is and get on about your business. I need a shave and a bath."

Vint shifted so he had a clear shot at the weasel, but he directed his comments at Kemp. "Fair enough. Do you know three diggers by the names of Russell, Meers, and Neff?"

"Should I?"

"Meers and Neff and some of their pards are all dead, and Russell will buy the farm directly. They were hired to kill Scurlock and Jim Hays, but they partly bobbled the job."

"So? Are you implying, Marshal, that I'm connected to their activities?"

"Not at all," Vint said. "I'd never accuse a man without proof."

Kemp's patience snapped. "Then what the bloody hell are you doing here?"

The Texan smiled. "We're huntin' us a gent who has lost a lot of teeth."

Every cowhand straightened. The skinny one scowled, meeting Vint's stare. "Do you mean me?"

"What's your handle, mister?" Vint asked.

"Matt Rash."

Allister Kemp displayed confusion and uncertainty for the first time. "Hold on, Evers. Everyone knows that Matt lost four front teeth a couple of years ago when Hurricane kicked him in the mouth. So what?"

"So the man who hired those miners lacked a heap of teeth, too."

"And you suspect Matt?"

"Could be."

The Englishman laughed. "Marshal, you amuse me. If the only clue you have to go on is faulty dentition, then half the inhabitants of the Territory will qualify. Dental hygiene is not exactly a byword on the frontier. My lawyers will make a laughingstock of you."

Vint did not take the gibe personally. "I'm not arrestin' anyone . . . yet," he said. "But I'd be obliged if Rash would come with Lee and me."

"Where to?" Matt Rash demanded.

"To visit Russell. He can identify the *hombre* who paid him to kill Lee. I'd like him to get a good look at you."

The skinny cowboy had the aspect of a wolf at bay. "What if I don't want to go?"

"I reckon I must insist," Vint said, flexing his fingers to accent his point. Several of the cowhands shifted and glanced at Jesse Bodine, their foreman, the man most likely to buck Vint if push came to shove. Bodine, in turn, glanced at the Englishman as if awaiting orders to cut loose.

Allister Kemp gave no such command. "I don't want any trouble today, Marshal," he said suavely. "If you want to take Matt along to see the digger, you have my permission."

"What?" Matt Rash exploded.

Kemp gestured. "Go with the lawmen, Matt. I'm afraid they have every right to request that you do. But don't worry. Everything will work out just fine."

Rash was not so sure. Flinty as a rat at bay, he looked right and left as if debating whether to make a run for it. "I'm the one they're accusin'. I think I should have a say."

"If you intend to remain in my employ, you will not make this difficult," Kemp said testily.

The outcome hung in the balance. Vint was tensed to unlimber should Rash go for his hardware. But an unexpected voice decided the issue, without bloodshed.

"Go with them, pard," Jesse Bodine said.

The weasel looked at Bodine, his twisted face showing that inwardly he wrestled for self-control. Then he shrugged and grew calm. "Whatever you want. I just hope the two of you know what you're doin'."

No one else objected as the lawmen mounted, flanked the reluctant cowboy, and rode off eastward as if making for Diablo. Once the buildings were out of sight, Vint nodded at Lee and they swung to the north.

"We're not stickin' to the road?" Rash asked nervously.

"No," Lee answered. "We'll save time by cutting across the ranch straight to the foot of the mountains."

Rash did not like it, Lee could tell. By taking the direct route instead of following the road all the way to the river and then bearing north until the cutoff into the foothills, they slashed hours off the time it would take them to reach the Russell claim. It would thwart any idea Kemp might have of sending riders on ahead of them to silence Russell.

Other than the thud of hooves and the creak of saddles, they rode in silence. Lee thought about why Kemp had not murdered Russell sometime during the past couple of weeks. It would have been the smart thing to do, and whatever else could be said about Allister Kemp, the man was as shrewd as a fox. He figured that the cattle baron must not have known that Russell was alive.

The oversight would cost Kemp dearly. Once Russell identified Rash, it would link the Englishman to the murder of Jim Hays, and for that Lee would love to see Kemp swing.

After many miles of waving grassland, sloping foothills rose into the stark mountains. They came on a narrow trail used for centuries by the Indians who had called the valley home before Kemp drove them off. It wound ever deeper in among the crags and ravines.

Eventually they turned eastward and were soon among the clustered tents and shacks that sprinkled the landscape. Since Lee knew where the Russell claim was located, he took the lead. As before, many of the pocket hounds glared in open hostility, especially at Rash, who, being a cowboy, was universally hated.

The sun was high in the sky when Lee spotted the site and rode down an incline to the clearing. "This is the place," he announced, puzzled that Claire did not appear to greet them. She would not wander far from her husband's side in the condition he was in.

Vint climbed down to stretch his legs. Matt Rash, fingering his reins, stayed in the saddle.

"Claire? Frank?" Lee called out. The same horrible stench assailed him, but this time he had girded himself. When no one replied, he took the liberty of parting the flap and going in. "Frank, I—"

The words choked off in the Tennessean's throat. Goose bumps prickled his flesh.

Both husband and wife were there, after all. But they were dead.

Frank lay in the same spot with the same stained blanket pulled up to his chin, his lifeless, glazed eyes staring at the top of the tent. Sprawled across his chest, a small blue hole in her left temple, lay Claire. A derringer clutched in her stiff left hand explained the bullet hole. Her eyes were closed, her face oddly peaceful.

Lee squatted and examined Frank. No gunshot wounds were to be found. Evidently the gangrene had finally taken its toll sometime the day before. Claire must have decided she would rather join her man in death than go on without him.

The woman's suicide touched Lee deeply. He never would have expected a Christian woman to take her own life, and he judged her act as more evidence of the abiding love she had for her fool of a husband.

Lee rose to leave when a troubling thought occurred to him. What if Claire had not died by her own hand? What if someone had shot her and arranged her body to make it appear that she had? Kneeling, he inspected her for powder burns. If she had shot herself, there should be smudges on her temples, traces of black powder in her hair. There were neither.

Then Lee saw a flannel shirt lying near Frank's shoulder. It had not been there during his last visit. Coincidence? Or had someone used the shirt to smother Frank Russell?

Profoundly upset, Lee stood and pondered. Maybe he was jumping to conclusions. Killing an innocent woman was a vile deed, certain to earn the culprit a necktie social in his honor. Would even Allister Kemp stoop so low?

Possibly. If Kemp was having Old Abe's operation watched, and if the Englishman had learned that Lee paid a visit to the Russells, disposing of the pair would ensure that Kemp could not be linked to the murder of Jim Hays.

Maybe Kemp had known all along that Russell was alive but had not acted because he believed Russell was going to die soon anyway.

A whinny outside reminded Lee that Evers and the cowboy were waiting. He wrestled with the dilemma of what to do. Matt Rash was now free to ride off scot-free, and that infuriated him. He was sure that Rash had been Kemp's go-between, that the skinny cowboy had donned miner's clothes and mingled with them in town, buying drinks and inciting them so they would play right into Kemp's hands.

A clever idea made Lee grin. It would only work, though, if Rash did not know the pair were dead, and from the cowboy's nervous manner, Lee doubted that he did. Leaving the tent, the southerner let out the breath he had not known he was holding.

"Is Russell fit enough to see Rash?" Vint Evers asked.

Lee faced the cowhand. "He sure is. Step inside, mister, and we'll find out if you're the coyote who went around masquerading as a miner."

Something inside of Rash snapped. "Like hell I will," he cried wildly, and went for his gun.

Some would say it had been unwise of the lawmen not to disarm the cowboy earlier. Matt Rash, though, had not been formally accused of any crime. Until the lawmen had cause to take him into custody, he was free to pack his iron.

Lee Scurlock slapped leather with a quick flip of his wrist, pulling his Colt as fast as he ever had. Yet his pistol was just clearing leather when the Texan's twin revolvers boomed with one voice.

Matt Rash was flung backward off his sorrel and smacked onto the unyielding ground. Landing on his left side, he rolled onto his back. Rash wheezed, sought to rise, and sagged limply. His revolver slid from fingers gone weak.

Vint moved forward, his smoking Colts held down low, both hammers cocked. The light of life was fading fast from the cowboy's dark eyes. "Can you hear me, Rash?" Vint said.

The weasel gazed blankly upward. His lips moved, but only crimson froth bubbled out.

"We need to know the truth, Rash," Vint said. "Clear your conscience before you shuck this life." He bent down. "Kemp had you pay some miners to bushwhack Scurlock and gun down Jim Hays, didn't he?"

Rash's head swiveled from side to side. He bleated like a stricken sheep, the froth spreading across his chin.

"Damn it! Speak to me!" Vint said. "If you don't talk, a lot of people are going to die. One word from you and I can stop the madness before it gets any worse."

The cowboy steadied himself. Looking at the Texan, he whispered feebly, "Come closer. Listen good."

Vint bent so his ear was above the other's mouth. "Go on. What can you tell me?" In his eagerness to end the bloodshed, in his haste to implicate Kemp before Rash died, he made the kind of mistake only a greenhorn would make, as he learned when the cold end of a pistol barrel gouged into his neck.

A feral gleam animated Rash. "Did you really think I'd turn on my pards?" he hissed. "I'm done for, but at least I can take you with me, bastard!"

A shot rang out. Vint jumped, expecting to feel searing pain and the sticky warm sensation of his blood gushing from his veins.

But it was Matt Rash who had sprouted a new bullet hole, above the ear. The cowboy twitched a few times, then lay quietly, taking the secret of his involvement with the miners into eternity with him.

"Damn!" Vint said. It was a serious setback, and the repercussions were bound to prove costly. He glanced at the Tennessean. "I owe you my life."

Lee was replacing the spent cartridge. "You would have done the same for me."

Holstering his six-shooters, Vint turned to the tent. "Now the best we can do is tie this varmint to the miners. Help me drag the body in there so Russell can get a good look at him."

Lee paused. The ruse had not worked out as he had hoped. "We have a slight problem there," he said, afraid that the Texan would throw a fit on learning the truth.

"What kind of problem?"

"You'd better have a look inside."

Brow knit, the Texan walked into the tent.

Lee waited tensely. It wouldn't surprise him if Evers demanded his badge. But how was he to know that Matt Rash would be stupid enough to throw down on a man with Evers's reputation? He'd expected Rash to surrender peaceably.

The worst part of it was that it left Allister Kemp free to continue scheming and murdering to his heart's content.

The flap parted. "Of all the harebrained, dimwitted, loco stunts I've ever heard of, the one you pulled takes the cake!" Vint Evers declared. Suddenly grinning, he clapped Lee on the shoulder. "But it was worth a try. You're an hombre after my own heart, Scurlock."

The levity was short-lived. Lee walked to a pile of tools and helped himself to a shovel. "I'll start on the graves," he offered. "But what do we do once we get back to town?"

"There's nothing we can do, pard, except wait, and hope that when the lid blows off, we're not caught in the blast."

Chapter Eighteen

A week went by, a week of relative tranquillity in Diablo, a week during which no one was murdered. There were only a few incidents the lawmen had to deal with.

One night a group of drunken miners decided to see who could shoot out the most windows. A few days later a pickpocket was caught in the act and had his arm broken by his victim. Several dogs were reported as being a nuisance, but they eluded capture.

There was one gunfight. A prospector accused a gambler of cheating during a game of five-card stud at the Dust and Nugget saloon. When the angry gambler made an insulting reference to the pocket hound's mother, the prospector drew a pistol and got off a shot that hit an innocent bystander.

The irate gambler produced a hideout, a modified Colt with the barrel shortened to two inches and the trigger guard sawed off. He fired once, but his aim was little better than his rival's. The slug seared the prospector's right cheek and nicked the leg of a man standing behind him.

About that time the rest of the patrons decided that enough was enough, and they pounced on the pair before anyone else could be hurt.

The drastic drop in the number of brawls and gunfights was directly due to the new town marshal. Vint Evers made it known in no uncertain terms that he would not abide the wild discharge of firearms within the town limits. It was also common knowledge that anyone who went on the prod must answer to him.

Few in their right mind would be so inclined. His skill as a shootist discouraged most hardcases. When fistfights broke out, his hasty arrival on the scene was enough to bring the combatants to their senses and prevent them from resorting to their hardware.

And everywhere the Texan went, he was backed up by either Ike Shannon or Lee Scurlock.

For Vint, it was business as usual. He had done the same time and again, in other towns.

Only this time there was a subtle difference, known only to Vint. For as he made his daily rounds, as he went about locking up drunks and breaking up fights and doing the hundred and one petty tasks that were part of a lawman's job, always at the back of his mind there gnawed the aching pang of failure that made him question not only his ability to serve effectively, but his very manhood.

Vint visited the Applejack only twice. On both occasions Nelly was tipsy. Each time she avoided him, although her haunted eyes marked his every movement, and it seemed to him that they grew more haunted as the days dragged by.

The peace and quiet lulled Lee Scurlock into thinking that maybe the worst was over. Maybe they had been all agitated over nothing. Maybe, just maybe, Allister Kemp was content to let the courts decide the issue.

On a bright, crisp morning eight days after Matt Rash was slain, Lee sat in the Delony parlor talking to the love of his life. They had spent every available minute together since her father was killed, and the more he saw of her, the more he wanted to see.

On this particular morning she was sharing family history. How she had been born in Indiana. How her father had practiced law there for several years before the urge to move west hit him. How the family crossed the Plains in a covered wagon and settled in Denver.

Jim's practice thrived. The family had a nice home in a well-to-do section of the Mile High City. Their future had looked bright and promising.

Then Allison's mother died. Jim became restless. Plagued by bittersweet memories, he had considered relocating. Diablo had fascinated him, and he had come up with excuse after excuse to justify paying Bob Delony a visit. Naturally, when Delony asked for help, he had selflessly gone to do what he could.

Now he was dead.

Lee fretted that talking about Jim would upset Allison, but she did not seem to mind. Seated across from her on the settee, he gazed into her wonderfully warm eyes and marveled that she should feel the same way about him as he felt about her. He half wanted to pinch himself to verify he was not dreaming.

For Allison's part, she was dizzily happy, yet plagued by guilt that she should feel so vibrant with life so soon after her father's death.

Still, when Lee was beside her, she could not help but feel as if she were floating on a cloud. She drank in the sight of him, her heart set to beating faster by the looks he gave her and by the gentle touch of his hard hands.

Allison had always heard stories about so-called "true love." As a girl, the tales had fired her with visions of romance, of a gallant knight-errant sweeping her off her feet and taking her off to live in his glorious golden castle.

In later years she had come to dismiss the notion as folly. True love happened to other people. It would never happen to her. She'd had no intention of ever marrying and settling down, because she honestly never expected to meet a man who would affect her as Lee had done.

Her? Fall head over heels for a *man?* The notion had been preposterous.

Yet now that it had happened, it made Allison realize that, she was no different after all from the tens of millions of women who had lived before her and the tens upon tens of millions who would live after her.

Men and women had been falling in love and rearing families since the beginning of recorded time; they would probably go on doing so for as long as the human race endured.

Now, Lee's hand clasped in hers, she ran a finger over his calluses and wished that it were night so she could lavish his lips with hot kisses. The thought made her blush.

"Are you feeling all right?" Lee asked, jumping to the conclusion that she must be coming down with something.

"Fine," Allison said hoarsely.

"Sounds to me like you've got a cold in the works," Lee said. "Should I ask Ethel to make you some lemon tea?"

"No need," Allison responded. To cover her embarrassment, she mentioned, "I've heard from my uncle. He's written to suggest that I go live with his family in Indianapolis. They have a spare room, and his wife has always been kind to me."

Lee blanched at the prospect of being separated from her.

"But not to worry," Allison soothed him. "I'm staying right here. Ethel and Bob have graciously offered to put me up until—" She stopped, reluctant to broach a subject that both had danced around but never addressed.

Lee sensed the truth, and froze. She was waiting for him to voice the most important question of their lives. But each time he went to do so, he choked, literally, on an unreasoning dread. Here he had already told Vint and Ike and even Allister Kemp that he fully intended to marry her, yet he could not bring himself to propose. It was too ridiculous for words.

Cold feet, some would call it. All he knew was that he felt like a skittish horse about to be ridden for the first time. He wanted to run and hide. A fine attitude for a grown man to take!

"I should be moseying along," Lee said. "Evers will be fit to be tied if I'm late again."

"Send someone to tell him you're sick," Allison proposed.

Lee smirked. "Why, Miss Hays, you brazen hussy! What would your pastor think?"

Huffing, Allison pretended to be scandalized. He playfully poked her ribs and she laughed, then, on an impulse, kissed him. At that they both flushed and an almost savage hunger came into his eyes. He leaned toward her to satisfy it. Unfortunately, the front door banged and excited voices trailed down the hall to the parlor.

Ethel and Bob Delony entered, arm in arm, beaming in delight.

"Bob!" Allison exclaimed, rising and smoothing

her dress. "You're back from Phoenix so soon?"

Delony could scarcely contain himself. "That I am!" he declared. "And with outstanding news!"

Ethel tittered. "He snuck up while I was tending flowers in the front yard. About scared the living daylights out of me!"

"What's this about good news?" Lee asked. "How did the hearing go?"

"Better than any of us could have hoped," Delony said. "Based on the preliminary work Jim did before he died, the judge disallowed every last one of Allister Kemp's motions."

"All of them?" Lee said in disbelief. So much for the judge being under Kemp's thumb.

Nodding, Bob moved to a chair. "Let me sit down. I've been a bundle of nervous energy since the hearing began, and I still haven't wound down." He pulled Ethel into his lap, and she squealed in mock dismay. "You should have been there. All three of Kemp's high-priced lawyers were strutting like peacocks. They really thought they had the upper hand." Delony sobered. "I only wish Jim could have been there to see the looks on their faces when the judge put them in their place."

Lee saw Allison sadden, so he took her hand and gave it a shake. She brightened, though not much. "Give us the particulars," he said.

Bob Delony wore a dreamy look as he recounted the events. "Judge Kramer turned out to be a nononsense jurist who was not about to let the wool be pulled over his eyes. He must be in his sixties, yet he's as spry as a spring chicken and as sharp as a steel trap."

"Bless him!" Ethel said. "This is simply marvelous!"

"Is it?" Lee wondered, but in the elation of the moment his comment was ignored.

David Robbins

"Judge Kramer disallowed Kemp's claim that the hills to the south of the valley and the mountains to the north are part and parcel of the Bar K," Delony detailed. "He noted that Kemp had never shown any interest in either prior to the arrival of the prospectors and the settlers."

"What a wise man," Ethel intoned.

"That's not all," her husband crowed. "The judge labeled as preposterous Kemp's bid for exclusive water rights to the Diablo River and all its tributaries. He was willing to grant limited rights for grazing purposes, but he bluntly told the lawyers that Kemp could not hog all the water for himself."

"How did Kemp's attorneys take the decision?" Allison asked.

"How do you think? They were furious, although they tried not to show it. They vowed to appeal and the judge told them to go right ahead, but that no court was ever going to side with Kemp."

Allison clapped her hands and spun in a circle. "We've won! We've won!"

"So much for Mr. Kemp!" Ethel agreed.

"Don't be too sure," Lee said, and this time they paid attention.

"What do you mean?" Allison said.

"Kemp won't take this lying down. He's not the type to waste months or years in a drawn-out court battle. I suspect that the only reason he has waited as long as he has to take stronger action is that he counted on winning legally early on. He wants the valley all to himself. He always has. So he'll do whatever it takes to get rid of the nesters and the prospectors."

Ethel stood. "What can he do? There are too many homesteaders and the like for him to drive them all out."

"Are there?" Lee said. The last he heard, close to

236

forty hands were on the Bar K payroll. A small army, and fully half were gun sharks.

Bob Delony frowned. "You're downright depressing, Lee. Here I hurried back to break the good news, and you have me thinking that the worst is yet to come."

Small talk ensued, until Allison clasped Lee's hand and excused them so he could get to work. As they strolled down the hall, shoulders brushing, she said, "Do you really believe Allister will start a full-fledged war?"

"Don't put anything past him. The man has a higher opinion of himself than anyone is entitled to." Lee adjusted his hat. "What really has me worried are his cattle."

"I don't understand."

"Evers brought up an interesting point the other day. When we were out at the Bar K, Kemp mentioned that he had moved all of his herds to the west end of the valley. Every single head."

"So?"

"So it's mighty queer for a rancher to congregate all his beef in one spot, especially when he has as many head as Kemp. Cattle should be scattered so they have plenty of room to graze and there's less chance of a stampede."

Allison saw the logic but not why the Tennessean was uneasy. "What purpose could Kemp have, then?"

"Vint reckons that Kemp wants the cattle out of the way, somewhere safe. It would be the smart thing to do if Kemp plans to go on the war trail."

"With you caught in the thick of it," Allison said, and suddenly wished she had not talked him out of being a gambler. She could not bear the thought of losing him so soon after they had found one another. Her grip on his hand tightened. "Please take care. I don't want anything to happen to you."

"That makes two of us."

Lee ambled south along Diablo's dusty streets. Because the town council had yet to provide a jail, the lawmen had moved into a run-down office south of Hell Street.

Every morning at nine the three of them met and talked over their plans for the day. Lee knew that he would be late—again. Even later today, because he had an important stop to make along the way.

On reaching Cedar Street, Lee spotted a group of five cowboys riding westward. Some of Kemp's hands, he assumed, and hurried to a leather shop across the street. The gray-haired owner glanced up from a strip of leather he was punching holes in.

"Deputy! You're mighty punctual."

"Tell that to Marshal Evers," Lee said, resting his elbows on the counter. "Is it ready?"

"As promised." The old gent stooped before a low shelf. "I molded the leather to the shape of the Colt, just like you specified. I also trimmed the top so you have quick access to the hammer and the trigger." Proudly holding up a brand-new holster, he added, "It's the smooth basket-weave design you liked. Your coat will never snag when you draw. Now that you're toting two irons, can I interest you in another gunbelt?"

"Excess baggage," Lee said.

The Tennessean unbuckled his own belt, attached the new holster, and strapped the gunbelt back on. The scabbard slanted, resting snug on his hip. Accepting the spare Colt he had lent to the craftsman, he slid it into the new holster, butt forward as he wore his Peacemaker.

After the spare had saved his life the night he was bushwhacked, Lee had decided that packing two

Diablo

guns was not as foolish as many claimed. Vint Evers did it. So did Jesse Bodine.

He wanted five or six extra shots he could rely on in a pinch, rather than wind up short and pay for it with his life. Reloading took precious time.

More than ever, Lee hankered to stay alive. Thanks to Allison, his prospects were rosier than they had been in a coon's age.

Even as the thought flitted across his mind, Lee remembered the three men on his trail. His future could hardly qualify as rosy until that score had been settled.

"Is the scabbard to your liking, young fellow?"

Lee gripped the butt of the pistol that had once belonged to Nate Collins and slid it in and out a few times. The heavy revolver unlimbered in a twinkling, as if the inside of the holster were greased. "It's perfect," he declared.

After paying the bill, Lee made a beeline for the office. As he rounded a corner, he nearly collided with Vint Evers and Ike Shannon.

"So here you are, laddie!" the gambler said. "We were beginning to think you'd eloped with lovely Allison and we'd never see you again."

"Just out of curiosity," Vint said, "are you ever on time for *anything*? Or should I—"

The Texan broke off, staring up the street. Lee and Ike both turned.

Nelly Rosell was hastening northward a block away. She wore a cape and hood, the hood pulled low so that it partially hid her face. But there was no mistaking her profile.

Vint took several steps. This was the first time he had bumped into her outside of the saloon in weeks. Guilt flooded through him, but this time he bucked it. Instead of turning tail, he hollered, "Nelly! Hold up a minute!"

David Robbins

To their utter surprise, Nelly clutched at her bosom, glanced furtively at them, then bolted like a frightened mare, holding the hood even lower.

"What the devil?" Vint said. He supposed that he had it coming, what with the shabby manner in which he had acted. But he was determined to speak to her, so he jogged in pursuit, his spurs jangling.

"Oh, hell!" Ike Shannon said. Every time his friend saw the blonde lately, Vint wound up trying to drink himself into oblivion. Even worse, Vint went around moping half the time, which made him easy pickings for anyone inclined to core his skull with lead. "Come on!"

Lee ran at the gambler's side to the intersection, then north to Hell Street. They were in time to see Nelly dash into the Applejack.

Vint drew up short at the entrance, torn between his burning desire to see Nelly again and fear of what she might have to say. He wouldn't blame her if she scorned him, wouldn't hold it against her if she cursed him for being the spineless coyote he was.

Ike Shannon and Lee arrived, the gambler seeking to spare the Texan more misery by saying, "It's pretty plain she doesn't want to have anything to do with you, Vint. Why don't we make our rounds and forget about her?"

Vint almost agreed. His lips parted and he was on the verge of walking off when remembrance of that delirious night spent in Nelly's company spurred him into shoving the door wide and stalking into the smoke-filled room. A knot formed in his throat, another in his chest. He found it hard to breathe and tried to tell himself it was the smoke. But he knew damn well it wasn't.

Vint was vaguely aware that Ike and Lee had followed him. He was scanning the Applejack for Nelly. She had to be there somewhere, but he saw no sign of her, which was doubly odd because at that time of the morning there weren't more than two or three dozen people in the whole place.

Ike muttered under his breath. He had seen that look on Vint's face before. A herd of stampeding wild horses could not keep the Texan from the dove's side now. And here they were, in the den of their enemies. His partner's timing was downright pitiful.

Lee felt a bit awkward being there. He imagined that Vint would rather see Nelly alone and was inclined to back on out and wait in the street. But Ike Shannon had practically pulled him inside, and he figured the gambler must know best.

As they stood there, Lee remarked, "Have either of you heard the news?"

"About you being fired and becoming a floor sweeper?" Shannon absently quipped.

"About the court case. Bob Delony just got back from Phoenix."

Both of them turned, though Vint kept scouring the saloon. "What's the news?" the Texan asked.

In brief, Lee related the details, and noticed Evers's lips compress tightly when he was done.

"The prospectors and sodbusters will be whoopin' for joy, but Kemp will be furious," Vint said. "I reckon he won't hold back now. He sees himself as lord and master of this here valley, and if he can't evict those he doesn't want here legal-like, he'll do like he did with the Indians."

"My thinking exactly," Lee drawled.

Ike saw the Texan's eyes widen slightly, and he pivoted in the same direction.

"What in tarnation?" Vint said.

They had found Nelly Rosell. She stood in a far corner, in a shadowed nook at the end of the polished bar, standing with her back to the noisy room and her hood over her head. It was almost as if she was trying to hide from them.

"Maybe we should take the hint and leave," Ike advised. "She doesn't want anything to do with us."

"I'll have to hear that from her own lips," Vint said, and headed toward the corner.

Snorting like a bull, Shannon shadowed him, beckoning the Tennessean.

Lee reluctantly tagged along. Whatever Vint and Nelly had to say to each other was their own affair. Some of the customers were staring, and that made him even more self-conscious. He didn't know how the Texan could tolerate the situation. If Allison were in Nelly's shoes, he'd go loco.

"Nelly?" Vint said, slowing near the bar.

"Go away," the blonde said timidly, her voice quavering, her head bent.

Vint stopped. "I'd like a few words with you," he said gently. "Please."

"It's best if you just leave," Nelly said.

Something in her tone—a forlorn tremor that hinted at abject despair and suffering—tore at Vint's heartstrings. He had to speak his piece quickly, while he still had the nerve. Taking a step, he laid a hand on her shoulder to turn her around. She resisted, and he had to use both hands. As she rotated, the hood fell free, revealing her face.

A pantherish shriek of sheer rage ripped from the Texan's throat.

Chapter Nineteen

"My God!" Ike Shannon blurted.

Lee Scurlock winced in sympathy for Nelly Rosell, whose face had been battered almost to a black-and-blue pulp. Her discolored left eye was swollen shut, her lips puffy and cracked. One cheek had been split and a nasty gash marred her left brow. Only her right eye had been left untouched, and from it gleamed cold fear as she gazed at the lanky Texan—fear that Lee suspected was more for the lawman's sake than her own.

A terrible change had come over Vint Evers. He stood ramrod straight, his whipcord body transformed into living steel. The muscles in his neck bulged, and the veins stood out as if on the verge of exploding. Hellish flames burned in his narrowed eyes, and his mouth was a ghastly slash of suppressed fury.

The Applejack had gone deathly silent. No one

spoke. No one seemed to even breathe.

Nelly broke the spell. She had dreaded this would happen, and had done her best to avoid it. Clutching at her lover's shirt, she pleaded, "Please! Don't do anything you'll regret! I'm not worth it!"

Slowly, tenderly, Vint Evers pried her fingers off. Then, with a studied casual air that was all the more chilling because of the awful scarlet flush that crept up his neck and the thunder that loomed imminent on his brow, he faced the bartender, who had turned to ice in the act of polishing a glass. *"Where is Frank Lowe?"*

The words crackled. They ripped the air like fangs, startling the barkeep into dropping the glass and recoiling. "I don't know!"

The Texan lunged, seizing the barman and hauling him over the bar. With a brutal shove he hurled the man to the floor, then loomed over him, his face a mask of doom. "Where is Frank Lowe?" he repeated.

Cringing in terror, the bartender tried to crawl away. "Honest, Marshal, I don't have any idea! He hasn't been in yet today!"

Vint cocked a fist, but suddenly Ike Shannon sprang, grabbing his arm. "Don't!" Ike cried. "Think of what you're doing! You're the law here. You can't—"

With a swipe of an arm, the Texan flung the gambler from him. Ike began to intervene again, but the lawman pointed a finger at his chest, just pointed and shook his head. The meaning was crystal clear.

Vint Evers whirled. Every person present either blinked or swallowed or jerked back. It was almost as if they could feel the pounding waves of seething violence being radiated by the wrathful apparition who stalked to the center of the room, raised both arms to the ceiling, and roared, "Lowe! Show yourself!"

The proprietor did not appear. No answer was forthcoming. Lee glimpsed Nelly, about to rush toward the Texan, and grasped her firmly but gently.

"Please!" Nelly begged. "He'll throw it all away on account of me!"

"She's right," Ike Shannon said. "No town will ever hire him again if he commits a cold-blooded murder."

Vint Evers was about to turn back when a beefy man playing cards caught his eye. It was one of the gunmen in Frank Lowe's personal employ, one of the bodyguards Lowe never went anywhere without. Like a cougar stalking prey, the Texan glided to the table. "Where's your boss?"

The gunman's blood had drained from his fleshy face. He licked his thick lips and had to cough before he could speak. "I haven't seen him today—"

Metal blurred, thudding on flesh and bone. The gunman was knocked backward, crashing to the floor on top of the chair. Blood poured from his split head as he struggled to sit up.

The Texan had streaked his right-hand Colt out and pistol-whipped the heavyset underling in the blink of an eye. Now, straddling him, Vint Evers raised the Colt for another blow. "Where's your boss?"

"Honest, I have no idea!" squealed the tough. "He gave me the morning off. I'm supposed to meet him here later this afternoon."

Vint hesitated. He had no doubt the man was being sincere; the gunman was too scared to lie. Shoving his Colt back into its holster, he bent and unbuckled the man's gunbelt, then tossed it aside. "Get out of Diablo. If I ever set eyes on you again, you're dead."

Visibly quaking, the man crawled backward, rising when he was in the clear. "I'm not about to buck you,

Evers. I'll do as you say, but I don't rightly think it's fair. I had no hand in what happened to your filly. Hell, I didn't even know until just now."

Evers pointed again. Gulping, the gunman sped from the saloon, and there wasn't a man there who would accuse him of being yellow. Hair-trigger death stalked the Applejack, and they all knew it.

The Texan spun. Briskly he strode to one of the rear doors and threw it open to vanish within. Furniture crashed. More doors slammed.

Ike Shannon growled deep in his chest and smacked the bar. "Damn him! He's playing right into Lowe's hands."

Lee still held Nelly. "How do you figure?" he asked. The way he saw it, Frank Lowe had made the mistake of his life. Most people could only be pushed so far. Sooner or later, if a man *was* a man, he would make his stand.

"Don't you see?" Ike Shannon said. "Lowe knew how Vint would react. Only an idiot would prod Vint into a fight, and Lowe's no idiot. He must have an ulterior motive."

"But what could it be?" Lee wondered.

"I don't know, and that's what worries me."

Nelly sniffled, listening to the smash of glass, to the man she adored bellowing for Lowe to show himself. "You must be right, Ike," she said. "Lowe showed up at my room last night, which he hasn't done in a long time. He said that he needed to talk, that it was important, and when I let him in, he began slapping me around for no reason. I fought back, so he slugged me."

"The bastard!" Ike snarled, his mind in a whirl. It was crucial that he find out what Lowe was up to before Vint's entire career was ruined by searing flames of jealous rage.

Just then another back door opened and out

stormed the Texan. He glared about him like a beast at bay, thirsting for the blood of his enemy. "Tell him!" he raged at the cowed patrons. "Tell Frank Lowe that I'm going to find him if I have to tear this town apart board by board!"

In the awful quiet that ensued, the rasp of the front doors opening caused half the men there to jump.

Framed in the doorway was a man in his fifties dressed in the typical homespun garb of the homesteaders. Crumpled hat in hand, dust and tears streaking his cheeks, he hollered, "Marshal Evers! Come quick! We need your help!"

Vint Evers took a few halting steps. Caught in the grip of a private tempest, his emotions boiling white-hot, he had to beat back the swirling tide of vengeance to focus. "What's that?" he blurted.

"Up in the hills!" the nester said, wringing his hat. "Masked riders are destroyin' our homes!"

All eyes swung back to the lawman. Vint Evers glanced at Nelly Rosell, then at the doors behind him, and finally at his own hands, which he clenched and unclenched. Swaying like a tall tree, he said softly, plaintively, "Not now!"

"Marshal?" the homesteader said. "People are bein' beat, and homes are burnin'. There's not a minute to lose."

Vint wavered. At long last he had let down the mental shield he had put up to blunt his outrage at Nelly's plight. At long last he had let his affection for her rule his actions. And now, when he had finally broken the chains that bound him, at the very moment when the woman he cared for needed him most, the bloodbath had begun.

Lee saw the torture his friend was going through, and felt deep sympathy. Any man who had ever loved a woman would feel the same. Duty or devotion? Which would the tall Texan pick?

The moment of indecision passed. Vint Evers strode to Nelly and clasped her by the wrist. "Your days of workin' for Frank Lowe are over. You're comin' with me."

Budding joy clashed with harsh reality in Nelly's breast. "But the contract I signed?"

"To hell with it!" Vint said, pulling her after him. "You told me once that you loved me, that you would go anywhere I went, and I'm holdin' you to your word. From here on out, we're two halves of the same coin. And I pity the hombre who claims different."

Ike Shannon hurried to fall into step beside Evers. "What are you aiming to do?"

"You need to ask?" Vint responded. "The nesters need my help."

"But you're the *town* marshal," Ike remonstrated. "The hills south of the valley are out of your jurisdiction. It's a job for a federal marshal or the Army, not for us."

Vint Evers never slowed. "It would take days for a rider to get word to the Army, days more for a patrol to get here. A federal lawman wouldn't show for weeks." He shook his head. "No, when I pinned on this badge, I didn't vow to protect some of the people some of the time. I gave my word to protect *all* of the people *all* of the time."

"But it's out of your jurisdiction," Ike insisted. "You won't have any legal standing."

Vint patted his left-hand pistol. "These are all the legal standin' I need."

Barreling outdoors, the Texan paused to thrust Nelly's wrist into the startled gambler's hand. "I'm countin' on you, pard, to watch over her until I get back. If Frank Lowe tries to take her, blow him to kingdom come with that big Sharps rifle of yours."

Ike was horrified at the thought of Vint riding off

to face Kemp's pack of killers alone. "Who's going to guard your back if I stay here?" he protested. It wasn't that he disliked the dove. He had nothing against her other than she was a prime distraction to Vint and might get him killed.

The Texan grinned at the Tennessean. "How about it, Lee? You feel like givin' Allister Kemp a dose of his own medicine?"

Lee was flattered by the confidence the famed lawman showed in him. And, truth to tell, he was itching for a chance to pay the Englishman back for the heartbreak Allison had endured, and the ambush. "There's nothing I'd like more."

Great billowing clouds of thick, dark smoke were visible from miles off. Borne high into the sky, they formed a hazy gray ceiling over the foothills that rimmed the valley to the south, shrouding the hills in false twilight.

A frantic exodus was under way. Scores of homesteaders were fleeing pell-mell. In wagons, on horseback, and on foot, men, women, and children, many dazed by the loss of their homes, quite a few weeping pitiably, filed urgently by.

Lee rode alongside Vint Evers, staring grimly at the terrified, anguished nesters, then at the dusty ribbon ahead where the line strung out for as far as he could see. On their right flowed the Diablo River, which bore westward at the southeast corner of the valley.

Off to the left a cabin was engulfed in crackling flames. Farther down the road another homesite lay in smoldering ruin.

"I reckon there's no turnin' back for Kemp now," the Texan commented.

Lee nodded, rising in the stirrups to scour the countryside for some trace of those responsible. Instead he spied a riddled sow and her eight young ones, flies buzzing thick over them.

A clattering buckboard approached. Vint Evers moved into the middle of the road and reined up. "Hold on there, hoss! I'd like a word with you."

The driver was a stocky farmer whose homespun clothes were sooty, whose face was layered with grime. His wife and two small children were with him, the children weeping, the woman in tears, too, but trying hard not to let her trickle turn into a deluge. The farmer halted, then glanced anxiously over his shoulder. "Make it quick, Marshal! They might be after us!"

"Who?"

Gnawing on his lower lip, the homesteader shifted to stare westward again.

"I need to know what I'm up against," Vint said patiently. "Tell me what you've seen."

"Hell on earth," the man answered forlornly. "Everything we owned is gone except for the clothes on our backs and this buckboard and team. And we would have lost them, too, if we hadn't been fixing to head into town when the devils struck."

Dejected nesters tromped past on either side of the wagon, one a mother with an infant clasped to her heaving bosom, another a homesteader whose back and left arm had been badly burned. Their eyes were wide with horror; they shuffled numbly along as if they were animated corpses.

"Tell me what happened," Vint prodded.

"A bunch of masked riders swept onto our place, whooping and hollering and firing in the air," the man said. "Some of them had torches, and they set fire to our house and the barn. When I tried to run inside for my rifle, one of them knocked me down with his horse."

"How many were there?"

"Ten or so, but we've spotted others since. There must be two or three bands of these Regulators, as they call themselves."

"They spoke to you?"

"A big one did. He told us that we were trespassing on private range, that after today the Regulators will kill anyone they find in these hills." The farmer wiped his sweaty brow with a sleeve. "I'm no coward, Marshal, but I'm not about to get myself killed, not when I have a family to support. They can have this damned valley, and welcome to it!"

Lashing his reins, the man hurried eastward, his children bawling louder than ever.

Vint trotted westward. "That Kemp doesn't miss a trick. I'll bet he appointed his whole outfit as Regulators, just so he can pretend to be actin' legal-like."

Lee knew all about Regulators from his days in Lincoln County. It was not uncommon when two sides were embroiled in conflict for one or both to set up vigilante committees. Regulators, they liked to call themselves, but they were vigilantes, plain and simple. It was done to lend their actions a certain degree of legitimacy.

"This accounts for all the cowboys," Vint said. "For the past week or so, groups of them have drifted through Diablo on their way to Kemp's spread. And I heard tell that he's been hirin' a lot of new hands who are better with guns than they are with ropes or brandin' irons. Now we know why."

Lee remembered the riders he'd noticed in town earlier. "What can we hope to do against so many?"

Rather than reply, Vint urged his bay onward, his expression cast in steel.

The number of refugees dwindled the farther west they went. Evidently most had already fled. Spirals of dark smoke curled skyward from dozens of burning buildings. It was as if the lawmen were passing through a war-ravaged landscape, blighted by a plague of human locusts.

In many low areas between hills the smoke was as thick as fog. It got into their eyes, into their lungs. They had to pull their hat brims low and cover their mouths with their hands.

As yet they had not come on any bodies, and for that Vint was grateful. Allister Kemp was being cagey. So long as the Regulators refrained from murder, the territorial authorities would be disposed to view the clash as a simple dispute over range. In that case, possession was nine-tenths of the law, as Kemp well knew.

The lawman came to a bend. Here the road skirted the base of a low hill thick with cottonwoods and willows. Through the trees Vint glimpsed six riders galloping from the west. "Quick!" he said, turning his mount into the stand and sliding to the ground.

Lee followed suit, loosening both revolvers in their holsters as he stepped back out onto the road. By rights he should be nervous, but he felt only an icy calm. No one had the right to set himself up as the Almighty, as Kemp had done.

Vint Evers adopted a wide stance smack in the center of the rutted track and pushed his hat back on his head. "I wish I had a greener," he said wistfully.

"A shotgun would be right handy 'long about now," Lee agreed, flexing his fingers.

Hoofs drummed loudly. In a swirl of dust, amid tendrils of smoke, the six riders swept around the bend. Voicing oaths and exclamations, the Regulators drew rein. Each wore a bandanna covering his face from nose to chin.

"Marshal Evers!" one declared.

Lee was as tense as an alley cat about to tear into a rival. By their size alone he knew that Jesse Bodine was not among them. Nor was Allister Kemp, which was to be expected. The Englishman would not soil his own hands when he could pay others to do his dirty work for him.

"What the hell are *you* doing here, Evers?" demanded a rider on the right. "This ain't your bailiwick."

"I'll be the judge of that," Vint said good-naturedly, but not a man there was blind to his poised iron frame, set to explode at the slightest provocation. "Can't help but notice your animals are all in a lather. Are you gents in a hurry to get somewhere?"

"We were," answered a cocky hawk in the middle, "but not no more."

The voice tugged at Lee's memory. His gaze narrowed as he noted the Regulator's blazing green eyes and curly blond hair. Those eyes were locked on him in intense hatred.

"As I live and breathe," the man said. "Just the *hombre* I've been itchin' to see again. I can't tell you how many times I've dreamed of buckin' you out in gore, Scurlock. There's unfinished business between us."

Vint Evers was watching the Regulators' hands. Long ago he'd learned that the old adage about always watching a man's eyes was so much bunk. Some gunmen, the really good ones, had a knack for adopting a poker face, for making their eyes go blank so they would not give themselves away when they grabbed for their hardware. "Do you know this jasper?" he asked.

"Allow me to introduce Nate Collins," Lee said. "He fancies himself a *pistolero*."

"Don't they all," Vint said with a sigh.

Predictably, Nate flushed with anger. "That badge of yours doesn't mean a thing out here, Texas. You'd best skedaddle while you still can. In case you can't count, there's six of us and only two of you."

Vint chuckled. Another lesson he had learned was that it paid to use his head. A mad enemy was a careless, sloppy enemy, so he responded, "Can I help it if the odds are in our favor?"

"Funny man," Nate bantered. He was savoring the situation for all it was worth. It wasn't every day that a man boosted his reputation by slaying a shootist of the Texan's caliber. The Tennessean was icing on the cake, as it were. Nate pointed at Scurlock's left-hand pistol. "Still packin' *my* iron, I see."

"You gave up your right to it the day you tried to kill me," Lee responded.

Nate's lips curled like those of a serpent about to strike. "Stealin' a man's gun is almost as bad as stealin' his horse. You can dress it up in words any way you like, but that won't change the fact it's mine, Reb. I want it back, and I want it back now."

An older Regulator shifted in his saddle. "What the hell are we palaverin' for, Collins? I didn't hire on to jaw people to death. Mr. Kemp will be waitin' for us. We'd best get this over with."

Smirking, Vint said, "So Allister Kemp *is* behind these raids. Much obliged for the proof I needed."

Upset by his blunder, the gunman growled, "I never claimed Mr. Kemp is behind anything. All I said was that we have to meet up with him later. That's hardly against the law."

Vint saw a man on the left edge a hand toward a Remington. "All right. Let's get this over with," he declared. "Unstrap your gunbelts and throw them down."

Brittle laugher burst from Nate Collins. "All this smoke must have addled your brain, Marshal. The only way you'll take our irons is off of our dead bodies."

"That can be arranged," Vint said.

Diablo

For several seconds the tableau froze, the tigerish forms of lawmen and gunmen alike rigid with impending violence. Nate Collins broke the spell by twisting to grin at a companion and pretending he was about to say something while lowering his right hand toward the new pistol on his hip. Then, in a burst of lightning motion, he drew.

It was the signal for the rest to slap leather.

Chapter Twenty

It was not all that unusual among the social circles of blue-blood easterners to hear them brand the lurid tales in the penny dreadfuls as bald-faced lies told for the benefit of dull-witted common rabble.

"No one could be that skilled with a gun!" they would say when reading the vivid exploits of a renowned gunman, completely unaware that many gunmen spent hours daily practicing their deadly stock-in-trade.

"No one could shoot a dime at twenty paces!" they would say with a laugh, oblivious to the fact that among the hill folk of the deep South, the feat would hardly merit attention.

For the plain truth was that those who lived and died by the gun made it a point to be as proficient as natural talent and dogged practice could make them. They honed their ability to a razor's edge, and beyond.

Diablo

So it was that men like James Butler Hickok, more commonly known as Wild Bill, could throw a tomato can into the air and put three holes into it before it hit the ground. Or stand midway between two fence posts on opposite sides of a country road and put bullets into both simultaneously.

Easterners scoffed. Blue bloods who had never touched a gun in their lives believed that they knew all there was to know about gun handling and marksmanship.

Ignorance has always been a breeding ground for arrogance. Those who don't know flaunt their empty heads, while those who do know nod theirs in silent understanding.

Had any of the doubters been present that hot afternoon in Diablo Valley, they would have shaken their heads in disbelief and been skeptical of their own senses. For what they would have seen was an uncanny exhibition of speed and accuracy in the opening moments of the gunfight.

Lee Scurlock whipped out his right-hand Colt and snapped off a shot that tore into Nate Collins even as the blond gunman cleared leather. The jolt threw Nate from his mount.

Lee heard Vint Evers cut loose, but he could not afford to hazard a glance to see how his friend was faring. He had plenty to occupy him.

For as Collins went down, the Regulator to the right brought a Smith & Wesson into play. Lee fired up into the man, then dived for the ground, landing on his right shoulder. Slugs smacked into the dirt around him. He rolled to make himself harder to hit.

The shrill whinny of frightened horses and the lusty curses of incensed killers were punctuated by the boom of six-shooters.

At the edge of the road, Lee shoved to his knees. And as he did, a gigantic cloud of smoke swirled

down around him, blotting out the Regulators and
Vint Evers alike. It happened swiftly. All of them
were enveloped in a span of seconds.

A few more shots rang out, then the gunfire died.
Horses pranced and nickered, but the men on them
were as quiet as churchgoers during a sermon.

The smoke burned Lee's nose. At the last second
he checked an urge to cough. Dozens of feet to his
left someone was not as diligent and paid for his
carelessness by having lead sprayed in his direction.
There was a grunt and the thud of a falling body.

Lee did not move a muscle, not even when a vague
shape reared in front of him. It was a horse. His right
hand elevated, but the pressure of his trigger finger
lessened when he realized that the saddle was empty.

How many Regulators were left? Lee figured at
least two, with maybe another two lying wounded.

A fluttering groan wafted through the cloud.
Someone was hit hard.

Spurs jangled nearby. Lee spun, but the smoky veil
hid whoever was stalking two-legged quarry. He had
to breathe shallow in order not to sear his lungs. His
eyes watered, and he wiped them with a sleeve.

The gray soup was so thick that Lee could not see
his hand in front of his face. Behind him a twig
snapped. Whirling, he waited for someone to appear.
A horse nickered instead, its position leading him to
suspect that it was Vint's or his.

The groan changed to a gurgling snarl, the sort of
death rattle a stricken bear might make. A scraping
sound attended it.

Then for the longest while there was no noise, ab-
solutely none whatsoever. Those horses that had not
run off were standing completely still.

The smoke eddied and whirled like currents in the
sea. Occasionally the veil would briefly part, allow-

ing Lee to see clearly for a few yards. No one appeared.

Lee tried to ascertain exactly where he was in relation to where the Regulators had been when the firing commenced, but it was hopeless. Crouching low to the ground, he sidestepped slowly, placing each boot down lightly so his spurs would not jingle.

Deep in the cloud a flurry of movement erupted. Someone cursed. A hogleg boomed. Another responded in kind, not once but three times. A heavy thump indicated that a man had lost his life.

Tempted to call out to learn if Evers was still alive, Lee bit his lower lip. An outcry would doom him as surely as if he walked up to one of the cutthroats and asked to have his brains blown out.

Lee took another step, and yet another. Without warning something wrapped around his ankles and clung fast. Startled, he glanced down into the ghostly visage of a human, a Regulator whose chest oozed blood but whose eyes flickered with vitality and menace.

"Got one!" the gunman cried.

Shaking a leg, Lee tried to dislodge the clinging hardcase. He might as well have tried to shed his own skin. Kemp's hired killer clung on as if for dear life. Lee snapped his Colt above his head to render the man unconscious. As he did, a form took shape before him. It was another Regulator, revolver leveled.

Lee was caught flat-footed. It would be impossible for him to lower his pistol and shoot before the Regulator did. The man's wolfish countenance creased in bloodthirsty relish as his revolver swiveled.

Three shots sounded. Lee flinched as if struck, but he was not the one who staggered backward with each retort; not the one who folded in half and keeled forward; not the one who sprawled lifeless in the dust.

Vint Evers advanced, smoke wisping from the barrels of both his expensive pistols. The left one barked again, and the man holding Lee's legs collapsed.

"Are you all right, pard?"

Lee nodded, deeming it unwise to talk until all the Regulators had been accounted for.

"I think that's the last of them," Vint said.

But he was wrong. Beyond the Texan reared a gun-toting centaur whose dark mount bore down on the lawman's broad back. Lee returned his friend's favor by working the hammer of his Colt twice.

An eyeball ruptured, a cranium shattered, and the Regulator crashed down almost at Vint's feet. The dark horse kept on going, the smoke swallowing it whole.

Quiet reined once more, broken by a canine whine. Lee moved so that he was back to back with Evers. Gradually, the wind stiffened. The shadowy gray blanket lifted and scattered, leaving a scene of carnage in its wake.

Six bodies littered the road and its fringe. Only two moved, one a scruffy gunman who was trying to crawl off despite a busted arm and a hole in his torso.

The other survivor was Nate Collins. Flat on his back, his knees bent, he continued whining until Lee stood over him. "Scurlock!" he spat through grating teeth. "May you rot in the deepest pit of hell!"

Lee said nothing. He reloaded.

Death's door yawned for Collins. His skin glistened like that of a slug. Only with monumental effort did his lips move. "Finish me, Reb!" Although his arms were outflung and his pistol was inches from his right hand, he made no attempt to grab it.

"Why should I waste the bullet?" Lee retorted.

"I can't move, damn it! You can't just ride off and leave a man like this!"

Vint Evers joined them. "You likely took some lead in the spine. Might be you'll linger for hours, might be for days."

Nate uttered a throaty growl. "Damnation, it hurts! If the Reb won't do me, then you pull the trigger, Texas. Surely you can't stand to see a man suffer."

Lee felt no sympathy at all. Collins had brought it on himself and now had to suffer the consequences. "You've got what you deserved."

Maniacal flames danced in the blond gunman's eyes. "And you'll get yours, both of you! Just wait and see! Sooner or later someone will collect the bounty."

"Bounty?" Vint said.

Contempt twisted Nate's pasty complexion. "Yeah, you heard right! Kemp is offering a thousand dollars for your hide and five hundred for Scurlock's. Be flattered, Texican. He had to offer twice as much for you or otherwise there wouldn't be any takers."

"So it's come to that," Vint said.

"Jesse Bodine aims to collect both bounties," Nate crowed, the effort flecking his lips scarlet.

"Where can I find your boss?"

"I'll never tell! You can go to hell!"

"You first," the Texan said casually. Slanting both Colts, he shot Nate Collins in the eyes.

Bedlam reigned in Diablo for a spell.

The influx of terrified homesteaders incited everyone to a fever pitch. Fueled by harrowing tales of fiery ruin, the town dwellers gave voice to collective outrage.

But they were not so mad that any of them mounted up and rode south to protect stragglers. Nor were any mad enough to go after the man responsible, although they all knew who it was.

Most prospectors and miners did light out, to the north, fearful that the Regulators would strike their claims next.

Will Dryer, one of the first nesters to have his home reduced to cinders, wanted to call an emergency session of the town council, but four of the members were absent, among them Old Abe Howard.

By the time Vint Evers and Lee Scurlock rode into Diablo toward evening, the pot had cooled to a simmer. Most everyone was indoors, gathered in stores, saloons, and other public places to discuss the crisis.

An air of raw tension gripped Diablo. Everyone could feel it. Even the dogs slunk off to hide, and cats were conspicuous by their absence.

The lawmen reined in their tired horses. Lee turned to survey the four animals bearing draped corpses, then tied the rope by which he had led them to a post bracing the porch overhang.

Vint was in a hurry. The entire ride back he had fretted about Nelly. Barging on in, he found Ike Shannon seated at a desk, cleaning a rifle. No one else was present. "Where is she?" he demanded.

"Sheathe your claws," the gambler said. "She's fine. But she didn't get much sleep last night and she could hardly keep her eyes open. So about an hour and a half ago I took her to our shack. No one will bother her there."

Vint's gut churned. Teego and those other killers had jumped him at their shack. "I'm going to check."

"Wait. Tell me what happened."

But Vint was not inclined to wait for anyone or anything. Brushing past Lee, he was out the door and turning right when a wall of citizenry stopped him.

People had converged from every which way. Some had seen the dead men being brought in, and word spread like wildfire. Townsmen, homesteaders, and a few pocket hounds formed a crescent that hemmed in the front of the building.

"Marshal Evers!" someone cried, inciting dozens to talk at once.

"One at a time!" Vint hollered again and again, but it was a losing proposition until Lee and Ike appeared, the Irishman cradling a shotgun.

The crowd quieted. A homesteader in sooty clothes who stood at the front raised an arm. "What do you plan to do about these Regulators, Marshal?"

"At the moment, nothin'," Vint admitted.

"What?" chorused a dozen throats. The spokesman swore and barked, "They've driven us from our homes! Burned us out! Killed seven or eight—!"

"Killed who?" Vint challenged him. Scanning the assembly, he demanded, "Did any of you actually see the Regulators murder anyone?"

Glances were swapped. Some fidgeted. Some muttered. But no one responded.

Vint stepped forward. "So far as I know, no one has been killed. Don't any of you go spreadin' stories to the contrary unless you have proof. Things are bad enough. We don't need a pack of lies makin' matters worse. You savvy?"

"I understand," the spokesman truculently answered. Others curtly bobbed their chins.

Gesturing at the bodies, Vint said, "Even with these six turnin' up their toes, thirty or forty more Regulators are out there yet. There's not much I can do against a small army that size with only two deputies."

The crowd stirred. "Appoint a posse!" someone suggested. "Run the stinking Regulators out of the country!"

"Now, there's an idea. Why didn't I think of it?" Vint said sarcastically. To the townsman who had spoken, he said, "I'll recruit you first. Are you handy with a shootin' iron?"

"Well, no," the townsman said. "I ain't hardly ever handled a gun."

"What about you?" Vint pointed at the farmer in sooty clothes. "You're so all-fired up to have your revenge. Can you shoot worth a damn?"

The homesteader grew sullen. "Not really. But I'm no gunman! My livelihood is crops and stock. That's what I know best."

"Which is just the point I'm tryin' to make," Vint said. "Where am I supposed to get this posse from? Thin air? I'm not about to lead a passel of you off to get yourselves rubbed out. We wouldn't stand a chance against a gun-wise outfit like the Bar K."

The Texan's logic was irrefutable. No one disputed him, although many grumbled.

"I'm doin' what I can," Vint reassured them.

"Doesn't sound like much to me," snorted a clerk.

In a flash the lawman grasped the front of the offender's shirt and shook him like a cougar might a terrified rabbit. "Are you on the peck, friend?"

"Who? Me?" The man gulped. "No sir, Marshal. I didn't mean no disrespect."

Capping his anger, Vint stepped back. Emotions had been worn raw, and it was up to him to set a good example. "I'm sorry," he apologized. "I reckon I know how all of you must feel. I'm doing what I can. You have to trust me. Spread the word among your friends. Stay calm for the time being. That's all I ask."

The delay had chafed at Vint's nerves. Touching his hat brim for the benefit of the ladies, he hurried around the corner, wishing he had wings on his feet like that Greek god a journalist had once told him about.

Ike Shannon nudged Lee. "Let's go. We're not leaving Vint alone for a minute. Until Kemp is taken care of, the three of us should stick together."

Lee tended to agree, but he also wanted to go see Allison. For now he was content to tag along, pondering deeply.

Should he tell Allison about the bounty on his head? She worried enough as it was; the bounty might prompt her into pleading with him to quit. And he couldn't do that, not when Vint and Shannon needed him so badly.

He figured it might be best to keep his mouth shut. So far, only Vint knew. The Bar K riders were aware of their employer's brazen gambit, but they were unlikely to spread the word. They wanted the money for themselves.

Kemp certainly wasn't about to tell anyone else. If the bounty became common knowledge, the Englishman risked having a U.S. marshal show up with a warrant for his arrest. A bounty on a lawman was a federal offense.

Allister Kemp. Lee had to admit that the cattle baron's strategy was brilliant. A grand design had lain behind Kemp's every move from the beginning, and none of them had been smart enough to realize it.

The Englishman must have learned that Jim Hays was coming to help Bob Delony and sent Collins, Gristy, and Morco to Wynn's relay station to goad Hays into a gunfight.

Lee scowled. When he had thwarted that plan, Kemp had invited him to the Bar K, then had Matt Rash dress up as a miner and hire pocket hunters to ambush him. That worked so well that Kemp had Rash do it again, hiring Joe Neff to kill Jim Hays, while another man bushwhacked Old Abe.

Kemp had cleverly hoped to divert suspicion by using miners as unwitting scapegoats.

David Robbins

The court action, Lee now firmly believed, had been a ploy from the start, a ruse to make everyone think Kemp was content to wage a legal battle when all the while the rancher was taking steps to launch a private little war. Why else had Kemp hired more gunmen? Why else had he herded his cattle to safety on the west range?

Lee should have seen it sooner. Similar tactics had been used by one of the factions in the Lincoln County War.

Like Murphy and Dolan in New Mexico, Kemp was cleverly covering his tracks, carrying out his master plan in such a way that none of the evidence directly incriminated him. By having his hired help do everything, Kemp kept his own hands relatively clean.

A jury would have a hard time finding him guilty if no proof linked him to any of the crimes his men committed. Hearsay would not suffice.

The wheels of frontier justice ground slowly. Juries were inclined to give the accused the benefit of the doubt in cases where the law did not have an ironclad case.

Kemp knew all that. Should he find himself in court, he'd simply claim that he had no hand in organizing the Regulators, that his men did it on their own. He was an accomplished liar. And as most everyone was well aware, a clever lawyer and a good actor could get away with anything.

Even the way the law was enforced in the West worked in the cattle baron's favor. In remote regions, like Diablo Valley, county governments did not yet exist, so there were no county sheriffs. U.S. marshals were few and far between, and they enforced only federal laws. A cunning lawbreaker need only worry about town marshals like Vint Evers, who were limited in how much they could do.

Diablo

A crafty man like Kemp could carry out his wicked designs with virtual impunity.

"There's the shack, laddie," Ike Shannon said, bringing Lee out of himself.

The plank dwelling was one of ten or so lined up in a row. An empty lot choked with weeds flanked it. Across the street stood a two-story frame building sporting a crudely painted sign: BOARDING HOUSE.

"I don't see Vint," the Irishman said.

"He's probably inside with Nelly already," Lee guessed.

Sure enough, the door creaked and the Texan and the dove emerged, arm in arm. They had eyes only for each other. He kissed her on the cheek and she brazenly planted her lips on his mouth.

Shannon coughed.

Vint Evers jerked back, a flush creeping up his neck. "Didn't hear you come up," he said.

The gambler shook his head in annoyance. His friend was behaving like a lovestruck kid, and it was liable to get him killed. "We should find somewhere safe for Nelly to stay until this whole business is over with. Maybe we could send her to Phoenix."

Nelly Rosell clasped her man's arm. "Not on your life, Ike Shannon. I appreciate your concern, but I'm sticking with Vint through thick and thin."

Shannon felt no need to mention that it was not concern for her that prompted his suggestion. The woman was a millstone around Vint's neck, a millstone that would drag the Texan down into an early grave if something was not done.

Lee Scurlock snapped his fingers. "I've got a brainstorm. Why can't Nelly stay with Allison? Ethel and Bob Delony won't mind, and she would be as safe there as anywhere else."

"I wouldn't want to put anyone out," Nelly said.

"It wouldn't be a bother. I can go right this minute and ask them."

"Not so fast," Nelly balked, torn by a sense of shame. The Delonys were a decent, upstanding couple, heavily involved in the new church. What would folks think if they took a soiled woman like her under their roof? "I need some time to think on it."

"What's to think about?" Lee responded. The solution seemed so obvious. He was going to say more when a gleam of light on the boardinghouse roof drew his attention.

Three cowboys were spaced along the roof's edge. Each was armed with a Winchester, and each was taking cold, deliberate aim.

Chapter Twenty-one

So perfectly coordinated were Lee Scurlock's reflexes that the very instant he spied the three riflemen, he exploded into action, angling both of his pistols up and out while shouting, "Evers! The roof! Look out!"

In a burst of tigerish speed, the Texan dove, bearing Nelly with him to the grass as the Winchesters thundered in lethal unison. Holding on to his sweetheart, Vint flipped toward the corner of the shack, seeking to get her under cover at all costs.

The cowboys were blasting away in earnest. Lee fired twice and saw one stagger. The tallest replied in kind, the slugs punching into the soil at Lee's feet as he skipped sideways to cover Vint and Nelly.

Ike Shannon crouched, bringing the shotgun to bear but holding his fire when he realized the range was too great.

In another moment Vint rolled Nelly behind the

shack, and suddenly the riflemen ducked out of sight.

"NO!" the Irishman roared, the Gaelic blood of his ancestors that flowed in his veins inflamed in berserk rage. "They're not getting away if I can help it!" Hefting the scattergun, he charged across the street.

Lee wavered, unsure whether to aid Shannon or to stay by the Texan and Nelly. The decision was made for him.

"Help Ike!" Vint yelled.

The Tennessean sped after the impetuous gambler, who had paused at the boardinghouse entrance to cock the twin hammers on the sawed-off American Arms twelve-gauge. "Wait for me, Ike!"

But the Irishman was not waiting for any man. Flinging the door wide, he vanished.

Swearing luridly, Lee poured on speed and bounded inside, into a well-lit lobby. Down a corridor on the far side raced Ike Shannon. Lee sprinted after him and saw the gambler dart into a room at the end.

Without warning a middle-aged woman stepped from a doorway in Lee's path. He nearly bowled her over, and had to grab her arms to keep her from falling. "Sorry, ma'am," he blurted.

"I never!" the woman huffed. "What is all this? Goodness' sakes!" Seeing his badge, she had the presence of mind to get out of the way.

Rushing on, Lee heard the blast of the shotgun. He reached the room, a tidy kitchen that opened onto an alley. Sprawled a few yards from the doorway was one of the riflemen, his chest shredded by buckshot. Lee leaped over the body.

Shannon was almost to the end of the alley, reloading on the fly. He glimpsed a shadowy form through the slats in a picket fence on his left and, spinning, emptied both barrels.

Diablo

A cannon could not have done better. The blast made a jagged hole the size of a watermelon in the fence. A shrill shriek greeted it. Rushing up, Ike peered through the hole to discover a cowboy missing the upper half of his head.

Just then Lee saw the third rifleman, the one he had winged. The man stepped into the open at the end of the picket fence and raised a pistol. Lee thumbed both hammers, the Colts bucking in his grip.

The cowboy tottered, his gun going off into the air instead of into the Irishman. Wordlessly, he crumpled and convulsed a bit before life faded.

Shannon was reloading again. Jogging past, Lee inspected the last rifleman slain. "I've seen him before. He rides for the Bar K."

"Was there any doubt?" Ike said. His only regret was that it had not been Allister Kemp behind the fence. "If it's the last thing I ever do, I'm going to kill the bastard responsible," he vowed.

"More will try to earn that bounty," Lee mentioned. "We won't have a moment's peace."

"Vint!" Shannon exclaimed, and was off like a thoroughbred, fearful that other cowboys lurked nearby, just waiting their chance. "Forget these vermin!"

Dogging the gambler was becoming a habit, Lee wryly reflected. They raced around the rear of the boardinghouse and back across the dusty street.

In the shadow of the shack knelt Vint Evers. Rocking back and forth, Nelly clutched in his blood-stained hands, he raised his anguished face to the heavens and broke into choking sobs. "They shot her! Damn their souls, they shot her!"

"It was awful, truly awful, all that shootin' and all those explosions," the grizzled prospector declared,

271

David Robbins

lingering terror making him tremble hours after the event. Dirt caked his haggard face, and he tugged nervously at his bristly beard.

"Tell us about it, man!" a homesteader prompted.

A murmur of assent came from many in the throng that filled the Applejack to overflowing. Miners, farmers, and assorted townsfolk crowded closer to the mahogany bar.

"Yeah, tell us!" a portly storekeeper said.

Near the entrance, their backs to the wall as a precaution, were Lee Scurlock and Ike Shannon. "We should have done something," the Tennessean lamented.

"What could we have done?" rejoined the Irishman. "Outnumbered and outgunned, we would have thrown our lives away for nothing." He patted his greener. "And I told you before. I'm not going anywhere so long as Vint is in danger."

Lee was not entirely convinced. He recollected vividly the distant thunder they had heard earlier while biding their time outside of Doctor Franklyn's office. Shortly after that the first bedraggled miners straggled in from the mountains, singly and in pairs, but growing in number as time wore on. They were as dazed and bewildered as the homesteaders had been, and with valid cause. The Regulators had struck again.

"Get on with it, McPike, damn you!" someone yelled.

The prospector nodded, fortified himself with another swig, then said, "All right! All right! Don't be rushin' me." He gulped enough whiskey to drown a burro, wiped his glistening mouth with the back of his left hand, and smacked his lips. "Ahhhh. That's much better."

"Did you actually see what happened to Old Abe?" a man hollered.

"That I did," McPike confirmed, "and I wish to hell I hadn't. Old Abe was the salt of the earth."

"Tell us what happened, you idiot!" bellowed a gruff listener whose patience had been frayed.

"Don't be so tetchy!" McPike countered. A surge of angry forms convinced him that he had better comply, and he quickly went on. "I was pannin' in the crick my claim is on, out west a ways from most of the other claims, when I heard all these critters comin' up the mountain. Like the sound of a buffalo stampede, it was, with all that poundin' and snortin' and such. And then all these riders appeared, fifteen or twenty or more, their faces covered, and wavin' pistols and rifles like they were on the warpath."

"Did they shoot at you?" someone called.

"Don't butt in," McPike responded. "Can't you see I'm tryin' to think."

"In that case we'll be here all day," a fellow miner cracked.

Hearty mirth resulted, and McPike scowled at the culprit. "I was struck dumb for a minute," he resumed, "not knowin' what was goin' on, and then they were all around me, bumpin' me with their horses and insultin' me and tellin' me to light a shuck for some other part of the country, or else." He ran a hand through his sweat-matted hair.

No one broke in this time.

"I got all huffy and told them what they could do with their threats," McPike detailed, "but they laughed and one of those fellers threw a lasso over me and the next thing I knew, by God, I'm bein' dragged from my claim. Dragged right over rocks sharp enough to cut a man wide open. Dragged through brush that tore like thorns."

The crowd hung on his every word.

"My ribs were fit to bust. I got the breath knocked out of me, and when I could sit up, I saw that I was all by my lonesome and those fellers were tearin' down my tent and bustin' my sluice."

"Regulators!" a farmer howled. "They had to be Regulators!"

McPike nodded excitedly. "That's what they called themselves, true enough. One jumped down, set somethin' on the ground, lit a match, and bent low. Then they all rode out of there like they were tryin' to outrace the wind." McPike faltered, sorrow turning his tongue leaden.

"And then what?" growled a callous soul.

"They blew my claim all to hell," McPike said. "The dirt and stones poured down on me like rain. I went over after the dust cleared, but all my gear had been blown sky-high or buried under tons of earth." He quenched his sadness with more red-eye. "Then those devils rode eastward, goin' from claim to claim, never missin' a one, firin' and cussin' and scarin' most of the boys out of their wits. Those that fought back had the stuffin' kicked out of them or were lassoed and drug until they half bled to death."

A more articulate miner took up the tale. "They blew up every last claim! It sounded like artillery, one explosion right after the other. Rock slide after rock slide they started, and they didn't give a damn."

Lee could envision the nightmare: the Bar K riders sweeping from site to site, the confused, frantic pocket hunters putting up a token resistance, easy pickings for the Regulators in the uproar, so stunned that they never thought to band together and fight back.

Although the prospectors and their ilk were a rugged, resolute lot, they weren't gunslingers. And although they were often fanatical about their precious ore, the sparkle and allure of wealth paled in comparison to saving their own hides.

"I didn't know what to do," McPike continued. "I

walked around half numb until I saw Old Abe's mine ahead. Them riders were swarmin' over it like bees around a hive. But they couldn't run Abe Howard off!"

"Did they gun him down?" a man asked, and the throng held its collective breath.

"No," McPike answered. "Abe had barricaded himself in his office. He shot a couple of those no-accounts when they tried to break down the door. That's when three or four of them snuck around to the side and planted some kegs next to the wall. I figured out what they were up to and shouted to Old Abe, but I doubt he could hear me for all the gunfire."

"Dear Lord!" a woman said. "You can't mean . . ."

"Afraid I can," McPike said. "I was maybe seventy yards away, yet I felt it when the mine went up. The ground shook under me so bad I could hardly stand. What was left of Abe's buildings came down in splinters, those bastards used so much powder." He took a breath. "Old Abe was blown to smithereens."

A hush descended, anger and revulsion marking every person.

Lee was mystified. So far Kemp had carefully avoided killing anyone. Had Old Abe's death been a mistake? Or was it a part of the cattle baron's grand scheme? After all, killing Jim Hays had been deliberate, and Hays and Howard were two of Kemp's most vocal critics.

Will Dryer, the head of the homesteaders, was a brave enough man, but with Hays and Howard gone, Dryer would be like a gnat trying to topple a grizzly. Just as Kemp, in all likelihood, had planned.

A miner climbed onto the bar. "Listen! There's more than enough of us here to teach those Regulators a lesson. I say we mount up and go after them."

"I say you're loco," replied another. "Didn't you listen to the marshal? We're not gun hands."

David Robbins

"Where is that Texan?" someone demanded. "Why ain't he doing something?"

"Haven't your heard?" the bartender, always a fount of gossip, responded. "His filly was shot. She'll live, they say, but Evers is over to the doc's, and he's not budging until she comes around."

"Wonderful! We're being blown to bits right and left, and our illustrious lawman can't tear himself away from some stupid whore!"

The remark was uncalled for, and Lee was prepared to say as much when a hand tapped his left elbow and he glanced around, startled to discover none other than Frank Lowe right beside him, alone.

"We need to talk, Scurlock," Lowe said.

Before Lee could respond, an enraged bellow tore from the throat of Ike Shannon, who shot past like a human bull gone amok. Grabbing the front of Frank Lowe's white shirt, Shannon slammed the short saloon owner against the wall.

Judging by Lowe's dumbfounded expression, he'd had no idea the Irishman was there. Entering, he had seen Lee near the door and gone over, neglecting to look around first.

Shannon was aglow with raw bloodlust. Shoving the shotgun into Lowe's gut, he propelled Lowe toward the doors. Lee went along, shaking his head at several onlookers who looked as if they were about to interfere.

Outside, the gambler pushed Lowe around a corner into a narrow alley between the Applejack and a dance hall. Uttering lusty oaths, Shannon shoved the other man against the wall.

"We need to talk!" Frank Lowe found his voice at last. He squirmed and reached to grip Shannon's wrist, freezing when the gambler thumbed back the hammers on the scattergun.

"All you need is a pine box, bastard!"

Lowe wriggled like a snake about to have its head staved in. "Wait! Wait!" he pleaded. "You've got to hear me out! It's important!"

"You miserable son of a bitch!" Shannon snarled. "Stand straight and take your medicine like a man. We have nothing to talk about, not after what you did to Vint's woman."

"That's wasn't my doing!"

"Liar!" Shannon roared, his arm tensing. He drove the shotgun into Lowe's stomach with such force that Lowe turned a sickly green and doubled over, sputtering, spittle dribbling from his mouth.

"I'm going to enjoy this," Ike Shannon said, taking a step back and leveling the greener.

Frank Lowe cast a silent appeal at the southerner, but if he was expecting the Tennessean to intervene, one look was enough to convince him that he would get no sympathy from that quarter. Sucking in air, he blurted two words, the only two that could have saved his life: "Allister Kemp!"

Shannon paused, raising his chin. "What about him?"

"He made me beat Nelly!"

"You lying sack of—"

"It true!" Lowe said shrilly. "Honest! Jesse Bodine and him came to my place late that night and Kemp told me to beat her silly or I'd answer to Bodine."

Doubt and suspicion smoldered in Ike's breast. "What kind of rotten game are you playing now? Why would Allister Kemp want Nelly Rosell harmed?"

"To get at Evers."

It was plausible, and it gave Ike further pause. "Talk, you four-flusher, and it had better be good."

Lowe nodded slowly, catching his breath, his arms pressed to his midriff. "All I ask is that you listen to what I've got to say. Then, if you still want to shoot me, be my guest."

"I'll give you one minute," Shannon said. "Convince me by then and you get to live."

Paling, the saloon owner talked quickly. "Kemp has gone plumb loco. He intends to drive the homesteaders *and* the prospectors out of Diablo Valley, and he doesn't give a damn whether the town is still here or not when he's all through."

"Tell us something we don't know," Ike said.

"The Englishman's crazy, I tell you! Stark raving mad. He's posted a bounty on Evers and Scurlock—"

Shannon cut him short. "We know that too." The shotgun gleamed as he pointed it at Lowe's face. "You have about thirty seconds left, mister."

Lowe licked his thin lips, staring in open fear at the twin barrels. "Do you also know why Kemp posted bounties on the Texan and the Reb, but not on you?"

Despite himself, Shannon became interested. "I've been wondering about that," he admitted.

"Kemp wants your friend Evers dead because he figures that Evers and Old Abe were in cahoots."

It was Lee who responded. "That's loco. Old Abe didn't trust Vint Evers any more than he did Kemp."

"Really?" Lowe snickered. "Well, Kemp saw it the other way. He figured that since Abe and Will Dryer voted to appoint Evers town marshal, they had to be working together."

"What else could they do, with Bodine the only other candidate?" Lee said. The revelation disturbed him more than he let on. Old Abe had detested the Texan, had even believed Evers would be partial to Kemp. And all the while, the Englishman thought the reverse. Both condemned the lawman without cause. Ironically, Vint's only interest had been in enforcing the laws enacted by the town council to the best of his ability.

"As for Nelly," Lowe said to the gambler, "Kemp wanted to prod your pard into being careless. He hoped that it would drive Evers over the edge, maybe turn everyone against him."

As devious as Allister Kemp had proven to be, Shannon had to admit that the plan sounded like something Kemp would cook up. "But he put you in the line of fire," he noted skeptically.

"Do you think he cares?" Lowe snapped. "That damn Englishman doesn't give a hoot about me, or about anyone other than himself. We're like the pieces in that game he likes to play, chess. He moves us around as he sees fit." Pausing, Lowe glanced at Lee. "Actually, there is one other person he's fond of. That filly of yours."

Icy fingers clawed at Lee's innards. "Allison Hays?"

Lowe nodded. "I guess he had big plans for her, and he became rattler mean when you came along and took her away from him."

"She was never his to begin with," Lee said.

"I know that, and you know that, but try telling it to him." Lowe shook as if cold. "Kemp is so far gone, he's not in his right mind. He put a bounty on you, Scurlock, because he wants you out of the way so he can move in on your girl."

"And me?" Ike asked.

"He told me that you're not worth the bother of a bounty," Lowe replied. "He called you an overrated nuisance."

"He did, did he?"

Some of Lowe's smug assurance had returned. Holding his arms out from his sides, he said, "Look, I took my life into my hands coming to see you. If Kemp finds out, I'm a dead man. So why don't you lower that scattergun before it accidentally goes off."

Shannon did no such thing. "Why are you being so helpful all of a sudden?"

"Because I want out of this mess in one piece. Kemp doesn't have any interest in the silver up in those mountains. It doesn't matter to him that the homesteaders south of here aren't really trespassing on his range. All that he thinks about is driving everyone, and I mean *everyone*, from *his* valley."

Lowe swore. "Hell, he's even turned on me, and I was supposed to be his business partner, to run the Applejack and our other ventures. But it turns out he doesn't care one whit about them, either." His jaw muscles twitched. "If that jackass drives all the homesteaders and the miners out, this town will turn into a ghost. I'll be flat broke in no time."

Lee stroked his chin. Lowe appeared to be sincere, and he was inclined to take the man at his word. Allister Kemp certainly had no need to accumulate more wealth. The baron was set for life. And if Kemp truly did see the valley as his and his alone, Lowe's story explained everything.

Ike Shannon was still not satisfied. "Why'd you come to us?"

"I don't want to be looking over my shoulder the rest of my life. I want to set things right with Evers and you. I know the Texan won't rest until he's hunted me down and paid me back. I want to make amends."

Reluctantly, Ike lowered the shotgun. Lowe made sense, but it irked him to have to be civil when he'd rather shove the scattergun down Lowe's throat and squeeze both triggers.

Lee saw a chance to glean more information. "How many Regulators does Kemp have riding for him? What does he plan to do now that he's driven the miners out?"

Frank Lowe began to speak, then froze, gawking

at the alley entrance, immobilized by shock. He
started as if he had seen a ghost and backed up, his
hands outspread as if to ward off a blow or a bullet.

Lee and Shannon whirled.

Death stalked Diablo. Death with seething gray
eyes, hatred chiseled in his sunburned features.
Death with black curls ringing his ears, and a black
sombrero pulled low. His hands were a heartbeat
from the smooth ivory butts of his pistols. "Stand
aside," Vint Evers said, his tone the peal of doom for
the man trying to wither into the wall.

Lee did as the Texan wanted. But the Irishman
stood firm, moving between the lawman and the saloon owner.

"Didn't you hear me?" Vint Evers said.

"I'm not budging," the gambler responded.

Ordinarily the Texan might have asked why. Now
he yelled violently, "Out of the way, Ike!"

"I can't allow you to kill him."

Vint Evers quivered with the intensity of his hatred. His elbows crooked. "You can't stop me!" he
raged, and his lethal hands swooped down.

Chapter Twenty-Two

Sunlight sparkled on the gleaming Colts as they sprang clear. Two hammers were thumbed back, two fingers curled around hair triggers. The barrels were pointed at Ike Shannon, who stood his ground without flinching, without fear. "Would you kill me to get at him?"

Conflicting emotions racked Vint Evers. He had never wanted to shoot anyone as much as he wanted to shoot Frank Lowe. A tiny voice screamed in his brain, *Kill!* But he held his fire, baffled and hurt. "Are you sidin' with this lowlife?"

"You know different," Ike said.

"Then what in the hell has gotten into you?"

Unease gnawed at Lee Scurlock. He felt that he should do something, but he also felt that he had no business meddling. This was between the gambler and the lawman and no one else.

Ike advanced to place a hand on his friend's shoulder. "If I let you fill him with holes, you'll step over that line you're always talking about. The line that separates lawmen from outlaws, citizens from cutthroats."

"He beat Nelly!"

"Yes, he did. And if anyone ever deserved to be planted, it's Lowe. But I know you better than any man alive, Vint. I know you'd never live this down. You'd never forgive yourself. Your days as a lawman would be numbered. It would destroy everything you've worked so hard to build up."

"So?" Vint said, but the spark of rampage had died and his wide shoulders sagged.

"So we're pards. I can't stand still while you throw your life away. Whether you agree or not, I'm doing what's best for you."

Vint lowered the Colts, but he made it a point not to look at Frank Lowe. He was afraid the mere sight would inflame him again.

"How is Nelly, by the way?" Lee asked.

"What?" Vint responded, the question derailing his whole train of thought. "Oh, Franklyn says she'll be up and about in a day or two. She came around an hour ago. The sawbones shooed me out so she could get some sleep."

"As soon as she's able, we're moving her to the Delonys'," Lee said. "I've talked to Bob and Ethel, and they're happy to have her."

Heartfelt gratitude choked the tall Texan.

"Are you calm enough now to hear what Lowe has to say?" Ike asked.

"I reckon."

Nervously, Frank Lowe came forward, but he did not fool anyone by standing slightly behind Ike Shannon. He finished with a surprising statement. "To prove myself, I'll help you turn the tables on Allister Kemp."

"How?" Vint asked.

"Simple. I happen to know where the Englishman will be at nine o'clock tonight. All you have to do is be there first, wait for him to show, and he's yours."

"And you expect us to trust you?" Vint's remark dripped cynicism.

Lowe grinned. "What choice do you have?"

Promptly at eight-thirty four grim figures emerged from the Applejack and walked northward along streets strangely quiet for once. Gone was the boisterous, rowdy, pulsing vigor that made Diablo so unique. In its place was a thickly somber atmosphere, reminding Lee of a wake. His hands rested on his pistols as he surveyed the false fronts and frame buildings.

"I don't see why I have to come along," Frank Lowe complained for the tenth time. "I've already done my part. Kemp expects to meet me at nine on Boot Hill. You be there instead, and finish it."

Vint Evers was a few steps in the lead, his wary tread that of a sleek panther on the prowl. "Kemp will be lookin' for you. If you're not there, it might make him suspicious."

"In the dark he'll never notice."

The lawman did not break stride. "You're comin', and that's final."

Lee Scurlock inhaled the muggy twilight air. It was spooky, he mused, so many empty streets. Rumor had it a lot of homesteaders and miners were calling it quits, that by tomorrow night fully a third of them would have packed up what few belongings they still owned, and left.

Will Dryer wanted to send a delegation to the territorial governor to plead for troops. While the idea had merit, other farmers and prospectors were against it. They did not want the federal government to get involved. As one pocket hunter put it, "Anytime they stick their noses in, everything goes to hell."

At Cedar Street a commotion caught their attention. A small crowd had gathered on the bank of the river.

"What the deuce is that all about?" Ike Shannon wondered.

"Let's drift on down and find out," Vint proposed. "We have a few minutes to spare."

A storekeeper spotted the lawmen when they were a block away. Dozens rushed to meet them, yells mingling in chorus: "Take a look at this, Marshal! Weirdest thing you ever did see! What do you make of it?"

The cause was the Diablo River. Something was drastically wrong. The river was ten feet narrower and half as deep. The robust current had tapered to a creeping snail's pace.

"Well, dog my cats!" Vint Evers exclaimed, bewildered. During the height of the dry season the river was known to shrink some, but never like this.

"Is it drying up, you reckon?" Shannon asked.

Lee Scurlock had no answer. It was unnatural. For some reason it filled him with vague foreboding. Nor was he the only one.

"This is an omen," an onlooker declared. "A bad sign of things to come."

Frank Lowe laughed. "What a bunch of yaks! By tomorrow morning the river will be its normal self."

No one disputed him, but Lee saw the glances thrown at Lowe when the saloon owner wasn't looking. As they trekked back up the street, strung out in a row so they could watch both sides and adjoining roofs, Lee commented, "Seasonal rivers and creeks dry up all the time, but the Diablo is year-round. Mighty queer."

"How can you go on about the stupid river at a

time like this?" Frank Lowe groused.

Vint Evers was tired of the turncoat's constant carping. "Seems to me you're a mite spooked," he said.

"Can you blame me? I could get myself killed helping you out. If something goes wrong, Kemp will have me strung up by my thumbs and flayed alive."

"Now, that would be a pity," Vint said with a smirk. The temporary truce grated on his nerves. His deepest desire was to punish those responsible for Nelly's being shot, and Lowe was near the top of the list.

The man did not know how to shut up. "I want the truth, Evers. Do you still aim to come gunning for me after you've corralled Kemp?"

"I haven't made up my mind yet."

"That's hardly fair."

The lawman regarded the dapper polecat coolly. "Count your blessin's. So long as you're still breathin', you don't have anything to complain about."

Lee took perverse delight in the glum expression Frank Lowe wore. It served the man right. He scrutinized the buildings ahead, especially shadowy doors and murky windows where gunmen might lurk.

In front of a general store a farmer and his family were busy loading supplies into a wagon. They would be one of the first to leave in the morning.

At the next intersection Vint bore to the right, deliberately staying in the middle of the street. "Let me hear your story again, Lowe," he said, more to annoy their unhappy ally than from any lack of memory.

"I've already gone through it twice."

"Then what's one more?" Ike Shannon prompted.

Lowe sighed. "Kemp sent word he wants to meet me at Boot Hill. The cowboy who relayed the message did not know why. It probably has something to do with our business holdings."

"Why didn't Kemp just ask you to ride out to his ranch?" Vint asked. "Why would he put himself at risk by coming into town?"

"What risk?" Lowe countered. "He'll have Bodine and some of his hands along, and they're loyal to the brand. As for your other question, he never had me out to his ranch before, so why should he start now?"

More quiet blocks fell behind them. Ike Shannon sidled over to the Texan. "What are your intentions if Kemp does show?"

"We'll try to take him alive and place him under arrest."

The gambler leaned closer. The brim of the lawman's hat concealed the upper half of his face. Ike had no clue whether Evers was being sincere. "You're not fixing to kill him?"

"Why do you sound surprised? You're the one who doesn't want me to cross the line." Vint tapped his badge. "I'm a lawman, Ike. It's what I do best. It's what I've always done, and what I'll do until the day I drop. And so long as I am, I must honor the law I serve. You reminded me of that fact."

"What are pards for?"

Vint smiled wryly. "You have more confidence in me than I do." He paused. "As for you, Lee, you did me a favor, too. I'd about decided that wearin' a badge wasn't worth the price I had to pay. That I was wastin' my life fightin' other people's fights. Then we helped those homesteaders, and I saw that we do make a difference."

A wistful longing to have his brother there at that exact moment stirred Lee deeply. Doc would be extremely proud. His being a deputy might lessen Doc's disappointment over the killing in Fort Sumner. Which reminded him—it wouldn't be long before the men who were hunting him showed up in Diablo. If he was smart, he'd get out of there before they did. But how could he just ride off? He had Allison to think of.

Fewer and fewer buildings lined the streets. Twilight had given way to night, and a myriad of stars glowed on high. A stiff breeze from the northwest rustled the trees, the grass, and the dust. Inky patches alternated with areas of lighter shadow.

Rearing up out of the earth like a primeval beast, Boot Hill loomed ahead. Starkly silhouetted against the background of heavenly lights, it resembled a monstrous squat toad about to pounce. Scraggy trees dotted the slope like a legion of spindly scarecrows. Everywhere were graves, mound after mound of raw earth. Many were unmarked, many more bore crude crosses, a few boasted headstones. A few reddish boulders added a touch of color.

In every last boomtown west of the Mississippi, in every cowtown on the Plains, was a special graveyard usually near the town limits. Buried there were the social outcasts, the countless unfortunates who died penniless or whose relatives were unknown.

Anonymous drifters, sodden drunks, wild cowboys, and deadly gunmen, dying in droves, buried with no markers or anyone to mourn them. Nameless victims of their own greed or lust or pride, they were the forgotten men.

Often, when a boomtown failed, when the gold or silver played out or the cattle started using an alternate trail, the dead were completely abandoned. The earthen mounds were worn by erosion, the crude crosses faded and cracked, and nature reclaimed the swatch of dirt man dared disturb.

Lee wiped his forehead as they neared the gloomy slope. Arizona in July was a scorcher; the heat had lingered. Or were his own nerves to blame?

Vint Evers halted at the base of the hill. "I reckon

this is far enough," he announced. They had to fan out. Once their trap was sprung, it would be his job to make sure that Kemp did not escape.

"There aren't many places to hide," Ike Shannon observed. The lay of the land did not suit him. Should the Bar K outfit show up in force, the cowboys would ride right over them.

Frank Lowe, for once, agreed with the gambler. "You can't stop here," he stated.

"Why not?" Vint asked.

Lowe pointed at a small bald clearing at the very top. "Kemp wants to meet me up yonder. All of you will be too far away to protect me if you stay down at the bottom." He opened his jacket to emphasize that he was not armed. "Remember, Evers, you wouldn't let me tote a six-shooter."

Lee shifted to scour their vicinity. Thanks to the pale starlight, he could see well enough to satisfy himself that gunmen were not sneaking up on them.

Vint gestured for Lowe to precede him. "Lead the way, then, mister. I'll be right behind you." To the gambler and the Tennessean he said, "Find a spot to lay low until Kemp gets here."

"Like hell," the Irishman said. "Where you go, pard, we go."

The Texan knew it would be futile to object. Lowe led them on up the slope, as nervous as a mouse in a barn full of cats. Dry grass crunched underfoot, spurs jingled softly.

Grave after grave lined their climb. Lee tried not to think of the grisly skeletons and decomposing bodies that surrounded them. Even so, the short hairs at the nape of his neck prickled.

It was childish, Lee told himself. Here he was, a grown man, scared to be in a cemetery after dark. Next thing he knew, he'd need Allison to tuck him into bed at night and hold his hand until he fell asleep.

Halfway up, Frank Lowe stopped. Apprehension had made him a nervous wreck. "Look, I've done my share," he said to Evers. "Let me go while I still can. Kemp will have me shot out of sheer spite if there's gunplay."

"How many times must I tell you?" Vint responded. "Tramp on up there and stand in the open where Kemp can see you from afar. Then leave the rest to us."

Sulking, Lowe complied.

Vint indicated gravestones on either side. "The two of you lay low. I'll keep watch on our bantam rooster until the lead commences to fly."

"We'll stick with you," Ike said.

"No." This time the Texan's tone made it plain that he would not abide another dispute. "By spreadin' out, we can catch 'em between us. Give yourselves breathin' space and everything will be fine."

Lee watched the lanky lawman climb higher. A string of whispered profanity came from the irate gambler. Edging toward a marker on the left, he unconsciously loosened both revolvers. "We'd better do as he says."

"You can if you want," Ike said. "But I don't trust that pimp. Vint trusts him even less. So what's he trying to prove by leaving us behind?" He continued to ascend.

So did Lee, but more slowly. It was the worst possible time to buck the marshal, and he'd rather do as they were told. Though he did wonder. Why had Evers gone on alone? Did the Texan smell a trap and intend to walk into it alone?

Shannon peered into the black patches that bordered the nearest graves, alert for movement.

Lee did the same, feeling as if he were a steel

spring about to uncoil. Frank Lowe and the marshal were now fifteen feet from the crescent rim. Suddenly the lawman stopped.

Eleven men had risen from concealment on the other side of the hill's crown, eleven smirking Bar K hands, all with six-guns adorning their hips. In the center reared Jesse Bodine, alight with triumph. Bodine looked down on the Texan like a wolf about to pounce on prey.

"Evenin', Evers."

"Bodine," Vint said calmly enough, then regarded the cowboys with cool indifference. "See you brought a few of your friends along."

"We caught you nappin', huh?" Bodine gloated.

"My eyes were wide open."

"Then why did you march on up here?" Jesse Bodine asked. "Surely you weren't thinkin' there would only be one or two of us?"

Vint ignored the question. "Kemp sure is workin' you boys to death. What with scarin' off the homesteaders, blowin' up the silver claims, and dammin' the river—"

"Doin' what?" Bodine said, perplexed. "We ain't touched the river. I saw it was low on the way over, but we had nothin' to do with that."

"Did you have anything to do with Old Abe being blown to kingdom come?"

"Of course not. Some of the boys got carried away when the old geezer shot their pards."

Vint Evers looked past the cowboys. "Where's your boss, Jesse? He's supposed to meet Lowe here."

The statement produced amusement, even laughter, among the Bar K riders. Bodine chuckled and looped his thumbs in his gunbelt. "Is he, now?"

"So I was told."

"Well, you shouldn't believe everything you hear," Bodine said, then winked at Frank Lowe, who walked to the pinnacle and placed himself at Bodine's elbow.

Lee Scurlock halted, fuming. Allister Kemp had used Lowe to lure them to Boot Hill. The townsfolk never came to the cemetery at night, so Kemp could have them disposed of without interference or witnesses. Once they were out of the way, there would be no one left in Diablo who had the grit to stand up to the Englishman.

Frank Lowe was upset. He gestured at Vint, Ike, and Lee. "Quit your gabbin' and dispose of these idiots like you were supposed to," he growled.

"What's your rush?" Bodine responded.

"This isn't no turkey shoot," Lowe said testily.

"And you're not the man I work for," Bodine said just as hotly.

Lowe did not back down. Stabbing a finger at the massive gunman, he said, "Why haven't you done as you were ordered? What in God's name are you waiting for?"

Bodine plainly disliked his dapper ally. In his anger he seemed to forget about the three men below; his own finger jabbed Lowe in the chest so hard that Lowe nearly fell. "Leave my job to me, mister."

"Then do it!" Lowe demanded shrilly. "Kemp ordered you to pick them off before they knew what hit them, but you let them waltz clear on up the hill. That's not doing your job, in my book."

Jesse Bodine straightened. "I'm not a yellow bushwhacker like some I could name," he said. "I don't gun men down from ambush."

"Then you're the biggest jackass who—"

The sound of Bodine's open hand connecting with Frank Lowe's cheek was like the crack of a whip. Lowe staggered and dropped to one knee, stunned.

"Are you heeled, you miserable pipsqueak?" Bod-

ine said, his hands hovering above the butts of his
.44s.

Wrath brought Frank Lowe to his feet, and had he
been armed he would have torn into Bodine like a
terrier into a mastiff. Making a visible effort to control himself, he said, "Kemp will hear about this."

"Who the hell cares?" Bodine said. "I don't answer
to him for every little thing I do." The big gunman
nodded at the lawmen. "As for them, I'll do what
Kemp wants, but I'll do it *my* way. You might be the
kind of low-down skulkin' bastard who would back-
shoot his own mother, but I'm not."

Frank Lowe had nothing more to say. Fists
clenched, he started to back off.

"That's right," Bodine said. "Why don't you mosey
along and go play with your painted ladies? Leave
the real work for those of us with backbone."

The instant that Lowe disappeared, a heightened
air of tension crackled invisibly on Boot Hill. Slowly,
almost ponderously, Jesse Bodine turned to Vint Evers. "Now, where were we?"

Vint shifted to the right a step so he was directly
in line with the other Texan. "You were about to ride
out of the valley and never come back."

Bodine laughed heartily. "Were we, now? I reckon
I must have forgot."

"There's no need for this," Vint tried one last time.

When Jesse Bodine responded, the mockery was
gone. "I'd like to oblige, Evers. I truly would. But
Kemp is offerin' a thousand dollars to the hombre
who cuts you down, and that's going to be me."

"Since when do men like us stoop to killin' for
money?"

Bodine was troubled, and it showed. "I've never
had a thousand dollars at one time in my whole life.
And there's this small spread up in Wyoming I've had
my heart set on."

"I see." Vint shrugged, then grinned faintly. "Well, Texas always did breed men."

Bodine nodded. "It's fitting this way."

The time for words had passed. Lee Scurlock tensed. He realized his mouth was dry, his palms moist. In the next few moments he might well die. He'd never wed Allison, never experience the joy of being her husband and rearing a family with her.

Like everyone else, Lee was riveted to the two Texans, awaiting the flash of movement that would determine his whole future. Or lack of it.

Chapter Twenty-Three

Seldom did gunfighters of the caliber of Evers and Bodine go up against one another. Both were confirmed man-killers, both were accurate even under fire, both were rattler-quick on the draw.

Seasoned gunhands liked to say that speed was second in importance to hitting what a man aimed at. But in this instance, since Bodine and Evers could shoot the head off a nail at ten paces without hardly trying, accuracy was a given. It was sheer speed that would decide the outcome. Whoever drew first stood to come out on top.

For a breathless span of seconds no one moved, no one spoke, no one seemed to breathe.

Then Jesse Bodine broke the spell by streaking his hands at his big revolvers. Vint Evers did likewise. And although Vint went for his guns a shade of a heartbeat after Bodine did, the two men cleared leather at the exact same moment and four pistols boomed in thunderous unison.

If Lee had blinked, he would have missed it. He saw both men sway. Leathery tough, neither went down. Both leveled their pistols again, but it was Vint Evers who banged off two shots first and Jesse Bodine who was jolted onto his heels and toppled like a mighty oak in a forest.

Even as Bodine fell, Ike Shannon vented a roar and rushed up the slope. He shot wide of Vint Evers in order not to catch the lawman in the spray of buckshot. His first blast flung two Bar K hands to the earth, both ripped and bleeding profusely.

The rest of the cowboys galvanized into action, clawing for irons, firing as fast as they could.

A leaden hornet buzzed Lee as he entered the fray. His pistols molded to his palms and he brought them into play. He sent two slugs into the gunman who had nearly taken his head off, two more into a cowboy taking aim at Vint Evers.

Gunfire boomed like thunder, rolling off across the flatland below. By now all the Bar K riders were shooting and dodging and shooting again.

Vint Evers rotated to the right and placed a bullet squarely in the sternum of a hefty cowboy, who then stumbled into a companion.

Farther down the line a scarred gunman had eyes only for the tall Texan. Skipping forward so he would have a clear shot, he fanned his Remington three times. At least one slug hit home, because Vint Evers stumbled and went to his left knee. The lawman raised his right arm to return fire, but someone beat him to it.

Ike Shannon saw his friend go down. Bellowing in rage, the Irishman charged past Vint, placing himself in the line of fire. The scarred gunman fanned another shot that missed. Shannon emptied his scattergun, and at that range the buckshot nearly tore the shooter in half.

The marshal was down. The gambler's gun had gone empty. Only Lee Scurlock had loaded weapons and was in any position to protect them. And protect them he did. Sprinting up the slope, he fired to the right and left, his pistols cracking in steady cadence.

Lee did not think about what he was doing. He did not consciously pick his targets. Self-preservation spurred him into firing on pure instinct, first at a Bar K hand to the left, then at another to the right, and then he whirled and squeezed off two shots at a lean cowboy who had clipped his hat. Pivoting, he saw a scruffy gunman pointing a pistol in his direction. His Colt hammered, adding a new nostril to the man's face.

Suddenly the firing ceased. Lee realized that it had, but in his razor-tense state he did not equate the quiet with a cause. He spun from side to side, seeking new threats, his fingers literally itching to pull the trigger.

"It's over, laddie. They played their hand and lost. You can relax."

It took a bit for Ike Shannon's remark to register. Lee looked at his Colts, then at the bodies littering Boot Hill. Finally it sunk in. Every last Bar K hand was down, most of them dead, a few moving weakly, a few convulsing. Dark stains framed many. A thick haze born of gun smoke partially shrouded the slaughter.

Near the center, Jesse Bodine stirred. He sat up, his cocked revolvers still in his hands.

Lee swung toward him. Ike Shannon whipped out a pistol. But Vint Evers looked up and called out, "Don't shoot! He's done for."

Bodine, oddly enough, smiled. "That I am," he admitted, and coughed. Blood seeped from his mouth and nose. "You shot me to pieces, damn your bones," he said to Evers with no malice at all.

"I tried my best," Vint said.

Jesse Bodine slumped forward but managed to lift his head. "Too bad we didn't meet a long time ago. You would have done to ride the river with."

It was the highest compliment any man could pay another. Bodine raised his glazing gaze to the multitude of sparkling stars, said, "They're so pretty, ain't they?" and pitched onto his face.

Ike Shannon slowly lowered his pistol. "Let's get you to the sawbones, Vint. How bad are you hit?"

There was no answer. The gambler and the southerner turned, to see Vint Evers lying stone cold on the dry grass.

The parlor in Doctor Franklyn's house served as his waiting room on occasion. Lee Scurlock sat in a rocking chair, hands folded, while Ike Shannon paced back and forth, making a shambles of his hat, which he kept crushing as if it were soaked and he had to wring the water out.

"How much longer can it take?" the Irishman complained, as he had every five minutes for the past half hour.

Lee was thinking of Allison, of how she would feel if he were the one under Doc Franklyn's knife instead of Vint Evers. He fingered his badge and came to a decision. Once Allister Kemp was dealt with, his days as a lawman were over. He had no hankering to put Allison through what Nelly Rosell was going through.

"Lowe and Kemp," Ike Shannon said. "If it's the last thing I ever do, I'm making wolf meat of both of them."

Lee stirred. "Kemp won't dare try anything else for a while. He's lost almost half his men already, and the word on the street is that a lot of others have lit a shuck for healthier climates."

"They're the smart ones."

A glance at the grandfather clock showed Lee that it was close to three in the morning. Evers had been in there for over five hours.

From behind the heavy green curtain that separated the parlor from the physician's work area came subdued voices and the occasional metallic clatter of instruments.

Lee yawned and stretched. No wonder he felt so tired. He wondered if Allison had stayed up to await his return. Mrs. Franklyn had kindly conveyed word to her when she went to fetch Nelly. Knowing Allison as well as he did, he wouldn't be surprised if—

The green curtain rattled to one side. Doc Franklyn wore a white apron spattered with scarlet. His hands and forearms were red to the elbows. New lines had been added to his seamed face, and he rubbed his eyes as he stepped out.

Lee was more interested in the figure lying on a large table. Bandages covered the Texan's chest and left shoulder; his eyes were closed, his chest rising and falling rhythmically.

Beyond the table sat Nelly, a white strip looped around her head. She held Vint's hand in hers, tears pouring down her cheeks, her eyes glistening with love and gratitude as well as the tears.

Shannon moved to meet the doctor. "Give it to us straight. Will he pull through?"

Doc Franklyn nodded wearily. "Your friend will live. Mind you, he won't be throwing a gun for months. He'll have to take it easy at first, with plenty of bed rest." Pausing, he indicated Nelly and spoke softly. "Her devotion is quite remarkable. She watched the entire operation without flinching. I daresay Mr. Evers will recover remarkably fast with her for inspiration."

"Vint will live," Shannon said almost under his breath. The next moment he groaned and keeled over.

Lee was nearest. Automatically, he leaped up and caught hold of the gambler before Shannon could strike the floor. His right hand made contact with a warm, sticky substance. When he pulled it back, it was slick with blood. "What in the world?" he blurted.

"He took a slug too?" Doc Franklyn exclaimed, as amazed as the Tennessean. "Why didn't you let me know sooner?"

"He never said a word," Lee replied. Together, they carried Shannon into the operating area and set him down on a sofa across from the table.

The doctor shook his head. "The darned fool. What was he thinking of?"

Lee knew the answer to that. Shannon always thought of Vint Evers first, always placed the Texan's welfare before his own. So even though Ike had been hit, he had kept it a secret until assured that Evers would live. The depth of their friendship was something to admire.

Franklyn stepped to a washbasin. "I want you to go home, young man," he told Lee. "I can tell that you're exhausted, and there's nothing more you can do here."

"But—"

"Please, I'm too tired myself to waste breath arguing. I'll send word as soon as I've ascertained Shannon's condition."

Nelly was staring at the Irishman. "How many more?" she asked no one in particular. "How many more before it's all over?"

Neither Lee nor Franklyn answered. Lee bade

them good night and departed, hurrying through the unusually silent town.

Diablo was as quiet and empty as Boot Hill. A drunk snored on a bench. A prospector and a dove walked arm in arm to the west, toward a cheap hotel.

Lee paused to take a deep breath of the cool night air. So much had happened in so short a time that he'd not had a chance to unwind since the day before. It was hard to believe that in a few short hours dawn would paint the eastern horizon pink.

The sudden drumming of hooves—many, many hooves—brought Lee around in a crouch. For a few seconds he thought that the Regulators had returned in force, although why they would approach from the east instead of the west escaped him.

The stark glare of light from an upstairs window played over a column of men, over their dusty uniforms and the banner one of their number held. Sabers rattled. Accoutrements clattered.

Lee blinked a few times, confounded. A tall officer at the head of the cavalry detachment spotted him and angled across the deserted street.

"Company, halt!"

The command must have woke up everyone within ten blocks. The officer stared at the Tennessean's badge and asked, "Are you Marshal Evers, by any chance?"

"I'm a deputy," Lee clarified, trying to count the troopers. It was hopeless. The file extended clear to the river. "Evers took three bullets. He's over to Doc Franklyn's—"

"The marshal, shot?" the officer declared. "Well, then, we've arrived in the nick of time." Removing a gauntlet, he swatted dust from his sleeve. "I'm Major Whittaker."

"Major."

"We've ridden day and night to get here. Let me

assure you that we will bring a quick end to the hostilities. The governor is aware of the disturbance and sent us to quell it."

Lee could scarcely credit his ears. The worst was over. Kemp's reign of terror was at an end. "How did you get here so fast? Did Will Dryer send word?"

Whittaker cocked his head. "Dryer? No, I don't recollect that name. A rancher named Allister Kemp dispatched a rider three days ago."

A lightning bolt could not have shocked Lee Scurlock more. "Three days ago?" he repeated.

"Mr. Kemp reported that a state of total anarchy exists here," Major Whittaker said. "Rogue bands of out-of-work miners have been terrorizing law-abiding citizens. Armed squatters have taken over part of Kemp's range. Bands of assassins have slain community leaders." The officer wagged a finger at the southerner. "I'm surprised that Marshal Evers didn't send word himself. This crisis is more than civil authorities can deal with."

"Kemp contacted the governor," Lee said, dazed by the implications.

"Didn't you know that Mr. Kemp and Governor Fremont are the best of friends?" Major Whittaker slipped his hand into the gauntlet. "Relay my regards to the marshal. Tell him—" The officer stopped as if struck by a thought. "Evers *will* live, won't he?"

"Yes."

"Excellent." The officer beamed. "Well, I can't dally. I'm under strict orders to reach Kemp's ranch without delay. I was told the Bar K is due west of Diablo. Is that correct?"

"You can't miss it," Lee promised.

"Thank you. As soon as we've verified that Mr. Kemp is safe, we'll be back to put Diablo under martial law." Major Whittaker rose in the saddle and hiked his arm. "Company, hooooooooo!"

Diablo

Lee stepped to the boardwalk and watched pair after pair of tired blue-clad soldiers trot by. The governor had sent enough to quell an Apache uprising.

Only when the last of the column melted into the darkness west of town did Lee bend his steps toward the Delony house. A terrible melancholy gripped his soul, mixed with spurts of baffled fury that brought lurid profanity to his lips.

Allister Kemp had won. The Englishman had outwitted them at every turn, had been one step ahead of them from the very beginning. No, make that *five* steps ahead.

Based on what the major had said, Lee guessed that Kemp had sent word to the territorial capital at Prescott asking for military help *before* he attacked the homesteaders and miners, claiming they were the ones to blame. The swift raids by the Regulators had been intended to uproot Kemp's enemies before the cavalry got there.

Since Kemp was a close friend of Fremont's, and since it had been Kemp who reported the "disturbance," the governor would naturally favor Kemp's version of events.

The man was the devil incarnate.

Sighing, Lee tilted his head back to relieve stiffness in his neck. Soon he spied the Delony house, a glowing square marking the parlor. Allison must still be up. He hurried, eager for her company.

In his eagerness and his fatigue Lee failed to hear the stealthy pad of feet behind him until they were right at his heels. Instantly he whirled, or started to, when immensely strong arms encircled his chest and arms. He was lifted bodily from the ground as if he weighed no more than a sack of grain. Stale breath laced with liquor huffed over his face. A voice that grated like metal rending metal snarled in his ear.

"Now I've got you, bastard!"

An iron knee drove up between Lee's legs. Excruciating pain exploded in his groin. He tried to grab a pistol, but his assailant shook him as a giant might a dwarf, shook him so that his teeth crunched together and his head swam. Then he was flung brutally to the ground.

"This is for my brother!"

A boot thudded into Lee's ribs, nearly caving them in. Pinpoints of light spun and danced before his eyes. He looked up but could not see the man's face for the shimmering fireflies.

"Nate Collins got word to me," the apish apparition said. Another vicious kick doubled Lee in half. "You shouldn't've killed Ed. No one does that to a Gristy and lives to brag about it."

Beset by a stifling fog of torment, Lee realized that his attacker was Ed Gristy's kin. A boot caught him in the back, flaring his spine with exquisite anguish. The man seemed intent on stomping him to death. Unless he did something, and did it quickly, he would never set eyes on Allison again.

Marshaling every ounce of strength in his steel-spring body, Lee lashed out with both legs. That he connected was borne out by the sharp snap that punctuated the blow and the crash of a heavy body beside him.

Fiery oaths filled the air. "Damn you, you nearly busted my knee!" Gristy roared.

Hands made of granite closed on Lee's throat. Fingers that could twist tree limbs apart gouged into his windpipe. Lee thrashed backward, batting at wrists as stout as oaks. Gristy sprang, straddling his chest, pinning him flat.

"Die, damn you!"

The fireflies faded. Looming above Lee was a ponderous face framed by a thick coal-black beard and lit by eyes that seemed to glow as red as those of hellspawn. Where Ed Gristy had been thin and puny, his brother was a hulking brute.

Dimly, Lee heard more footsteps. Another apparition flowed out of the night, this one wearing a patterned dress. Pale fists swung at Gristy's head.

"Stop it!" Allison cried. "Let go of him!"

As casually as if he were swatting a fly, Gristy swung an arm and sent her sprawling. A surge of new power gushed through Lee, fueled by rage so potent that, twisting sharply, he hurled Gristy off him and leaped erect.

The human grizzly rebounded in the blink of an eye. Steel glittered dully in the starlight, slashing in a savage arc.

A knife! Lee backpedaled, and the tip sliced into his shoulder, though not deep. Out of the corner of an eye he saw Allison rising. Fearing that she would try to help again and be fatally stabbed, he moved to place himself between Gristy and her.

Gristy must have guessed his intention, because the man darted in like a striking snake, flicking the knife at Lee's chest. Lee blocked it with his left forearm. For tense moments they strained shoulder to shoulder, wrist against wrist, Gristy striving to lock his other hand on Lee's neck, Lee's right hand fumbling at his hip for his right-hand Colt.

Just as Lee touched the pistol, Gristy shifted and flashed the knife at Lee's belly. By sheer accident the blade was deflected by the rising six-gun. Gristy snapped the knife high for another stroke, but before it could descend Lee shoved the barrel of his pistol against the bigger man's abdomen and fired.

The shot was muffled. Gristy tottered backward. The knife fell at his feet and he dropped a hand to his own pistol. It was halfway out when Gristy buckled, his eyes rolling up into his head as he gave up the ghost.

Allison leaped into the southerner's arms. "I kept looking out the window for you and saw this commotion—" She broke off, overcome by relief, sobbing softly.

Tears moistened Lee's neck. He closed his eyes and held her close, his breath catching in his throat. If she had not shown up when she did, he would be dead. That she would throw herself at a murderous brute like Gristy to save him was a marvel beyond words. It demonstrated, more than anything else could, the full depth of her love. He never wanted to let her go.

"I was so worried when Mrs. Franklyn told me about the gunfight at Boot Hill," Allison said. "And now this!"

Lee lightly kissed her hair, swallowing hard. "This won't ever happen again," he vowed. "As soon as Vint is back on his feet, I'm hanging up my guns. For good."

Allison's response was to smother him with hot, passionate kisses.

Epilogue

The town of Diablo died a lingering death. Diablo Valley withered and faded into a footnote on the pages of history. If it was remembered at all, it was due to the Diablo Valley War, as historians would one day dub the conflict.

The military took over. A commission was set up to get to the bottom of the bloodshed. Headed by Major Whittaker, it showed a strong bias toward Allister Kemp.

Because the homesteaders did not have legal title to the land they had farmed, those who stayed were denied permission to rebuild their homes.

The miners fared little better. Most had filed claims, but many of the sites were buried under tons of rock and earth. The few who did go back up into the mountains reported that the creeks they had panned and relied on to operate their sluice boxes had all dried up.

David Robbins

Disgusted and penniless, most of the ore hunters left to seek their fortunes elsewhere.

The drying of the creeks mirrored the shrinking of the Diablo River. Over a three-month span, the once mighty waterway shriveled to a trickle and eventually stopped flowing altogether. Without water, Diablo could not endure. Six months after Kemp started his private little war, the town was an empty shell.

Why did the river dry up? Two ideas were bandied about. Some blamed it on the blasting done by the Regulators. Everyone knew the river was fed by a source high in the mountains. Speculation ran rampant that the blasts had somehow affected the underground water table.

The second train of thought blamed the death of the town on the Almighty. According to this version, Diablo had been a den of debauchery and sin to rival those of Sodom and Gomorrah, and the Lord had smitten it in his righteous wrath.

Before the town died, several events of note took place.

Two weeks after the Boot Hill gunfight, Ike Shannon was approached on Hell Street by three haggard men on horseback. Ike's wound had been minor, and he had been back on his feet in no time, sharing duties with Lee.

The first thing Ike noticed about the riders was that they had ridden a long distance. The second thing was the badge each wore. "Howdy, gents. Can I help you?"

The lead rider removed his hat to mop a sweaty brow. Sunburned, leather tough, he wore a pearl-handled Colt that had seen a lot of use. "Are you the marshal?"

"Deputy Shannon at your service. Vint Evers is the marshal here."

The man smiled. "Well, now, this is a piece of luck.

308

I know Vint from way back. I was born and raised in Texas not ten miles from where he lived. We're old friends."

"And who might you be?"

"United States Marshal Coe."

Ike idly stared up the street and saw Lee Scurlock and Allison Hays enter a store. "What brings you to Diablo?" he asked.

Coe leaned on his saddle horn. "I'm after an hombre who killed a deputy sheriff at Fort Sumner. We lost his trail on the Painted Desert. But he was driftin' in this direction, so he might have passed through."

"This gent have a name?" Shannon asked, not all that interested until the lawman responded.

"Scurlock. Lee Scurlock. He's related to Doc Scurlock, the gunman. They're brothers."

Ike glanced up the street again. Lee and Allison had not reappeared, but they might at any moment. "I've heard of Doc," he admitted. "You say this Lee gunned down a deputy?"

"Yep," Coe said, and frowned. "It's a dirty business."

"How's that?"

"There are plenty of witnesses who swear that Scurlock was forced into slappin' leather. I reckon you've heard about the Lincoln County War?"

"Who hasn't?"

"Well, the Scurlocks rode with Billy the Kid for a spell. They accepted the amnesty and stopped fighting. But the deputy, who was related to one of the men Billy the Kid killed, braced Lee in a saloon. Called him every name in the book, then tried to slap him around. Scurlock pushed him away, and the deputy went for his gun."

"Sounds to me like the shooting was justified," Ike said, trying hard to hide his nervousness. A figure appeared in the store's entrance. It was Allison, and Lee was right behind her.

Coe shrugged. "I'm just doing my job. Do you happen to know if Scurlock has passed through your town?"

Shannon saw the young lovers step into the sunlight. All Coe had to do was turn and he would see them. "Tell you what. Why don't I take you to see Vint? He's laid up at the doc's." Without waiting for them to agree, Ike started down the street, away from the general store.

"What happened to him?" Coe asked.

"I'll let Vint tell you all about it."

By a roundabout way Ike escorted the lawmen to the physician's, then waited on the porch with the deputies for more than an hour. When Marshal Coe emerged, he walked straight to his weary horse and mounted.

"Leaving so soon?" Ike asked.

Coe nodded, to the surprise of the deputies. "We have no reason to stay. Lee Scurlock died in a gunfight with a man named Nate Collins. I have to get back and file my report so the manhunt will be called off."

"But, Marshal," one of the deputies said, "after coming all this way, what will it hurt to stay the night?"

"It's been ages since we had a bath and a decent meal," added the other.

"Sorry, boys," Coe said. "We'll stop at that relay station east of here." Touching his hat brim, he said, "*Adios*," and, flanked by his mystified deputies, departed.

That night Shannon told Lee of Coe's visit, and Lee promptly went to visit Vint Evers. Ike did not know what was said, but when the Tennessean walked out, his face shone with gratitude.

Diablo

It was two weeks later that the last killing in Diablo took place. Frank Lowe had turned up shortly after the troops arrived. He closed his saloon and was arranging to travel to Tombstone to open another.

On the night before Lowe was to leave, he was strolling down Hell Street when someone in an alley he was passing called his name. Bystanders saw him turn, then scream. Some of them were sprayed with gore when his head was blown to ribbons by a shotgun blast. The culprit eluded capture.

The last wedding in Diablo was a double affair. On October 1, 1880, at the Delony home, the minister united Allison Campbell Hays and Lee Tucker Scurlock, and Nelly Amber Rosell and Vinton Darby Evers, in the holy state of matrimony.

Both couples lingered in Diablo until the town was nearly empty. They were on one of the last stage runs out, along with Ike Shannon. In Wichita, Kansas, they parted company, the women hugging and crying and promising to write every month.

Vint Evers took Nelly to Colorado, where they started a thriving ranch. Nine months after their house was built, Nelly gave birth to a robust boy, the first of four children they would rear during the decades they were together.

Ike Shannon gambled for several years, drifting from boomtown to boomtown. Ultimately, he made his way to California, where he settled in Los Angeles. In his seventies he became a technical adviser on the sets of Western movies, lending realism to Hollywood fantasies.

But the Irishman journeyed to California long after the final act in the Diablo drama was played out.

At the time Lee heard the news, he lived on his own spread in western Montana, a week's ride out of Missoula. Allison had given birth to a baby girl four months earlier. On a cold, blustery winter's night, as

David Robbins

he sat rocking their daughter to sleep in front of the fireplace, Allison read to him from a newspaper he had picked up on his last trip into town.

"Now, this is interesting. A new boot and shoe store has opened. It says here that they carry the finest assortment for women this side of the Rockies."

"That's nice," Lee said dreamily. Lulled by the warmth and the tender feel of the infant on his chest, he was ready to doze off himself.

"Goodness gracious!" Allison exclaimed. "A can of tomatoes is going for a dollar and twenty cents! That's outrageous!"

"Canned goods are always pricey this time of year," Lee reminded her.

"You sound tired. Maybe we should turn in early tonight."

"Good idea." Lee sat up, fondly admiring his daughter's cherubic features. "Beth is in dreamland already." As he went to rise, his wife gasped as if stricken and pressed a hand to her throat.

"Dear Lord!" she blurted, the strongest oath she ever used.

"What?" Lee said anxiously, not knowing what to make of her dismay.

"There's a story here about Allister Kemp."

Lee stiffened. The last he'd heard, the Englishman had been forced to sell his stock and relocate after Diablo Valley turned into a dust bowl. Word was that Kemp settled in southern Wyoming and was heavily involved in local politics. Rumor had it that he might run for the U.S. Senate. "What about him?"

"I'll read it to you," Allison offered, and cleared her throat. "Murder most foul. A prominent Wyoming rancher has been slain by an unknown assassin. Fifty-six-year-old Allister Kemp, who moved to this country at an early age from England, was shot from ambush four nights ago on his ranch west of Cheyenne. A dozen ranch hands were with him at the time, but none were harmed."

"Does it say how it happened?"

"I'm coming to that," Allison said, and resumed reading. "The Laramie County Sheriff's Office reports that Kemp was on his way to Cheyenne when the shooting occurred. His assassin apparently was hidden on a ridge over a thousand yards to the north and killed Kemp with one shot to the head." She paused, glancing up. "A thousand yards? Is that possible? Can any rifle shoot that far?"

"An old Sharps Big Fifty could."

"Aren't they the guns used by buffalo hunters?"

"Mostly. What else does the paper say?"

"Kemp's hands attempted to track the assassin, but they lost the trail in a snowstorm. The Laramie County Sheriff's Office is still investigating. So far they have no solid leads." Allison finished and turned. "I know we shouldn't sit in judgment on others, but that awful man got exactly what he deserved."

"Amen to that."

"I wonder who could have done it."

Lee Scurlock did not reply. Carrying Beth as if she were a fragile egg, he rose to take her to her crib. And as he walked from the room, his face curled in a broad smile.

WILDERNESS GIANT SPECIAL EDITION:

PRAIRIE BLOOD
David Thompson

The epic struggle for survival on America's frontier—in a Giant Special Edition!

While America is still a wild land, tough mountain men like Nathaniel King dare to venture into the majestic Rockies. And though he battles endlessly against savage enemies and hostile elements, his reward is a world unfettered by the corruption that grips the cities back east.

Then Nate's young son disappears, and the life he has struggled to build seems worthless. A desperate search is mounted to save Zach before he falls victim to untold perils. If the rugged pioneers are too late—and Zach hasn't learned the skills he needs to survive—all the freedom on the frontier won't save the boy.

_3679-7 $4.99

WILL HENRY

JESSE JAMES
DEATH OF A LEGEND

Beneath the bandanna, underneath the legend, Jesse James was a wild and wicked man: a sinister and brutal outlaw who blazed a trail of crime and violence through the lawless West. Ripping the mask off the mysterious Jesse James, Will Henry's *Death Of A Legend* is a novel as tough and savage as the man himself. Only a great Western writer like Henry could tell the real story of the infamous bandit Jesse James.

_3990-7 $4.99 US/$6.99 CAN

Dorchester Publishing Co., Inc.
65 Commerce Road
Stamford, CT 06902

Please add $1.75 for shipping and handling for the first book and $.50 for each book thereafter. NY, NYC, PA and CT residents, please add appropriate sales tax. No cash, stamps, or C.O.D.s. All orders shipped within 6 weeks via postal service book rate. Canadian orders require $2.00 extra postage and must be paid in U.S. dollars through a U.S. banking facility.

Name _____

Address _____

City _____ State _____ Zip _____

I have enclosed $_____ in payment for the checked book(s).

Payment <u>must</u> accompany all orders.☐ Please send a free catalog.

MACKENNA'S GOLD

WILL HENRY

"Some of the best writing the American West can claim!"

—Brian Garfield, Bestselling Author of
Death Wish

Somewhere in 100,000 square miles of wilderness is the fabled Lost Canyon of Gold. With his dying breath, an ancient Apache warrior entrusts Glen Mackenna with the location of the lode that will make any man—or woman—rich beyond their wildest dreams. Halfbreed renegade and captive girl, mercenary soldier and thieving scout—brave or beaten, innocent or evil, they'll sell their very souls to possess Mackenna's gold.

_4154-5 $4.50 US/$5.50 CAN

THE CROSSING

By the Bestselling Author of *The Bear Paw Horses*

Jud is the son and grandson of famous Southern generals. He was reared in the genteel Virginia traditions of his widowed mother, but life on a Texas ranch has molded him in the harsh ways of the frontier. In the deadly Confederate campaign to secure the region, Jud sees brave men fall with their guns blazing or die from naked fear. But he is of better stock than most, and he'll be damned if he'll betray the land—and the woman—he loves just to save his own worthless hide.

_4084-0 $4.99 US/$5.99 CAN

ATTENTION PREFERRED CUSTOMERS!

SPECIAL TOLL-FREE NUMBER
1-800-481-9191

Call Monday through Friday
12 noon to 10 p.m.
Eastern Time
Get a free catalogue;
Order books using your Visa,
MasterCard, or Discover;
Join the book club!

Leisure
Books

Love
Spell